GIVE HIM A STONE

By the Same Author

Such Waltzing Was Not Easy
The Entombed Man of Thule
Count a Lonely Cadence

GIVE HIM A STONE

A NOVEL

BY GORDON WEAVER

Crown Publishers, Inc.   New York

Inquiries should be addressed to Crown Publishers, Inc.,
419 Park Avenue South, New York, N.Y. 10016.

Printed in the United States of America
Published simultaneously in Canada by General Publishing Company
    Limited

A portion of this novel first appeared, in somewhat different
form, in the *Denver Quarterly*.

Library of Congress Cataloging in Publication Data

Weaver, Gordon.

    Give him a stone.

    I. Title.
PZ4.W3628Gi [PS3573.E17]   813 ·.5 ·4   74-34055
ISBN 0-517-51897-X

To the Memory of My Father,
Nobel Rodel Weaver, and for My Wife, Judy,
and My Children,
Kristina Katherine and Anna Lynne

If a son shall ask bread of any of you that is a father, will he give him a stone?

Luke 11:11

I know all human flesh must die, but a man may live many years for all that.

Henry Fielding, *Tom Jones*

I

Son, listen: I would have you know my father. But not the facts,
the details of what I tell you. Trust my memory no more than I do
(I make up what I forget). Pay no attention to the answers your
aunt or uncle will give you if you think or care to ask. Forget the
few photographs I keep: he is—was—not the sullen boy who
glowers into the sun on the porch of the Indiana farmhouse, rigid
already in rebellion against his heritage. He is not the cocky
ballplayer, arms on the shoulders of two anonymous teammates,
nor the slender World War I soldier, mock-serious, sitting on his
bunk, pretending to play a violin for the camera. He is not (and
this is how my memory's faulty eye sees him still) that aged man
with too-big ears, grayed temples, false teeth that fit too-clearly
uncomfortably in his mouth. The double chin, swollen paunch,
tell you nothing of him. Disregard the fading letters, bold block

1

letters, black ink, on yellow sheets. Those are only his words. Of my father I want you to know, not what I know, but what I feel, which is all that can ever be true. Listen, then. Better, see.

What I ask is not easy. We recede in time. Yes, your mother exists then, but she is not your mother. Then, I have never known her, and there is not the most remote chance I ever will. You? Of course not. You simply are not, and then, in this then-time, there is no faintest reason or argument or probability to imagine you will ever be. It is not easy.

Your Aunt Jane has not, I think, changed greatly. She was younger, slimmer, with fewer and shallower wrinkles at the corners of her eyes, no flecks of gray to conceal in her hair under blonde rinses, but the same cold cast of distance that keeps you from kissing her until you are told to was already in her blue eyes. Then, as now, she smoked cigarettes incessantly, the ashes falling unnoticed to smear her skirt or burn a rug. Her children, your cousins, were, of course, only babies then. I pass over her husband; I know no more of him than you do (pictures, a smiling man in a blue uniform)—I know only his facts, feel nothing.

As now, she was very often present, yet not of or in our lives. She did not talk to us (myself, Arn, our mother) as much as she commented, wisely or sarcastically, on what we said. She has always been very helpful, to everyone. I suspect, and it is only suspicion, that she understands better than anyone, now and then, that if only she would allow herself to come close to us, touch, she would tell me things about my father that would dissipate and destroy all I feel, all I mean to share with you now. She may have loved him even more than I, but her life has taught her prudence, caution, a fear dissembled in detachment.

She was the same. She blows cigarette smoke up and away from herself, in a stream, tilting back her head and rolling her eyes toward the ceiling in a way that makes me feel the tangled complexities and absurdities of meaning in experience that will always be beyond my innocent interest and grasp. Jane, then, was only younger. She would not tell us if she could.

Your Uncle Arn, who bursts now into your life only two or three times a year, laden with expensive gifts, a cynical and vigorous humor, a contempt for me he is too unsubtle to hide even from you, was then a very young man. Forgive him, for he is affluent, if not rich, and childless. Then: he is tall and quite handsome: he wears old military uniforms with the chevrons removed, leers unashamedly at any woman, goes off evenings to swill beer with friends I never meet. He reveres no authority, values his future in dollars. He knows (and sometimes recites for me) an unlimited number of dirty stories, and when he steps outside, invariably clears his throat with loud, exaggerated noises, and spits viciously into the nearest gutter or bush.

I never (then as now) presume to question or doubt him, and have not lost this awe. I remember: when Arn—your Uncle Arn—rises from a chair, wherever he sits, he stands straight, rotates his broad shoulders briefly, lifts his chin to stretch the muscles of his corded neck, then reaches casually down to his crotch to adjust the hang of his penis in his shorts. This is always, this half-conscious prodding of his sex, and for me, then, it is the most magnificently masculine gesture I have ever seen. Timidly, unbelieving, I swear myself to emulate him in some distant adolescent future, and of course I never do.

Do not ask your uncle. He has lost himself in becoming what he is. He could not tell you if he would.

And our mother, Jane's, Arn's, mine. Do you remember your grandmother? I thought not. She would not have helped us. She is somehow less real than he, my father, to me. Yet hers was the presence, in the world of facts, that persists through all that time, and beyond it. Had I been denied her, as I was denied my father, I might care to unravel her meaning for myself, for you. Her voice comes to me, strident and angry. I see the set of her teeth, edge on edge, at the mention of his name. I imagine her, frantic, pained, over long-distance wires as she tries to call me back from that pointless flight with my father. I feel the cut of her shriek as she lunges from behind a screen door to claw at him, the day he returned me. She is lost in the scuffle on that porch, when your uncle struck his father. She is another story.

Now my father. It is not easy. Particular to general, general to particular, what difference does it make? I have facts, but must qualify them. Like the photos, the old letters, they do not suffice. I shall lie when I have to.

Example: his name was Oskar, like me, like you. But he never used it, was seldom called upon to answer to it in my hearing. He hated this foreign, anachronistic identity more than you or I can pretend to. I can muster insistence, be proud of it, but he neither could nor would. He was called *Buck*. Buck Hansen.

Always, he signed himself Buck (strong, black block letters—as in the letters on yellow paper). Somewhere on the back seat of that huge Chrysler, among the rest of the salvage he carried when he fled, was a long box of his business cards. I filled my pockets with them ("Help yourself," he said, "twenty-five years up the spout."), pretended they were playing cards, shuffled them, made broad fans of them until my small hands could hold no more, read them over and over again to abate the boredom of our long hours on the highway. I traced the embossed letters, my eyes closed, or during the long night on the Pennsylvania Turnpike, with the pads of my fingertips: *Hansen Engineering Company. Engineering Sales and Consulting. St. Paul, Minn.* Two telephone numbers, home and office. In the lower right-hand corner: *Buck Hansen.*

Also on the Chrysler's cavernous back seat, his latest edition of the *Engineer's Handbook.* I read the columns of logarithms until my eyes dizzied me. On the flyleaf, those black letters, *Buck Hansen, 1945.* He carried a small, needle-sharp pocketknife, to clean his nails, remove the metal slivers that worked out of his fingers (embedded years before my birth, when he worked a lathe in a machine shop), or turn small screws in delicate mechanisms. Its silver panels were engraved, *Buck,* on both sides. His tie clip was made to order, *Buck,* in flowing letters, flat and shiny against the wide, bright-colored neckties men wore that summer of 1946. His cuff links were *BH* monograms, of heavy-gauge stainless steel. On the back of his wristwatch (my sole inheritance: the Masonic symbols, until I bought a new band, caused strangers to approach me, say "Hello, Hiram," or ask "Where were you hit on the head?" taking me for their lodge brother) he had scratched *Buck* with the point of his knife. There, do you see? He was Buck Hansen.

I remember: in the Chicago suburb where we went first, the man he saw to beg help (my father had trained him, years before, before engineers all went to college) said, edging toward refusal: "The smart cookies made their piles while it lasted. It was one swell hell of a war, Buck." My father nodded emphatically, knowing he could expect nothing.

On Long Island, in Mineola, when at last we reached the end, where he thought to find another chance, another life, before she knew he was broke, Lillie Broadfoot (she would have been his third wife) comforted him. He held her hand, fingers interlaced tightly, as if it were a final lifeline. She stroked his forehead with her long, white fingers, nails scarlet, saying, "Buck honey, you look so tired, I swear!" He could only sigh by then, not yet sure it was already over.

On his brother's farm (my Uncle Thurston, your great-uncle) outside Goshen, Indiana, where we rested before our big push east, where he grew up, even there he was Buck Hansen. His brother (I wish I could imitate the thickness and richness of his Swedish accent for you!) said to him, "I almost forgot you don't like being called your name, not since a kid, ain't that right." My father grinned, shaking his older brother's hand, perhaps grateful for that kindness, since there would be no others.

But names don't matter. Understand from this that even to know his name, this fact, is to know nothing of him. I am named for him (as you for me, and for him), but he seldom called me *Oskar*. Never in his letters. See how little the very fact of our name can mean?

Others (just as meaningless). Born: 1896, Goshen, Indiana (this makes him 49, this summer, which is all I know of him). Occupations: farm boy, machine shop clean-up boy, machinist (tool and die maker), tool designer, design engineer, machine tool salesman and engineering consultant. Military Service: US Army, 1918-1919, Fort Sill, Oklahoma. Married: Anne (née Tanberg), 1919, Chicago, Ill.; children: daughter Jane, born 1921, son Arn, born 1925, son Oskar Jr., born 1937; divorced, 1944, Milwaukee, Wis., remarried, Irene (née Peterson), 1944, Minneapolis, Minn., deceased, 1947. Politics: Republican. Hobbies, Skills, and Interests: musician (semiprofessional), piano, violin, banjo, guitar, spoons, ham bones; baseball (semiprofessional), first baseman and outfielder; general mechanics (professional competence); good and plentiful food and drink; women. Unusual Experiences: kidnapped youngest son, June, 1946, returned son to mother June, 1946, no formal charges filed.

So much for facts.

Now, closer.

He was a big man. No, no bigger than I, not as big as Arn. But my father had . . . he was a big man. In my memory's eye he towers, always, over me. I stand, only a shadow of his substance, my head back to look up at the steep wall of his chest and stomach. He is always stooping to speak or listen to me, reaching down with arms big and solid enough for me to climb like trees; he stands against the sun, half eclipses it, throwing me into a perpetual shade that somehow both warms and obliterates me. My father stretches up on the horizon of my past, the sole durable feature outcropping in that landscape.

I remember: his hands. Yes, much like mine, but his fingers were not so slender, and his skin was a fine shade darker, the hair above his knuckles and on the backs darker and thicker. On his right hand the first and second fingers were stained above the first joint by years of smoking. Even the nails were a rich orange brown. "See what it gets you?" he said when I asked. "Learn from your old man and don't ever start." When his hand was close, on my shoulder or touching my hair, my cheek, I could always smell the faint, delicious odor of tobacco.

He wore two rings, the gold Masonic symbol, set against dark red onyx, on his right hand, and a large diamond in a plain silver setting on his left, in place of a wedding band (my mother continued to wear hers to her death, saying it was so tight it would have to be sawed off, and that was too much trouble). He seldom spoke of the Masons, but the diamond was an investment, a resource to pawn if the day ever came; he had lived long enough to value even absurd preparations for disasters.

We stopped once, somewhere in Ohio, to eat, refuel the Chrysler, and make long-distance telephone calls. A number was busy (I do not remember if it was Lillie Broadfoot's beauty parlor on Long Island or the sanitarium in Minneapolis where Irene, his second wife, was dying very slowly of an embolism). He stepped from the outdoor booth, took my hand in his (the cup of his palm swallows my fist) and led me into a small jeweler's shop.

"Can you give this a quick clean?" he said to the jeweler. He twisted the ring off, held it under the man's nose. Like a brilliant drop of clear water on my father's finger, it seemed larger and heavier in the pale, delicate hands of the jeweler. Wearing sleeve garters to keep his crisp white cuffs out of his work, the jeweler slipped his glass into his eye and examined the ring.

"That's quite a stone you have there," he said.

"It'll do for something to hock on a cold day," my father said. "It's got a nigger in it you'll see if you look close."

"Ah," the jeweler said, nodding and removing his glass when he spotted the flaw deep in the gem, a fourth as big as a grain of pepper. "I'll give it a scrub." He went to the back of his shop to scour it under a faucet.

My father winks at me, bends over to whisper in my ear (I see him now, looming enormous near the ceiling—the shop's walls seem to bend with him!). "That'll give him something to talk to the old coots at the general store about," he says softly under the noise of the running water. The corner of his mouth smiles, showing the gleam of a fleck of gold filling between two teeth, and he winks again to be sure I understand. This is secret to ourselves, the two of us.

In our private knowledge, I expand, straighten, puff with the glory of sharing with him. The jeweler returns, drying the ring in his handkerchief. My father gives him a quarter (it smacks sharply on the counter top). He slips it on his finger, deft as a parlor magician, then straightens his arm, spreads his fingers and admires his ring. The silver setting catches the sunlight from the display window. "Think that'll get us in some of the best places now, big boy?" he says to me. The jeweler laughs for him. "Now let's us go see if Ma Bell is still on the job," he says, and we leave, the jeweler turning back to his crowded bench.

My hand inside his again, we went to telephone; the pale jeweler, his exotic glass, his elastic sleeve garters, the puzzle of wheels, springs, screws on his bench, the dozen-or-more wrist-watches, tagged and hanging from wooden pegs, the displays of bands and bracelets and pins—they remain with me, of me, surrounding and subordinate to my father, with whom I now share some essential and exquisite wisdom of the manner and being of small-town Ohio jewelers and jewelry shops. The wisdom is part of us, me, and I of it, all in the presence in memory of my father.

Do you see?

His hands. They transmit a power to me I can never know in myself. We are on the farm outside Goshen. My father's voice breaks my reverie (am I thinking momentarily of my mother, brother, sister? Are they somewhere now on the highway south of Milwaukee? Contacting police? Will the farm be rushed in the night, or in the next minute?). "You need your ears lowered there, sonny," he says. My Uncle Thurston says the barber is only minutes away. "The hell you say," my father says, "what's he need a barber when his father's on the job? You dig out the old man's tools and I'll show you barbering plain and fancy. Unless you hocked it to get past a bad winter."

"We don't throw nothing away around here, Buck," his brother says. The box of barber's tools are found by Thurston's wife, my Aunt Marie. Though she was not Swedish, she did look Swedish—she is a grim woman, does not approve of divorced people, speaks little to us, fears her husband will lend his brother money, is busy in kitchen, yard, and vegetable garden. I have little of her.

"Will you look at this," my father says. I sit on a chair, atop a volume of Rand McNally, a picture album and scrapbook, and a Swedish Bible with hard leather covers, locked shut with a brass clasp. My father ties a patched bed sheet (nothing is thrown away) around my neck, flowing to the floor, my hands folded tightly in my lap—somehow I know this is important. As he snugs the knot and runs his finger around my throat to smooth the cloth, I smell the fragrance of his cigarettes. "Man could work his way across the country with half this," my father says.

The box is wooden, painted black, made by my grandfather ("He was some old country Swede cocker like you'll never know," my father said.). There are two clippers, the steel dull-finished, handles curved gracefully to fit the hand. Several of the long, needle-nosed scissors; my father puts his fingers in the loops at the end of the handle and snaps the air crisply; one has short and blunt blades, with ragged teeth, for thinning. The hard-rubber comb tapers to the width of a rat's tail, the teeth so fine I can barely see light through them when I hold it up in front of me. There is a whisk and two shaving brushes, two crockery mugs, and in a separate case with an inlaid lid, two straight razors. Beneath it all lies a leather strop, dried, cracked, useless.

"I'll be damned," my father says. "You remember him in front of the mirror every Saturday morning, Thurston? Rain or shine, cold enough to freeze your fanny blue, face all lathered up, shaved his face so close it glowed like an apple."

"I do," his brother says.

"Hard-headed square-head Swede sonofabitch'd do anything to hold two bits out on the barber—remember how the farmers lined up in town on Saturday morn—" he begins to say.

"Don't be cussing your pa in front of your own boy, Buck," his brother says. His wife leaves the kitchen; she will not abide such words.

"Agh," is all my father says, snapping the long scissors next to his ear, as if to get the feel of its trueness. "Watch this," he says, and reaches out with his free hand to set my head at the proper angle for him to work.

His hand descends, fingers spread, over the top of my head, grips me at temples and base of skull, his palm over my crown. I feel pressure, and with his wrist he cocks my head to give himself the best view. The pressure releases . . . with the comb he raises tufts of my hair, the scissors clicks in my ear, the strong flutter of his fingers visible in the corner of my eye . . . my hair falls in swatches to my shoulders, slides down to rest in the bowl formed by the bed sheet in my lap. "Like downtown," he says to his brother.

But I am still feeling the shape and pressure of his fingers—I thrill with the quivering awareness that his hand is strong enough to crush my head like an eggshell if he wished to, and with the sure faith that nothing on earth could make him do it. Because he is my father, and loves me.

Hair in my lap is a small heap. His sleeves are rolled back to his elbows; when he stands back to inspect his work, I see the blue tattoo of a woman's head on his thick forearm (it is some sort of Miss Liberty, found on the arms of many veterans of the first war, I am told). His fingers rest gently on my throat, where my blood pulses close to the skin, as he guides the heavy clippers now, cold against my skin, at my nape. Again the long scissors, and he takes hold of my jaw to turn my head sideways to him, trimming near my ear; again I exult in the tactile promise of his implicit power.

"Tell me now I can't cut hair," he says to his brother.

"I'll grant you that okay," Uncle Thurston says. The whisk dusts my neck, ears, forehead. Is there any witch hazel in the house? he wants to know. Of course there is, Aunt Marie shouts from the next room, and brings it. He shakes it into his cupped hand, slaps and massages it roughly into my scalp, wipes my neck and ears with it: the clean freezing of my skin makes me tremble.

"El finishing touch, as they say in Spain," he says. My hair is slicked forward over my brow, witch hazel fumes filling my nostrils, eyes watering slightly. He stands back, squinting, comb in hand, to sight the precise engineer's line that will be my part. "That'll be two bits, never mind the tip, I'm a relative," he says, holding the concave shaving mirror up for me to see.

In the mirror, my eyes distorted, bulged, my hair glossy, pores visible, I see myself as glorious as his satisfied, posed smirk assures me I must be—because I am his, he has made me, just as he has shaped the lay of the hair on my head. "Where can a working man wash his hands, brother?" he says to Thurston.

It is this power in him I want you to feel, son, through me. Dormant, I still knew it, all during our journey that summer. And often, I saw it flash. His energies were volatile, and I never knew how they might be directed.

In Chicago, our first stop, I thought we were hurrying to reach Cal Rocker's house, to put distance between ourselves and Milwaukee. He stopped suddenly on Clark Street. "Could you handle a meal about now?" he said.

"I thought we were going to see Cal Rocker."

"We are. Right now I want to show you the best Mexican restaurant in the world. Your mother ever make chili for you? You don't know what chili is until I show you where your old man used to get it back before the world went to hell and gone. La Nortena," he said (it means, I have taken the trouble to learn, "the northerner," feminine gender). He drove again, almost recklessly now, "I can damn near taste it," he said. "I think about it and I can damn near smell it and taste it." That is what I mean here: listen, think, smell, taste—feel!

La Nortena was a tiny place, the windows filmed gray, the ancient floor uneven, tiles missing here and there. The linoleum counter was pitted and worn black in spots. Except for one swarthy, sideburned man who sulked in a booth, dropping cigar ashes in a coffee cup from time to time, we were the only customers. There were no napkin dispensers or sugar bowls; only salt, pepper, and clear-glass bottles of chili-steeped water, plugged with the same sort of sprinkling spout my mother used to dampen laundry before ironing. The menu was chalked in Spanish on a streaked blackboard above the back counter. There seemed to be only one lavatory, with an arrow painted on the wall to point the way, labeled Caballeros. Flypaper, encrusted with its victims, dangled close to our heads from the ceiling. The counterman was very old; he snubbed his cigarette carefully out against his apron, then tucked the snipe behind his ear as my father ordered.

He spoke eagerly, rubbing his hands together, rolling his lips, probing his dentures and the soft insides of his cheeks with his tongue when he paused to consider each item.

"Chili," he said, "you're still pushing chili I hope. Two big bowls, but go easy on the hot stuff for the boy here. *Burritos*? You have *burritos* today? Two, green chili. Two apiece is the idea. Large order of flour tortillas. You have some of the red stuff, taco sauce, besides this?—" pointing at the pepper-water on the counter— "so far so good. You like a salad? Go on, you need your greens. No salad today? *Guacamole* then. No? The hell you say. Oh, and *chalupas*, that's the ticket." The swarthy man in the booth stared out past us at the empty street.

When it was before us, steaming and pungent, my father unbuttoned his suitcoat and swept the tails back, like a pianist sitting down to a concert. He breathed deeply, once, leaned forward on the stool, and began to eat. He was a man of appetite, if you understand me.

"Dig in," he said to me, picking up his spoon. I cannot recall how much I ate of the spicy food: I watched my father most of the time, while the counterman joined the dark lounger in the booth, their soft Spanish a background to my father's loud chewing and swallowing.

He ate with gestures: in one hand, he holds a hot *burrito*, poised over the chili bowl while he dribbles clear pepper-water over it. A quick twist of the wrist is necessary to point it toward his open, approaching mouth without spilling. His bite is enormous: where half the *burrito* had been is only a crescent-cut stump, the green chili mash, flecked with smatterings of beef, exposed. Still gripping the spoon in his other hand, his jaws and temples moving as he chews, he dabs at his lips with his knuckles. Swallowing with a thud deep in his throat, he breathes loudly through his nose as he gathers momentum for the next bite. Dipping into the chili with his spoon, he raises it, heaped high with red brown beans, sucks it in. Without breaking the rhythm of his jaw, he ducks his head to dry the tear that forms in the corner of his eye on the shoulder of his jacket.

"Mmmmm," he seems to intone as he eats, to me, to share his gusto, or to himself, to savor it. Midway, he stops, sets down his spoon, places his hands on his hips and breathes deeply in and out, like a runner preparing for a sprint. "Dig in, boy," he says to me, "nobody holds back in this boardinghouse," and reaches for a tortilla, folds it around his extended finger, and with his chili spoon, fills the trough with *guacamole*.

"Jesus," he said to himself, shaking his head as if in disbelief when he finished, "I'll live to regret this." Paying (there was no register; the counterman lifted his apron to put the money in his pocket), he questioned the counterman about his menu. Why did they no longer serve *tostadas*? What ever became of the fat woman who made tortillas on the stone in the front window in the old days? They ought, he advised, to lay in some taco sauce; the pepper-water was murder. In the Chrysler again, he told me he had acquired his taste for Mexican food while serving at Fort Sill, Oklahoma. "Before your time," he said, "and most everyone else's for that matter."

Though I ate little, I felt as full as he. He stabbed at his dentures with his thumbnail, stifled belches with his clenched fist, lit a Pall Mall and spewed smoke out the open car window in long sighs of complete but momentary satisfaction. "Jesus!" he said.

"What's wrong?"

"Heartburn. We'll stop at a drugstore before we check in our hotel. Bromo and some Tums I'll be a new man." Like so much of his energies, he had wasted the edge of his appetite on something self-destructive, but he never ceased to believe in remedies. Driving to the drugstore, to the hotel, he lapsed into a silence of discomfort, and, I think, recrimination. Many times, that summer, he told me he was trying to lose weight.

And drinking: we are in a cocktail lounge not far from Cal Rocker's home. It is called Sans Souci, the sign outside of multicolored neon, which is new then. For a short time, I am absorbed by the first television set I have ever seen, mounted high on the padded wall at one end of the long, marbletop bar. It is late

11

afternoon, the bar almost empty. I hear the sound of silverware being laid from the adjoining dining room.

My father and Cal Rocker are standing sideways between the fixed stools at the bar. The bartender, immaculate in a tight red corduroy vest with silver buttons, listens carefully to them, as if they are important men, and their conversation contains vital secrets he can exploit if only he gets them straight. Their drinks are on the bar, their cigarette packages and lighters, and two not-quite-careless piles of coins and bills. There is more glow than real light from the concealed fixtures in the backbar. Cal Rocker is younger than my father. His hair is blond, he is shorter, slimmer, never not-smiling. He has just spoken, interjected his brief wisdom into my father's endless, emphatic address; Cal Rocker has just said that it was one swell hell of a war.

My father dominates. One foot is on the polished rail, knee cocked. His other leg supports him, hip a mound on which he rests one hand lightly. The other elbow is on the bar, fingers relaxed, Pall Mall burning, smoke curling up and over his wrist. His jacket open, thrown back, his paunch hangs, collar open, tie loose. "I hope to tell you," he says, "I paid forty thousand and better in income taxes three years running, and I've got the papers to swear to it what's more." The bartender shifts his chewing gum to the front edges of his teeth, bites hard (out of envy, regret, awe?), Cal Rocker bends at the waist in deference. "Skoal," my father says, and is all motion.

The shot glass is level before his lips (smoldering Pall Mall still in his stained fingers). He tips his head, only a few degrees, the glass is empty. It raps on the bar, he motions with a thumb (imitates a spout), the bartender is pouring, Cal Rocker is draining his last, ice-diluted dregs, a fresh Pall Mall is in my father's lips. The drinks are poured, the bartender invited to join, my father says, "Skoal!"

They drink, his arm sweeps, his lighter clicks, he explodes smoke. "You goddamn bet you!" he says. I am frozen in this corner of time, where somewhere close there is the first television set in the world, the clatter of silverware being laid, a glowing light that suffuses myself and a gum-chewing bartender and a man named Calvin Rocker, this summer of 1946. At the center, orchestrating us, giving us life only as we respond to him, is my father, whose meaning (hence mine) embodies itself in Pall Mall cigarettes and shot glasses of amber whiskey (which he calls schnapps, no matter what it is) and the insanely large and meaningless amounts of money he has paid in taxes to the federal government during the recent war.

Cal Rocker gave him no money, and drinking meant the morning, sick, my father bent over the sink in our hotel room, wearing only baggy shorts and sleeveless undershirt, letting the water run cold from the tap on the back of his neck. "Never never never never again, I swear so help me Christ!" he said. I am sent out to buy Sal Hepatica to ease his misery.

What I tell you, son, is that he was what he was with affirmation. What he could not accept was that nothing was sufficient beyond its moment. And this knowledge scalded him. Still, he would not embrace it. And his anger could be both wonderful and violent. He would not submit, and that is something, after all.

We are driving: it is in a city (Milwaukee, Chicago, Hammond, Gary, Cleveland . . . always eastward, toward Lillie Broadfoot). The Chrysler is hot, the wind from the scoop and the open windows like the warm draft from a wood stove. The radio is always on—Truman, strikes, the singing of Georgia Gibbs, Connie Haines, Jo Stafford. My father sits very still behind the wheel, the inflated rubber pad he sits on of no use in easing his sciatica or his hemorrhoids if he moves. As he finishes his Pall Malls he flips them out the cracked wing. He glances occasionally into the rear-view mirror (watching for Sheldon Rotter, the Jewish deadbeat chaser who has pursued him since the day he fled Saint Paul? I am not to meet him until after Lillie, on Long Island). My father clears his throat, coughs sometimes so fiercely that his face reddens and he ends in deep wheezing. Then there is the heat again, the radio, the click of his lighter, until whatever is happening inside him has grown too strong to hold in any longer.

Someone passes him too quickly or too close, cuts into our lane, brakes abruptly, stalls when the light is green. My father erupts.

"Ugly bohunk sonofabitch!" he screams. "Black boogie bastard!" "You damn kike-looking yid heeb!" he bellows into the close heat. "Stupid cunt, if you can't drive, park!" he roars into the face of a mild-looking woman with blue-tinted hair as she pulls her prewar Lincoln alongside. "Get to goddamn hell out of my way!" he shrieks at the back ends of Hudsons and Packards and Buicks.

We pass through the cities and towns heading east, and my father curses them horribly as his hope gives way to despair and

13

the frustrations of the instant. Leaving Goshen, we pass a dull-faced farm boy, slouched on a tractor that hogs the center line and leaves clods of dirt in its path. "Draft-dodging, tax-dodging goddamn farmer Dutchman!" my father brands him as we pass, leaning across the seat to yell out the window. The farm boy does not even blink, high on his tractor, but I recoil into the far corner of the seat, face burning, terrified, not of my father or his words, but of the fear that makes him hate so quickly and easily. I wish to fade, dissolve into the humid, sticky air, because I do not want to live in so horrible a world. "You don't want to go around repeating everything I say, you know," he said to me.

He believed in force (I do not, only, I fear, because I find so little in myself).

"What the hell," he says to Cal Rocker and an attentive bartender, "selling is physical when we get right down to it, right? I'm serious. Ask yourself, Cal, how do you sell a man? I'll tell you, you damn well sell him when and if you overpower him, that's when. Look at yourself, ask yourself. You sell, and you sell because when you walk in on a man you're bigger than he is. And Buck Hansen does it the same way, and I've sold some in my day I hope to tell you. You walk in on him and he gets up and you bull in on him. You speak louder and deeper and clearer than he does, and you grab his hand and wrench hell out of it. I'm talking psychology now. No matter if he's five inches taller and fifty pounds heavier, you overpower him. You make him know you can kick his keester up between his shoulder blades if it suits you. You make him know it because you make your*self* know it!" He jabs with his orange brown fingertip; the bartender lowers his eyes, overpowered.

In the desk room of the Mineola Municipal Police Station, I saw him fight, in June of 1946.

They have removed the handcuffs from Ben, Lillie's brother. He is emptying his pockets before being led to a cell (Lillie waits outside, still weeping, covering her blackened and swelling eyes with a wet washcloth, in the Chrysler). My father already understands the situation. He holds me loosely by the hand. An officer with a clipboard lists Ben's possessions.

"You ain't keeping me here overnight, are you?" Ben says.

"We'll see," says the police officer. I have never been in a police station before.

"I guess you know to keep away from Lil," my father says.

"You can tell my bitch of a sister for me—" Ben says before my father reaches him.

14

It was not much of a fight. They grappled, separated, swung wildly at each other, their punches missing or glancing off, and then the policeman stopped it. He aimed at Ben's head with his club, missed, and broke his collarbone. He swung a second time as Ben was falling, missed again, and broke the fourth finger on my father's right hand, shattering the second joint. I think I did not move; it seemed to me to be safe there so long as I did not move.

"Goddamnit, Buck," Ben said, unable to get up.

"Get up, I'll clean your damn clock," my father said. He held his broken finger, raised it to his mouth to blow gently on it.

"Now you don't want to start anything," the police officer said. He kept the club ready, trembling.

"When I hear that kind of talk I want action," my father said.

I never feared him. His violence terrified me because I had never known it existed before, but with him, I felt protected by it, even if the world would no longer be safe for me to move in again (in Milwaukee, the day he returned me to my mother, he neither defended himself nor retaliated when Arn struck him).

My Uncle Thurston boarded a riding horse on his farm, son—yes, while we were there. It was a big horse, a buckskin, with a long head, panels of big yellow teeth, eyes that rolled madly when we approached his stall. He stamped nervously, yanked sharply on his halter rope, twisted his neck to glare at us when we came around behind him. My father edged into the stall next to him, but I stopped, afraid of being kicked and bitten. "Come on," he said, "I'll show you how we tell his age by his teeth."

"I don't want to."

"He's just as scared of you as you are of him."

"He'll squeeze me against the wall," I said.

"The hell he will," my father said. He put both hands on the buckskin and pushed. "Get on over!" he said, and raising his hand, smacked the horse on the fat of his rump; it sounded like a gunshot, and the buckskin seemed to buckle under it. The horse snorted, laid back ears, but moved. "Yagh!" my father commanded, and moved him to the other side of the stall, and I walked in beside my father, and we examined the buckskin's mouth to determine his age. What should I fear with him next to me, holding the horse's head still, pulling back the thick black lip?

But all this is nothing, son, unless you know the love. This, and that he could delight me (playing an ancient banjo at the farm: "Here's a hot Eddie Peabody number, sonny."). And shame me—ask your Uncle Arn, ask Jane, they will tell you of shame.

They mean nothing unless there is the love. What illustration will prove this to you?

It is the middle of night, and I wake, perhaps from a bad dream I cannot remember clearly enough to put away. In the dark I do not know where I am, that this is the seldom-used room on the second floor of my uncle's farm in Indiana. I am naked except for undershorts, and though it is June, very cold. I shiver and huddle on the narrow bed, and do not hear the even breathing of my father, asleep across the room.

I remember now what he—what we have done, think of my mother, brother, sister, and begin to cry softly without wanting to. I do not want to be alone, naked and cold, do not understand why I am here in this dark and strange place. I fear nothing specific, only that there is nothing I can reach, touch, that I know, that will tell me what and why I am. I bite down on my fingers, afraid to hear my own cries, but they cannot be stopped, and I am the more terrified by them.

"Oskar?" my father says from his bed. "What's the matter?"

"I'm cold," I say when I can speak.

"Come on over here with me."

"I can't see you."

"Just get up and come to my voice. Come on, it's warm here." The bare floor is cold; I walk in the dark, only a few steps, and there is the hulk of my father in his bed, up on one elbow, holding the covers open for me like a warm cave. "Snuggle up," he says, and I hear the half-asleep quality of his voice now.

He drops the light cover over me, and I inch close to him. I lay my head in the hollow of his shoulder, and he brings his other arm across me, his hand close to my face, where I clasp his fingers with both my hands. His chest and stomach and hairy leg touch and warm me the length of my body. We say no more, and soon his breathing tells me he is asleep. I lay, gently embraced, and soak away my coldness and terror in his love. And soon I sleep, to wake on my Uncle Thurston's farm, near Goshen, Indiana, the summer of 1946.

Do you see? He loved me. He loved me enough to steal me. And to return me. He was my father.

Listen, son.

II

He arrived the day we moved back into a house, to live, my mother said, like decent people again.

I lay awake in my cot in one of the two finished attic rooms we rented from Mrs. Spaulding. Since the end of that old life, so old, so *past* that it was not mine in memory, not mine except in the chemistry of associations, smells and textures and echoed phrases indistinctly heard, the three of us lived. And I do not, dare not, count any of that past—my sister's marriage, the war, my brother's departure for training in the Army Specialized Training Program, the divorce, the death in action in the Pacific of my sister's husband. It is history, not mine. I begin here, in Mrs. Spaulding's attic, awake in my cot, my hands on my chest, outside the covers, as my mother always cautioned me when I went to

17

bed, listening. First alone, my mother and I, then with Arn joining us after his discharge. I listen to Arn and my mother decide on the new life for us.

It began in anger and frustration. Quickly, our landlady, Mrs. Spaulding: dowdy, dark-haired upper lip, unshaven legs, dyed jet-black hair that sets off her sallow face to disadvantage, worn slippers on her feet, seated at her kitchen table, Sacred Heart on the wall above the sink, a dried palm frond stuck up behind it, the room steeped in cooking odors. Mrs. Spaulding's bland greed is quite as firm as my mother's bitter intensity. I sat on the cold attic stairs, halfway between the landing and the open door of Mrs. Spaulding's warm, brightly lit kitchen below.

My mother carries out the ritual of rent-day, her check sealed in a dime store envelope for presentation. But Mrs. Spaulding, her greed winning over her timidity, is upping the ante.

"You and the little guy was one thing, Missus," she says, "but I didn't count on no big fellow coming out of service." It is an uninteresting voice, thick with the sediment of routine, of coarse meals simmered long over gas jets, of sleepy midnight shuffles in those shabby slippers to the bathroom, where the plumbing explodes and vibrates upward to my half-dreaming ear. I listen, visualize her sorting mounds of dirty laundry to soak in the clammy basement tubs.

My mother: "There's still an Office of Price Administration that makes laws about what rents can be." Her voice is all edge, a sharpness that can so easily quaver, break, disintegrate.

"Truman don't tell me what to do, Missus. It's my house and I can charge what I feel like. I guess you can always leave if you don't like it. You got no complaints about me. Did I say anything when the daughter comes over and leaves the kids run over my head all day? Do I say anything when I worry you'll leave the hot plate go and burn us all up?"

There is a short silence: I envision, there in the chill dark of the stairs, my mother cutting her losses of spirit (only *now*, understand). She sets her teeth carefully together, wrings the fingers of one hand in the other, narrows her eyes behind her bifocals. Her chair scrapes as she slides it away from the table.

"That's jolly darn well what we'll do then," she said. I am up and off, quick and quiet, in my cot before she reaches our adjoining rooms at the far end of the attic, warming myself on the glow of my own breath in my cupped hands.

"Missus? Missus? Okay, if that's how you want it," calls Mrs. Spaulding up the empty attic stairwell.

18

And still awake, the beginning, through my mother's weeping at the single table in the other room, through her subsiding gasps and hiccups into the hissing stream of her eternal recriminating dialogue with herself; through my brother's return from a night at a tavern meeting of the Fifty-two-twenty Club, the making of coffee on the electric plate that haunts Mrs. Spaulding's cataclysmic fancy, through the debate over the housing shortage, down-payments, the mortgage market, the scratch of paper and pencil that goes on into the night. I listen, and this is my beginning.

"Why not? What's to stop us?" Arn said.

"I don't know. I just don't know. I have to have something to hope for. What's the use if you can't hope for anything?" my mother said.

"It all works out on paper," my brother said. "Don't take it so hard," he said. "It all works out, doesn't it?"

They have reckoned without my father.

Moving day. In the immediate postwar sociology of the city of Milwaukee, we are risen. From deep in the lower East Side, where Lake Michigan breezes are polluted by a paper factory and a coal yard, the neighborhood teeming with Poles and Italians made loud and aggressive by inflated wartime wages and travel, and worse, clots of Negroes, teen-agers who pilgrimaged each night across the river to the Palomar Roller Rink—we flee this and go north. The high, square-cut houses were built by the original waves of Germans, the refugees of 1848 and after, who will, this year of 1946, in their last show of strength, elect their last socialist mayor. We move to Cramer Street.

(Yes, *now* it is in decline, the larger houses converted to nursing homes, the smaller racked and torn by hordes of college boys and student nurses who live commune style; nobody paints, nobody mows lawns or shovels walks, and winter chuckholes gape on into summer before street crews come this way. My brother Arn, his eyes keen for investments, would dismiss Cramer Street.

We are at work. My mother is within, too busy to feel or speculate the past life of the bare floors, the grimy outline-ghosts of pictures, a calendar, mirrors on the walls, the blind emptiness of windows without shade or curtain. Slashing with a razor blade, she opens the neat tape on boxes scrounged from IGA, A&P, National Tea stores three years before, each labeled on top and side in black crayon, retrieved now from storage, carted in from the rented trailer by my brother and myself.

She is dressed for unpacking, or gardening, or mucking in a

19

ditch, sufficient to any task, because for her, her life, ours, all is renewed today. She wears an old housecoat, safety-pinned where two buttons are missing. A handkerchief is tied around her forehead for a sweat-catcher. Her feet are bare. On hands and knees, she wields the razor blade, tears open the boxes, surveys contents, empties some, calls to me to take others to basement or bedroom or kitchen. And all the while her lips move, the flow of sibilant whispers rises and falls, shifting tempo to meet the scale of exultation or depression brought on by those cardboard containers of her, our, once-dead, now-revived past.

While she speaks, however softly, the angry narrative-of-then, and my brother Arn is silent and grim except for grunts and curses uttered only outside, out of her hearing, my impulse to memory shouts inside me, to me, bitten by recognitions I cannot understand or articulate. These *things*, emerging as box flaps open like vault doors, stacked, strewn, call out for my response, but I can only touch and wonder, and wait, like any child, for the dim but potent future to give me wisdom and a tongue.

She stops, working and muttering, only when a lock of hair falls over her eyes. She will try once or twice to blow it back, then reaches up to push it away with the back of her wrist, careful not to touch herself with her dirty hands. Rarely, she pauses long enough to straighten her back and reach around to press one of her kidneys, sighing loudly in relief.

Though we have propped front and back doors open, forced jammed windows up, there are no breezes from the lake, and our new house heats like an oven in the untimely morning June temperature. Inside, the air seems to hang in layers, the texture of flannel, plugging my mouth and nose. Dust motes float slowly in the rays of blistering sunlight shafts at the windows. On the porch, shielding my eyes with one hand like an Indian scout, heat-shimmers radiate from the softened asphalt surface of the street in either direction. My face and neck and arms are slick with sweat, my tee shirt pasted to my chest and stomach and back, and a hot, moist itch torments my crotch.

Arn, wearing an old Army Air Corps uniform shirt, interrupts every effort to wipe his eyes on his shoulder. The pale khaki cloth is dark with sweat crescents in the armpits, and a subtler shade on the sleeves where his buck sergeant's chevrons have been removed.

(He washed out of the ASTP program—too nervous for flying. To see him now, competent and corpulent, you would not think him plagued with nerves, but he sees expensive doctors

20

periodically to prevent the perforation of a duodenal ulcer—oh yes.)

Standing on the porch, I watch him horse the boxes out of the rented trailer, onto the strip of parched grass between sidewalk and curb. His brass belt buckle catches flecks of sun like a jewel, and his guttural swearing is not quite audible in the heavy air. I shiver, instinctively, as a horse dislodges flies, unwilling to embrace the day or the work, turn and go inside to wait at my mother's elbow for commands.

"It's hot," I said, unable to bear the burden of mystery in her private conversation.

"I know it's hot."

"I wish I could be outside or do something."

"Well you can't. I need you."

"I wish we weren't even moving today."

"Stop it!" She rose to one knee and glared at me. Her tolerance for whining is low; for blasphemy, nil.

"I just wish I could go outside and play or over to Jane's or something," I said. I brace myself for a head-snapping slap, a deliberate and methodical licking, or worse, the rage of rant and tears, menopausally insane, that will make me cry with her for guilt, and will, surely, bring my furious brother in to whip me. But I am lucky, or perhaps her need for this new stability for us all is too great to allow for diversions, even for my bratty balking.

"You can't," she said, "because I need you here. I won't have any more of this, do you hear me? Not now, not today. Now are you going to be a help or are you going to make everyone miserable with your crying? Answer me."

"I'm going to be a help," I said, as I knew I must. She leans so close to me I can feel her breath on my face; there can be no question of my willingly harboring the least grain of dissent or rebellion.

"All right," she said. Arn came in.

"What the hell are you doing, Os?"

"I can't carry heavy ones," I said. The hard corners of the boxes stabbed me in chin and chest and the soft insides of my arms.

"The hell with that noise—"

"You needn't use that language," my mother said, but too wearily, automatically to interrupt him.

"—there's a ton of little crap you can carry. Let's get with it. Come on." I trail after him, coming no higher than the small of his

21

back (I dream a violent, physical revenge on his sweating shoulders, for that answer-full future time when I will be, miraculously, as large, larger than he, but know in the instant of dreaming how futile my vow is, that I will never grow up to him, never). Behind us, my mother's whispered commentary resumes smoothly.

Does she simply react to each item revealed when a box springs open in her hands? Is she only a charged plate of dormant memories to no more than spark when struck? Or does she—as I do, now—take sides, thrust herself actively into the stored dramas, and refight old, undecided or lost battles? If I could have heard! But my child's ear was too dull to separate the voices that surfaced and sank on her lips, and so all this, this much, is lost.

We walked out on the porch, Arn swaggering and sullen, myself resigned like a trussed prisoner, and he was there—there, backing his Chrysler up to the nose of Arn's Ford, was my father . . . come without warning, to break the day, the world, into the thousand jigsaw fragments (my legacy, my treasure!) it is, since, my business to reassemble. He came and changed, if not the world, then the eyes I saw it with.

He arrived, and nothing is the same.

How it happens: all in an instant, yet, seen now, which is how it has become (*is*!), arranged on a frozen continuum as solid as sculpture.

Arn stops at the edge of the porch steps, places his hands on his hips, and I bump full face into him, but there is no irritated scold or threat. I push off, like a night swimmer maneuvering around a hulk submerged in murky waters, and see my father's Chrysler at the curb. First it is just the long maroon car, the bug screen over the grill, the nose of the hood, the windshield, all speckled and smeared with insects, the streaks of mud sweeping back from the front wheels, the Minnesota license plate, the shadow-figure of the man behind the wheel, the rear windows showing the heaped cargo on the back seat (life-salvage, looted out of Saint Paul), a curtain of shirts and suitcoats hanging on the collapsible bar just behind the front seat, the faded **A** sticker (for gas rationing, his for traveling the Midwest, selling a machine that made a part of a machine that made a part of something to make war).

—all this, and more, more, more, but instantaneous, now frozen, seen at last!

Arn stiffens, squints, sucks at his lips; remotely, I feel his

22

hand come out to take my shoulder and hold me back, as he might if there were a traffic accident or a dogfight.

The driver's door opens, he steps out, his head rises over the roof of the Chrysler, and an arm comes up to wave, sleeve rolled back. Arn looks back over his shoulder at the front door for a sign of my mother, and looses me.

I ran down the steps to him. I did not cry out, did not speak. His head disappeared for a moment as he bent to reach back inside the car for the jacket lying on the front seat. Holding it, giving it a shake to unfold it, like a flag of hoped-for truce, he came around the front of the car to meet me. He hopped the curb, as if longing to break into a lope, but I reached him, just as some sound . . . not *Dad* or *Daddy*, but some sound of like meaning and force, found my lips.

He lifted me, before I might run into his legs, grabbed me under the arms and hoisted me over his head, then swooped me down to his chest and folded his arms over me. Swallowed, clinging with knees and legs to him like an infant, I heard him speak my name, muffled, blunted as it came through the bones of his jaw. His moustache and the incipient stubble of his cheek scratched my throat and ear, the strength of his arms hugging away my breath, keeping me from speaking still.

"How's my big boy," I heard him say. He turned in a circle once, and I saw Arn start down the steps toward us, and behind him, the flash of my mother's housecoat at the front door. Turned fully, he saw Arn approach, so lifted me again, out and away from him, where he held me suspended, then set me carefully down and reached out his hand to Arn. Now I could stand back, apart, see, and listen.

"Hello, Arnie," he said. His voice was weak, not with fatigue, but faintness, trepidation, suspended, as his arm remained outstretched to my brother for a second of total isolation. Then Arn put out his hand and took it. They clasped and released, did not shake.

"Hello, Dad," Arn said.

"So how's it feel to be a civilian?"

"I been back so long I can't remember," my brother said, and took a half step backwards. My mother came out on the porch, reached the stairs, stopped and looked down as if to count them carefully before proceeding, then came on. Then my father stepped back, my mother near, and he stood alone, like me, waiting.

Waiting, I watch, and feel with him this great, hot void of

23

doubt. I tremble. I fear, as he does, that there will be not even a civil welcome, possibly not even the formal words of recognition, and if there is not, then this moment of being with this man who is my father will not really occur. It will happen only as something forbidden, utterance, memory, existence—like the past. Insofar as I feel, and so know myself, an identity in relation to him, his once-removed reflection, then any denial of him is denial of me. All this I know, then-now, in this sweltering and pulsing fraction of time that I make, in writing this, forever.

"Hello, Anne," he said to my mother. His voice is further reduced, shadow of its shadow, words croaking.

"Hello, Buck," she said. She stopped exactly beside my brother. Her hand drifted toward me, fingers spread to take mine, and I moved toward her, knowing my necessary instinct as I instinctively obey. Her hand is warm and sticky on the back of my neck, but I must wait to know what will or can be. I would not—then, now—be surprised to see my father sink to his knees on the grass, mouth open wide to wail for mercy.

(This is to see . . . this is *seeing* how fast he and I are locked together in time; this is understanding why we can, must mean so much to each other. I tremble with him, held close at my mother's side.)

He looks like: well . . . a man who has come a long way to find something. But, having forgotten, perhaps, what it is, and arriving, knows at least this is not it—his quest is obscure and irrelevant, his reception indifferent if not hostile. He might, he feels, have spared himself the trouble, but those consequences are exactly what he had fled. He looks like a man . . . *reduced* is the word. Nearly as tall as Arn (my child's yardstick), a slump has come into his shoulders. He cannot hold his chin up high enough to erase the dewlap, feels his arms and hands dragging him down. This is where, when, I realize that people age, that a man (with luck!) will see the time when he is less than he was, and in that knowledge, torment himself with yearning for that former self. He cannot recover losses, cannot abide self-awareness, never hope to arrest the certain path of his future. He looks like all this.

More: His hair is still dark, but graying at the temples, above and behind his ears, and beginning to thin, the sun shining through it as if it were a frail net where ruffled by his hand. His face is burned with the wind and sun of the long drive from Saint Paul, his features pinched by the gradual vise of middle age (he is forty-nine years old). More subtly, the general sag of cheek, lip, jowl—the bone-deep imprint of sadness and regret. His moustache and the long night's bristle of his beard are quite white.

His dress shirt is pale blue, pin striped, sleeves rolled back far enough to reveal dark grizzled hair on his muscular forearms, and a portion of the blue black, fading, blurring tattoo on his left arm. His collar is open, crumpled, a wide, brightly flowered necktie hanging down his chest like an apron, the knot twisted off-center. In his breast pocket bulge a package of Pall Malls and a Zippo, and next to them the clip of his Parker 51 fountain pen. He has smoothed his suitcoat, laying it carefully over his right arm like a stage-waiter's towel. His paunch swells the front of his wrinkled shirt, rolls over his belt, the shirt coming untucked all around. His trousers are badly wrinkled from the drive, the toes of his shoes scuffed and dusty. He half opens and closes his mouth, as if testing a piece to speak; a fleck of gold inlay winks in his teeth. His wristwatch band is decorated with Masonic symbols. On the ring finger of his left hand is the large imperfect diamond he will pawn before the month is over (even the man who refuses his history desires to leave a heritage!).

We stood there in the heat of noon, my father breathing loudly through his mouth, a whistling, huffing sound, and then Arn cleared his throat and leaned to spit in the gutter. I felt my mother start, as if she had been dozing, shocked awake, her arm tightening as she resolved to deal with him.

"How did you know where to find us here, Buck?" she said. My father shifted his feet, stood a little more erect before answering.

"Sister," he said. "We still drop a line back and forth every so often."

"Now I didn't know that," my mother said.

"Well, look—" Arn started to say, turning away to the boxes on the lawn, the trailer.

"We're moving into a house again!" I blurted—I had to speak, to give him, myself, every chance.

"I can see that, sonny," he said.

"I've got work to do," my mother said. She turned back to the house.

"I guess you can use a hand with the heavy stuff," my father said to Arn. My brother bit his lip, gestured at the stacked boxes as if he could easily levitate them up the steps if he wanted to. My mother stopped on her way to the house, looked wildly,

25

hopelessly at Arn, then turned and walked quickly up the steps, stomping on each step as if she doubted their substance.

"I'm helping too!" I cried, seeing we had won. For the time being, at least, they—mother, brother—were retiring to wait and pick another moment or day to do combat. I ran, grappled with a box too big for me.

"Don't strain yourself," Arn said to me.

"Ease off, boy," my father said, plucking the box up under one arm. "No problem, couple of strong backs." He faced the house, flexed his shoulders, breathing deep.

I watch him expand. He runs a hand through his thinning hair to straighten it, gives his tie a hard yank, using thumb and forefinger like a wedge, spreads the wings of his collar even wider. He steps up to the trailer to take a carton from Arn, deep-breathing like a weight lifter, sucking in his paunch, chest bigger and bigger. He jams his shirttails into his trouserband, hitches them up. "Load it up," he says to Arn, holding out his massive arms. We have, temporarily, won.

"Have you got the big things in yet?" he asks.

"The storage's supposed to deliver today sometime," Arn said. He spoke no more to our father until after we had finished.

We work, my father and I. The sweat runs so freely down his face and neck, soaking his shirt, that he removes it; I marvel to see the unremembered mat of hair, pepper and salt, that thatches his chest like a knitted dickey between the two shoulder loops of his undershirt. His upper arms and shoulders are an unhealthy, bloated white against his sun- and wind-burned face and forearms. Large brown moles dot his shoulder blades. I push myself to keep pace with him, absorb his rhythms, dizzy and close to fainting with exhaustion and uncertain delight.

The trailer empty, Arn drove off to return it to the rental lot. "It's not so hot inside," I said. "We can get a glass of water if you want to."

"All righty," he said, but hesitated at the porch steps until I could get in ahead of him.

"Come on."

"Give an old man a break," he said softly. "When you're my age you'll see what I mean." He followed. My mother, hearing us, moved to a back bedroom.

We waited together, for Arn's return and the storage company delivery van, walking back and forth in the living and dining rooms, our route laid out for us by my mother's arrangement of the boxes, lids standing open like pairs of poised wings. He wiped his face with his fingers, snapped them against his trouser leg, and following my lead still, examined the contents of boxes with me.

"It's kind of small, isn't it?" he said, looking toward the back of the house, where we could hear my mother at work. He spoke low enough to prevent her hearing.

"It's lots bigger than Mrs. Spaulding's. Were you ever there?" I spoke to him as if he were my own age. I knew this man, knew he was my father—I was nine, but had not seen him for nearly three years, and before that he was on the road, selling—I circled him, I think, as I would have any neighbor boy I might have bumped into outside.

"I just meant it's smaller when you get inside and look it over good."

"I can remember some of this stuff from before," I said. I picked up a large silver lazy susan that rattled when I turned one of its tiers. "I think I remember this." I tried to see us all sitting down to a meal, but could not—there was no before, no eating meals, going to sleep in beds, going places in the car (the Chrysler?).

"So do I, boy," he said. "I don't suppose your brother has any smokes laying around loose, mine are out—" but I did not answer. I found a carton marked *Oskar's Things*.

"Here," I said. "Here's some of my stuff. Look!"

I pulled out a tarnished bugle, a pair of cowboy's chaps; beneath them lay a xylophone, red, silver keys cushioned with black felt. "Look!" I cried, "Look! I don't even remember this!" Tied in a bundle were four knobbed sticks for playing it. "I don't know how to play any music," I said.

"Here you go," he said. He lifted the heavy xylophone out of the box, one-handed, as if it were papier-mâché. He sat on a box, testing it gingerly to see if it would hold his weight. Then he laid the xylophone across his knees. I handed him the sticks, and he cut the string with his pocketknife.

"What can you play?" I said.

"Anything you want to hear."

"Just play anything. I can't think of any songs."

" 'Roll Out the Barrel,' " he said like an announcer. He tried the balance of the sticks, waved them grandiloquently over his head, wrists and fingers suddenly turned rubber—for a split second he seemed to go away. His eyes focused on nothing somewhere near the ceiling, and in the dreadful, thick heat and silence of the

27

dining room of my mother's new house, he listened. Then his head dropped with the downbeat, his heel thumped the floor, and he played a flawless, jumping "Roll Out the Barrel." The last echo receded and disappeared.

"Can you do any more?"

"You bet you. Name it."

"Just do some."

"Stop me when you recognize this one," he said, played, but I did not know it.

"What was it?" I asked.

"Think a minute." He hummed part of it. "No? 'Cow Cow Boogie.' No?" I shook my head. "You ought to. Your brother played it fifty times a day on the piano . . ." He stopped. Again he seemed to go away from me, the cluttered dining room. We heard the swishing noise of my mother sliding a box across the bare floor in the back bedroom.

"You really don't remember?"

"No. I don't think so. I don't know."

He began to weep, his eyes filling, speaking rapidly and unevenly, and he sat still, the red xylophone on his knees, sticks in his hands. "Fifty times a damn day. You don't remember the baby grand piano, do you? Arnie used to come in there with his friend—do you remember the Federson kid? They wore their letter sweaters and saddle shoes all the time when they went out together. He'd sit there and pick it out on the piano, they even traced the picture off the sheet music . . . don't you remember the house? I plunked down cash for that house—nobody ever bothered telling you that about me, did they? You had all those Wheaties model planes strung up on the ceiling in your room, Jesus, you had all of them . . . that was one hell of a house, boy," he said. He choked, wiped at his eyes, set down the xylophone sticks and groped for the handkerchief balled in his hip pocket.

"Don't," I said. I was two or three feet from him, glowing in a fire of terror and embarrassment to see this man, my father, blubbering, blowing his nose again and again, covering his eyes from me when he could not stop himself. I was afraid to put my hand out and touch him, as though there would be some paralyzing, destructive static that would collapse the walls and bury us.

"Oh my Christ," he said, and set the xylophone on the floor. The keys rang faintly. One of the sticks rolled away from his foot. "Jesus," he whispered, then pressed his knuckles into his still-flowing eyes, lowered his head, snuffled loudly.

"Isn't Arn back yet?" my mother called before she entered, giving fair warning. He got up quickly and went into the front room, out onto the porch, the screen door banging once behind him. His coughing faded as he walked off the porch. "What's going on?" my mother said when she saw me. I touched my face, felt the wetness of my own unconscious, sympathetic crying, my runny nose. "What's the matter with you, Oskar?" she said.

"I remember all this stuff" is all I could think to say. She took my arm and shook me.

"What's he been saying to you? Answer me! Did he make you cry?" She looked toward the front windows for a sight of him.

"No," I said. "I don't know. I was looking at all this stuff. He played some songs for me."

"I heard it." Her face was reddened, filmed with perspiration. "Go wash your face and hands," she said, releasing me. She went into the front room, after him.

"Don't make him cry again," I said, coming after her.

"I said get in the bathroom and wash your face," she said. "I'll make him something, I promise you," she said to herself as I watched her leave the house. I will not imagine what she said to him.

When I came out of the bathroom she was back at work on her hands and knees in the dining room. She did not look at me.

"Where is he?"

"Out on the porch." She ripped the linens free of the box, threw them onto her shoulder in one violent, snapping motion.

"Can I go see him?"

"Of course you can. You're not in prison."

His back was to me. He was smoking, had put his shirt back on, looking very calm, but he started when I spoke. "It feels good to splash your face with cold water."

"You bet you."

"You can go in and do it too if you want to," I said. I could see no traces of his weeping in his face. He was paler, if anything.

"Thanks but no thanks." His Pall Malls and Zippo were balanced on the porch railing. "Oskar?" he said. "Did your mother ask you what I said? Did you tell her anything I said in there?" He was very embarrassed.

"No. She asked me, but I didn't tell."

"Then I thank you for that." He looked away. "I'll thank you in advance if I can count on you not to repeat anything I ever say."

"Okay." He looked at me.

"Not to anybody. Not ever. Can I bank on you?"

"I promise," I said.

"Good boy. When you're my age you'll appreciate it," and he looked away from me again.

"Why?" I said, but then Arn came around the corner in the old Ford, and a few minutes later, the storage warehouse van with our furniture, and there was work to do.

I only watched. My father worked with Arn; the van driver and his assistant, two very black Negroes, made another team. My mother supervised, identifying what rug went where, directing the placement of chairs and tables and floor lamps. I watched, sometimes following close upon my father as he took one end of the sofa or the platform rocker, sometimes hovering near my mother, who muttered sharply now, of rugs that would have to be pulled back to wax floors, of furniture not appearing to have been adequately covered (as the contract stipulated), of lazy Negroes who took their jolly sweet time doing anything. Gradually, the house defined itself. The sun mercifully went behind clouds, lights were turned on. The house grew its pattern of rooms, and I began to feel that naturalness would take over . . . the last things would be carried in, we would clean up, eat dinner . . . life would begin, and then go on, always.

"Stove and icebox's all's left," the Negro driver said. His work shirt was drenched a dark blue with his sweat, his face and arms gleaming as if greased. His assistant was no more than fifteen or sixteen. His eyes large, round, surprised, as if he had never seen white people before. He never said a word.

"Get out your dolly and we'll wheel her in," my father said.

"Don't need no dolly long's I got me," the Negro said.

"You're kidding me," my father said. But he was not. We all went out to see it. He wrestled the old Norge refrigerator (older, then-now-forever, than I am) to the van's tailgate. The boy looped a canvas strap around it and over the driver's head, across his chest. "I still don't believe it," my father said.

"Seventeen years I done it," the Negro said, "just you keep the door open on me." He locked his fingers together on his chest, closed his eyes, grunted, leaned forward. He trotted two or three frightening, tiny steps, caught his balance, bent nearly double, and then walked with slow and deliberate placements of each foot, up the walk, across the porch, into the house. The boy walked behind him, steering and lifting the corners lightly to keep the balance.

"I'll be damned," my father said. "I'll be good goddamned."

"Man's in shape," Arn said, twitching his biceps and pectorals.

(The word, or the thought, *strength*: I see a glistening Negro carry a Norge refrigerator on his back, and am good-goddamned as long as consciousness exists.)

I watch: my mother looks at me to see if I listen to what my father says. "You dolly," the Negro said, "bus' up the motor. Don't nothing get no hurt this way."

I stayed in the kitchen with my father when the others left. He leaned against the counter under a bank of cupboards, staring at the lengthening ash on his cigarette.

"He's strong, isn't he?" I said.

"I'd say so."

"Could you carry it if you had to ever?"

"Not on the best goddamn day I ever saw. Not on your life."

"How's come?" I said.

"How come what I can't carry as much as that nigger: Maybe because your old man's no nigger." The ash fell off his cigarette. He scattered it on the linoleum with the toe of his shoe. "There's a whole hell of a lot of things I'm not, sonny." He held the cigarette under the tap and dropped it in a trash bag my mother had put out on the counter.

"Come on," he said, prodding me out of the kitchen, his hand like a warm, dry rock against the small of my back, "let's go watch your nigger lift that stove." I felt I had shamed him with my interest in the Negro's strength, much less my admiration.

The van left, and we were all in the dining room, waiting. I was close to him. No one sat.

"So when's chow?" Arn said, and, "You starting to digest yourself in there, Os?" He swiped at me, to dig me in the stomach with a finger or dutch-rub the back of my head, his smile strained. I ducked behind my father. He would not risk bumping him to catch me.

"We can't go out to eat like this," my mother said. She looked at her dirty hands, touched her brow with her wrist, but I knew she meant: not together, with my father. She had waited, and this was her moment to oppose him, to fight again. My father made a point of coughing, sniffing loudly to clear his nose of dust.

"I can pick up something for sandwiches at the delicatessen if you'll drive me," she said to Arn. "Get washed and come along, Oskar," she added quickly, as if she had just noticed and remembered me.

"Can't I wait here for you?" I said. My father stepped to a window to look at the house next door.

"If you like," my mother said. Arn jangled his car keys and looked hard at me as he went out with her. My father sat down then, but did not speak, nor could I think of anything to say for several minutes. I picked up the old bugle and blew a shattering, raspberry blast. He jumped in the rocker where he sat as if I had stuck him with a needle.

"Loud," I said. "How about playing some more songs?" I pointed at the xylophone on the floor in the corner.

"Some other time," he said, and, "Am I a goddamn stepchild to eat off a dirty plate on the back steps?"

"What?" I was poking in another box on the dining room table. This one held miscellaneous hardware, small metal parts and hand tools.

"You don't turn even a nigger out without a meal," he said. I did not answer. He was building something, gathering and sharpening the small and unspoken insults of my mother and brother, mustering them to cover and relieve his hurt. "You'll never live to see the day Buck Hansen refused to buy a round or stake a panhandler to a meal," he said. I was afraid he would get up and throw his chair. I hunched my shoulders against whatever might come. "Not so much as where are you staying, have you had your dinner, kiss my sweet patootie, Buck Hansen," he said.

"What's this!" I cried to divert him. In the box of nails and screws and files and hacksaw blades lay a pistol, its finish a pitted gray, one of the hard-rubber grips cracked. I picked it up and held it out to him.

He said, "I guess that was mine once." He took it from me, laying it on the flat of his hand. It was a bulky .38, once the property of a machine tool company in Chicago, where my father worked as shop foreman, long before my birth, during the Depression. Issued to a watchman, the man was laid off in a cutback without notice, and before the personnel manager had a chance to request its return, he sold it cheap to my father to get even with the company for laying off a family man without warning or compensation. "See," my father said, "here's the ammo."

There were three bullets in a Bull Durham drawstring sack,

neatly, in my mother's fashion. With his teeth, he pried open the knot, emptied the bullets onto the dining room table, reached out to keep them from rolling off. He broke the gun open and loaded it, then lifted it, one eye closed, aimed into the kitchen. "Pow!" he said. "Got him, Tom, dead center," like the Ralston radio show. "It's nothing to fool with," he said, and laid the pistol on the table. He folded his hands in his lap and closed his eyes.

"Should we go outside or do something?" I said.

"What the hell for?" he said.

"I think I'll go outside and look around. I want to see if there's any kids live around here." I started to go.

"Oskar," he said. His voice was unnaturally deep, his chin almost resting on his chest.

"What?"

"If you go outside and leave me here alone by myself," he said, "I think I'll shoot myself with this gun." He had not unfolded his hands, did not raise his head. I could not tell if his eyes were open or closed. I laughed, once, hard, half hysterically.

"I have to go outside I think," I said.

"I'm afraid I'll kill myself if you leave me alone," he said. I walked back to him. Close, I saw he shook in short, regular spasms, as if he were holding himself to keep from flying apart. I waited, thought only that Arn and my mother would return soon and save us both.

See him, son:

Buck Hansen sits: for the man in the middle of the earthquake, no reality is firm. The unrelenting heat of this strange, lifeless house, the final and frightful relief promised in the rusting .38 pistol on the nearby table, the starkly terrified breathing of the nine-year-old boy, his late and accidental child, hold no horror like the immediate past. In the sanitarium bed he cannot pay for, in Saint Paul, Irene, wife of his casual and mechanical adultery, wastes to a hag's death. Her flesh melts, she shrivels, her face a skull mask, begs him for mercy he can neither feel nor bestow. Her breath is sour in her convulsing mouth; a glossy clawhand lifts to clutch coldly at him. His business creeps to a strangled finish in the musty office of a decaying building. An old rolltop desk flows with due bills, letters of regret and refusal. The electricity disconnected, a tomb dust of failure settles on the cheap-deal furniture, irrelevant rubber stamps—he carries away, a thief in the night, anything of value to hock for getaway money. Buck Hansen is some ghost without the power to haunt. Anne shames him, a faded picture of a plain girl in their wedding portrait. Overdue

33

alimony and child support. How much time and life will it take to preserve something here? His daughter smiles cynically in the comfort of her own tragedy. Arn is a man already, bursting with stupid confidence, quick to play judge and executioner on request. And this boy, frightened by his own ignorance? Hope glimmers like easy mockery—Lillie Broadfoot in black underwear, blood red lips and nails, wet, groping kisses; a thug-brother Ben at her side, drunk on Buck Hansen's lies of big deals yet to come. And somewhere, pray God still back in Saint Paul, sniffing a cold scent, the skip chaser Sheldon Rotter in a new Studebaker. Oh Jesus, God, thinks Buck Hansen, what did I ever do to you?

"Mom's coming," I said. He looked up, released his hands.

"Put that away," he said without looking at the gun.

"It's loaded."

"Oskar . . ." But I was running to meet them on the porch, and to break my promise to him, never to tell—as I break it now, again and forever.

"He's going to shoot himself if we leave him alone!" I shouted. "Hurry!"

"Damn you! Damn you!" my mother screamed, running past me. Arn grabbed me before I could follow her.

"Get in the backyard," he said through his closed teeth. He pinched the back of my neck so hard I squealed at the pain. "Get out in the back until I tell you to move, so help me," Arn said, and I went. "Mom," he said, and ran in after her.

I do not know how long I waited in the yard. Time is nothing and everything to children. First I only wept, and when I had passed the cause of my misery, and the misery that is caused by misery, I hiccuped to a stop, through the necessary stages of embarrassment and wonder. My face caked with dirt and sweat and tears, drying to a plaster, I leaned against the house to listen, but heard nothing beyond the rumble of shouting voices, as indistinct as the past. I came away with my clothes smeared with the white powder of the disintegrating coat of paint. Then I heard the front door slam, my father starting the Chrysler, the screech of his tires as he pulled away from the curb.

I wandered back to the weathered, leaning one-car garage that creaked in the very late afternoon heat. I stayed for a while in the shade of the new-blossoming crab-apple tree, and then opened the gate and walked over to the brick trash burner that jutted into the narrow alley. The odor of the dry ashes in the burner seemed to clear my head.

I wondered if the huge steel, horse-drawn garbage wagons could squeeze past, or would they park out in front and the men use the opportunity to search for wild mushrooms to take home in their lunch buckets. Would we still take from the Luick Sealtest Dairy here, or Borden's, and would it be a horse and wagon or one of the new trucks? I looked up and down the alley carefully, but there was no one. Were there *any* kids in this neighborhood?

The Chrysler just appeared in the alley, as if he had been parked at the end of the block, out of view, waiting for the right moment, my crying over, when I reached the balance of boredom and curiosity, about to venture out in the neighborhood or back inside to ask for a delicatessen sandwich. There was a little roar of the engine, and there he was, coasting to a halt opposite our open garage, hidden from the view of anyone in the house.

He stuck his head out the window. "Oskar," he said, pulled back inside, leaned across the seat and opened the right front door for me.

I went around the front of the car, but stopped short of touching it, not sure if I was disobeying my brother. "Arn made me stay outside," I said.

"He forgot I'm still his father, no matter what, that's all," he said. If he had been angry, or cried again, reached for me, cursed, I might have run inside to report it, but he spoke calmly. He had been somewhere (gas station rest room?) to clean up. He wore a fresh shirt, his hair wet, combed. "I just came to see you," he said. "We didn't get much of a chance." I nodded, as if memorizing, expecting to be quizzed later.

"Are you going to die if you're alone?" I said.

"My trouble is I think I'll live," he said.

"Are you going away again now?"

"I have to, boy."

"Are you coming back?"

"I couldn't say for sure either way." Did the law haul a man back to his wife's deathbed, to face civil judgments? Was there a slot, a job, waiting in Chicago? Would his brother offer sanctuary in Indiana? Was Lillie, on Long Island, a dead end or a fresh start? How could he have said?

"I never see you much I guess," I said.

"That's one main reason I came."

"It didn't work so good," I said. He straightened up behind

the wheel, raised his head to peer through the branches of the crab-apple tree at the house.

"Goddamn," he said.

"What?"

"Nothing." He reached for his Pall Malls. "Want to take a little ride with your old man?" He flipped open his Zippo, winked at me, spun the wheel to light it with a theatrical snap of his fingers. The flame popped. "You ain't seen nothin' yet," he said. The inside of the Chrysler filled with fragrant smoke.

"Where to?"

"You name it, you got it." He put the car in gear.

"We could go over to Jane's house if you know the way," I said. He hesitated only a second, looked once more at the apple tree, the garage, the peak of our new house.

"Like the man said," he said, reaching out, his arm like a scoop to clear room for me on the seat among the road maps, toilet kit, cigarette packs. "Hop in."

I got in and he leaned in front of me to grab the door, close and lock it. "Where to said the chauffeur," he said. He winked again, touched my ribs with his elbow, ashed his cigarette out the cracked wing.

"Jane's house," I said, and we laughed. He accelerated, ducking as we passed the backyard gate. There were no faces in the windows to see us leave. "Do you like our new house?" I said.

"Oh, it's a doozy," he said. "No doubt about it. Absetively, posolutely," he said.

III

My sister lived on Milwaukee's South Side, halfway across town from Cramer Street, among the thick, rough swarms of Poles who manned the assembly lines at Nordberg's and Allis-Chalmers and Allen Bradley. She moved there shortly after her husband enlisted in the Navy, in 1942, because rents were lower, and to be close to Nordberg's, where she worked until just before V-J Day, a Rosie the Riveter on the graveyard shift, supplementing her government allotment and, as the wartime propaganda put it, freeing a hypothetical man to fight for his country. The allotment checks went into savings, the savings designed for the new postwar life that was to begin when her husband returned, the new life that never did begin for my sister Jane.

And there she stayed, after Nordberg's laid her off (for union activities—there were, I'm told, real communists lurking somewhere behind the scenes), after the government's ten thousand dollars came in to join all those accumulated monthly allotment checks in the savings account. My mother didn't like it. It wasn't, she said, any kind of neighborhood for decent people's children to live in. There wasn't any need for it.

Once, the war just over, Arn still in Europe, Mrs. Spaulding pushed my mother close to too far—worried about our use of the hot plate, complained of my footsteps overhead, something—and my mother threatened to move out. Jane offered to take us in if she really meant it.

"No thank you," my mother said. "I have no desire to learn Polish. I suspect I'll hear it soon enough from my grandchildren if things go on." Jane dropped it without another word. She smiled, or smirked, or opened her mouth to let cigarette smoke drift up over her face, and changed the subject entirely. She had her reasons, but they were no one's business but her own.

We crossed the Sixth Street viaduct, the air immediately pungent with the smell of dung from the stockyards in the valley below us, richened with the appealing odor of yeast cooking at the Red Star plant, suppliers of the city's breweries. On the other side, the change was sudden. There were more taverns, several to a block sometimes, signs in their windows quoting the day's special price for a boilermaker, and we ran into a wall of industrial racket. Behind the frosted glass of factory windows, the light of cutting and welding torches flared. I looked up at the clock on the Allen Bradley plant tower. The Army and Navy E flag, a landmark for me on all the Sunday afternoon streetcar trips I made during the war with my mother to visit Jane and her children, was gone.

"Mom doesn't like polacks," I said.

"Is that a fact," my father said. "I can't say as how I'm specially partial to them myself."

"How's come?"

"This is neither the time nor the place," he said.

"But how come Jane lives over here then? Where they all live."

"Maybe she likes them. I'm just kidding you. I don't know. I guess she worked over here, didn't she?"

"Not any more though."

"You're right," he said. "I'm not an expert on the subject."

"I don't think Jane likes polacks either. She doesn't like Mr. Lenski, I know."

"Could be. Poles," he said. "Polack doesn't sound so hot."

"It stinks here," I said. "Pee-you!" I held my nose, half clowning.

"What's that?" He poked in the full dashboard ashtray to see if it was smoldering. "Oh." He turned to his window and sniffed the smoky, metallic air. "It does that. They built a hell of a lot of hardware here for the war, boy. Let me tell you."

"But if it's over now," I said, "and she doesn't work here anymore, and she doesn't like polack people, why does she still live so far from us?"

"Search me," he said. We crested the hill on Howell Avenue, the Nordberg plant jumping into view, and he turned off to get to Rosedale Avenue where Jane lived. "Don't ask me to try and figure out your sister, boy," he said. "I just don't have the answers to that."

Rosedale Avenue was entirely row housing, cramped lots with tiny patches of hard dirt for lawns, the buildings separated by narrow, cracked sidewalks leading to small backyards, an alley, and behind them all, the Greenbaum Tannery, its lot cluttered with pallets of heaped, salted cowhides that stank in the sun. Jane's block ran to a dead end, a steep, weed-grown bank, behind which ran the tracks of the Milwaukee Road. (I remember, on Sundays, wartime visits, climbing the gravel bank, standing to watch and count the number of freight cars, wave to the engineer and fireman, the signalman on the caboose, trying to memorize as many names as possible, painted on the cars: Burlington, Great Northern, Wabash, Rock Island Line . . . laying my ear on the slick surface of a rail, feeling pulled in by the deep humming that must be an approaching train . . . once, perhaps inspired by Mr. Lenski, who told me of a boy found, cut in two, near the roundhouse, I piled stones on the rail, shuddering with anticipation of the imagined derailment and wreckage, but kicked them off when my mother screamed to me to come away . . .)

"This must be the place," my father said, setting the hand brake.

"Have you ever been here before?"

"Not in your memory," he said. It was a small house, like all the others on the block. Her downstairs apartment was really a converted basement. The Lenskis—her landlord was a Milwaukee Road brakeman—lived above. His sons were delinquents, brought home often in squad cars for stealing auto parts, truancy, raiding other boys' garage-roof pigeon coops in the neighborhood. One was named Jerzy, a delight and a puzzle to me every time I heard it pronounced. His wife was a starvation-thin woman who cried loudly when she was beaten, or when she tried and failed each Saturday night to carry her burly, insensible husband up the stairs after the night's drinking at the Polonia Lodge.

In the middle of the three front windows of Jane's apartment, their sills at ground level, she still displayed her gold star flag. "I'll be damned," my father said, stopping to stare at it.

"It's for my brother-in-law. He got killed."

"I know what it is."

"I don't remember him."

"I do. Come on, let's face the music." Before I could think to wonder, or ask what music, Jane opened the door, waiting for us, prepared.

She wore a heavy, quilted bathrobe, despite the heat, wrapped close, tightly belted, firmly knotted. In the fingers of one hand, of course, was her burning cigarette. Her face was puffy, eyes swollen, as if she had just gotten out of bed. Her long, blonde hair was only pinned back out of her eyes and off her neck, instead of in the single, ropelike braid that hung to her waist, uncut since before her husband's death. She swung the door open as I reached for the knob, as my father searched for the nonexistent button to ring the bell.

"Hello, Jane," my father said.

"Well look who all's here," she said, looking at me. "Come on in, Daddy," she said, "it's hot out there."

We step down into Jane's living room, dark behind shades drawn to resist the heat, the air a little dryly stale, our eyes slowly adjusting. She turns on a table lamp. The room gives an impression of abstinence, penny-pinching, caution. The furniture, scarred end tables, frayed doilies on the worn arms and backs of upholstered chairs, the collapsed sofa cushions, a small radio with a cracked, discolored plastic case, the napless carpet—it cried secondhand, relatives' attics, church rummage sale, Goodwill. All the ashtrays are full to overflowing, and in the light from the lamp, smoke hangs in dead layers. Every available surface, table, radio, the telephone desk, bears a picture of Richard Hackbarth, her dead husband. I have no memory of him, none.

One is only a Kodak snapshot, trimmed with a scissors to fit an oval frame. Richard Hackbarth sits astride a motorcycle, booted, the straps of a white cloth helmet dangling on his shoulders, goggles on his forehead. Another, enlarged, is Richard Hackbarth and, by some mystery of time before my time (so mystery to me), my sister Jane, side by side on a bridge railing, holding hands, their hair blowing in an invisible wind. On the telephone desk is Richard Hackbarth's official Great Lakes boot camp graduation portrait. Jane has had it tinted. It is badly, terribly badly done. His eyes are depthless marbles of glossy brown, his skin a nauseous orange, teeth like lacquered cubes of sugar, the blue of his seaman's jumper almost black, his hat a halo of impossible, dimensionless porcelain-white.

"Sit down, Daddy," she said. "I was more or less expecting you. Mother called me."

"Did she now," my father said. He sat heavily across from her.

She has saved everything. In her spare closet hang his suits and jackets, the kind once called sporty, or even zoot. I have found the cloth cyclist's helmet and the goggles, buried beneath her lingerie in a dresser drawer. In the telephone desk, locked safely away from her children, are the rolled, rubber-banded drawings Richard Hackbarth did as a hobby. He liked to design fanciful automobiles, but they all have rumble seats, all look a little like Pierce-Arrows or Cords. My father did not like him.

He called Richard Hackbarth a jitterbug (they entered dance contests, sometimes won, and the trophies are packed, carefully wrapped in cheesecloth). He called him brainless, directionless, strongly opposed their marriage. They eloped across state lines to Greencastle, Indiana. And now Richard Hackbarth is dead, and my sister has elected this strange, hidden life, and my father sits here across from her, running from his own life, in a direction he has only half decided upon as yet.

"Where are the kids?" he asked to break the silence when Jane would not.

"Out. Babysitter," she said. "I thought you might be coming. Mother didn't say you would, but I thought you would from what I heard of it. I told you not to go over there."

"I see. You only heard her side of it."

"What I didn't think was you'd ingbray imhay." I pretended not to understand.

"I don't see the harm," my father said.

"You don't? You better look at it from her side for a minute," she said.

This is my sister Jane. She is tall, slender, blonde, attractive, looks even younger than she is (twenty-five this 1946 summer)—unless you look into her eyes. Like the crudely tinted eyes of her dead husband in the boot camp portrait, hers tell you nothing. Except that there is much you cannot be permitted to know. She can, as she will now, with our father, share portions of a common past, if need be. But she has choked off her ability, or willingness, to trade in any and all that begins with the death of Richard Hackbarth. She dutifully brings my niece and nephew across town to be grandchildren to our mother. She will talk prices or politics or the unreliability of public transportation, but always, behind her beautiful blue eyes, there are secrets, dimensions of understanding, inside stories that she betrays with no more than a snicker, a sardonic look into a vista she denies the rest of us.

A parttime legal secretary in the evenings since her layoff at Nordberg Manufacturing, she has holed up in this basement apartment with her children. (A vague sum: her hair is a hard-edge marcel for her high school graduation, class of 1939, her unsmiling face in the rear row of the Song Club, a certificate attesting to her proficiency on the piano, my mother's structured anecdotes—"Nobody could dance like your sister Jane. She had music in her blood. That's how she met her husband. No, I know you don't remember him.") Here, she takes her stand, knowing what she knows, determined to be efficient, to survive in that knowledge. Let others look to themselves.

She stubs out her cigarette, reaches in her robe pocket among wadded tissues (she is a private weeper, never public) for another. My father fumbles for his Zippo, stretches to light it for her. She exhales, nodding casually, a woman accustomed to accepting small masculine gestures, courtesies, but caring little for them. This is my sister Jane: I must guess, create, what I cannot know.

"It was a mistake, I hope you know that," she said to our father.

"Meaning what exactly?" he said, glancing at me. I pretended absorbing interest in the dial of the radio, the picture of Richard Hackbarth and Jane, in the toes of my shoes.

"Going over there," Jane said, "especially on a day like this, moving in, when she's trying like hell to get back on her feet." Her voice hardens as she speaks, discovering anger as she recalls our mother's telephoned, near-hysterical report. "She doesn't know you've got company with you, you know. When she finds out there's the devil to pay for everybody, I promise you."

"I didn't come to get in a discussion about your mother."

"What did you come for then, Dad?" She sits back, deep in the sprung sofa, crosses one leg over the other, smooths her robe over her lap as if preparing herself hurriedly against any pretense he may attempt. The room is dim with their cigarette smoke, and they stare at each other like opposing lawyers about to present briefs.

"My God . . . " my father said. And what should he say? He can only rely on the mix of half-lies and half-truths that is the substance of my knowledge of him, that hairball of feints, evasions, and false fronts that is my task to untangle if I will seek understanding. What else could he say?

"Irene and I are going through the wash," he said.

"You don't say," Jane said softly. Then, a sharp, ugly sneer spreading slowly across her mouth, mockery flowing into her chill, beautiful blue eyes, she laughed. Then she choked on her cigarette, bending almost double on the sofa, racked with long, lung-deep coughs, holding her cigarette away to keep from burning herself or the sofa. My father lowered his head, ran his fingers through his hair, looked at the worn carpet between his shoes until she recovered. Her eyes were damp with the exertion of coughing. She swallowed hard to find a voice, but the terrible smile of her vindication had not left her face. "Do tell," she said, swallowing, sniffing, stubbing her cigarette out in the nearest dirty ashtray, reaching at once for another in her robe pocket among the Kleenex. "I'm not hardly going to believe this," Jane said.

"Damn funny to hear some people tell it."

"We don't all see it exactly like you do, Daddy."

"No doubt."

"When you go about making a mistake you really make a whopper, don't you," my sister said.

"Sometimes your life's full of them." If he sought sympathy, she would not give it.

"That's for a fact," she said, and then, suddenly loud, on the verge of tears (no, she will not cry, ever!), "Oh hell!" He started on the edge of his chair. "Are you serious, Dad?" she said. "Do you want me or Mom or Arnie to say we're sorry for you and Irene? Do you want us to be responsible when she lets you down?"

"Nobody let anybody down," he tried to interrupt.

"Well I'm not. I'm not sorry for you, if that's what you're asking for, and I don't think for a minute Arnie or Mother is either." Ask me! Ask me! I want to cry out, as dead to them in this instant as the framed photo of Richard Hackbarth I hold in my hands, a small, small piece of the world that is not destroying itself in front of me. Ask me: I'll be sorry for him.

The story? How common. Mundane. Yet special, particular for me, us, my son. Though I repeat it ten times ten, you cannot *know* it. No. Nor can I. We cannot know it, but all the same, we must make it ours! Gather the fragments scattered in questions answered and ignored in years following; collect, assemble, shape, discern. Now, flesh out the bones, let them breathe. See, it moves! It is ours. Because we have made it. Where the truth is dim, the fact contradicted or lost, we must fabricate. Listen.

We must imagine what we do not know. Who can ever *know?* It is all a lie, but in it, of it, we make our truth. He was my father. You are my son. I stand between you, telling his story, mine, making it yours if you will but listen. Listen. I know only what I can imagine, what I *feel* as truth. We must not, dare not stop at fact—I tell you this lie, but if you can believe, if you will believe, then it shall be our truth, and give us reason for our living. *Listen.*

For Buck Hansen, 1942 is one hell of a good year. You damn bet you, with the tax receipts to prove it. It's so good it takes a little while before he can really believe it. There are moments when it all kind of hits him between the eyes. There are moments when he sits in the engineering offices of jerry-built shops, thrown up at government expense to produce for government cost-plus contracts, when he has finished his pitch, and he can't help but look helplessly into the eyes of the purchase agent sitting across the table from him in shirt sleeves and open collar, and he wonders what in hell ever made him think he could get away with it.

Buck Hansen, sitting here nice as pie and talking about sums of money he can't even imagine—he looks helplessly into the face of the purchase agent across the table, and Buck Hansen asks himself, who in hell's half acre do you think you're kidding, and he fully expects to get tossed out on his keester. But the purchase agent only thumps the papers with his knuckles, or clears his throat, and says "Can do" or "Looks kosher from here," because when it comes right down to it, all that matters to these hobo engineers is cost-plus, and nothing at all seems to matter to the federal inspectors who okay contracts. Buck Hansen unscrews the gold cap of his Parker 51 and says, "Let's get your John Henry," and he has a commission so big he can't really believe it, all the way on the road to Parsons, Kansas, or Davenport, Iowa, or Gary, Indiana, where the next jerry-built shop on his itinerary, built at government expense, waits for him.

Every week or ten days or two weeks, he rolls home to the big new house in Milwaukee, with maybe three days of dictation to knock off in the district office, and there are more of those moments.

He stops to look back at his Chrysler, big as a boat, the motor ticking under the hood as it cools, and he looks at the '41 Plymouth the company bought for his wife because he'd be on the road so much, and he looks at the big new house that is still unreal after the years in Chicago apartments. The lawn is wide and green, and two tall, symmetrical evergreens flank the front walk, and evergreen shrubs hide the foundation, and there are French windows all the way around this wonderful house. He hefts the heavy grip in his hand, squeezes the leather briefcase under his arm to make it squeak, lets himself stand between the tall evergreens an instant to feel the hang and quality of his sharkskin suit.

It hits him like a mallet, and he remembers when it came his way after the steady, grinding years in the shops in Chicago, the hopping like a frog on a griddle to keep his head above water while the Depression tore good men to pieces all around him. After that, when he got his crack at it, he tried to talk with Anne about it, just to get a handhold on it, and it was no good talking to his wife about what and how he *felt*. There was nobody else he could talk to, and he ended up feeling foolish, calling his brother long-distance at the farm in Goshen.

Buck Hansen smiles, standing between the tall evergreens, hidden in their shadows, imagining Thurston rolled out of the sack to answer the phone, sure only death in the family or the last trumpet justified late phone calls. "Is the family okay, Oskar?" Thurston said. "What's wrong?" He felt like a fool, like a ten-year-old running to his big brother for protection, but he got it out.

"They want me to sell, Thurston. They want me to be a salesman."

"What's wrong? Can't you sell?"

"Of course I can. I just wanted to tell you about it, I guess. If I told you how much money they're talking about you'd think I was stiff. I'm not just kidding you, brother."

"So go be a salesman. You can do anything you want, can't you? That's what you always told me, anyways."

"I guess maybe I just wanted to tell you the news. Forget it, Thurston. Go back to bed. I'm sorry I woke you up," Buck said.

"How's Annie? How's your family, Buck? You getting along any better with your daughter, I hope?"

Buck Hansen gets out his key to open the front door of the big new house in Milwaukee. Anne will come to the door, almost at once, and it will be a wonder to him, a thing not easily believed,

45

that in the midst of all this that has happened, that still, after all that he has become, it will still be the same Anne. Anne Tanberg from Hambro, Illinois, wearing a worn housecoat, her rapidly graying hair coming uncombed, wearing old, broken shoes because it does not pay to wear good shoes to do the housework; she will be there in the midst of all this new wonder that Buck can at moments not quite safely credit.

If it is late, Anne will be sitting up special to meet him, darning or reading by a single light in the large living room. She will make a meal, and talk . . . complain that Arnie doesn't do as he's told quickly enough (Buck must talk to him), lament, subtly, that their daughter will not come to the house when Buck is home, urge him again to do something to end the estrangement (yes, a girl, a woman, has to go her own way when she marries, but Buck Hansen will not forgive her marrying a zoot-suiter jitterbug nobody who runs off to join the goddamn navy with a wife and two babies to support). Anne will have saved something cute the youngest has said. He thinks briefly of his youngest child, only a few years older than his grandchildren, and it is all the more wonder.

If it is not difficult to go through these moments of disbelief—they come, they pass, and he is sure who he is, that he is the same man he has always been, it does not, just the same, always seem right. He looks about himself and sees all the new wonders that have come about, and then remembers that he is in his forties and a grandfather twice, that he has on the one hand a son already taller and broader in the shoulders than he is, on the other a small boy strangers would think too young to be his son, and Anne, who is somehow fantastically still the same Anne Tanberg of Hambro, Illinois, only older . . . it does not seem somehow right. Why could it, for example, not have happened sooner?

It is the rarest, the most unexpected, the most glorious thing that has ever happened to him in all his life, but it is so strange, not quite right in so many small ways, that when he comes to total the year 1942, it has been one holy hell of a good goddamn year, but Buck Hansen is not at all sure it will last, the newness of life in and around him.

But it seems to. 1943 is no different. He is on the road in the enormous Chrysler, an A sticker giving him unlimited gasoline, and besides, he knows places where ration stamps are not required for gasoline, or for tires, or for shoes or meat or cigarettes either. It is Anne who saves stamps to help their daughter out, Anne who buys a cigarette rolling machine and a sack of Bugler, when Buck can get all the Pall Malls he wants. Anne flattens their empty tin cans to cooperate with the scrap metal drives. Anne saves fat to turn in to the butcher for meat ration points, and Buck does not bother to tell her how silly he knows it all is.

1943 just goes on with it. He is on the road to Muncie and Detroit and Anderson and Minneapolis, and cost-plus is the magic behind the machines he sells. The machines that make a part of a part of a machine that makes something for the war, and it feels now like it will go on forever. He only knows how far he has come, how different it all is, when he goes ninety miles out of his way one afternoon to see his brother on the farm at Goshen.

"That's some car," Thurston says.

"The only way to travel. I'm sold on Chryslers. When they start turning them out again I'll be in line, I hope to tell you."

"How you getting all this gas for this running all over the place, Oskar? I get me two gallons a week, besides for the tractor."

"It's for business," Buck said. "It's who you know, anyway. Haven't I always told you that? You never believe me when I tell you a thing, will you." They sit on the ancient glider in the shade of the back porch. If Buck hadn't thought to bring a bottle of rye in his grip, he'd have been stuck with potato schnapps or his sister-in-law's lemonade. "Drink up," Buck says. "There's plenty more where it came from. What's more, I know the place."

"You know darn well I ain't one of your drinkers, Oskar." Shading his eyes with the palm of his hand, Buck can penetrate the heat waves that shimmer over the unpaved county road that connects them, if you go far enough and turn enough corners, with the town of Goshen. As it gets closer he makes out the Amish surrey, a second horse tethered behind it. "I'll be goddamned," Buck says. "When the hell's the rest of the world going to get them do you suppose?"

"Why should it?" his brother said. "They keep their own ways, don't bother nobody."

"Draft-dodging sonsabitches."

"Come on. That's dumb," Thurston said.

"Come on my fanny," Buck said. "You forget I got a boy in now. Since May."

"He ain't in no danger going to that school, is he?"

"I was in once myself too, don't forget."

"You saying something's wrong because I stayed home to help out our Pa? Besides, all you done was fly whiskey over from Texas and sell it, you told me," his brother says. Buck looks at his brother. He is always annoyed to find that there are qualities of hardness in him, qualities he respects, as a younger brother always retains some vestige of respect or fear for his elder, simply because he is the elder, always has been, will be.

"That was different," Buck says. "You weren't dodging the draft." The Amish surrey has long since passed on the dirt road, the dust raised by its high wheels settling back.

"You never paid enough attention to nobody but yourself long enough to find out what I was doing," his brother said. "A man doing so good like you say shouldn't get so bothered, Oskar."

"Sometimes I envy you, brother," he says, but does not mean it. Over his brother's shoulder he sees his sister-in-law Marie, spying on them from the small pantry window, checking to see how much of Buck's rye they are going to drink. He stays for dinner, but counts the trip a bust. No matter how many ways he brings it up, neither Thurston or Marie will ask him how much money he is making this year of 1943. The hell with it anyway, Buck Hansen thinks as his Chrysler leaves the farm, Goshen, behind in the dust of the unpaved county road.

There are some changes in 1943. In early May, Arn is admitted to the ASTP program for pilot's training (Buck is pleased—he was a flying sergeant in the first war, though he got no farther in the rickety Spads than Texas, where he flew to pick up booze in crates, moonshine, for his barracks-mates at dry Fort Sill). Arn is called to report for schooling before his high school class formally graduates. They gather, Buck, Anne, the little boy, and for this occasion, Jane and her babies too. Anne and Jane weep because Arnie is leaving, and the little boy weeps because his mother and sister weep, and the babies cry because they are uncomfortable and unattended. Buck takes his son's hand, and hugs him, waits for unwilling tears or the choke of emotion to strangle him, but they do not happen. There is something so inevitable, and thus natural, about it, and if Buck thinks of anything it is his own departure for the first war, and of how different, how much better these Army Air Corps uniforms look than his did. He gives his son more money, at the last moment, than he planned to. His old man, Buck Hansen reflects, gave him his unspoken curse, and would have thrown in a boot in the tail with it if he'd been spry enough.

And Richard Hackbarth is killed and buried at sea in the Pacific, and the formal estrangement of Buck and his daughter is over. Now, when he returns from the road, Jane and her babies are often there, but it is not much better between them. Jane will speak, ask him if he did well, was the driving rough, but her presence is oppressive. Anne will flee frequently, upstairs to their bedroom, to cry, hard and silent, at their daughter's plight, the innocent fatherlessness of the two small grandchildren, and the whole atmosphere of the big and wonderful house in Milwaukee seems to combine against Buck Hansen, to make him feel that he is supposed to feel some guilt or contrition for his dislike of Richard Hackbarth, his opposition to their marriage. He is damned if he will! It ought, the intangible death and burial at sea, to make things better, return them to normal, but it does not. And he does not like to hear Jane say to her children, "See, Granpa's home. That's your Granpa, see?" Buck Hansen is only in his forties. If he'd make up his mind to take off a little weight, he could pass, he believes, for a good deal younger.

There is still some delight in the returns home from the road. It is good to sit at the new stainless steel and Formica kitchen table, to be waited on by Anne while he talks of sales, commissions, personal triumphs over men he secretly suspects are better men (he could not say how) than he is. Anne is impressed, and even Jane, if she is about, will leave her children, bring her cigarettes and coffee into the kitchen and listen politely, ask the kind of questions that let him say just about what he wants to. And it is some delight to watch his little boy tear through the compartments of his grip to find the presents Buck has brought home for him from the road trip.

It is the road, the hours in the swaying, powerful Chrysler, the sales pitches that always work because nobody needs to be sold, the packing away of contract agreements, the whole new life, that is finally larger and more real. Anne, Jane, Arne, his little boy, Thurston and Marie, the years in Chicago machine shops, quickly diminish. It does not surprise him greatly, when he bothers to think about it, that there should have been an Irene Peterson.

It might be any hotel, almost any woman, but it is Minneapolis, and Irene Peterson sitting at the bar in the lounge, having some difficulty with her cigarette lighter.

He swears (or will swear) that he never tries to fool himself, no matter how he lies to anyone else. She is not attractive. She is no idea of a mistress that he has ever nourished. It is enough that this is the new life that he has trouble believing in, that Irene Peterson is, that she, as well as any other, can help him to believe, to know, to take hold on it and make it his for certain.

She is too tall (for Buck's taste). She is too thin. She is

decidedly flat-chested, potbellied, her hips too wide for her height and weight. Her skin is too pale, the veins in the backs of her legs, her neck, the insides of her wrists showing through a grayish blue. She wears a lot of makeup (Anne wears almost none), rouge and face powder, eyebrows plucked and replaced with the thin, arched, too-hard lines of a pencil that does not exactly match her hair. Her eyes are blank, unpleasantly magnified by glasses just a bit too thick to keep from noticing them. She dresses well, puts her money on her back, but good clothes do not look well on her. She wears steep high-heeled pumps that torture her incipient bunions. The cheap costume jewelry she buys is always too large or bright for her wrist or neck or ears. She can look pretty good, sitting at the lounge bar, stupidly snapping a Ronson with no flint in it, but is older than she will ever admit to. "Let's not get talking about people's birthdays, Buck," she says in the lounge of the hotel.

Later, after the second or third night together, at another hotel, she gets as close to the truth as she ever will (she cannot, for Christ's sake, hold her liquor worth a damn!). "I'll be honest with you, Buck. I'm not twenty-nine anymore. I'm not even thirty-nine."

"So what are you?"

"Cut it out, damnit!" she shrieks.

"Just keep it down to a low college roar, will you," he is forced to say. Nearby people at the bar and in the dining room turn to stare, smile, shake their heads. Buck hustles her out as quietly as possible.

Much later, he discovers her rich brown hair, long, carefully waved, is a dye job to conceal wide streaks of premature gray. But he never kidded himself that Irene was any beauty queen, nor that she was any too bright. He had to explain to her how it is a lighter can't light without a flint, and if she'd ever heard of a cost-plus contract, it couldn't be proved by Buck Hansen. She did not know how to drive a car, could not cook so much as an egg decently, and while she knew there was a war on, she thought it had something to do with the first one because the Germans were mixed up in it both times. He tried talking politics just once. He let it drop when she promised to take his word for it to vote against Roosevelt next election. It was the first she'd heard, if she was telling the truth, that Roosevelt was part Jewish. She promised to get her mother, her only relative living, to quit voting for Franklin Delano Rosenfeldt. He had to explain the joke, too.

What she did (besides crawling in the hay without making a

50

federal case out of it, or turning too soupy on him) was to listen to him like he had the gospel. And Buck Hansen talked to her, in hotel bars, in the Chrysler on short business trips when she started going along for the ride, in bed (she was nothing special that way either—however much she'd been around, she wouldn't talk about that either). She listened. He talked, and she sat there, never taking her eyes off him, listening, her blank eyes behind those slightly-too-thick lenses fixed on him as if she couldn't possibly blink for fear of missing something vital. Irene Peterson, about whom Buck Hansen will not bull himself, listens, and he talks.

"The nearest I can figure it," says Buck Hansen, "is the war. Sometimes I feel like it was waiting for me, or I was out in cold storage somewhere, waiting for it to happen, only I couldn't have told soul one it was going to happen if my life depended on it. I'm serious. You know my life. The more I think about it, it all works up to it, the war, now. You following me? You do that, when you get old enough or something, you get to the right point in time. You look, Christ, I look back and try to see how one thing leads to another, what all. One time it looks like so much dumb luck, slop, another, you look again and it dovetails. You know what I am, Irene? I'm a goddamn dyed-in-the-wool hick. I mean that seriously, the best way. Someday, I ever get the chance, I'd like for you to see where I came from. Jesus!" He laughs, to think what Thurston and Marie would think, say, do, were he to drive up the unpaved road from Goshen with Irene Peterson sitting up high on the seat next to him like nobody's business.

"You know what I'm trying to tell you about?"

"I don't know, Buck. I guess so. I'm not always so sure I always get you when you're being serious."

"Not by a long shot. It sounds screwy as hell, I grant you. The hell with it. It doesn't come out to six bits to rub together, but it fascinates the bejesus out of me. If you could have known my folks. My old man for instance. My mother died when I was a kid. Go ahead, guess what kind of an old man I had. Seriously. Just try and describe him from what you know about me. Go on."

"I can't, Buck. Honestly, how should I know," says Irene Peterson.

"You could at least give it a damn try," Buck says, irritated, but he relaxes in the fact that he never believed she was any whiz kid on brains in the first place. "Have another schnappser," he says, or "Take a gander at that map and see how close we are, my hind end's killing me," or, "It doesn't amount to a hill of beans any way you cut it. Turn out the light." And she drinks up, or reads the road map for him, or simply waits quietly to see if he will start talking again.

"I'm not letting any grass grow under me," says Buck Hansen. "How long you think this war is going to last? You got to be a man with a plan, like somebody said someplace once. You get a chance, and you either jump it or you hold tight and rot. I'm not kicking, but I don't dare let myself sit still. This bubble's going to break sooner than later. Where do you think I'll be, this, this job, when it's all over?"

"When what's over?"

"The war, damnit."

"I don't think I know what you mean, Buck."

"I'll tell you where. Out on my ass in a snowbank if I don't make do to do it any different. You think I'm planning to live on the road all my life? You damned right not. And all a man's got is all he ever had, himself, himself, and maybe if he's lucky, like I've been lucky, some contacts here and about and then he's got what he can make out of it. You can bet your sweet Aunt Fanny I'll be ready when it comes due. What's so damn funny?"

"Aunt Fanny," says Irene Peterson.

"It doesn't take a whole hell of a lot to amuse you, does it?" She is very easily hurt, and this too he likes. He'd have to hit Anne over the head with a club.

"Come on, Buck. I can't help it if I think something's funny. Don't start picking on me, please. Why do you always do that?"

"Forget it," he says, because he would rather talk, and be listened to, than hurt her at this moment. "Don't start the damned waterworks, there's no call for it, you hear me?"

It is because he has hurt her, and has to do something good enough to make it up to her before she will forget it that he promises and makes good on taking her along this time when he heads back to Milwaukee. But for that (he will think often in future), Anne would never have been any the wiser, nobody hurt, nothing . . . none of it (he thinks often in future when he seeks more intensely for a cause, the cause, of it all).

He never knew exactly how it got to Jane. Cut it any which way, it started on its way because Buck Hansen couldn't keep his big mouth shut about it. He may have told as many as a dozen men about Irene, on the road, in the district office in Milwaukee. "The invitation's swell, hunky-dory," says Buck Hansen, "but just on the Q.T., she isn't Mrs. Hansen. There is a Mrs. Hansen, but she's not her. If it bothers you we can call it off, but I like to keep that sort of business straight. The fact of the matter is I counted

on you not being the sort of man would make a fuss about it."
Most often, they did not. One dozen, maybe two, who could
remember how many people he told?

The only one he was positive about, letting out the news that
Irene was in Milwaukee, at the Schroeder Hotel, was Cal Rocker.
Which he could forgive himself telling if he was honest with
himself (he will make great efforts to be honest with himself in
future). He'd known Cal Rocker since Adam was a corporal, since
Chicago, when Buck Hansen was a master tool and die maker at J.
I. Case, and Cal Rocker came to work as a blueprint detailer,
nineteen years old, only a few years older than Buck's son, Arn.
What he knew about machine tools he knew from Buck Hansen,
and what it came down to was Buck feeling a very real sense of
responsibility for him. Buck Hansen brought him along to
Milwaukee once he got his feet on the ground in the new job, and
once Cal got his draft deferment settled in Chicago, he took to it
like a duck to water.

Cal Rocker, who was a snot-nosed twenty-six- or -seven-year-
old, would have been detailing blueprints, or maybe apprenticed
to some bohunk machinist, if Buck hadn't taken care of him, and
here was Cal Rocker already making his big move to get in on the
fast and fat end of the gravy, some big deal with a couple of kikes
or whoever, going in business for himself at cost-plus back down in
Chicago. The long and short of it was that Buck felt like telling
this kid something to set him back on his heels, just so he'd
remember who was who, and when. So he told Cal Rocker that
Irene was in town with him, staying at the Schroeder Hotel while
Buck was spending his nights with his family in the big new house
with French windows.

"You're kidding me, Buck."

"The hell I am."

"I guess you aren't. What does a fella say? I'll be damned. I
guess I just never imagined you that way. I'm really surprised. You
always seemed to get along so well with your wife, I mean."

"Who said I don't? The world's not that simple, son. Relax, it
happens in the best of families."

"I reckon it does," said Cal Rocker, who did not take the
news in just the way Buck wanted him to. He did not ask
questions about Irene, where Buck met her, when, details. He just
grinned a smart-aleck grin and shook his head like Buck had told
him he'd done a Brodie off the Brooklyn Bridge.

"You damn tootin' it does," Buck said. "Give yourself time,
you're hardly dry behind the ears. Who knows, the big city of

Chicago may corrupt hell out of you. Look out those hebes don't skin you alive when your back's turned." They both could laugh then. Buck was not sorry he told him, only disappointed that it didn't do what he wanted it to. He made a little silent, secret prayer that Cal Rocker's partners in Chicago would strip him to the bone and boot him out in the cold.

Jane knew Cal Rocker slightly, but he could not believe Cal would have told her. Whatever, whoever, Jane found out, and that was it.

Which is not to say it was all that simple. It wasn't. He naturally got to staying out on the road a good deal longer than before; a swing through the circuit of his customers was not complete until he'd backtracked to Irene's apartment in Saint Paul, which meant an extra four hundred miles plus on the Chrysler, an extra two days or three, in Saint Paul. And he found excuses to see customers in the Twin Cities, which all meant he came home less often than before, stayed fewer days than before. Nobody in the district office in Milwaukee cared, not what with the volume Buck brought in each trip, and Anne did little more than remark he seemed to have no time at all left for his family—she could put up with anything, she said, because she knew how much it meant to him. Jane had her own responsibilities, and Arnie was gone, but Oskar, it seemed like to her, might as well almost have no father at all, Buck was gone so much.

It did not get to him so much with Anne. Somehow, without it being a formal thing that he'd settled in his mind, he had broken completely with her now. Somewhere along the line she went on, the same, and he went his way—this, the new life. She was still Anne Tanberg from Hambro, Illinois, and whatever he was, it wasn't Oskar Hansen from Goshen, Indiana. And he had no regrets about that. Christ, he could look in a mirror and see how far he'd come!

He did not think much about Arnie, once he was gone. He had been mad as hell—they went, Buck, Anne, Jane, the little boy, to see Arn's high school class graduate. The principal made a brief general remark about the boys, half a dozen or more, who could not be there, but did not so much as read their names. Anne cried, and Buck waited forty minutes to get the principal alone to give him hell for it.

"I'm sorry, Mr. Hansen was it? I understand how you feel. All I can do is apologize. I should have known better."

"Sorry's not half good enough. You remind me of the jerk was principal of the hick high school I had to sit through until I got fed up. Sorry won't help the boy's mother out there, and it for damn sure won't cool me off. I ought to knock you on your fanny!" The principal looked at him for a second like he expected just that, and then he walked away without speaking. "You son of a bitch," Buck said almost audibly, but that meant nothing. What he was thinking of was what the hell right he had to sound off, what with Irene and all. And he was thinking of the principal of Goshen Township High School, who he had told to go to hell one fine day in the spring of 1914. But that passed very quickly.

Jane scared him a little. Often, she came over from the South Side early in the morning, packing up her kids and a ton of gear to take care of them for a day, right after getting off the graveyard shift. When Buck rolled in from the Twin Cities, she would be there in the living room, smoking, worrying a cup of Anne's egg coffee, clutching a balled-up hankie in her free hand, watching her children at play on the rug as if they were going to disappear if she let up for an instant. Her expression was drawn, yet strong, from having been without sleep for too long. "Hello, Sister," he might say, surprised by her presence after thinking mostly of Irene all the way home to Milwaukee.

"Hello, Dad. Rough trip?"

"No worse than some I've seen. You look a little fagged yourself." He did not kiss her. Sometimes he left quickly, went to the kitchen to see Anne. Sometimes he stooped to hug his grandchildren. Rarely, he sat to talk to her, waiting on Anne to hear his voice and come in from the distant kitchen, rooting for her to hurry and get him loose of his daughter, who frightened him just a little.

"Make a lot of money, did you?"

"A little here, a little there. How's yourself?"

"I'm keeping body and soul."

"Do you? Can I talk to you seriously for a minute, Jane?" He was not sure, later, if he was sincere, or if he meant to buy up her allegiance in advance, just in case. Because she scared him a little. "Or am I off your list for good, is that it?"

"Of course you can. Don't talk so silly."

"Then just tell me if you can why you insist on this. If it's the money, you know goddamn good and well you can come to me. Do I have to tell you how much your mother would like you to move in here? Christ, I'm gone so much—"

"Not a bit," his daughter said. "I don't need your money, and I do need my own place. I mean that the best way I can, Dad."

"Okay," he said. Anne was coming now from the kitchen. "Cut off your nose to spite your face. I'm sorry I didn't get along with your husband. I can't help that. Forget I said anything," Buck said.

"That's not it at all. Let's leave things alone, Daddy, okay?" She was already beginning to smile, to be ready when Anne walked into the living room. But it seemed like more to Buck, as if she knew a whole lot more that she was saving for the right time and place. Which was foolish. She let him have it right between the eyes, without a second's hesitation, when she found out what he figured only Cal Rocker could have told her.

"Come here, you," Buck said, grabbing his grandson. The boy squealed and kicked his feet in delight. He was something to hold onto with Anne coming in the room, and Buck hit with the foolish thought that his daughter was going to blurt out something disastrous.

The little boy, Oskar Jr., was just that. Like Buck's grandchildren, he was just so small, young, that it made no sense at all to think about him at all in connection with Irene Peterson.

It was like a rehearsal, thinking about it later. It was up in Minneapolis, shortly before he more or less set up a permanent base for his road work in Irene's Saint Paul apartment. Buck was awake. He had gotten in late from Duluth last night, called Irene to meet him, the reservation for two arranged a week earlier. The business in Duluth had not been good, and he was tired. They had a drink out of the fifth of rye carried in Buck's grip, and went to bed. He expected to sleep long and late, but he was awake early, lying on his back, without remembering waking up. He put his hands carefully behind his head, not wanting to wake Irene beside him. His eyes were open, the ceiling a dark nothing above him, thinking of nothing in particular, still tired, when the knock came.

At first he was angry only because he would have to get up, take his hands out from behind his head, frustrated because he could not yell to whoever it was to get the hell away from his door because that would wake Irene, and he did not want to wake Irene, or talk, or move. The knocking stopped only momentarily, began again before he was out of the bed. He rose very slowly to keep from jostling Irene, laid the covers back very gently. He was in his shorts and undershirt, but the knocking started up for the third time, so he did not grab for the robe lying across his open grip on the floor near the bathroom door. There was a short, dim hallway with a vanity mirror. He had a quick, horrifying look at himself, gray stubble on his jaws, hair sticking up in all directions like spikes, eyes puffy.

He unfastened the chain Irene insisted on hooking before she turned in, as if cat burglars would rob them while they slept. "Holy jumping Jesus!" he said softly when he had trouble with the doorknob. He had been lying awake, a little tired still, but feeling fine, resting, thinking of nothing in particular, and now he was up, his bare arms and legs cold after the warmth of the bed, his nose clogged, head fuzzy, all the sour taste of openmouthed sleep on his tongue and in the back of his throat. He threw open the door so hard that it banged against the wall. Irene said something as she woke.

"What the hell do you want?" Buck said. It was a young man, about Arn's age. He was a good half a foot shorter than Buck, very slender and delicate looking. What enraged Buck immediately was the cleanliness, the neatness of the young, frail man, the clear, small eyes, the sense he radiated of wide-awake alertness, a cheerful confidence, a tight, active vitality. The young man carried a briefcase, held something up toward Buck as he spoke. The lights were on in the hotel corridor. Buck realized he was squinting terribly against the blast of light, and he was embarrassed to be standing in his underwear before the clean young man dressed in a suit and tie.

"Good morning," the neat young man said. "I'm out talking to people today. I think you might be interested—" He did not seem to see Buck's wrinkled shorts, his bare limbs, the state of his hair. Buck focused on the paper the young man held close, higher, for him to see. *The Watchtower*. It was very fast, but when he thought about it later, it was more than just being madder than hell at being rousted out of the sack. It was shame. Shame that he would not accept, would not take lying down. It was one hell whole of a lot more than knocking the frail young man around for being nosy, a pesty son-of-a-bitching Jehovah's Witness.

He never actually hit him. Buck grabbed him by the tie, his lapels, he grabbed him under the throat with one hand, grabbed the hand and wrist that held the *Watchtower* with his other hand, shoved him straight back across the corridor and jammed him up hard against the opposite wall. Through it all, the Jehovah's Witness never lost his relaxed expression, and he never dropped his briefcase or the copy of the *Watchtower* that Buck tried to wrench loose and jam in the young man's face. Through it all, the Jehovah's Witness kept repeating, "Excuse me, sir, I'm very sorry, please sir."

"You goddamn psalm-singing son of a bitch!" Buck roared in his face. He got a good hold on him with both hands and rocked him against the corridor wall again and again. "You pious goddamn bastard, I'll break your skinny sonofabitching neck for you. I've got a boy your age out for bullet bait to save your goddamn hide, you draft-dodging bastard!"

"Buck? Buck, what is it?" Irene said. Buck wheeled around to see her, spinning the Jehovah's Witness with him. Irene stepped behind the hotel room door, wearing only a nightgown. She stuck her head out again to see what was happening. "What is it, Buck?" Without her glasses she looked like a blind woman. Her hair was smudged out of shape from her pillow. The skin of her neck and shoulders was a dull dead-white, the polish on her nails a shrieking, obscene scarlet.

"Close the damn door. Get the hell out of the doorway!" He let his fingers release the young man's jacket.

"I'm very sorry," he said, twitching his narrow shoulders, stretching his neck to get his shirt and jacket to hang back in place. Buck turned on him.

"You come at my door again, so help me God, I'll kill you." The Jehovah's Witness backed away, as easy and confident looking as ever. Buck toyed for a moment with going three steps, catching, letting him have it within an inch of his life.

"Buck, please come back in, please?" Irene said from behind the door.

"What's going on?" The man came out of the room next to Buck's. He was wearing pants and shoes, but bare to the waist, a tall, very thin man with a shiny, hairless chest, tiny, dried-looking nipples. His hair was freshly plastered down, his face half shaved, thin swaths of shaving soap showing the tracks of the open straight razor he held carefully away from his body in one hand. He carried a bunched hotel towel in his other hand. "What gives?" he said. The Jehovah's Witness kept moving, backing sideways like a crab, turning, disappearing silently down the carpeted stairs. The tall, thin man with shaving soap on his face shook his head, as if he had witnessed something pathetic or disgusting. He turned and reentered his room, closed the door behind him. Buck, alone in the well-lit corridor, dressed in baggy shorts and undershirt, clearly heard the tall man hook the chain and snap the lock on his door.

"Buck, are you still there?" Irene said. He could have been

standing alone there in the corridor only a few seconds, but it was very intense, still seeing the man's straight razor. He had not seen a straight razor . . . since when? His own father had shaved with a straight razor, once a week, Saturday mornings, hell or high water. Buck remembered the first time his father let him use it, hovering close to him, Buck standing over the basin of hot water. They were on the mud porch, off the kitchen, and it was cold on the porch, and steam rose in swirls out of the graniteware basin. Buck shaved his face for the first time in his life—he was what, sixteen?—careful lest his hand waver and lay his skin open, lest his father correct him. *Am I doing it right, Pa?* he thought he had said. What had his father said?

The tall, thin man with the straight razor was like having his father see him like this. Jesus God! Buck Hansen thought at the wash of raw, child's shame that hit him. "Buck?" Irene said. She stuck her head out again.

"Will you get to hell in there like I told you?" he said, and pushed the door roughly open, slammed and locked it behind him. Irene was about ready to cry. She sat on the bed, huddled, her hands clasped in her lap, shoulders moving in random spasms, her head down. She looked repulsive to him. The nightgown hung very loosely. Her feet were gray, insteps laced with raised, blue veins. Her bones stuck out at her elbows, her shoulders, the base of her neck. Her hair looked dirty, and her voice sounded as if she had a bad, nasal cold.

"Buck, will you please tell me—"

"Knock it off!" he said. "Just shut your trap and forget about it. No skin off your nose at all, so be quiet. Don't start your damn maudlin yammering at me, goddamnit!" Then she did cry, a long, nose-honking, messy harangue. He did not go near until she wore herself out and went into the bathroom to clean up.

He stood in the middle of the room, his toes and fingertips growing colder and colder, trying not to see her, smoking one dry, choking Pall Mall after another. What, he asked himself, if that had been Anne at the door, or Arnie, or, God help us, Jane? What would his own father, dead almost twenty-five years, have said or done if he'd found Buck like that? Holy jumping Jesus. Give me a goddamn break! Buck Hansen said to himself.

Through Irene's sloppy crying, he tried to listen for the sound of the tall thin man in the next room, to hear if he would strop the razor before putting it away in its case. And that night, Buck Hansen had his first dream in which his father, dead twenty-five years, watched him. Buck did nothing in the dream.

He lay on the floor in some strange, empty room, and his father stood over him, watching him closely. *Hi Pa*, he said to his father, but his father said nothing. When he woke the next morning, the alarm set to get him on the road early for Milwaukee, he thought to tell Irene about it, make up at the same time for being rough on her the day before. But she slept through the alarm, her mouth open wide, and did not wake until he was on his way out the door with his grip in his hand.

"I wish I could come with you, Buck," she said.

"You're not even out of bed. I'm late as it is."

"I meant sometime."

"Sometime. We'll see," he said. Not on your best damn day, he thought. What if that had been somebody else at the door? Never, he promised himself.

But he broke that promise before long, and that was about it. Had he spread it to anyone else besides Cal Rocker that Irene was staying at the Schroeder? The only difference was—thank the Lord for small favors—that he was not in the hotel when Jane went down to blow everything to hell and gone. Irene called him at the office, about the time he was wrapping things up to leave. He planned on stopping at the Schroeder for an hour or so, then going home to the big new house that he still wondered at a little.

1943 is still one hell of a good year for Buck Hansen. He has the tax receipts to prove it. If the end of a life, one kind of a life, is not counted. "I hardly know how to tell you this," Irene Peterson sobs, "your daughter, Buck. She was here. Here at the hotel. She got my room from the desk. Why did you use your right name, Buck? I thought she was going to hit me. She called me all kinds of dirty names, Buck. Can she make me go away, Buck? She told me to get out of Milwaukee or I'd be sorry for it. I'm *not* lying to you, Buck, honest! Your daughter." It takes, it turns out, forty-six years to make a life, but it goes up the spout in a couple of weeks, a few months to get it all down on paper.

"If you will stop," says Buck Hansen to his wife of twenty-five-odd years, "if you will stop for one solid minute at a time and let me explain myself."

"You be damned and go to hell," says Anne Hansen, née Anne Tanberg, of Hambro, Illinois; he would never have believed there was this in her. "You're a dirty pig! You make me sick to look at you, and your children are ashamed to know you for their father. Get out! Get out of this house and get out of my life! Damn you to hell, damn you!" Jane will not see him. Between them, Jane and Anne, they take care of Arn.

60

I do not know how to say what I feel, writes Arn. *I talked to Jane on the phone at the base telephone office. She told me most of the facts there are I guess. Mother wrote me twice since I talked on the phone to Jane. I do not know what I am supposed to say to you. When people talk to me about their father I do not know what to say to them about mine. If I knew I would. I wish I could make myself talk to you about this it would be better than in letters. I feel almost like I do not have a father at times.*

"She can have the house," says Buck Hansen. "She can have her alimony, and the support for the kid. She can have whatever she wants," says Buck Hansen to a lawyer who if he is not a yid at least looks like one. Named Meyer, so impossible to be sure. "That's why we're meeting, isn't it?" says Meyer who looks like a yid even if he is not one.

"You'll do what the law tells you to," says Anne, who in the end surprises him all the more by refusing alimony and taking only twenty-five a month for the little boy.

"She could have picked me clean," says Buck Hansen to Irene Peterson. "She could have hauled me up on the beach and let me rot dry. Be grateful for small favors, like the man said."

"Does it mean I won't see you now, Buck?"

"What in hell's name are you talking about?"

"I thought if you blamed me for it you'd be through with me now," Irene says.

"What good would blaming you do me?"

"I was afraid it was all over between us," Irene Peterson said.

"Don't holler before you're hurt," said Buck Hansen.

With the little boy, it did not even make common sense. Buck squatted on his haunches, his hands on the boy's shoulders. The boy, much less understanding what was going on, did not even sense Buck's seriousness. There wasn't a hell of a lot Buck could say, with Anne watching like a chicken hawk no more than ten feet away, in the dining room of the big, new, wonderful house in Milwaukee, the last day Buck Hansen saw the inside of it.

"Will you be a good boy for me?" Buck said.

"Sure. Where you going this time?"

"A long way. Pretty far away, for a long time I think."

"Will you bring me something again when you come back?"

"You bet. Give me a big hug and a kiss now. That's my big boy. Oh, you're strong! That's my good boy. Be a good boy."

"Are you crying, Daddy?"

"No. Certainly not. Not on your life." He stood up, his knees cracking, and he touched the boy's hair, hoping he would follow him to the door, but he did not. If he had, Anne would have corralled him. Buck did not look at her, did not speak. He went out and got into the Chrysler and headed for the Twin Cities and his new life.

The next year (and 1944 was better than ever!) Irene started putting the bite on him to make her honest. He would not have, except that he was laying plans to set up in business for himself, to make his pile the way Cal Rocker was making his down in Chicago. When a man made a new life, he might as well go whole hog, Buck Hansen thought. So he married her as soon as his final divorce papers came in from the Family Court of Milwaukee County. Which, marrying Irene Peterson, was one of the dumbest, sorriest things he had ever done, Buck thought (not so much later).

"Nobody's feeling sorry for Buck Hansen!" my father said loudly.

"Then what!" Jane shouted back at him. "What! What can we do for you? What do you expect from us? For the love of Christ, we don't have anything left for you here, Dad! There's nothing left of any of it, for any of us, don't you see that? You threw it all away, and we can't any of us make it up for you again." She did not cry. My mother fell easily into hot, grudging tears; Arn retreated to coldness, an awkward, cheap resentment; if my sister Jane released her hurt, she did it without letting anyone see it hurt her.

"I didn't come here begging a goddamn thing," my father said. He may have meant it, if only for the instant in which he said it. "The past is past," he said.

"Amen," Jane said.

"I'm not even fifty years old yet, and I'm by Christ not going to live the rest of my life like some old coot with nothing but his rotten goddamn memories of what's over and done with to feed on while I wait around for the undertaker to haul me away."

"Dad," she said, looking at me, "little pitchers."

"The hell with what's been," he said, ignoring her, me, up now, striding back and forth in front of her, waving his arms. "If all I cared about was that I'd still be busting furrows on my old man's farm." He continued to pace, to challenge more than berate the past, almost smiling now at the memory, I think, of his father's farm in Indiana, at the vision of himself, perhaps, transported intact, between the handles of a plow, chucking at a team of horses. "What the hell's the use," he said.

62

"I was about to say the same thing," Jane said. He stopped pacing and stood in front of her. She did not uncross her legs under her robe, did not change her expression, let the ash grow long on her cigarette until it fell in her lap, where she let it lay.

"I thought I could count on you, Sister," he said. "That's my mistake. I never looked for anything from Arnie or your mother. With good reason. You I could write and get an answer. I thought you cared if I lived or died or disappeared somewhere out hell's half-acre. I won't make that mistake again."

"Now who's feeling sorry for himself, Dad?" The long ash on her cigarette, white as snow, forming a gentle arc as it grew, splashed into her lap, but she did not brush it away.

"You never got over that in the first place, did you?" he said. "You never forgave me for it. Hackbarth," he said. "Are you satisfied now? You got enough of my hide to suit you?"

"That's not true."

"True my sweet—" he began to say when Jane's telephone rang.

"That'll be mother," she said.

"I give a good goddamn."

"There was a call for you earlier, this morning," she said as she got up to answer the telephone. It rang beside me on the desk, again and again. "A Rotter somebody, long distance from Saint Paul," she said. My father said nothing about this. It was the first I heard of the Jewish skip chaser, at that moment somewhere on the highway north of Milwaukee, after my father. My father moved to the front door, forgetting me for a moment I think. It was my mother on the telephone.

"He's here," Jane said to her, watching my father. "Both of them. Yes, he brought Oskar here with him. I don't know that. I'll tell him, Mother. I'll tell him."

At my name, my father looked at me, reached his hand out; "Come on boy," he said.

"Dad," Jane said. She laid the receiver on the desk, my mother still talking, and came after us as my father opened the door. It was strange; the brilliant sunlight was gone, the afternoon over, the sky dull, dusking. "Leave him here, Dad," she said. "Arn can come and get him. Don't make things worse."

"In a pig's eye," he said. "I'm still the boy's father. I've got rights too. You know what your trouble is?" he said, pulling away from her, yanking me sharply along, as she touched him. "The trouble with you is you forget I'm still your old man, no matter what, and that still counts for something, by God, in my book!"

My sister stopped outside her door as we continued down the walk and got into the Chrysler. My father pushed me in, slammed the door, went around the front of the car to get in.

(In my memory, sparks are struck by the blows of their words: the postman slips his delivery through the brass slot in the front door, and the floor shakes as my father half runs heavily to reach it before anyone else, to intercept letters from Irene Peterson if she is so foolish as to write him at home . . . I am under the dining room table, playing with tin soldiers once my brother's; my father follows after my mother, "It wasn't *dastardly!*" he pleads.)

"Why are you doing this to us!" my sister shrieked.

"Tell it to the Horse Marines," he said. He put his thumb to his nose, extended his fingers and waggled them at her—at the repetitious row housing of Rosedale Avenue, at the city of Milwaukee, the world that was not Buck Hansen's, and wanted no part of him, had no place for him. The warm tires squealed as he took corners too fast.

"Dad," I said. "Dad? Daddy. Hey, Daddy."

"What?"

"I didn't forget."

"What's that?"

"You're my father." He looked at me, looked back at the street we drove, looked at me again. He pointed his finger at me, dug me softly in the side, winked.

"You bet. How'd you like to take a trip with your old man, son?"

"Where? I guess so. Sure."

"Anyplace they'll have us, huh?" he said. "And I know a few. Hold onto your hat. I don't get to town often," he said, "but when I do . . . *bang!* goes the egg money!" He winked again, and I laughed.

IV

"Daddy? Dad?" Now we had left the streets I recognized. I did not know where I was. He drove grimly, both hands on the wheel, leaning forward slightly, as if it were raining or foggy, the road treacherous. The Chrysler's upholstery, red leather with panels of plaid fabric as coarse as raw wool, tortured my bare legs, the car's interior baked by the sun as it sat outside Jane's house. But the sun was setting, the air coming in the hood's windscoop and the open windows beautifully cool and moist. "Dad." I spoke for reassurance, to hear myself, to hear his reply, to make manifest that no matter what had happened, what strange part of the city we passed through, he was there with me, and I with him, safe no matter what.

"What is it?"

"Are you mad at Jane?"

"That's not exactly the word for it."

"Are you mad at Mom and Arn?"

"Let's get off this, shall we?" He let loose of the steering wheel with one hand to fumble in first one shirt pocket, then the other, for his cigarettes. "Scout around on the seat there and find me my smokes, will you, sonny?" He sneezed and coughed violently after he got one lit. "I'm going to give this up one day, see if I don't," he said to himself.

"Dad?"

"Yeah."

"Are you mad at me at all?"

"Hell no. Jesus name, boy, you're with me now. Come on, talk about something else."

"Who's Rotter? The man Jane said called you at her house."

"Glory," my father said, and checked the rear-view mirror. "You hear all the good ones, don't you? Some other time and place." I think he drove a little faster, eye on the speedometer to see how much over the limit he dared.

"Can't I talk about that too?"

"Why would you want to? Give your old man a break."

"Then what can I talk about?" I may have sounded as if I were about to cry. I was only stymied.

"You know what a skip chaser is? A collection agent?"

"No."

"See what I mean?"

"Tell me."

"A yiddie sonofabitch," he said, "and pardon my French."

"What does he do?"

"He's a creep who makes his living chewing a man's bones. You been told never to kick a man when he's down or his back's turned?"

"Japanese sneak attack," I said.

"You bet you. A skip chaser is a Jew bastard who makes a living kicking people when they're down for the count, get it?"

"No."

"Put it this way. Know what owing money is?"

"I think so."

"Your old man owes some money. A skip chaser comes for your throat to get it before you can pay it off like a white man, if you see what I mean."

"Who do you owe money? A kid owes me a dime, but he moved away."

"That's neither here nor there, but you get the idea."

"Why is he a Jew?"

"Because that's what he is. A Sheldon Rotter is a Jew is a Jew is a Jew, would smell as sweet, etcetera. Because no white man worth his name would do it."

"I don't get you."

"You know how your mother doesn't like Polish people so hot? Polacks, right? I don't like Jews. Let's change the subject, huh?" I looked out the window, but we might have been in another city.

"Sonny," he said, "are you with me?" I did not understand what he meant.

"Sure."

"Want to play a game? You ever count cars when you ride along like this? You know what different kinds of cars look like? You know what a new Studebaker looks like? The brand-new ones that look funny?"

"Coming and going," I said. "I know a kid's dad has one. He thinks they're neat."

"That's the ticket. We'll play a game. Whoever sees a new Studie yells out like a stuck pig before the other guy, get it?"

"How's come?"

"Tell you what I'm gonna do. Just to make it interesting. For every Studie, new one, you see before I do, I'll give you a penny. One cent American. If it's green, you get a nickel. Sound good to you?"

"But I get the penny every time still if it's not green?"

"Damn straight. Deal? Deal," he said. "Okay, starting now. You got to keep your eye out if you want to get rich. Hop to it." The Chrysler speeded up. We went on, through the streets I did not recognize, and I watched, until my eyes ached, for new Studebakers. For the new, green, 1946 Studebaker of Sheldon Rotter, the Jewish skip chaser who was after my father for his bad debts.

Why me? Buck Hansen got to asking himself frequently, along about the spring of 1946.

He was forty-nine years old, and knew damned well he looked every day of it. If not more. How did I let that happen? he wondered. He'd paid no attention, and this worn-out, shot-to-hell body had crept gradually up on him, jumped him, become him. He took to looking at the few photographs he'd held onto when he was divorced. The semiprofessional athlete he had been in his youth was an anonymous stranger, a lanky, gangling, smirking, smart-aleck in a baseball uniform complete with a Connie Mack hat. He concentrated, tried hard to get past the sun-squinting, skinny punk in the baseball uniform to the inside of him; to get inside himself the memory of what it had been like to be that wiseacre baseball player in the bad team photograph. But it was no dice. He could sit hunched over the picture, straining like a man trying to pass a peach pit, and all he got was himself, forty-nine years old, feeling ready for the boneyard, holding an ancient photograph in his shaking fingers.

He felt ready for the glue factory half the time. He believed, all his adult life, that he was more-than-average attractive to women. When he entered a bar, a hotel lobby, a business office to face a receptionist, anywhere women were present, he always perked, deliberately, as if it were an obligation to live up to as good as he could look. Now, he lacked the energy, whatever, believed women found him old, and worse, could not always make himself care. His gut was too large and soft to suck up and hold in; he was forced to wear his suitcoats unbuttoned to keep from looking like a stuffed penguin. His forehead was permanently and deeply frown lined, his neck creased, and his dewlap no longer disappeared when he raised his chin. The gray in his hair, at his temples and above his ears, was too uneven to look distinguished. Worse, he was losing it. He examined his comb and brushes with horrified anticipation, afraid to estimate how much loss was normal, healthy, how much the sure handwriting on the wall for Buck Hansen's crowning glory. And there was no damn way to figure that and come up with justice by anybody's book. Flowing out from under the Connie Mack cap of the punk ballplayer could be seen the wild, thick thatch of dark brown hair, healthy as pasture grass. He tried to recall the hereditary formula; but his mother's father (seen last when Buck was eleven, the old cocker near eighty) was full headed, his own father as hairy as a goat the day he died. No justice for love or money!

Ah! His moustache, once as trim and precise as the Arrow Shirt man's, was white. His beard had gone snow white on him.

Buck Hansen tried to resist it, but he was exceedingly tired, and could not seem to rest up. An evening of pure relaxation, a *Time* or *US News* on his lap, listening to "Amos 'n' Andy," Mr. Anthony, "It Pays to Be Ignorant," Fred Allen, and other favorites, did nothing for him.

Chain-smoking seared his throat, clogged and irritated his nose, made his chest ache and resound with rales, his eyes water. His fingers and toes grew cold as lumps of ice. His hemorrhoids tingled unpleasantly, his tailbone was sore (five years on the road behind the wheel to thank for that!). His head throbbed, and his stomach growled like a sewer drain. If he indulged in a few bottles of beer or a cheese and sausage snack, he got gas at once. Liquids went through him like a dose of salts, like he had no kidneys left. His ankles swelled in the evenings, and varicose veins in both legs drove him frantic with scratching. Jesus God! Buck Hansen thought.

At times he was sickened. The backs of his hands were not yet liver spotted, and the veins, though prominently raised, did not show blue. But the first two fingers of his right hand were forever stained a dark orange brown from the smoke of thousands of Sweet Caporals, Twenty Grands, and Pall Malls. Even immediately after washing his hands in his wife's scented toilet soap, he could raise the fingers to his nose and smell the stomach-wrenching, nose-tickling odor of stale cigarette smoke. It lived in his clothes, in his car, in his office, in the walls of his apartment.

Undressing to take a bath, he might look back over his shoulder and see his ghostly white, elephantine buttocks and thighs in the mirror, be reminded of some carnival fat lady, Dutch nudes. Sitting in the tub, he had only to glance down to be revolted by the thick white tires of his enormous middle, like the pleats in an accordion bellows made of human skin. To stare at his somehow emaciated feet, toes twisted and horned with callous, was no relief. It was like looking at the bare feet of a stranger in a public sauna, and he was compelled to close his eyes and shudder inwardly.

Most often he ignored himself, but there would come severe tests when his imagination felled him like a polled ox. He removed his partial plates, dropped them in a glass of water and baking soda to soak overnight. Something made him lean close to the medicine cabinet mirror, lips sucked back in over his gums. At best, he saw an idiot, a clown, something out of *Snuffy Smith*, a face fit to play a hillbilly in a Warner-Pathé newsreel short on the Ozarks.

At worst, the wasted, sunken face of a corpse, ready for the undertaker's cosmetics. His partial plates, magnified and dulled by the water, leered at him from the tumbler like a skull's grin.

"Oh no you don't," he said to the bathroom mirror. And made efforts to fight back. For a while, after the long winter broke, he skipped lunch and walked for an hour about the busy commercial streets of Saint Paul. The area crawled with one-legged, one-eyed, one-armed panhandlers, pros who worked the circuit from Chicago through Milwaukee to the Twin Cities, and Buck's arches ached to beat the band, but he stuck to it most days. He was not the kind of man had any trouble telling a bum to get the hell out of his way if he didn't want to pick himself up off the sidewalk in about a second and a half.

Though he never finished the carton, he did change to vile-tasting Sano cigarettes, and he used a denicotine filter holder for a few days, until it got left and forgotten somewhere between the office and his apartment. It made him look, he thought, like a wop anyhow. He even printed, underlining the letters, the resolution *Buck Hansen will quit using coffin nails* on his desk pad. He used saccharine in his coffee, co-salt on his food to lick the swelling in his ankles. He borrowed his wife's nail brush and scrubbed the two fingers that held his cigarettes with a vinegar solution. He dosed his indigestion with Sal Hepatica. All this he did, and believed he might have done more—stopped smoking, cut out beer, dieted. "Not on your life, goddamn you," Buck Hansen said to himself in the bathroom mirror, feeling himself renewed by the firmness and intensity of the challenge thrown in the face of the broken-down old cocker snarling back at him from the glass.

But when it became clear that events combined against him, Buck Hansen gave up the struggle and fled for his life.

The gradual failure of Hansen Engineering intensified, suffocating more rapidly as it became more impossible to estimate, much less guarantee delivery dates without military priority on sales. With the end of cost-plus, industry was retooling in other directions, cutting back, going conservative. There might have been a chance if that goddamned Pendergast-machine Truman had not prolonged price and profit controls. The gang of creditors snapping at Buck's heels stopped inviting him down to their offices for discussions of refinancing and new payment schedules that always ended by upping the ante on him. They got on the telephone now, at the office, at home, and they stopped being polite. He opened very little of his business mail.

The family of his first marriage was a blind alley. The first he'd heard from Anne since the divorce was a snotty note dunning him for a late child-support check. His daughter had loosened up enough recently to talk to him on the telephone and answer his letters. Thanks to Jane, he knew when Arn came home from

Europe. As for the little one, he trusted Anne to poison him against his father at the earliest possible convenience.

Irene, his second wife, went suddenly and inexplicably off her rocker, maybe nudged by what she suspected about Lillie Broadfoot, Buck's new woman. And Lillie Broadfoot, who he'd taken up with on his last business trip east, seemed to have cooled, at least a mite, toward him. How much was a man supposed to take?

Why me? Buck Hansen often asked himself. What in hell did I ever do to deserve this? He never could come up with an answer that satisfied him, so he ran, to save his very life.

His escape was triggered at last by a series of horrible dreams and a growing morbid preoccupation with death that he could not get himself free of, alone there in the apartment after Irene was in the loony bin.

The dreams were about sex, most of the time, and his father was usually in them. In one, Buck was in bed with Lillie—he knew it was Lillie, but it did not look like her; she was hairy, hair growing thickly on her stomach and thighs. She laughed and coaxed Buck to come close, touch her in the crotch, but each time she approached she reached out to clutch viciously at his balls, and he pushed her away, finding his arms suddenly without strength, his groin very exposed, vulnerable to the hand that looked like an old woman's hand, with long yellow nails. His father stood at the foot of the bed then, watching and shaking his head, clucking his tongue the way he did if he saw an animal mistreated or a piece of farm machinery misused. His father wore work clothes, bib overalls, yet wore a high collar, his cheeks shaved, hair combed down with water, as if he were going to sit for a picture. *You, Oskar, I be damned*, his father's voice said, but he did not open his mouth, the words coming from somewhere, above and behind him. *It's not so bad, Pa*, was all Buck could say to defend himself, all the while writhing weakly to escape the ripping hand of the beast-Lillie-woman in bed with him. When he woke, his heart was thumping, and he very delicately reached down to touch himself and be sure he had not been maimed. He peered at the foot of his bed to be sure his father was not really there.

In another, he was squatting at the side of a dirt road somewhere near the farm. It was hot, and Buck was fully dressed, tie, vest. He was very hot, but did not sweat. He wondered why he did not sweat, and he wanted to peel off some of his clothes, but knew that for some reason he neither should nor could. His stomach hurt. Then his father was there, some presence that was his father, without face or figure or dress. His father said, *I seen you from way back there, Oskar,* and then waited as if for Buck to speak. Buck knew he could not.

In another, he dreamed again that he was in bed, and next to him was some woman—not Lillie or Irene or Anne—but a woman he knew well from someplace. He felt her touching him the entire length of his body, shoulder to ankle, and her hair was against his cheek. He lay there a long time, waiting to turn over onto her, but waited without knowing why. Then he turned, and she was still there in the bed, and he knew she expected him, but his father lay next to him now, and she was someplace else. When he woke he reached out and felt Irene's empty pillow, the cool space of the sheet, to be sure he was alone in the bed. He was ashamed of his erection.

Psycho, he thought, and blamed it on Irene's crack-up, but the dreams came anyway.

Worse, because he was awake and still unable to control his thoughts, were the visions of his death. They came without warning, so real they were like recent memories, and he was afraid he half enjoyed them.

First thing every morning, he had his bowel movement. Half awake, the echo of the Big Ben alarm still clacking in his head, he got a cigarette lit, grabbed the current copy of *Time,* and shuffled to the bathroom, coming more awake and alert with each mechanical step. The carpet nap felt good on the soles of his bare feet. Seated comfortably on the commode, shorts draped down over his feet, he let the cold water tap run to wash away the ashes as he reached up from time to time without looking, to flick them into the sink. He read the magazine randomly, skipping whenever the whim struck him from movies to politics to science. He liked to examine the news pictures first, read the cryptic captions, then dig into the text of the article to see how the caption was lifted, how it related to the story. Inevitably, there were one or two fits of wracking smoker's cough. It started that way.

He drew too deeply on the cigarette, or held it carelessly so that the smoke floated up in his face. There was a spasm very low in his throat, and the hacking convulsed him. He coughed from deep in his chest; his throat seemed to want to burst. His eyes felt bulged, ran tears, and his face turned crimson. He dropped the magazine, threw the cigarette in the sink, held on to the edges of the toilet seat with both hands to keep his balance while his body rocked, his head snapping forward with the violence of the deep coughs.

It passed, but this time he did not get up, wipe himself, and get with washing and shaving. He stayed on the commode, weak, slowly getting his breath, swallowing, wiping at his wet eyes, sniffing. And he imagined himself shocked into a first-class heart attack by the coughing, saw it clearly. The hacking hit him, and at its peak his chest felt like a red hot ingot was drawn through him. He imagined himself stiffening, his tongue protruding, losing his handholds on the toilet seat, collapsing on the cold tile floor. He calculated where his head would be likely to strike (the pipes under the sink, the baseboard molding).

The picture was complete, terrifying: Buck Hansen in a tangle on the bathroom floor, bare, unclean ass sticking up in the air, tongue out, hair uncombed, eyes open and glassy, skin cold, rubbery to the touch. He got off the commode slowly, waiting for the first rumble of the explosion in his chest. He made a point, all morning, of breathing deeply and deliberately, and it was a good hour before he let himself light another Pall Mall.

He feared his own rages, for they were most likely to bring something on. He was afraid to swear and ball his hands into fists at another in the daily string of business disappointments, afraid to scream out at the bushwa spewed out on the radio by some politician, afraid to roll down the window in the Chrysler and give holy hell to some stupid sonofabitching driver who got in his way. At last it came over him one evening when he was sitting, quiet and relaxed, feet up, with a bottle of beer. He had plopped down, bushed, without bothering to open the drapes or turn on the lights. He sat in perfect peace in the semidark, feeling the fatigue ooze out of him. Then he saw his own funeral. He lay in a coffin, the plush lining bunched up around his head. He adjusted the image of his face to account for the undertaker's work, colored his skin an orange rouge, flattened his eyelids, folded his dead hands over his stomach. He was about to go on to the flowers banking the casket, the decorated ceiling of the funeral parlor, the stream of people who came to pay last respects. He was caught by his hands, folded over his stomach as he sat in the big easy chair, and he could not go on with his vision until he lifted one hand and touched the back of the other with it, to see if it did not feel like a dead man's.

When crocuses bloomed in residential Minneapolis gardens, and he spotted his fourth robin of spring on a lawn in Saint Paul, Buck Hansen knew he must run if he was not to die.

The last full day, a Saturday, he holed up in the apartment, shades down, drapes drawn, to make final plans.

It wasn't so bad. Action, even if only imminent, liberated him from his own fears. The telephone rang several times in the morning, and again in the late afternoon, but all he had to do was wait it out, thumbing his nose at whoever was clamoring for a hunk of Buck Hansen's hide. Once, around noon, as he sat at the kitchen table eating a fried egg sandwich and a raw tomato for his lunch, the buzzer sounded from the foyer below. Buck sat still, leaning over the plate, the warm sandwich in his hands, not chewing again until it stopped. He had started to eat again when he heard someone coming down the hall. Whoever it was used the brass rapper on the door, then knocked with his fist. He didn't let himself start chewing again until the sound of the footsteps going back down the hall had vanished. Luckily, he'd turned off the radio before he went into the small efficiency kitchen to fry his egg. That was the only real scare all day.

Most of the time he listened to the radio. He had two cartons of Pall Malls and a nearly full case of National Premium beer that he saw no reason in leaving intact for the building super—whoever —when they got around to letting themselves in with a passkey. For snacks, he found a can of Planter's Cocktail Mix on a high shelf in the kitchen cupboard, and there was a sack of fresh tomatoes in the refrigerator vegetable crisper. He ate them with salt substitute, a remnant of his concern with weight, blood pressure, and circulation. When he packed his grips, early in the evening, he put the co-salt in along with his Sal Hepatica and his saccharin tablets. It gave him that kind of faith again: to be going, taking action, made him sure he would straighten his health out, first chance he got. One thing at a time, but everything, given a little time!

While he ate his dinner, a cube steak, a sliced tomato, and a bottle of National Premium, he studied his road maps, spread out to one side on the kitchen table. He decided on and traced routes with his fountain pen. He started to run hot water for the dishes before he realized it made no difference. He left them, stacked, and went into the living room with the maps to make the necessary calls. Before lifting the receiver and asking for the long-distance operator, he put his cigarettes, an ashtray, and his address book where they would be handy. He opened another bottle of beer, took a long drink, and asked the operator to get his daughter's number in Milwaukee.

Wouldn't it be a kicker, Buck thought as the operator went to work, if something happened to me right this second, here and now? He tried to smile at his own sense of irony, but it was too frightening. He waited for a stroke to cut into his brain behind his eyes, an explosion to erupt in his chest, then made himself quit it before he lost all his nerve. That's the way, he thought, you end up in the booby hatch. And then he could smile, just slightly.

"Hello, Jane," he said when she answered.

"Who is this, please?"

"Your father. Buck. I suppose you'll tell me you can't remember what I look like either," he said.

"Will you hold it just a minute, Dad? I'm giving baths here, and if I don't sit on them I'll have the tub all over my floor."

"This is long distance, you know," Buck started to say, but the clunk of Jane's receiver laid down told him she had gone. He was angry for a moment, that she should let him hold a line while the toll charges rolled just to yank her kids out of the water. Then he remembered that he was going, was all but on the move already, and the phone bill would never be paid. He lit a cigarette and pulled on his beer. She took her damn sweet time anyhow.

"I'm sorry," she said when she got back. "Dad?"

"I'm here."

"I didn't think you'd want me to let one of them drown. Butchie's really still too small to be left alone in the water. His sister's just mean enough to dunk him if I'm not there."

"Certainly," he said, "I understand completely. Think nothing of it."

"Are you mad?"

"Hell no. Damnit, don't start that kind of thing, Sister. I didn't call to spar with you."

"Whatever you say. How are you, Dad?" She was always polite, the same in her letters. He wondered if she had forgotten what she had done to him.

"I'm fine. I called to find out how you were. How's the kids?"

"Do I owe you a letter or something? Oh, forget it. We're fine, Dad." There was a pause, as if she had no more to say, or were thinking, frantically, of something to say—Buck spoke quickly, afraid she would matter-of-factly say good-bye and hang up on him.

"I've appreciated your letters one hell of a lot, Sister." When she did not speak at once, he went on quickly. "It helps a man to know at least one of his kids hasn't written him off for good and all."

"Dad."

"I mean it. No matter what happens to a person, you know, if he has children he's still interested. You ought to know that if anyone—"

"Dad, this is costing you money," she tried to say.

"Tell me about my children, Sister," he said. "Do you see Arnie? How's Arnie? Has he changed a lot in the service?" He struggled to keep the maudlin quaver out of his voice, to resist the need to swallow and blow his nose. Not this, he told himself. Get up on your hind legs, Buck! he urged himself.

"He's fine," Jane said.

"Does he talk about me to you?"

"Once in a while. Do you really want to talk about this? I can't get him to write you, Dad. Nothing's changed that way. I don't think Mother lets him forget it, if you know what I mean."

"I think I do. You could say I do, yes."

"They're moving, you know," she said.

"No, I didn't know. Have you got the address?" He wrote it in his book as she dictated. How was Anne expecting him to send the support check? "The reason I called, Jane," he said, "one of the main reasons I called, was to let you know I may be down that way before too long."

"Don't go to see Arn, if that's what you're asking, Dad."

"I'll keep it in mind. What about you? Can I come to see you?"

"If you think you want to," his daughter said. "If you think it serves anything. I've told you how I have to live with this, Dad."

"You have for a fact," Buck said. He could hear one of her children nagging her to be allowed to talk on the telephone. "So maybe I'll be seeing you. If circumstances allow, and all, huh?" He wanted her to say: come. Come, Dad. Daddy, I want you to come and see me! She did not.

"These kids are pulling me apart here," she said. "This is going to cost you a mint, Dad."

"How's Oskar?" he said quickly. "How's my little boy, Jane? Tell me about my son, Jane! Don't hang up on me. Does he talk about me ever, Sister? Does your mother say anything about me to him?"

"Dad—"

"Please, Sister."

76

"He talks about you. He wonders where you are, I mean, why you aren't there, I suppose. Mother doesn't tell him anything like you think, if that's what you're thinking. Dad, I have to hang up now. Really." He could hear both his grandchildren squawking close to the phone now. He did not hear his daughter say good-bye, because he was crying hard, shamelessly. He dug for his handkerchief as the operator asked him if his call was completed.

When he hung up, he went to the bathroom to wash his face. After he was sure he was all right he made the mistake of going in the bedroom to check his grip to see if he had his son's picture. He couldn't find it, remembered it was down at the office. He could get it tomorrow, stop on his way out, but it made him weepy again, and again he went to the bathroom to rinse his face, and stared into the mirror, water dripping off his chin, and cursed himself. "A grown goddamn man," he said aloud. "Will you stand up like a goddamn man and fight!" he said. Shortly, it was over, and he could go in the living room and place the next call.

It took a little longer. He had Cal Rocker's phone number, penciled on the back of his business card, but when he got it it turned out Cal had moved since he last heard from him. He got the new number from the Chicago information operator, and a little girl answered, very exact, polite, and Buck asked her please to let him speak to her daddy, Mr. Rocker.

"Buck?" Cal said, "Buck Hansen. Where the hell are you calling from? Are you here in town now?"

"No, Cal, still up in the woods. I tried your old place, but they tell me you pulled stakes."

"That was months ago." His voice was very clear, very loud. "I'll be damned. I thought we'd see a lot more of you, Buck. Hell yes. I don't even operate out of the same place, man. I've moved up, Buck. New building, bigger and better, built myself a new house."

"I'm glad to hear that." It hurt him to say it.

"And I don't forget how much of it I owe to you, Buck. It was one swell hell of a war, wasn't it? Honest to God, I remember all the time, you sitting there and telling me to get off my duff and out of the drafting room because cost-plus was going to make a lot of men a lot of piles. Do you remember talking to me like that, Buck?"

"I do indeed. It's nice of you to say so, but you better give yourself a little credit."

"Me and a couple of those sheenies used to get your goat so bad. Remember? You know what I mean though, Buck. So what's up with the best machine tool salesman in the Midwest? You coming down to see us here or not?"

"As per usual, Cal. Samo samo, I'd have to say. That's why I called you. I'll likely be in Chicago soon. I'd like to have a few hours of your time if you can spare it, Cal."

"No appointment needed. You know that, now. We can put you up right here at the house. Hell, we got room to burn. I'll be insulted if I don't hear from you *mach schnell*. Right?"

"Since you put it that way, Cal," Buck said. So all his luck was not gone out the window after all. He'd gone over half a dozen names before he picked on Calvin Rocker, all men who owed him and could be counted on to admit it. Cal was a good choice. It sounded like he was sitting pretty, able to give Buck the leg up he needed if he was going to save himself. Still, it hurt. Buck Hansen on his hands and knees to a slightly-better-than-average tool designer who had no business anywhere above a small shop in Chicago Heights. Still, it gave him the boost he needed to call his brother in Indiana. Buck got another bottle of National Premium from the refrigerator.

Sitting in the apartment, listening to the terminals clicking to connect him with Thurston, he could close his eyes and see the small square stucco building in Goshen that was the telephone exchange office. He could remember when it was a dairy store. He pretended to be driving, following the telephone wires down the main street, past the little park on the right (where Buck's name was listed on the white and gold honor roll with the others who were in the first war), the movie theater on the left, out of town and down the highway. Saturday night, late, the taverns, the theater, the two restaurants, the A&W Root Beer stand would all still be open and doing business. The Amish would have long since cleared out, gone home in their buggies and their Model T's. He followed the road to the four-way-stop junction with the state highway, then a mile beyond it, turning off on a dirt road that led to the truck farm where he was born and raised, where his brother and sister-in-law, childless, lived as if nothing had happened in the world in the past fifty years. Buck had not been back since before he and Anne were divorced. "Good Christ," he said, swallowing, wiping at his eyes. "What the hell's happening to me?" He couldn't remember why he should have wanted to speak to his brother.

"Hello. This is Thurston Hansen speaking here." He pronounced his name *Tor-sten*, like an old Swede farmer just off the boat. How could a man, Buck wondered, live his life like that? "Who is this?" Thurston said.

"It's me. It's your brother, Buck."

"Will you believe me," he heard him turn from the phone to say to his wife, "it's Oskar calling us up."

"How you doing, Thurston?"

"It's you, Oskar," he said, as if not really convinced. He could hear Marie whispering to his brother. Buck imagined them in long nightshirts (skullcaps too?), alarmed by a call at this hour of the night. Buck almost laughed, pushing his vision to Thurston, nightcap and gown, sleepy eyed, holding a lit candle, like the Fisk tire ad. "I guess we're fine here, Oskar." He pronounced it *Aws-core;* it set Buck's teeth on edge. "What's wrong? Is something wrong that you're calling us up here like this?" his brother said.

"Not a bit of it," Buck said. "I'm fine and dandy. I just wanted to see if my welcome was worn out yet or not."

"What do you mean, your welcome? Are you in some trouble, Oskar?" He could see their heads close together at the wall phone's earpiece, Marie craning her neck to hear too. Buck laughed.

"I'm in no trouble. Not so's you'd know it, anyway. I'm maybe going east in a few days, and I want to stop by and visit you and Marie if it's not too much trouble for you." There was a silence; Thurston would cover the mouthpiece with his hand while he discussed it with Marie. Marie was a goddamn Dutchman, which meant it would be her at the bottom of it if his brother told him to get lost.

"You been back and forth east lots of times, Oskar, all them postcards you send us. You never stopped in before. You never called to ask if you should stop in."

"I never had time before," Buck said. "Why are you so damn suspicious of me, Thurston? I don't want anything from you. I'm not going to put the bite on you for money, for Christ's sake! I just want to come and see you and see the place where I grew up. Is there anything wrong with that? Thurston?" There was quiet while they debated again.

"I guess not," Thurston said. "I guess you got the right to visit this house no matter what's all gone and done with, Oskar." *I guess not.* He sounded, voice and words, like their father. *I guess not.* Old Anton Gustav—ask the old man for a dime after an afternoon weeding vegetables, until your back broke and your head split from the heat of the sun, "Can I have ten cents, Pa?" *I guess not*. "You still there hearing me?" his brother said.

"Hey, Thurston," Buck said, "do you ever think about the old man? Pa. Do you ever think about Pa, brother? I had a dream about him just the other night. I think you were in this one too—"

"What you talking about? Are you telling me your dreams or some crazy thing, Oskar?"

"Forget I said it," Buck said. "I'll be seeing you then, maybe, huh? Give my love to Marie, brother."

"We'll look out for you, Oskar. You sure you got no big trouble of some kind?"

"Not at all. Good-bye, Thurston."

"I mean," his brother said before he could hang up, "we ain't been in touch since you messed up your family and all. No hard feelings on that though, Oskar, okay? I was just wondering. Marie was wondering too. If that woman is coming with you. You still living with that other woman and all, Oskar?" He could imagine Marie was wondering, like she'd never get back to sleep tonight if she didn't get all the dirt.

"I married that woman, Thurston. And no, tell Marie relax, I'm not bringing her along. I'm not, for a fact, living with her anymore. She's in the hospital at the moment. Got all that straight now?"

"I guess so, Oskar."

"And will you do one favor for your little brother?"

"What's that?"

"Stop, for the Christ's sake, calling me Oskar, will you? Can I count on that?"

"Whatever you like. You better say good-bye now. This is gonna cost you a lot of money I bet."

"Money's no object. Good night, brother." When he put the phone back on the cradle he was near tears again. "In the goddamn Jesus love of Christ's name!" he said. He stared straight ahead, at nothing, for several minutes. And then he called Lillie. He'd saved her for last. He had her number memorized.

Saturday was the big day in her beauty parlor, open till nine, and it was ten or ten-thirty, he knew, before she could get away. The first night he'd stayed with her had been a Saturday. Buck waited outside in the Chrysler, smoking and wondering just how far, where, this was going to lead. Guilty one moment, he was angry at himself the next for doubting his instincts and his right to make a little happiness for himself before his life was over. She stuck her head out the door and told him to come inside and have a look at the shop. Buck was impressed. She had a dozen dryers, a long counter with a wall-length mirror behind it where her customers could sit and admire themselves while their hair was being combed out. Spotless sinks and gleaming fixtures, a huge display cabinet stocked with shampoos, home permanent kits, comb and brush sets. She employed four girls full-time, and two others who came in to help on Saturdays and before holidays, Easter, Christmas week. He had never yet worked up the gall to ask her what she was worth, but his guess was it came to a fair-sized plenty. Her brother Ben had a small piece of the business, but how much, exactly, Buck didn't know either.

"I'm sorry, sir, that number does not answer," the operator told him. That Saturday, Buck asked her where she'd like to go, and she said why not just go back to her place, it was so late. That was the first night.

"Keep trying, please," Buck said, but still there was no answer. He had her try the beauty parlor. Lillie might have stayed extra late to clean up instead of leaving it for Sunday, or maybe she and Ben were working on the books, payroll, something. That Sunday, the morning after their first night together, Ben had come upstairs from his flat to see if his sister was ready to go over to the shop and clean up. Buck was embarrassed to be found by her brother, drinking coffee in his bathrobe, but Ben Broadfoot acted as easy as if he had not the slightest idea Buck had slept with Lillie.

"I'm sorry, sir, that number doesn't answer either." Buck had the Mineola operator find Ben's number, but there was no answer there too. Where the hell was she? It was an hour later on Long Island. What was she doing out at this hour!

"Cancel the call," he said. Not being able to talk to her depressed him, but he would call again tomorrow, out on the road. He needed Lillie Broadfoot. He needed her worst, most of all, more than anything. To hell with his kids, Cal Rocker, his brother—he needed Lillie Broadfoot.

Tired now, his head thick with beer, tongue raw, throat sharply sore from smoking, he lay down on the sofa, his travel alarm set. He fell asleep immediately, but woke shortly after midnight from a dream about Irene.

At first they were together in a room like the nursing home, but it was really some sort of hospital. Buck was the one who was ill, though he felt fine. Irene had come to stay with him, and they lay on white hospital beds, fully clothed. *It's my job*, Irene said. *I feel fine I told you*, Buck said. They argued about her staying in

81

the hospital with him, and then they were eating a meal off a cafeteria tray. They both wore hospital gowns, and Buck was afraid someone would come in while he ate and see his rear end sticking out of the gap in the gown. He tried to eat faster, but whatever it was fell off the strangely shaped fork he used. Irene was trying to eat as fast as he did. She smacked her lips, food falling from her mouth back on the metal tray. Now Buck was threatened twice, by the gap in the back of his gown, by the embarrassment he would feel if someone came in and saw Irene's manners. Her head was down so close to the tray that he could no longer see her face. She scraped frantically at the tray, a terrible noise that would attract someone. He was afraid her glasses would fall into the food. *Where are your specs?* he said. He wanted to curse her for her swinish manners, but was afraid his voice would draw someone who would come in and ridicule him for leaving his fanny bare. Then Irene was standing on his bed. He was afraid she would fall off if he tried to move away. *Okey-doke,* she said, *now we'll see once and for all,* and she began to take her clothes off—she wore street clothes again. Buck covered his face to keep from seeing, but spread his fingers to peek. Then she was sitting, or lying, now on an ordinary bed or a sofa, but it was still somehow in a hospital of some kind. Her face was covered by her hair hanging down. Buck picked at her hair, smoothing it, trying to get to her scalp. It repulsed him to touch her hair, but he had to do it for her for some reason. *If you start crying on me so help me I'll belt you one,* he said to her. Somewhere in this he spoke to his father—when he was looking at his father he was certain he had expected him. *Fresh vegetables*, his father said. *You don't know when you're well off, do you?* Buck laughed at him and said, *Don't tell me your sad stories, squarehead. Who you calling a name!* his father said, and it was his brother then, not his father. *You want to fight me?* Thurston said. Buck was very glad to be lying on a bed next to Irene, free of his brother, who would beat him if he tried to get up. He could feel the lump of his wallet under him, knew it was full of money, but he felt too heavy and tired to reach under himself and get it. Irene giggled, and she said, *Okay, the card room's good enough for me any day, buster.* And quickly she flopped from her side to her back and closed her eyes, but she continued to giggle, mouth twitching. Then Buck knew this was their funeral, by some great mistake, and he would have to close his eyes and fold his hands on his chest. He was afraid his skin would feel too warm if anyone touched him. Irene could not stop

82

sniggering to herself. He wanted to tell her to shut the hell up. He would have to lie still, play dead to avoid embarrassment. He closed his eyes and tensed, waiting for the first mourner to reach out and touch his face. His face itched.

When he opened his eyes, awake, he knew at once it had been a dream. He knew where he was, what he intended doing. He went over the dream, then went over the steps he planned for morning. He turned his pillow over, laid his cheek gently against the cool underside, but the dream would not get out of his mind. "Ha ha ha," he said, loudly and deliberately. Finally he got up to smoke and take a leak, and at last, along about four in the morning, he made his only local call, to the nursing home where Irene was staying.

"I'd like some information about a patient. A guest. Mrs. Irene Hansen. She—"

"I'm sorry, sir. I'm not allowed to release any information of that kind over the telephone. May I suggest you—"

"Look, young lady, this is her husband. I want to know—"

"—not without specific authorization from her physician—" She wasn't even listening to him.

"Who the hell you think's footing her bill, Yehudi?" he screamed.

"—I have no authority to—"

"Go to hell!" he said, cutting her off before she could say more. But it worked to drive away the feeling the dream had left in him. When he raised the shade in his bedroom, dawn light was just blurring the horizon. It was Sunday, time to make his move.

It was only a little past eight o'clock when he left, but already warm enough to make him sweat as he carried his grips down the back way, out to the Chrysler. A garage came with the apartment, but he had not used it the past week. A garage was where someone went, nosing around to attach an automobile. He parked the Chrysler a block and a half away, where no collection agency leg man was going to find it and slap a plaster on it. He needed the car. Give him an automobile he could count on, and a good man was never down for good. Nobody was pulling him under to stay as long as he could move, keep moving. If it moves, it's alive—bank on it! And he could count on the Chrysler.

He had plunked down a company check for it the day he went to work on the new job, just a few weeks before Pearl Harbor. There were fifty thousand plus miles on it, but give it a wash and a simonize, and it looked like it just rolled off the assembly line. The tank was full, oil changed, greased, a hundred and eighty horses under the hood and a set of four new recaps, scarcer than hen's teeth, on the wheels. Buck Hansen knew how to take care of an automobile. He'd made his pile on the road, and by Christ he would do it again if God or whoever gave him half a chance.

Grips locked in the trunk, it took two more trips up and down the stuffy back stairs for the rest of his clothes and the portable Motorola he'd originally given Irene as a birthday present. He'd considered clearing out with all the household appliances, toaster, mixmaster, vacuum cleaner, but they were more trouble than they were worth to a secondhand dealer or a hock shop. He locked the apartment and dropped the key in the super's mailbox. On his way back through the hall to the stairs he thought he heard his phone, but it was too late now. He got in the Chrysler and drove to his office in Saint Paul to pick up his son's picture, and to see what there was left worth carting off. He looked forward to getting out on the highway, where he could open up the windows, put the speedometer on seventy, and get some real relief from this heat. It was going to be a scorcher.

I did not recognize the streets, and as it grew dark, they began to look all alike, and the world shrank to block after block of houses with vague, dim porches and yards, the rectangles of their windows lit. The street lights came on, and then it was very dark. There were lighted windows in the houses that bulked darker against the dark sky, and sometimes we stopped for a traffic light, and there were the small islands of light that were drugstores and groceries still open. In the dark shell of the Chrysler's interior, my father's cigarette tip glowed when he puffed, and the dash panels glowed, and his breath whooshed as he exhaled, and it was no longer uncomfortably hot in the car. I do not remember it that way, but he must have driven back across town, by a strange, uncertain route, approaching the neighborhood of my mother's new Cramer Street house, or perhaps he simply drove streets, not in any conscious direction, while he made up his mind, finally and articulately, to take me with him on his flight. We drove a very long time in the city, and at last it was totally night.

"Daddy?"

"What's that?"

"I can't see to do it anymore."

"Do what?"

"I can't watch for the Studebaker cars." I had not seen any, had not won a single penny. "It's too dark. I can't see what colors a car is."

"That's okay," he said. "He can't see us either. That's a daytime game we'll play. Okey-doke? You getting chilled from my window?" He closed the wing. "Wrap yourself up in my coat there if you need it," he said. And then we drove some more, and it must have seemed darker as we left the city, the houses spacing out, street lights less frequent, but I do not remember that gradual leaving of the city. I did not know until we passed the farm market, at the six-way intersection on Highway 41 (Gone. Of course, now, it is gone. I do not know what has been put in its place—everything looks so much alike now.).

"Hey!" I cried. My father started, looked quickly, several times, at me, back at the road, at me. "That's the farmer market," I said. It sat on an enormous triangle of land between the converging roads. It was brightly lit with lights that extended out from the shed roof, like billboard lights. There was no name; the lights shone on a white signboard, running the full length of the shed, the board somewhat amateurishly painted with enormous, swollen watermelons, some halved and quartered to show their bright red meat, the black seeds arranged in perfect patterns radiating out of the centers. The lights illuminated melons, yellow orange ears of shucked sweetcorn as large as melons, pea green cabbages and heads of lettuce highlighted with silver blue drops of water to keep them fresh. Purple turnips, black, shining eggplants, radishes, dark green peppers, cream colored eggs. The sheds were open in front, produce heaped in stalls, and in the gravel tip of the triangle were parked the customers who came from all over Milwaukee, and the pickups of the truck farmers who drove in daily to set up shop.

"That's the farmer market," I yelled. "We're going away! This is the way we go away!" I began to scream and bawl like an infant; I knew, fully and clearly, that he was taking me away . . . where? Somewhere. He was taking me away, and I was more frightened than I have ever been, before or since, in my life.

(Something is wrong here: he may have slowed the car—he did not stop—but somehow we are there in the car, the lights of the farm market casting their excess into the Chrysler; my father and I are fully lit, we see each other clearly—the moment is expanded, slow motion. There is the white signboard with all the grotesque fruits and vegetables depicted in garish colors. The produce farmers leaning on their stalls, wearing overalls, work-shoes, hats, hidden partially by the shadows of the overhanging shed roof. Customers, walking slowly, reaching out to handle and pinch the produce. The crunch of car tires, pulling into the gravel triangle—the traffic converging there may have slowed us. And I have screamed *We're going away*! I bawl like an infant, knowing he is taking me. The moment is expanded, forever, free of the realism of time and place.)

"Please," my father said. "Please stop that now. I can't drive and watch out for the traffic if you carry on. Boy. Oskar, please." He reached out with his right hand—we are past the green market, again immersed in the dark—to grope, find me, comfort me with pats and strokes. It felt like the frantic pawing of an overfriendly dog, one big and awkward enough to be dangerous to a small child.

"I have to go home!" I cried. "Mom's going to be mad, Arnie's probably looking for me!" I imagined them, waiting for me on the front porch of the Cramer Street house, my mother, arms folded, mouth set firm, eyes bursting to weep when I was close enough for her to slap me and rage. Arn stands behind, to one side, nervously flexing his pectorals and biceps, running the point of his tongue over the inside of his mouth, waiting for the moment to carry me inside to one of the half-filled bedrooms, close the door, and there among the stacked cardboard boxes, in the room with no curtains or shades on the windows, whip me without mercy. And Jane. What is Jane thinking, doing, in her cloistered basement apartment? She smokes incessantly, watches her children with only half an eye, preparing on her tongue words that will shatter me in their brutal delicacy once I am before her. "What's going to happen when I get home so late?" I cried. "What's Mom going to do!"

"Don't you worry," he said. "Come on now, cut it out. That's my big boy. What's to fret about? Listen to me a minute, boy. Look, here we are, we're in Dad's big car, aren't we. We're out on the open road! Who's to bother us? Who's to say what we do? You're right here with the old man, ain't so? Here," he handed me a handkerchief, "blow," he said. "Wipe your tears. That's my big boy. There ain't a thing in this whole world you got to worry about so long as you're with your old man, right? That's the ticket. Blow hard."

"Mom doesn't know where I am," I said.

"All things in good time. Just stick the hankie in the bag on the floor. We got to be getting you your own hankie here, don't we?"

"I'm cold now," I said, and he rolled up his window. And now we were out of the city, going south on Highway 41. There were only occasional farmhouses, the telephone poles that rushed at me in the Chrysler's headlights, and now, signs giving the distance to Bobby Nelson's Cheese Box, Fossland's Restaurant, the state line, where Arn had driven us once, all of us, to buy oleo across the border in Illinois, where there was no tax on it and they could sell it already colored. I concentrated, read Burma-Shave jingles, the meter of the lines blocked out by the spacing of the red-and-white signboards, accentuated by the slap of our tires as we crossed asphalt seams in the pavement. I do not know why I stopped crying, why I was no longer so afraid. With the windows closed, the car was like some child's fort, a cozy and secret place shared only with my father. The heavy Chrysler rocked and dipped pleasantly. Outside, very far away, the black, clear sky was strewn with brilliant stars that winked like the tip of my father's cigarette when he drew on it.

I began to feel tired. As we talked, I must gradually have fallen closer and closer to sleep.

"Where are we going, Dad?"

"Where? Anywhere. Everywhere. You name it, I got it. There's a yahoo in Chicago I want to see, but he can go to hell in a handbasket if you give me the say-so. We can go any damn where we want, son! Hey, you dozing off on me?"

"I'm sort of tired now I think."

"We'll stop and sack out first chance we get. Keep your eyes open for me. I need your help, Oskar."

"But I mean, when are we going back? Will we go back tomorrow?"

"Back? Never look back if you can help it. Remember that. I'm serious. Hell, full speed ahead, damn the—what's the matter now?" I must have come close to crying again.

"When can I see Mom? I want to see Arnie again. I want to see Jane!"

"Calm down," he said. "Listen to me for a sec, will you? Do you need the snot-rag again? I want you to listen to me, boy."

"I am."

"God only knows I never planned this. Do you understand me? What you have to understand, I'm on the ropes, see? Your old man's reeling like a drunken sailor. Get me? I'm in bad shape at the moment." As he spoke he kept his eyes on the road ahead, talking as much to himself, for himself, as to or for me. He paused sometimes, long enough for me to wonder if he was finished, and it was time for me to say something. He paused to light cigarettes, to crack his wing and throw them out on the road (then, or maybe some other night on our flight, I knelt on the seat, looked back out the rear window, watched the red orange cigarette ash shatter, skip and blow out behind us, disappear). He paused to cough, to clear his throat, blow his nose, adjust his bottom on the inflated rubber ring he sat on, to flick the dashboard clock with his fingernail, be sure it was working.

"This is not the time or the place for you. You can't grasp it, I know. You're just not old enough, you're not . . . I can't make it clear for you, God help me. I'll tell you something, a word to the wise from your old man. Never do anything I ever did. Okay? If you lay your head in the corner like that you'll fall asleep on me, boy. I'm tired myself. I am beat. Bushed. More than I can say. I've had it up to the ears, and then some. You'll know when you're my age. There comes a time you got to stand up on your hind legs or else you're ready for the glue factory. I'm on the edge, boy. It's do or die for me right now, you understand?"

"Like you said you were going to die if I went outside before?" He did not seem the same man with the pistol, in the Cramer Street house.

"Something like. I want," he said, and he did not speak for some time. "I don't know exactly what the hell it is I want. I got nothing, is my problem. I grew up and got old and all of a sudden, blooey! Know what I mean?" I shook my head. I don't think he looked. "It's like magic," he said. "It's all gone, almost like it was all at once. Like a dream. Irene . . . do you know who Irene is?"

"Your wife. Mom said," I said.

"Nothing. There's a gal out in New York—this is no time or place for you. Someday you'll see what I mean. Are you conking out on me?"

"No. I'm real tired." Now we passed Fossland's Restaurant off to our right, its sign starkly red against the blackness, the floodlit lot carelessly jammed with semitrucks and trailers. And now, we crossed the state line into Illinois, past the World's Largest Gas Pump, a sham structure big enough to provide a warm-up room for the attendant in winter. "I probably have to go to sleep," I said.

"The thing is," my father said, "you're all I've got right this minute, boy. You're mine, as much as you're your mother's. Divorce be damned. You're mine. You're my son, no matter what else. That's why I need you with me. Do you see that? Am I making any sense to you, sonny?" I don't know what I said. Or if I was too close to sleep to speak at all. I rested my head against the steadily vibrating door, covered myself with his jacket, pulled my legs up on the seat. "Give your old man a break," he said. "When you're my age you'll know what I'm talking about. I've got my rights too," he said. "I love you." And then I must have slept.

"Wake up, sonny," my father said. I woke, cramped and chilled. My eyes itched, and one foot had gone to sleep beneath me, needles of circulation showering in my toes as I tried to sit up. The car door was open, my father standing outside, leaning in over me. The night air felt very cold. I meant to get out, to join him, but he held me there, half in, half out of the Chrysler. "Hold on a sec," he said. "Are you wide awake, boy? Can you hear what I'm saying to you?"

"I'm cold again." I searched the seat for his jacket to cover myself, but he was wearing it now. I thought at first we had stopped by the side of the road. Crickets chirped in the long grass, and there seemed to be no light other than the inside dome that went on when the car door was open. I blinked and rubbed at my itching eyes. "I have to go to the toilet I think," I said.

"In a minute. Listen to me good now. We're going to sack in here for the night. Can you wait here for me while I get us a cabin?" he said. I tried to get out of the car again, but he held me back. I straightened up on the seat and looked out the windshield. We were parked in a ring of six or seven small rectangular cabins. Each had a small light up over its front door. They had no windows. On the end, to the left, was a house, dark except for a small wing jutting out into the court.

"Where are we?"

"Near Chicago," he said. "Can you wait here while I go in and line up a bed for us? Come on, boy, wake up and talk to me."

"I have to go to the toilet. Bad." He sighed, looked at the wing housing the tourist cabin office, out toward what must have been the highway (it is near Great Lakes, where you would turn off the freeway today—no, no, it is no longer there).

"Okay. Now listen. Can I count on you not to spill the beans if I take you in with me? Are you listening to me?"

"I don't know. I have to go." His fingers tightened on my arm.

"Damn, I'm going to get you to a potty here in a second. Will you promise me not to say anything to anybody when we go inside to register? That's my good boy, give me your promise." I think it was then I remembered where I was, what had happened, what we were doing. The coldness of the night was accentuated by the shrill, metallic chirping of the summer crickets in the grass. The partial ring of tiny cabin lights was like a path leading to the door of the office—the lights in the wing made me think it must be warm in there. My father bent awkwardly over me, his large, heavy hands still resting on my shoulders. His breath whistled in his throat, and I smelled tobacco smoke on his clothes, his skin. He had put on his jacket, pulling up his tie to close his shirt collar, run his fingers through his thinning hair to straighten it. He frowned, the deep lines in his forehead, between his eyes, at the corners of his eyes, running down from his nose, drawing the corners of his mouth down—he looked frightened. I knew then, there in the courtyard of those shabby tourist cabins, that I could destroy him by refusing him. And I realized I might save him, if only for myself.

"I won't say anything, Daddy," I said.

"Good man." He grasped my arms, my elbows, hoisted me easily, up and out of the car, swung me clear and set me lightly on my feet, took my hand. "Come on, ace," he said, "let's get us a bed and find you a john pronto."

And so I was not *running away*. I had run away, two or three times, I think, from Mrs. Spaulding's house. At some real or imagined injustice at my mother's hands, at some hard word or casual swat from my brother, I had simply walked away from home. Run away. Once, I intended to walk to Jane's and ask to live with her. At least once, I remember, I was merely going away, no destination in mind. Once, I do not remember which, I circled Mrs. Spaulding's house at a distance of two or three blocks for several hours, and returned at last to sit on the front steps, exhausted and disgusted, until my mother came out to call me in. And once, I was picked up by two smiling police officers in their squad. They questioned me, then returned me, like the lawless Lenski boys who lived upstairs of my sister, ignobly, to my mother, who thrashed me while Arn watched.

This was not *running away*, any more than I was kidnapped. I had been taken, yes, but he would have returned me the next day if I insisted. I know this! But I had agreed, there at the tourist cabins. I had joined him. I thought of my mother, of Arn, Jane, my niece and nephew, as I stumbled at his side, so drowsy only his hand holding mine kept me from falling, my eyes bleary, foot still tingling, bladder burning. I thought of them, but was not sad or frightened. I was going with him, wherever he might take me, however long we might be gone, because I knew he needed me if he was to live. Because it came to me as we were entering the office wing, that, though I did not know him, that no matter what had happened, he was my father, after all.

The woman may have been asleep. Her head was down on her arms. She jerked up quickly as we came in, looked at us, or past us, blinking, as if she had been dreaming and the sound of the bell over the office door had merged nicely in her dream, the way the clatter of an alarm clock will be a siren or a scream if the dream requires it. She looked at us, but did not seem to see us. "Can I help you? My God, what time is it," she said. She wiped roughly at the corners of her mouth.

"What we need is two things," my father said. "One, and pronto, where's the nearest privy for my boy here? His back teeth are floating, so he tells me." He squeezed my hand. She blinked and wiped at her mouth, then turned her head and nodded toward the hall leading back into the house. My father released my hand and pointed me, started me with a touch on the seat of my pants.

"There's a string for the light," the woman said behind me as I set off.

"Two," my father said, "your best beds for me and the boy here. We've had a hell of a day, and tomorrow's liable to be worse before it gets any better." I found the light, relieved myself, wavering over the bowl like a drunk, closing my eyes against the glare of the light reflected in the porcelain. My father picked me up when I came back. The woman put on a sweater and came along to open the cabin for us. I watched her over my father's shoulder, his hands on my back like warm pads. She looked like Mrs. Spaulding.

"Be careful if you're going to smoke cigarettes," she said as she left.

"Up yours," my father said too quietly to be heard by her, and to me, "Go ahead and crap out on the bed while I get the bags." I sat on the bed while he was gone. He pulled the Chrysler around behind the row of cabins before he brought his grips in. He had to hide the car in case anyone, police, Sheldon Rotter, came snooping. "It ain't exactly the Ritz, I'll grant you," he said when he came in. I sat with my hands folded, warming them between my thighs.

"Mom's going to be sad," I said.

"What?" He had already stripped off his jacket, unbuckled his belt.

"She'll think I'm running away or something." He buckled his belt and reached for his jacket.

"Where are you going?"

"Over to wake that old bat up to use her phone if she's got one. This place looks like the dump I was raised in." He kicked with the toe of his shoe at the open door of the old-fashioned dressing table. "That's where we used to keep the thunder mug in the old days. I'll have to use that john myself. I wouldn't be surprised to find an outhouse out back somewhere."

"Are you going to call Mom?"

"I am not," he said.

"She'll be sad if she thinks I'm lost."

"I'll call your sister if you'll give me half a chance here. Go ahead, climb in bed, I'll be back in a jif." But I waited for him, sitting on the edge of the bed. And now there was nothing more to worry about—my mother would know what I was doing; it would be all right, no matter what.

(No, I cannot say I knew this, thought anything at all about what was happening—what could I have understood? I was nine. I say it *now*, construe it as I must, and it is our truth. It suffices.)

I closed my eyes and waited for him, unwilling to cope with the clammy, worn linoleum on the floor, the beaverboards tacked over joists to make walls, the single, bug-filled, milky light fixture in the middle of the room, the rough blanket on the bed that screeched if I moved even slightly. I shut my eyes and hunched my shoulders, clasped my hands tightly between my thighs for warmth, and while I waited for him to come back, I ordered the new universe. I was with my father (must I not be, then, safe?) somewhere near Chicago. I was with my father, and we were going . . . somewhere. A yahoo in Chicago he needed to see. Good enough. Jane: in her basement apartment, very strong and safe with her children and the pictures of Richard Hackbarth. My mother is in the Cramer Street house, but she has Arn to help her unpack and put away all the things in cardboard cartons. Jane, Arn, my mother, the city of Milwaukee . . . all rest secure, in good order, and I am here with my father.

"Did you call Jane?" I said when he returned.

"Indeed I did." He seemed short of breath, his chest heaving, flushed, as if he had been out running.

"Is it okay?" He sat on the single chair, put his head in his hands.

"Oh boy oh boy oh boy," he said.

"Dad?"

"You really did it up brown this time, Buck, didn't you," he said. He shook his head, his breath whooshing in his palms, whistling between his fingers. "Oh Jesus God, now what do I do!" he said.

"What did Jane say? Did she say it was okay? Is she going to tell Mom where I am?" He took his hands away from his face and looked at me; I thought from the sound of his breathing that he might be crying, and I was prepared to cry with him—I was with my father, and if he wept, I had no chance in this new universe. But he was dry eyed, the flush gone out of his face.

"Who?" he said. "Jane. Maybe someday I'll let you in on it. What she said. They can go whistle up a stump, huh? Let's get ourselves between the sheets, boy." I watched him undress, fascinated.

He sat next to me on the edge of the bed to take off his shoes and socks. The socks were almost as sheer as a woman's, decorated with hourglass designs, held up by ankle garters—I had never seen them before. His feet were dead white, as if they were made of stone, marbled with dark blue veins, the toes enormous, knobbed, the nails yellowish white, gnarled; it was some miracle to see them move as he wiggled them. "Them dogs is burnin'," he said, standing to remove his shirt and drop his trousers. Again I was shocked at the puffy, taut paleness of his skin, the moles speckling his shoulders, the pepper-salt thatch showing on his chest between the shoulder loops of his undershirt. But now he skinned the undershirt up, over his head (dark brown tufts in his armpits!). The hair on his chest tapered beneath his breastbone, ran to his navel, where it spread again, disappearing into the waistband of his trousers—his stomach seemed to swell even larger, the navel a dark, deep, hairy pit. He made claws of his fingers, kneaded his enormous belly as if it were a mound of stale dough, probed his navel with a fingertip. "Aaagh!" he said. He looked down, saw me staring. He winked, inhaled with a sound like wind, sucked up his stomach (it disappears, up under his ribs!), his chest rising until it nearly touched his lowered chin. Elbows out, hands folded into fists, biceps jumping, he turned to one side, back again to me, stiff necked. "Any girls on the beach?" he said, choked, exhaled with a blast of breath. "I'm a mess," he said. "I'm putting myself on a diet and exercises here the next day or two."

In his baggy shorts, he went to his grip for pajamas. "We'll need to get some pee-jays for you," he said. "It won't hurt you to sleep in your skivvies one night." His legs seemed too small, thin, for his torso, purple lumps of varicose veins showing through the curly hair on his calves and lower thighs. He put on the pajama top first, then stepped out of his shorts, awkwardly, uncertainly perched on one leg like a crane, squinting up at the light fixture as he jerked his foot free (I have one quick, simultaneously horrifying and thrilling glimpse of his scrotum hanging free, the blackness of his coarse pubic hair. Like my brother, he fondles himself unconsciously after pulling up the pajama bottoms.). "Come on," he said, "get undressed and into bed so I can douse the light."

He stood over me, took my shirt and short pants, my socks and shoes, laid them carefully on the dresser top. "In you go." He threw the single pillow on the floor. "Gives you a widow's hump," he said. "Watch your posture now and you'll never regret it when you're my age." He folded the top sheet neatly over the edge of the rough blanket. "Looks like war surplus," he said. He held the covers open for me like the fly of a tent, and I scurried into bed. The sheets were a cold, damp envelope. I drew my knees up, nestled my hands into my crotch, put my lips to the sheet and blew a spot warm for my ear. He crossed the cabin and turned off the light.

The floor seemed to shake as he recrossed the cabin. Then the bed dipped as if it were a thrown trapdoor, the shriek of the springs almost covering the grunt he gave, getting under the covers. He flopped heavily from his side to his back (I bob with the movement of the mattress, a weightless pea on a tilting plane), locked his hands behind his head, and blew out his breath, long and deliberate, as though clearing his lungs of another day's impurities.

"You okay?"

"I'm pretty good I guess."

"Sleep tight. See you in the morning." We were quiet for a moment, and then he said, "Do you say prayers when you go to bed?"

"Sometimes I do. If Mom says, I do. Not all the time."

"Do you want me to help you? I mean, do you say them out loud to your mother, or what?"

"I don't always say them."

"You're the boss."

"Sweet dreams," I said. My mother said it to me, every night, when I kissed her good-night.

"What?"

"Sweet dreams," I said. "It means have a good dream." He snorted, a sort of laugh. "You can say it back," I said. "I say it back to Mom when she says it to me."

"Do you now. Coming back at you then. Sweet dreams, boy. Come on, let's get some shut-eye. Got covers? Good man. Kick me if I snore." Then we were quiet. I must have fallen asleep for a short time, then wakened easily and gradually. The bed was warm and comfortable now.

"Daddy? Dad," I said, and when he did not answer, reached out and touched him.

"Wha—?" He jerked awake, sat up, pulling the covers off me. "What. Did you yell or something? What's the matter?"

"I just wanted to tell you something." He peered at the door, as if he expected to see morning light seeping under it, or to hear someone pound on it for entrance, break it off its hinges, police, Arn, Sheldon Rotter.

"Do you have to go potty again?"

"No. I just wanted to tell you something." He coughed, sighed, lay back down, adjusted the covers back over us.

"Okay. Let's hear it. We should be asleep."

"I'm really with you," I said. "What you asked before. I wanted to tell you I was really with you. Okay?" I expected him to say something, to be glad, but he was quiet for a long time. "I'm sorry I waked you up," I said.

"I guess I was having a dream," he said.

V

I woke to my father's coughing. He was out of bed, seated on the cabin's single chair, still in his pajamas, the shirt unbuttoned, hacking terribly. He sat forward, elbows on his knees, pale mound of his stomach exposed, racked by his chest-deep coughs. When a spasm passed, he sat, breathing deep, wheezing, stomach heaving, swallowing, wiping at his eyes. Then he would begin again, the depth and intensity of the seizures building, until he moved like a man having a muscular fit, head bobbing, shoulders bucking, face scarlet. It ended with his head between his knees. He looked up and saw me watching.

"Good morning there," he said.

"Are you okay, Dad?"

"What? Oh, hell yes. This is how I get started in the morning.

It takes me a while to get my wind, you know." He got up, still wheezing, found his trousers, got his handkerchief, put it to his nose and blew until his eyes seemed to bulge. It sounded comic, like the squawking honk of a duck lure. He shook his head as he blew, as if he were trying to twist the end of his nose off in his fingers. When he finished he sat down to deep-breathe again, clear his head of the dizziness brought on by the exertion. His complexion faded slowly.

(See the resignation, the lassitude. Without me, I believe, he would not be able to rouse himself, begin.)

"Dad."

"Better get up and get dressed, boy."

"Where are we going?"

"Chi," he said. "Anywhere. To hell out of this dump. Oh, you'll like it." I dressed, shuddering at the chill held in the beaverboard walls; when he opened the door, the sun rushed in on us like a warm breeze. "I'm going over to settle up," he said. "Can you lug one of those grips to the car, or do you have to go to the bathroom before we get started?"

"I think I can hold it for a while."

"Be right back." I had never carried anything so heavy, massive, as his suitcase. I half dragged it, its rigid side thumping me with each step, almost hard enough to knock me off my feet. I reached the Chrysler, hidden behind our cabin; it was beaded with dew, the windows silvery opaque. I felt myself sweat a little from the work, but I stood next to the suitcase while I waited for him to come, proud of myself for having made it.

"It's real heavy," I said when he came.

"I'll say." He opened the trunk and tossed it in after the other he had brought. "Always travel light as you can," he said. "You never know when you have to make a fast getaway." And then we were gone from the unnamed tourist cabins somewhere north of Chicago, not so far from Great Lakes. I watched the landscape as we drove away, thinking that I must remember to tell Jane that I had been near Great Lakes, where Richard Hackbarth once was—she would be glad, I thought, to hear it. Except to cough up phlegm between cigarettes, stick his head out of the car far enough to spit clear, he was silent as we drove into Chicago.

"Are we going to see the yahoo?" I said.

"The which? Rocker," he said. "You got it. Right." And after a moment in which he looked very closely at me, "Now let me give you a little tip. It isn't always the best policy to repeat anything and everything you say in private to other people. Know what I mean? So I trust you won't call Cal Rocker a yahoo when we see him, right?"

"What's a yahoo?" He laughed, let go the steering wheel with his right hand to reach over and touch my hair.

"That's neither here nor there," he said. "The point is, if I make some kind of crack, there's no good in your repeating it to every Tom, Dick, and Harry we run into, okay?"

"What if I don't know always if it's a crack? Is that a wisecrack?" I understood that this was intimacy—and I desired it. If I could get this clear, we would be so much the closer, sharing a private compact, and this I wanted very much, as we reached the outskirts of Chicago.

"If you have any doubts, just ask. Better, good policy is for you to speak only when spoken to, once we get into this, huh?"

"Okay."

"Now," he said. "I'll give you the poop on this so you can know what's what. Poop. Inside information. Got it? Good man. Your old man," he said, lighting another cigarette, "is trying to pull off a little deal here. And not so little when you come to think of it, either. Now this Cal Rocker yahoo is okay. I mean, he's all right. He owes your old man some big favors from way on back, see? You know, you pay attention good here, you could learn something valuable. Interested?" I nodded. I had to go to the toilet again, badly by this time, but I would have held it to the point of insensibility rather than interrupt. (Do you see? I wanted this! My father speaks to me, as freely as if I was not there, and in listening we become one in his schemes, his dilemma . . . listen.)

"If it comes to talent," he said, "your old man is a fair jack-of-all-trades. But if there's one thing he's good at it's knowing how to set up a deal, see? I use psychology. This Rocker yahoo—" he winked—"is only sort of more or less expecting me. Which is exactly the way I want it. You'll see how I go about it. Pay attention, someday you'll have something worth money, no matter what you end up doing. You know what you want to be when you grow up yet?"

"No," I said.

"Don't let it worry you." I had, of course, never thought of it, worried about anything like it. At nine, there was no future—all was present, and the dim, haunting flickers of the immediate past. Future begins, time begins, with my father. "I'm forty-nine years old," he said, "and I still don't know what I want to be when I grow up. That's a joke, son," he said when I did not laugh at once.

"I think Arnie's going to be a teacher when he goes to college. Or else business he's going to study," I said.

"The hell with that noise," my father said. "That's fine if you're an old lady spinster with nothing better to do. You watch your old man, I'll show you how to handle people in this world. It's better than any college education. I never even graduated high school," he said, "and I never once regretted it. You pay attention, keep your trap shut and your eyes and ears open, you'll see what I mean."

"I will."

"You feeling a little cruddy from that fleabag we slept in? We'll be checking in a good hotel here in a minute, we'll get us spruced up, don't worry."

"Aren't we going to see Cal Rocker?"

"You darn tootin'. See, that's what I mean. Here's a point. We can't go see a man to do a deal looking like we're the ragman's kids, can we. Not on your life. You have to look right if you want to feel right. Would you lend a man looked like me twenty bucks if I asked you for it?" He had tried to comb his hair in the cabin, but it was still tufted, uneven. He had not shaved. The stubble of his beard was nearly snow white, two days' worth. He wore the same shirt and suit from yesterday. I felt suddenly unclean. "Certainly not," he said. "Watch, when I get through with us we'll look like we came out of *Esquire*. That's a point to remember. Never give anything away on your appearance. It can make you or break you." I repeated it, again and again, to myself—I would never, *never* forget it! "Make the best of what you got, because all you got is what you are," he said.

I would never forget! I had already forgotten that I had to go to the bathroom.

And then we were on Clark Street, and he stopped and said, "Could you handle a meal about now?" And we went to La Nortena restaurant, ate a breakfast of Mexican food that upset his stomach. And then we went to the LaSalle Hotel, checked in, and prepared our appearances, ready to handle Mr. Calvin Rocker.

(No, I had never eaten chili for breakfast before. Nor since. That is not the point. Of course, my mother, your Grandmother Hansen, fretted over my meals, consulted illustrated charts depicting a nutritious and impossible Basic Nine Foods necessary to each day in a growing child's life . . . no, I did not think of this, felt no wonder or guilt, as we sat eating chili and burritos in the La Nortena restaurant on Clark Street, in Chicago, this day in June, 1946. The point is: my father.)

I see, now, in this vision of memory, how he comes alive this day in Chicago. It begins with the deadly, painful smoker's hacking in the chill cabin near Great Lakes, donning stale, wrinkled clothes, driving out without washing, shaving, brushing his teeth. Perhaps there is (surely there is!) soreness in his throat as he proceeds to chain-smoke, and stiffness, cramps from the lumpy mattress, the feeling that dirt, and time, and circumstance have caught and engulfed him. Does he consider returning me to Milwaukee?

But I ask about the Chicago yahoo, Mr. Calvin Rocker, and with his own voice, his own absurd desire, his need, my father re-creates himself to live another day. It is not chili for breakfast, not nostalgia for a place he knew *back before the world went to hell and gone*; it is appetite! For one more day, he has made himself believe. A man who believes, lives. A man who lives, hungers, and he who can hunger *must eat!* He has made himself live another day, in a world that no longer needs or wants him, and now we have begun, with a breakfast of chili, the careful and confident process of *handling* Cal Rocker, and no matter how it ends, he, we, are alive!

And do you see, I can almost believe I am responsible. At the least, I share, and at most, I am proud for having given him the chance. I carried the suitcase to the car, I asked after the Chicago yahoo—I am with him all the way.

"Now watch," he said, "this is all a part of it. You even ever stayed at a hotel before? You'll get a bang out of it." The LaSalle Hotel dominated the street. Its sign was three stories high, parallel to the building front, *LaSalle* spelled out in letters stacked like blocks, and at the top and bottom of the massive sign, *Hotel*. At night, the letters were marked with light bulbs, hundreds of them. He swung wide to avoid the line of foreign-looking Checker cabs at the cabstand, then cut back in sharply to park directly in front of the marquee. On the front of the marquee was a banner, *Air Conditioned*, the letters painted to resemble blue white blocks of ice, icicles drooping from each one; on the two sides of the marquee, the banners read *cool*. "Relief in sight," my father said, snugging up his tie before he got out. "Watch. And remember, mum's the word."

How could he have looked so different as he approached the doorman? Yet, he did. He was suddenly taller, his waist slimmer, chest higher, shoulders back, chin up. The doorman's cap was unexceptional, but his coat was glorious at a distance. Closer, the braid on his epaulets was tarnished, a button missing, an elbow crudely mended. He touched his cap to my father.

"Okay, admiral," my father said, reaching for his wallet, "I'll tell you what I need." The doorman bowed as he took the two dollars my father extended, the bills held between two fingers, folded the long way. "Your man, number one," my father said, "to lug in our bags and the rest of the clothes you see hanging there. Two," he unclipped the ignition key from his key ring, handed it to the doorman like it was a coin, "somebody to get the buggy to a garage for a wash and wax. And I mean a good one. My boy and I just blew in here from Saint Louis—" Mum, I repeated to myself, was the word—"and we've got a ways yet before we're home free. Something good on the wax, too, simonize, Blue Coral, you get the general idee, huh?" The doorman bobbed, saluted. The cuffs of his trousers were mud spattered, the gold stripe coming loose on one leg, the heels of his shoes badly run over. "Now show us the way to register and we'll be no more trouble to you." I marched in behind my father, as confident as if I were a field marshal, the doorman, a simpering aide, holding the heavy door open for us.

The marquee banners were deceptive—the rooms of the hotel were air conditioned, but the central lobby's moist heat was relieved only by the wide blades of the overhead fans that turned at irregular speeds, stopping, starting with a whirring sound, drifting slowly on momentum. It was that kind of hotel.

And that was part of it, my father would later explain. We are here to handle Mr. Cal Rocker, and everything works to that end. So, blow into the Blackstone or some ritz on the North Shore, Cal Rocker is going to wonder why Buck Hansen is working so hard to spend his money like a Sunday-rich nigger. Nope. The LaSalle is the ticket. It's a good hotel, the sort of place a solid man checks in when he wants comfort and service for his money. The LaSalle is a good hotel without thinking it's the Waldorf Astoria or the Royal Hawaiian, and Buck Hansen and son (Cal Rocker must be made to think, must think *without thinking about it*) stop there as easy and natural as water finds its own level; even though (of course) they can afford the Waldorf if push came to shove. It is part of it: when Cal says, where you stopping, Buck? we (he) reply, the LaSalle—it's right on your way when you come in. Psychology.

The LaSalle Hotel has a doorman, even if his braid is tarnished, his coat mended, his nose and cheeks laced with boozer's veins. The bellhops do not look clean and enthusiastic like Philip Morris Johnny. They are men as old as my father, heads and hands too large for their uniforms, the uniforms soiled, as if you could lay them over a clothesline, like rugs, and beat clouds of dust out of them—the bellhop who trots after our bags (my father passes him a dollar bill with the grace of a stage magician) has blackheads all over his face, and eyebrows that grow together in a solid, shaggy line across his brow. But the LaSalle has bellhops with stiff, high collars and pillbox hats strapped under their chins. The lobby carpets are faded by feet and sunlight, the fringes are fraying, but the designs are authentically Oriental. The furniture is comfortable, if old, and the planters are full, if untended. There are brass spittoons, even if nobody empties or polishes them daily any longer. The desk man wears a white shirt and a tie, though his nails are bitten, his hands unwashed (my father uses his own pen to sign—the gold cap gleams, the ink jet black, signature an effortless flourish). The maids, aged (they remind me of Mrs. Spaulding), wear aprons and hairnets that do not cover their hair.

"I'll take the key," my father said. "Where's your tonsorial parlor? Barbershop to you."

"Aren't we going to our room?" I ask as I follow him to the barbershop off the central lobby. "Will we get to ride in the elevator, Dad?"

"You bet you," he said. "All in good time. First things first. You got to start at the bottom and work your way up through it. Keep your eyes peeled."

There are five chairs, two barbers on duty, a Negro shoeshine boy, all unoccupied. "Look alive, here comes one," my father said loudly as we entered. It was as if they had been there forever, created to be there, wait for him, our arrival. One dropped his magazine, sprang out of his chair, snatched a striped apron from the arm of the chair, snapped it open, stood at the ready as my father doffed his coat, handed it to the Negro, and seated himself like royalty on a throne, bored but at perfect ease, possessing the privilege to be bored.

"The little boy, too?" said the second barber, smiling, his hands folded over the stomach of his off-white jacket.

"He'll do for now," said my father. "We'll get his ears set out before too long, I guess." He stretched his neck, moved his chin from side to side as the barber pinned the apron. "Grab a mag and sit tight," he said to me, and to the Negro, "Give the boots a lick and a promise there, will you?" The Negro slid his stool up to my father's feet, began to daub polish on his shoes with his fingers, whistling almost inaudibly. The second barber did not go back to his chair, but stood like a soldier at parade rest, hands clasped behind his back, looking at nothing out in the central lobby, rocking slightly on his toes and heels, as if, any minute, a whim of my father's would send him away, set him in motion, out on an errand.

I found *Life* or *Time* or *Police Gazette,* a prop to hide behind while I watched.

It is like watching a play, a pageant. The tile floor and walls, the wall-length mirror behind the row of chairs, the porcelain sinks, the chrome and steel fixtures, all seem to focus light on my father, who sits above everything, everyone. At his feet, the Negro, spine hunched almost in a curve, rubs polish into shoe leather, begins to buff with a brush, now humming something that serves as celebration. The unoccupied barber is solemn, yet very alert, a sentry, bodyguard. My father's barber moves steadily around his head, his feet making nervous little half-steps and shuffles. A long comb stuck over his ear, another in his breast pocket, still another in his hand to fluff up hair for the scissors that never stops clicking. And my father, totally oblivious to them all, one hand free of the apron to hold his Pall Mall, pays attention only when he glances casually down to jar the cigarette over the ashtray ingeniously set in the armchair, precisely in expectation of his coming.

"Just a trim," he says to the barber. "Nothing off the top. Cut it close around the ears. It keeps the gray from showing. You get the idea." To the Negro, "Let's not shine my socks too if we can help it." To the other barber, "So what's new in the Windy City? Summer's worse here than it is in Saint Louis. I hope to tell you. Drove all goddamn night rather than hole up in the dumps you find between there and Chicago. Just close around the ears, don't skin me. I didn't order white sidewalls, now did I?"

How long can a haircut last? In the barbershop of the LaSalle Hotel, in June of 1946 . . . forever, clearly.

"Shave too, sir? Shampoo?"

"I guess not. When I find a barber I think knows how to use a straight razor properly, I'll give him a crack at my gullet," my father said. The barber snickered, obligatory, as the apron was removed. The Negro finished with a final, ear-opening pop of his rag, slid back out of the way, still seated on his stool. My father stood, faced the wall mirror, combed his hair with his own comb as the barber whisked his shoulders. "Not half bad if I do have to say it myself," my father said. The giving of money is flawless.

The bills again extended as if they were litmus paper held up to check for something suspected in the atmosphere. My father raises his hand, fingers joined, palm out, like a traffic policeman saying halt, freezing the barber as he digs in a drawer for change that is now his to keep. The Negro holds his coat for him, receives a half-dollar, slipped back to him as surreptitiously as a lover's note. I follow my father out into the central lobby, with all the sense of moment of a ring bearer in a wedding procession. Behind us, the barber, the Negro, surely vaporize, or, the source of power that animates them withdrawn, stand like statues, for eternity, or until . . . no, for eternity, because my father will never return.

"Why did you say Saint Louis, Dad?" I asked as we headed for the elevators.

"What nobody don't know won't hurt them, boy," he said. "Like Satchel Paige says, pitch with a whole mess of loosey-goosey moves. It confuses hell out of the opposition."

"Who's Satchel Paige?"

"Later," he said. "Now we really get down to work." Another Negro steps in ahead of us to operate the elevator, this one old, his hair like a mound of soapy bubbles. He might have been invisible as we stepped past him. My father gave him a quarter as he let us out on the floor. "It's not so much throwing your money around loose as it is laying it around you with the right people at the right time," he said when I asked him why. "You'll see," he said.

The bellhop with blackheads had been in ahead of us to turn on the air conditioner. It was mounted in one of the windows looking out over the hotel's marquee (pressing my cheek against the cold glass, straining my eyes, I could see the front edge of the massive sign, a score of light bulbs part of the letter A). It was as large as a dresser, throbbing and humming, shuddering every so often as it changed cycles. A thread was tied to the vent grating; it stood straight out in the flow of cold air (my arms goose pimples, my head began to ache, if I stood directly before the grating), quivering like a filament carrying an electric current. "This is more like it," my father said, unlocking his grips. "Now I could stand about a year of this, huh?" But it was not refreshing; the icy flow from the vent faded to a clammy greasiness on the far side of the room, the air smelling slightly burned. I wanted always to sneeze, and wished for a long-sleeved shirt. My father picked up the phone. "Room service, *mach schnell*."

"Here we go," he said, opening the second grip. He unbuckled a strap and gently lifted out a tan summer-weight suit, hung on the mini-hanger that came with the grip. "How's that hit your eye, sonny?" It was a fine suit.

"Slick," I said.

"You said it. That," he said, "is a suit to go see a man in. Prewar, and mister, they just don't make 'em the way they used to. Some styles never go out, let me tell you." He laid it tenderly on the bed, turned back to the open grip, slowly pulled back a zipper to get at an inner compartment. "That came with two pairs of pants and a vest," he said.

"It's real nice."

"Strictly *Boul Mich*," he said. "You don't horse-ass around with a man wearing a suit like that, I hope to tell you. And," he said, "ah!" Carefully, slowly, as if it were a platter of hot food balanced on the palm of his hand, he gingerly withdrew a flat package, brown butcher's paper tied with string. He nipped the string with his pocketknife and folded back the paper. It was a white shirt.

"Can I have the cardboard? Arn gives me his if Mom doesn't want it. I draw on them sometimes and make stuff."

"There isn't any," he said. "I've got a chink up in Saint Paul does my shirts. Did, I should say. This is the last of the Mohicans. Starched to a fare-thee-well." He nudged the package to the center of the bed, returned to the grip. "The com*plete* man," he said, and took out a small box with a rubber band around it. Opened, he held it out to me. "Take a gander." The cuff links were square, flat blocks of highly polished stainless steel, BH cut into each one in a plain, block initial. The tie clip spelled *Buck* in flowing, bold letters, a facsimile of his handwriting.

"They're real nice. They're keen," I added when he continued to hold them under my nose, waiting for more.

"I made those," he said. "I made the links on a lathe, right here in Chicago, before you were even thought of, I might add. The other I had a jeweler make up for me, over on Division. I suppose I could have made it for myself if I'd taken the time." He laid the jewelry out on the dressing table. He stood looking at them, then at me, and I felt I had fallen short of what he needed, what I owed, if I was to make . . . well, if I was to be *responsible*. "Play your cards right," he said, "and these'll be yours someday."

"I don't wear ties," I said.

"I mean when I'm dead and buried." He said it very casually. Then the old Negro elevator operator knocked on the door. "It's open," my father said. While my father spoke to him, the old Negro continually nodded his head, shooting his eyes about the room, eyewhites curdled yellow, at me, at the open grips, up at my father, down at the money being laid in his streaky orange palm. "Find me a tailor and get this spot-cleaned and pressed. First class though, know what I mean?" He handed him the suit, slipped the hanger over the Negro's thumb like he was hanging it on a wall hook. "And see I get that hanger back. That's mine. You know a good schnapps when you see one? A decent rye. I don't mean snooty, I mean just a good, decent rye won't rot my tubes. Okey-doke? And a bucket of ice cubes at the same time. This is for your trouble." He took another dollar out of his wallet and stuffed it in the breast pocket of the Negro's jacket. I could see in the wallet; he held it so the Negro could see in it. It looked like a lot of money—a Philadelphia bankroll, he told me. When he had his money, turning to leave, the old Negro smiled, pulled back his thick, purplish lips, exposing horse-sized teeth as yellow as the whites of his rolling eyes.

"You act like you never saw a nigger close up before," my father said when he had gone.

"I guess I didn't."

"I'm not blaming you, don't get me wrong," he said, "but I don't suppose it's nice to stare at anybody, is it? Good enough." Then it was time for our showers. "Neat and clean," he said, "head to toe. Tell you what. You won't be needing a shave—" he lifted his chin and scratched the white stubble on his throat with his fingernails—"so I'll bathe first. Okay? When that nigger gets back we'll see about some stepping-out clothes for you. You might as well get out of those dirty clothes, they're for the incinerator first chance we get."

I took off my clothes, but it was too cold in the air-conditioned room, so I followed him into the bathroom and sat waiting on the toilet-seat lid, warming myself in the steam from his shower that dewed the walls and fogged the mirror. On the shelf above the sink, he had laid out fresh underwear (Fruit of the Loom, the oranges, grapes, in full color on the label!), and next to it, laid open his traveling toilet case (twin military brushes, barber's comb, toenail clippers, file, tweezers, like dentist's tools prepared for an extraction). He closed the shower curtain, but I had a full view of him as he shampooed and lathered, his eyes squeezed shut, stepping in and out of the needle-spray of the showerhead.

Another revelation, mini-epiphany (but of what? to what end?): a great Babe Ruth body, looking oiled in the coating of water and soapsuds. Balloon buttocks and paunch, hard sticklike

106

legs, white knobby feet, corded tanned forearms, soft mole-
flecked shoulders and back, chest hair plastered flat, glossy against
his skin, scalp shining through the flattened thinning hair on his
head—he tips back his head, fills his mouth with needles of
steaming water, gargles, lurches to spit into the tub drain—he
works a small bar of hotel soap into a muff of lather in his hands,
reaches down and engulfs his groin with washboard strokes; he
sees me watching, smiles, breaks into song—"Asleep in the Deep,"
digging his chin deeper into his chest, bending at the waist for each
progressively basser note, cocking his head to the wall to catch the
full resonance, one hand, fingers webbed with soap, to his ear like
a radio announcer, a tobacco auctioneer, a parody of deafness . . .

"You sing pretty good."

"Can't hear you!" he shouts through the curtain of water,
shakes his head, grins. I draw my feet up on the toilet seat, warm
at last, hug my knees, as he fades in and out of the steamy mist
swirling in the bathroom, a Hamlet's father.

(Mini-epiphany meaning nothing! I do not care, so long as it
is mine. Ours.)

He shuts off the water suddenly, steps out, a dripping
amphibian, towels himself roughly, oohing and ahing like a
porpoise. "Good, good, good!" he cries to me, his image in the
mirror. "God*damn* that feels good!" he cries to me, the mirror.
The hair on his head, chest, legs, fluffs like silk. He sets the
temperature of the water for me, holds back the curtain while I
step in. "Wash off the road, boy." It is like dozing, like those
delicious, impossible-to-retain moments of half sleep while falling
asleep in a clean bed. The water is a warm blanket that ripples
down my body. I watch him continue the process of his
re-creation.

Shorts and undershirt on, he gets a bottle of Lucky Tiger
from his grip. "You can't buy this stuff in a drugstore. Sold by
barbers only." He dribbles an exact quantity into his hand, slaps
his hands together to spread it, shakes the excess into the sink,
lays fingers to his scalp and works it in. His hair shines, flops in
strands. "Too much and you smell like a French floozy. You want
to massage your scalp, sonny. Show me a bald man, I'll show you
a man with a scalp tight as a drum. Circulation's the ticket if you
want to keep your hair, boy." He combs his hair forward, parts it,
squinting into the mirror, ends up with short strokes, touches to
get it perfect, leans forward over the sink to inspect, tipping his
head up, down, to each side. "Look good?"

"Sure."

"Damn bet you." From the grip also, his Rolls Razor. "Next best thing to a straight razor," he says. "My old man used a straight razor all his life. I learned on one. Safety razor ain't worth the powder to blow it to hell." He strops the razor in its bright, chrome case, the clack of the blade against the red leather echoing like circus clown slaps in the bathroom (the slug-white flesh of his upper arm shivers as he works the razor in its case). Assembled, the razor gleams like a scalpel. From a mangled tube of Molé shaving cream, worming onto the bristles of a wet shaving brush. He lathers his face with brisk, circular motions. The cream erupts on his cheeks, jaw, lips, into a thick mass of white foam. Then the bright Rolls Razor sweeps up his throat, down his cheeks, around his mouth, leaving clean, pink skin in its path. He brings it to perfection, lifting his chin, stretching the loose skin with two fingers; he puckers his lips, pulls his face to one side, the other, ends with tiny, delicate strokes on the points of his jutting chin. He leans close to the mirror to examine once more, rinsing the razor clean under the hot water faucet.

"Smooth as a baby's behind."

"You cut off your moustache!" I cry, head out of the curtain. He looks back at me from the mirror, smiles.

"Hell, it put an extra five years on me. I look like a new man." Almost, he does. He towels his face clean, then rummages in the toilet kit, brings out lotion. "Plain witch hazel," he says. "I don't want to smell as good as Rocker's wife, now do I?" It makes his face shine. "Brush twice a day if you want to keep your choppers, son." Again, I think of a magician: thumb and forefinger grip his upper teeth, move, remove his partial plate, lay it on the sink, an ugly half-circle of gold wires, prongs, very real-looking teeth. The lower follows. He sees me watching in the mirror, turns, sucks in his lips, face collapsing like a deflated bag. "Thee wha' I mean?" he lisps from the caved-in hole of his mouth. I do not know if I dare laugh, or if I want to screech.

But when he has scrubbed them, rinsed them, reinserted them, he looks, almost, like a new man. "You better get out of there and get dry, I think that's our nigger," he said. He paused to stick out his tongue, flatten it, observe it in the mirror. The shower off, I heard the old Negro knock again on the door as my father went out to open it. "Wrap yourself in a dry towel," he said when I came out, "I sent old Stepin Fetchit down to get you some new duds. Let's hope you don't end up looking like a jig's kid, huh?"

He completed himself with the fresh clothes. The socks were

standard, hourglass design, held up with garters. If he looked ridiculous, in socks, garters, shorts, buttoning the clean white shirt, it was only for an instant. Trousers on, new-shined shoes on and laced, shirt tucked in, I began to see it. The tie was plain brown (shit-brindle brown, he called it) to complement his suit. He slid his arms carefully, slowly, into the coat, brought it up on his shoulders with a shrug. Then stood in the middle of the room (I am freezing, tugging on the rough hotel bath towel to cover more of myself!) to shoot his cuffs (the monogrammed links spring into visibility!), run his thumbs around his waistband (the last shirt starched by the Saint Paul chink crackles!) and give the knot of his tie a last snugging. Last, he extended his hand to slide on his wristwatch, held up the proper fingers to receive the Masonic and diamond rings, clipped his tie. "How do I look?" he said.

"Real nice. Fancy," I said. It could not have been adequate. Nothing could, for what he felt, what he needed.

"Are you chattering your teeth? Move out of the way of the air conditioner if you're cold, for crying out loud." He went back to the bathroom for a better look. "*Boul Mich*," I heard him say to himself.

"That's a neat suit, Dad," I said when he came out, trying again, knowing I could not succeed.

"You bet," he said. "In this suit I could borrow a sawbuck off that coon if I was to put my mind to it, boy."

The Negro returned with clothes for me (a long-sleeved polo shirt, dark slacks, two pairs of socks, underwear). It would do for what we had to do to Cal Rocker, my father said. He would get me properly outfitted in time for anything else that came up. He was ready, after fixing himself a rye-and-water highball on the rocks, getting his cigarettes and an ashtray close at hand, lighting one, resting it on the lip of the ashtray, getting the slip of paper with Cal Rocker's number out of his wallet.

"Give a listen," he said as he waited for the operator to connect him, for the switchboard at Cal Rocker's plant to give him Cal's secretary, for Cal to pick up his phone. "I'll show you how it's done."

—And there he is: the complete Buck Hansen. He looks almost a new man. Oh, he looks very good! His hair does not seem to be going quite so gray, the black showing Lucky Tiger highlights. His face has color, the skin has a witch hazel sheen. The Saint Paul chink's shirt moves against his body as though it were molded of sculptor's plaster. The tan of his expensive prewar summer suit absorbs light, the texture an illusion like weightless suede. His trousers are hiked before he sits to preserve the knife-blade creases. The garters do not show. With his free hand he rotates the highball glass (ice cubes rattle pleasantly). Smoke from his burning Pall Mall streams up to be caught, dissipated by the air conditioner's flow. This is no man to sit with his head between his knees in a shoddy tourist cabin near Great Lakes, Illinois, near-broken by chronic morning cough! No man to grimace into a hot sun, wondering at his welcome; no man to plead for mercy from a bitter daughter—this is Buck Hansen, and he has the perfect right to be, because . . . because he *is*. And what is more (*I* know, then and now!), he knows he has the perfect right to be this, his existence. Because he feels it so. There in the LaSalle Hotel, as Cal Rocker lifts the phone from its cradle on his executive desk.

"Hello, Calvin me boy," my father said; he straightened up on the chair, uncrossed his leg, set his drink down. "Who the hell else would it be barging into your busy day? By Christ, I told you I'd be by, didn't I? You damn bet you. The hell you say—" There is no Calvin Rocker on the other end of the line. No voice, person there for me to imagine, construct. There is just my father, the center of the hotel room, the rest dim (I am dim, an agent of perception, no more). These words are a stream of my father's words, needing no ear but mine to hear them, no voice to answer. "Not so bad," he said, "the road's always a bitch, but I'm used to that, I guess. I ought to be if I'm not. I'm at the LaSalle. Sure, you know. One fleabag's like another for me, boy. Now that sounds right neighborly of you. I always said you'd turn out all right if they could get you to wear shoes, didn't I." He shared a laugh (I smile, watching him, though it means nothing, no joke, to me) with Cal Rocker. "Hold on while I write all that down, will you?" He removed his fountain pen, the telephone wedged between his chin and shoulder, uncapped it. "Skokie?" my father said, "that's pasture land out there, isn't it? What are you, a goddamn gentleman farmer? The hell you say. We'll get started before too long or I'll never find it in the dark. Oh, say, Cal. I've got my boy with me, you know." And now there is a voice, a Cal Rocker on the other end, because my father speaks of me, and he must be there to hear it. Do you see? "No, no," he said, "the little guy. Junior. That's him. It has at that, hasn't it? You won't know him, I promise you. I hardly know him myself. You bet. Okay, Cal. You got it."

Setting the phone gently down, my father gave me an exaggerated wink, forming a circle with the thumb and forefinger of his free hand. "In like Flynn," he said, poking my stomach.

"I'm your junior, aren't I?" I said.

"You're what? That you are. It means we have the same name."

"I know," I said. But I had never heard it said—*junior*. Never before.

"We've got to get going before long," he said. "There's one little thing I want you to do for me." He rummaged in the drawer, tossing the Gideon Bible out on the bed, envelopes, stationery. "Here we are." The LaSalle Hotel supplied postcards to guests; the pictures showed the enormous sign, the marquee, but there were no air-conditioned banners up when the picture had been made. My father printed the address. "Here," he said, handing me his pen, "I want you to write something."

"Who are we sending it to?"

"Your sister. Read the address. Just tell her you're fine or something. Anything you want. Go ahead." I took the fountain pen; it felt delicately balanced, seemed very long, as if the cap would stick up, waving awkwardly, over my shoulder as I bent to write. "Do you write writing or do you just print?"

"I can write pretty good. What should I say? Aren't you going to call Jane again and tell her where we are?"

"Damn, boy," he said. "Phone calls cost money, you know? Look, we'll send her the card today. We'll mail it right down in the lobby on our way out to Rocker's house. He lives way to hell and gone now. Jane'll get the card tomorrow or the next day latest."

"She doesn't know where I am now," I said. "Mom doesn't know where we are!"

"By tomorrow you should be on your way home, what with a little luck. See? If you're not I'll call your sister like I did last night, deal? Any breaks and I'll have you packed off to your mother tomorrow. Promise."

"Will I see you again sometime?" I asked. But he was calling the desk, asking for the bell captain to check on the Chrysler. So I wrote: *Dear Jane I am fine I am with my daddy I am having fun Oskar* (no pen writes so smoothly, it glides over the postcard, the letters assertive, jet black!). "Is it okay?" I asked when I handed it to him.

"Perfecto," he said, adding a note of his own for Jane,

blowing on the card to dry the ink. "You must get good marks in penmanship." He read it again as he capped and put away his pen. "Do you spell your name with a *k*?" he asked.

"Sure."

"I could have sworn we changed yours to a *c* when you were born. We gave you a hell of a sweet handle too, didn't we," he said.

It was a long way back out, north, to Skokie, Illinois. I remembered my father's remark on the phone, *gentleman farmer*, and wondered if Cal Rocker would have a barn, silo, pigs, horses. We passed fenced fields, wooded acres. Traffic lights became few and far between, dusk fell. I was glad to be out of the hotel room, warm again, clean and comfortable in my new clothes. I sniffed the sleeve of my polo shirt often, to see if it would smell different—my mother had once said that Negroes smelled different than we did (dogs could sense it immediately!). I held my head very still, careful not to brush against the back of the seat, after my father combed my hair for me—the few, heady drops of Lucky Tiger on the comb seemed to fill the car with perfume. Beside me, smoking, my father retained the glory of his fresh suit, shirt, thorough toilet.

"Ready to put on the feed bag?" he said. "I can promise you we'll get a good feed, if nothing else."

"I'm not too hungry yet. I ate a lot before." The Mexican food, as my father had predicted, stuck with me. He had dosed himself twice with Sal Hepatica before we left the hotel. His faint, stifled burps punctuated the silence as we drove. Not bad manners, just good beer, he said the first time.

"Well I hope to Christ you won't come out with that when we get to Rocker's. Will you?"

"I won't say anything," I said.

"That's not what I mean. Hell, I'm not the goddamn Gestapo that you can't open your mouth if somebody speaks to you, you know." He looked at me. "Listen, this is a real important night for your old man, boy: Are you listening to me?"

"Yes."

"Okay. Let me give you a few clues here. Some wise words to the wise. Like when we checked into the hotel, see? You're going to hear me maybe say some things aren't strictly kosher. True. I'll be counting on you not to make a liar out of me in front of Cal."

"I won't. I won't say anything."

"Damn. That's exactly the point!" He slowed the car.

"You're going to have to talk a little, you know. I don't want you to sit around all night like a bump on a log. You're a good boy, hell, you know how to talk to people when you meet them, don't you? Don't you?"

"I think so."

"Do you know enough to shake a man's hand when you're introduced?"

"I know how to shake hands."

"Let's see. How do you do it? Go ahead, shake." He threw his cigarette out the wing, extended his hand to me. I took it, feeling the glassy coldness of his Masonic ring. "What do you do, just hold the man's hand in your mitt? Give it a pump. Give it two. Let him know he's having his hand shook, see." He let go of my hand. "Okay, try her again. This time, try to give it a squeeze. It's not a contest to see who's strongest, but you want to let him know he's got hold of a man there. Pump it. There you go." He released me. "Remember that when I introduce you to Cal Rocker. You lay your hand out like a slab of warm mush, a man thinks he's got some queer or an old lady there. You can do it."

"I'll be sure and remember." My hand tingled from the squeeze he gave it, from the lingering presence of his touch. I wanted to lift it to my nose and smell it, but did not.

"Same goes for his wife," he said.

"I shake her hand too?"

"If she puts hers out you do. If not, just say pleased to meet you, some such. Got it?"

"Pleased to meet you."

"Good. We're having dinner, so ixnay on how full you are, or we ate Mexican food in a greasy spoon, all that, okay? Just let me do all the talking about where we've been, what we've been doing, etcetera, got that?"

"Are you going to tell the lie about Saint Louis again?" He did not answer for a moment.

"No," he said. "It's not exactly lying, either."

"Fibs," I said.

"Call it what you like. Look now. Get this straight in your head. Your dad's in a bind, see? He needs help bad. Cal Rocker can fill the bill if everything goes right for us tonight. It looks good so far, but this is the clincher, see? How far we get tonight depends on how well your old man talks, see? I'll no doubt have to fabricate some, but it's all to the same good cause. You want to get back to your mother and all tomorrow, don't you? Like I said?"

"I guess so. Sure I do."

"Then keep quiet when you see I'm spinning some yarn or whatever. God help me, boy, I need help. Bad. I'm banking on you not to snafu the whole shooting match for me. Please." He began speaking while trying to watch me, looking away from the road as much as he dared, but ended looking straight ahead, as if he could not let me see his face. "We get through this and I'll buy you something swell to take back home with you."

"It's okay," I said.

"What is?"

"You don't have to buy me anything. I'm helping you anyway. Aren't I helping you, Dad? I mean I'm just being a help, no matter what else or anything."

"That's my big boy!" he said, and reached out, gripped my thigh with his fingers. "You and me, kid," he said, "we can lick the world, I'll tell you."

Now we were out of the city. There were no street lights, very few cars, and it was getting darker. He stopped the car suddenly, put his arm over the back of the seat, backed up to a side road we had just passed. He pulled over on the wrong side of the road to be able to read the sign, rolling down the window. The sound of crickets, the fresh smell of country, came into the car. I was afraid a breeze would muss my hair.

"Hoity-toity," he said.

"What?" He rolled up the window, cramped the wheel, turned up the side road. It was dark, blacktop, the trees on both sides growing almost together in a canopy over the road.

"Indian Hills Circle," he said. "There hasn't been an Indian here for a hundred and fifty years, and I'm damned if you could find a hill high enough to pee off of. It took some hebe developer to think that one up." There were no hills, but the land did roll gently, and both sides of the sharply winding blacktop road were heavily wooded. When we turned into a curve, the Chrysler's headlights swept a wall of trees and wild shrubbery. Once, off to my side, I thought I saw a pair of glowing animal's eyes. "A dog most likely," my father said, "could be a coon or a possum up a tree I suppose. I don't think you'll find deer running wild this close to the city."

And then there was a circle. It would have been very picturesque from the air, I know: a winding road moving through the thick woods, leaving its freedom to bend to the right in a long, perfect arc until it returned upon itself suddenly. And here were, not street lights, but floodlit porches, huge homes starkly white,

114

shuttered, gabled, their walks signaled with coachlights at the rounded curbstone. "Holy balls, he must be an effing millionaire," my father said.

"It's like a park," I said.

"Let's see if we can find which one he's hiding in." We circled once, completely, before my father saw the house number. It was mounted on a small white cast-iron standard near the edge of the lawn. They reminded me of homes in Milwaukee suburbs, Fox Point, Whitefish Bay, Lake Drive, where my mother liked to cruise just before Christmas to see the lighted decorations—there was a prize given every year, and the winning home had its picture in the Sunday *Journal*. "Let's get him," my father said, turning into the wide driveway. "Let's skin him alive!"

"Roger Wilco," I said, and we laughed. There were two cars in the drive, one of them a prewar station wagon, its wooden body waxed, blond brown in the Chrysler's headlights. As we stopped, another porch light came on, and Mr. Calvin Rocker came out to the front door to greet us.

"Buck?" he said. He was silhouetted by the light from the doorway. My father took my hand to walk to the door.

"Last time I looked," my father said.

"I thought it'd be you," Cal Rocker said. "What in the—" His silhouette ducked back inside, and then still another outside light sprang on. The light sat on the edge of the garage roof, showering us, the driveway, the three automobiles, in bright light. "I'll be goddamned," Cal Rocker said, sticking his head and shoulders back out the doorway. "I thought that was your old clunker. Christ, Buck," he said, "when the hell you going to break down and buy a new car. You've had that heap since before the war, isn't it?"

We reached the door, and my father put out his hand, shook with him. "They don't make them like they did," he said. "I wouldn't have one of those jalopies they make now if you paid me into the bargain. What's that you have there, is that a new Packard?"

"Packard," Cal said, "that's a Cadillac, Buck. The station wagon's Carol's."

"How are you, Cal?" my father said. They shook hands vigorously, and Cal Rocker put his hand on my father's shoulder.

"Just great. Come on in now. I thought sure you'd be first in line for the new models." He held the door open wide for us.

"I want you to meet my boy," my father said. "This is my youngest son, Oskar."

Cal Rocker: he is not as tall as my father, but much younger. He bends sharply, as if he were bowing formally, to meet my face as I put out my hand to him. What he thinks is a smile on his face—it could as well be a teeth-baring snarl, a wince at sudden internal pain. His teeth are very white, very even. His hand is very dry over mine. My muscles set all the way up my arm to my shoulder as I give him a squeeze (is my father watching? does he approve?). I pump, once, twice, and nearly pull loose of Cal Rocker's warm, dry hand. His handshake is limp (do I look at my father in shock?). I think to say something, *pleased to meet you*, but that is reserved for Mrs. Rocker—my father has left me no words, unprepared.

"I'll say I don't recognize him," Cal said. "Boy, you were knee-high to my knee the last time we met." He reached out again, straightened up now to his full height, to touch my head. I dodged, but not quickly enough to avoid my hair being mussed.

"Turn your back on them they shoot up like weeds," my father said. As Cal stepped behind us to close the door, I saw the metal monogram **R** riveted to the front of the heavy door. It was the kind of door that closed quietly, that swung easily for all its weight, without a sound until the muffled *chunk* when the latch caught. He stepped around me, put his hand in the middle of my father's back to guide him into the living room, and I followed behind them. My father was lighting a cigarette.

Cal Rocker: he is not as tall as my father, but much younger, and there is something wrong. He cannot smile a real smile (the cords in his neck are forever tensing, relaxing, as his smile-not-a-smile clicks on and off his face all evening, like a flashing sign). His hair is very blond, receding, a widow's peak like a peninsula in the exact center of his smooth forehead. Two or three times he dips, bends, sits, and I see the bald spot, the size of half a dollar, at the precise crown of his head. He looks like a trim man, he is a trim man ("Golf?" my father said. "Never heard of him." "It's great," said Cal Rocker. "I get out three, four mornings a week. I was going to invite you out, Buck. We joined this little country club they have out here. Oh, it's great." And he set his feet, did a lazy, slow-motion swing from the tee for us). He is trim, but when he sits his soft middle collapses over his belt. He stands, and the waistband of his trousers is bent over by his spare tire. He is much more casually dressed than my father.

From the moment we entered the large living room (it seems to stretch, like a great hall, back, back . . .), we were only formally welcome supplicants. We came through the archway, and

116

there I saw us all, frozen in the mirror, its frame a gilded swirl of spear-shaped leaves, on the opposite wall. It must have been ten or twelve feet long, and leaned slightly, from the top, toward the floor. I was afraid it would fall if our voices were too loud.

We are defeated. The walls are the exact color of my father's prewar summer suit. We are done.

My father and I were apart (my hand creeps back into his). The tan, prewar summer suit, so fully sufficient to itself, to any purpose, in the LaSalle Hotel, was here, in this thickly carpeted, warm, ticking room, the suit of a supplicant—a road salesman come on bad times, a beggar of hope, a man who dreams wildly because there are no reasonable dreams left to him. And I. I was a pale, indifferent boy, without charm, without humor, without even the freshness of innocence to face them, as my father had to. I tried to hide from the Rocker family, and from my ignominious mirror-self, by holding my father's hand and sidling behind the protective pillar of his leg.

Cal Rocker, deceptively trim and not-smiling, stood in the middle, a go-between for these obtrusive visitors with his wife and children. Mrs. Carol Rocker is almost beautiful. She was also blonde (but hers is peroxide!), and genuinely thin. Her hands folded at her hip, one foot model-like, before the other, she too not-smiled. Her dress was plain, and she had not taken off her short apron, but somehow (the vulgar diamond on her finger? the stilted posture? the elaborate upsweep of her shimmering bleached hair?) she fit, like the chairs, the low coffee table, the grossly gilded frame of the mirror, in the new opulence of the house.

"Well, hello there, Buck," she said, stepping forward, extending one diamond-laden hand to my father, the other very carefully placed on her husband's wrist—she will not cross a void to us.

"There's my gal," my father said. I was dumbfounded to see him kiss her (she receives it, turning her head to present the plane of her cheek, closing her eyes, not smiling). "And this is my boy, Oskar," he said. She knelt, one knee, glossed with nylon, emerging at the hem of her dress. Her fingers are long, very thin, tapered, nails unpolished, as lifeless as wooden dowels.

"Pleased to meet you," I murmured—where was my father?

"That's cute!" she said, standing. "He's shy!" In the white lobe of each of her small ears was a silver white, minuscule pearl.

Then we could dissolve, from the diorama of our isolation in the mirror to the upholstered chairs, the plump cushions of the sofa beneath the precarious mirror. "Go on," my father said, half whispering, "park yourself on the couch there. You don't want to stand by me all night." Mrs. Rocker repeated: I was shy. And they could laugh and dissolve to chairs while Cal Rocker ran through the menu of drinks available.

Except for his daughters. Three of them ("Takes a man to shoot the balls off them," my father said, later, when Cal said they hoped to try once more, for a boy). They were a set. Three girls, the oldest nearly my age, all blond, in pink dresses with bows behind that stood out like wings, lacy collars and puffed short sleeves and black patent leather shoes with straps that reflected light like polished onyx. They did not smile at me. They were like butterflies, ready for mounting on felt boards, or like twirler toys needing sticks, like bridal flower girls waiting patiently for their bouquets.

"What'd you have," my father said, a frosty highball in his hand, "the two the last time I saw you?"

"Oh no," said their mother, "Laurie must have been born then."

"We *were* planning on stopping after two," Cal said.

"You and me both," my father said, "but—"

"Accidents will happen," Cal said.

"I hope to tell you," my father said. I looked at him (my mouth drops open: am I an accident? But no, I could not have understood what they were talking about!). And he looked back, one furtive, ashamed apology, I think.

"There's time for another drink if you boys want it," said Carol Rocker. The oldest daughter (her name? I cannot remember, do not care) presented herself for my glass, but I shook my head. I do not think I more than tasted my cola, touched it to my lips, but did not drink. My father, saying he could not fly on one wing, gave his glass up to Cal.

Cal Rocker: he is a success (no, no, I am not a success. Nor was my father, of course not. Yes, Arn, your Uncle Arn, is a success too. But the cost. Do not overlook what he pays for it. That's all I ask of you.) There can be no question of it, and without conscious cruelty, he rubbed my father's nose in it. I watched, and I saw the cost.

"So can I get you to admit you were wrong, Buck," Cal said.

"How's that? Wrong where?"

"Those hebes!" he said, laughing. He leaned back in his chair, raised his arms, spread them, swept them to indicate the furniture, the room, the house, the parklike, sequestered neighborhood where, today, the Cal Rockers have trebled, quadrupled, exploded in a profusion beyond imagination or comprehension.

"Hebes?" my father said. "Hebrews you mean?"

"Look at him," Cal said to his wife, "he won't budge an inch, will you, you son of a gun!"

"If you'll let me in on the joke," my father said.

"You must be getting old—" my father's face became monumentally serious—"you're losing your memory, Buck. I'm talking about all those warnings you gave me to watch out for my partners, the ones were going to gut me. You know damn well you remember. You remember him, hon, old Buck's always giving the Jews hell. Sure you do."

"I may have at that." Over the rim of his glass, my father's eyes moved to take in the room.

"Wouldn't old Jack Perlmutter just love to listen to this guy talk about the Jews," Cal said to his wife. "It tickles hell out of him, I've told him how you used to rant about all the damn kikes taking over the world and all—"

"I thought I spoke in confidence, I guess," my father said. He had put his glass down. Were we going to stand up, denounce them, leave? I prayed for it!

"Who the hell can you trust anymore, huh, Buck?" Cal said. And my father laughed with him. I looked at the set of three daughters to keep from seeing my father's face.

"It's about time to sit down for dinner," Carol Rocker said, rising, smoothing her apron.

"Come on, Buck," Cal said, "quick, bring your drink with you. I want to show you the house." He looked at me. "You want to stay here with the girls?" I got up quickly, carrying my glass of cola, and followed them on the tour of the house.

It dissolves, like our static grouping in the wall mirror. It loses coherence, comes in bright, exact flashes, distinctly remembered lines of dialogue. We toured the house, guided by Cal Rocker, who leads us, beyond a sense of time, through corridors, room to room, up and down stairways, the house stretching impossibly in all directions, a house fit for the most ambitious dream of the striver after success. Somewhere along the way, I found my father's hand again, did not release it until we sat down to eat.

"I designed the kitchen myself," Cal said. "Looky here." Stained walnut cupboards, chrome fittings . . . oh, everything! Electric burners that pulled down from the wall, like small leaf tables; a garbage disposal beneath the sink, growling dryly at the touch of a button; the blades of a blender, recessed, set in the Formica counter top; an oven set in red bricks, chest high; cannisters for flour, sugar, coffee, shaped like miniature barrels, the walnut staves bound in burnished brass; sinks so white and smooth they hurt my eyes to look at them; wonder of wonders, a carpeted kitchen, dark blue to raise the robin's egg blue walls and ceiling—all of it leaping into brilliance made by indirect fluorescent tubes that popped and sputtered until they warmed up. "Any woman in the world'd give her right arm for a kitchen like this," he said.

"I daresay," my father said.

"It's neat," I had to say.

Room to room, we went swiftly, my father tugging me after him, jerking on my hand if I began to fidget whenever we stopped to listen to Cal describe in detail. It blurs: a master bedroom— "Here's where the lord and master sleeps," Cal said—with a bed large enough for the entire family, walk-in closets with doors that glided almost noiselessly on lubricated tracks, end tables and vanity and dressers matching; a quick look in to a bathroom (rug, toilet seat cover with shaggy nap like the fur of a wild animal, a step-in shower, the frosted glass door decorated with tropical fish, bubbles, seaweed). A room for a washing machine and a mangle and a sewing machine—"Carol's got a colored gal comes in a couple times a week to help her with it all. The only drawback, Buck, is the place is too damn big for one woman to run right." A door, a light, "Watch your step here, men, this is steeper than I wanted it." We descended to the rec room. And I knew we were defeated. What had we to offer against all this? The cream-colored tile floor had, in its center, in beige tiles, a monogram R.

"You need someplace to hold a convention, just give me a ring," Cal Rocker said. And all my father could do was look nervously around for an ashtray to drop the cigarette that threatened to burn his fingers. "Right over there," Cal said. He went behind the bar. "We can build us a short one before Carol gets after us." My father helped me up on a padded stool, sat next to me, pretending to watch Cal make fresh drinks, but he had no heart left to look at anything.

"So how you making it, Buck?" Cal said.

"I'm living."

"Will you admit you were wrong, just for the hell of it? About my partners?" He never stopped not smiling.

"I guess I'd have to, wouldn't I?" My father looked up at the ceiling. It was laid with acoustical tile. The dots in each panel seemed to dance when I looked up. Cal Rocker let my father go with a laugh.

"There she is," he said, pointing to the framed architect's drawing of his new plant. It was long and low, the grounds broken here and there with perfect architect's shrubs and trees. "We got the sonofabitch for ten cents on the dollar for what the government put it up for," he said. My father could only nod. "You were right, Buck. Godalmighty, it was one hell of a good war if you knew which end was up!" My father drank and wiped his mouth. "I wish to hell it was daylight," Cal said, "I'd like for you to see out back. I had a guy build a playhouse for my kids. It looks just like this, the real house, from the outside." That was something I would have liked to see. My father shrugged and swirled the drink in his glass. "Maybe you could get out tomorrow—oops! No, hell, I can't get away long enough tomorrow to get back here. You wouldn't know it," he said, twisting to look at the architect's drawing, "but we're right on the edge of boogie-town, way out south. How long are you staying around, Buck? You never said."

"That depends," my father said.

"On what?"

"On how interested you are in doing a little business." He looked at Cal Rocker, and Cal Rocker held his not-smile, and then suddenly he laughed very loud, tipping back his head (I see his wet, pink tongue, the backs of his even, white teeth!), slapping the bar with the flat of his hand.

"You old bastard!" he said. He grabbed my father's shoulder, shook it. "Come on, grab your drink, Carol must have dinner waiting. Come on, we don't want to talk business tonight. I want to hear all about what you're up to there in the sticks, Buck."

And then, until we left, I remember only very little things. (Yes, we ate dinner; I remember several firsts. My first dinner with ice water in special goblets, my first sterling gravy boat with a matching ladle, my first slice of something called torte for dessert. My father accepted second helpings. I ate something of everything, afraid my manners were poor in contrast with the set of three exquisite little girls, whose free hands never left their starched laps.) Bits and pieces:

"How's Irene?"

"Fine. Same as usual, I guess."

"I'll bet she misses you."

"I don't remember her saying, but I'll take your word for it."

"What are your older kids doing now, Buck? Your daughter was widowed, wasn't she?"

"She was. She works. I don't keep close tabs on them; they're free, white, and twenty-one."

"The boy, what's-his-name, Arnie, he must be out of service long ago."

"He's going to school, I hear. Planning to, anyway."

"You still have your own company, Buck?"

"Certainly. That's why I'm down here."

"Tell you what. You promise not to talk business, we'll get together tomorrow, deal?"

"Whatever you say," my father said.

"More coffee?"

"If you please," my father said. He held his cup out, and he ate second helpings, but we were defeated, and I knew he knew this. The hope, the belief, was gone out of him. Gone out of his talk, out of the crisp hang of his tan suit, out of the set of his clean-shaven face.

There was more coffee, and bubblelike snifters of amber brandy back in the living room, and I was invited to go with the three girls to their playroom (I imagine toy boxes built like pirate chests, life-size dolls astride hobby horses, nursery rhyme decals on the walls, but do not think I saw it on the grand tour), and I declined. The Rocker daughters left. There was more talk, but I could not listen any longer.

"Take your shoes off," my father said.

"Oh, let him, Buck," Carol Rocker said. I was falling asleep, had put my feet up on the couch.

"It's late," Carol said.

"I'll finish my drink and we can hike," my father said. Then I did sleep, and whatever else passed between them I missed.

I woke because I was getting wet. Cal Rocker was carrying me to the Chrysler, my father ahead of us to open the door, and it was raining lightly. I woke, being carried like a baby, my face held close to Cal Rocker's chest. I opened my eyes, drops of rain pelting my face, and looked directly up into his straining face. His white even teeth were bared, the cords of his neck standing out; it was very like his smile, and I nearly smiled back automatically. His cologne was diluted by the cool night air.

"Right in here," my father said, holding the door open, and Cal set me gently on the seat, slipped his hands from under me.

"What's all that you've got stowed in the back seat?" he said before my father closed the door. I did not hear his reply. Cal trotted back to the front door, disappeared, then his head emerged with his wife's beside it. They waved, together, as if rehearsed, as my father got in and backed the Chrysler out of the driveway. As the front of the car lifted when the rear bounced into the road, the headlights hit the house's chimney. I saw the black monogram R; the house was too new for ivy to have grown that high yet.

"Dirty goddamn sonofabitching bastard," my father said softly as we left the parklike circle of homes ("two surgeons, a guy in the real estate game, and one, so-help-me, gangster," said Cal Rocker of some of his neighbors).

"Dad?"

"I thought you were asleep." It began to rain harder. He drove very fast for the winding blacktop road.

"I was I guess."

"Then go back to sleep. I'll wake you when we get to the hotel. I don't feel much like talking right this minute."

"Can I ask you one question?"

"If you have to. Shoot."

"Am I going home tomorrow?"

"We'll see."

"Did you handle Cal Rocker, Daddy?"

"That's two. You said one. Go back to sleep."

My father put me to bed in the LaSalle Hotel room, then stayed up very late, drinking the bottle of rye. In the morning, when I woke to the sound of the taps running in the bathroom, there was only an inch or two of whiskey left in the bottom. I got up and went in the bathroom to use the toilet. He stood at the sink, dressed in his underwear, his head under the flowing faucets. He did not see me until he turned off the water, raised his head, hair flattened, dripping, running down over his chest. He only looked back at me from the mirror, did not say good morning, ask if I had slept well.

"I guess today I'm going home," I said.

"Don't count your chickens before they're hatched." He threw a towel over his head, rubbed his hair dry. As I used the toilet, he moaned.

"What? Did you say something to me, Dad?"

"I said never again," he said. "You wouldn't understand. Get yourself dressed. We're going to meet Cal Rocker after lunch if I can manage it."

"Do you still have to handle him?"

"Just do like I tell you," he said. "I'm beginning to think I'm the one's being handled here." We dressed—the tan suit has lost its

123

luster, the creases broken, the tail of the jacket wrinkled, the soft texture of the material hardened; he had sat up in it most of the night, drinking. But we dressed, and after two abortive calls, he reached Cal Rocker, and Cal Rocker agreed to meet us after lunch. "We may just come out of this smelling like a rose yet, kiddo," my father said.

We are in the Sans Souci Bar, near the end of the bar, where I can hear tables being laid with silver in the adjoining dining room for the dinner service, where I can see the first television set in the world. The bartender is immaculate in a red corduroy vest with silver buttons. He listens carefully to the conversation, attentive to the gestures calling for refills. Cal Rocker has said what a swell hell of a war it was, and my father, in a brief recapture of the glory that only he has for me, has spoken the short litany of his faith in man—*the man,* as the source of all success. Cal Rocker and the red-vested bartender nod agreement, as if awed by the simple profundity of it. And once more, their glasses are empty.

My father nudged his glass with the back of his hand, made a pouring motion with his thumb for the bartender, drew a circle in the air to indicate Cal's glass as well.

"No, no," Cal said, "not for me, Buck. Pass me. Hell, I've got to be going." He stood away from the bar, hiked his trousers, made a stab at tucking in his shirt, twisted his wrist to see his watch, reached for his money on the bar. My father had one foot up on the rail, leaning heavily on one forearm on the bar, jacket open. He stood up straight very quickly, dropped the butt of the Pall Mall smoldering in his fingers, ground it out on the floor under his shoe. He took another step away from the bar, as if he feared Cal might bolt for the curtained door, and he must block his way.

"The hell you say," he said. "You just got here. We haven't even talked."

"Come on, Buck," Cal said. He got his bills lined up, tucked them carefully into a moneyclip. The coins were left for the bartender. "Come on now," he said. He buttoned his jacket.

"Come on what?" my father said. "What the hell do you mean, come on. I want to talk business with you. Why in hell do you think I drove five hundred miles—"

"You said you might stop by, Buck, you said you had business."

"I said I needed a few hours of your time!" my father said. He turned and looked quickly at me, then back at Cal Rocker. I thought he might ask me to swear to it. The bartender stopped chewing his gum, staring at my father (yes, there were other people in the Sans Souci Bar; the after-lunch crowd had gone back into the Loop, gone back to work, gone, but there must have been at least a few left, farther down the bar toward the door, at a table, in a booth, but I did not see them, do not remember them).

"You've had more than a few," Cal said. My father glanced at the empty glasses, as if the number of drinks were referred to. "Come on, Buck," he said.

"I won't beat around the bush," my father said. "I'm dead serious. I want to be heard. You owe me at least a hearing, for Christ's sake!" Cal Rocker's smile-not-a-smile disappeared from his face, replaced by something real, personal. It was as if he were preparing his mouth to spit. "At least give a man a Chinaman's chance to speak his piece," my father said. "I've got some ideas, you know."

"Buck," Cal said, "it isn't like I don't have the vaguest idea of what's happening with you, you know."

"What in hell are you talking about? Meaning just what, tell me."

"I see a lot of people, Buck," he said, "and a fair enough number of them get in and out of the Twin Cities, you know. What do I have to say to you, Buck?"

"And what do your smart-ass sonofabitches tell you about me? Some more of your kike associates, no doubt." My father looked again at me. Was I supposed to smirk knowingly with him? The bartender cocked his head at those words, raised an eyebrow.

"You see?" Cal Rocker said. "That's you all over again, isn't it." Was I supposed to nod with Cal Rocker? "I've got to go, Buck."

"That's what I like!" my father said. Now he turned again to me, to the bartender, to the room at large (I do not remember the other people, what they might have thought at seeing him this way). "A real friend. A real good friend in need. Ask for a break and get your teeth kicked in. I sure do love to find out who my friends are!"

"So long, Buck." He started past, but my father caught his arm. Cal Rocker looked down at my father's hand on his arm as if it was something dirty a stranger had thrown at him, spattered him with. "Come on," he said.

"I'd been thinking about a merger, what a merger, I've got a mess of contacts, all over, you know that," my father said. He put his other arm around Cal, as if he meant to hug him. "There's intangibles," he said. "Why in hell do you suppose an outfit sells goodwill and good name when they fold up—*sells* it! I don't come empty handed, mister!" Cal lurched, my father's arm dropped away, but he held on to his sleeve.

"Get off me," Cal Rocker said. And now there was nothing on his face, no not-smile, nothing. He did not look worried or angry. (I? I sit on my stool. I watch.)

"I'm asking you to help me, Cal. You owe me something. I started you off for where you're at right this minute! Who was it told you to get on the bandwagon when the getting was good? Buck Hansen's who!" Cal grasped his trapped arm, tugged, but my father held him. "Capital!" he said. "I'm fresh out of capital. My credit's dried up, man! I'm being squeezed, see?"

"You and everybody's brother, read the papers," Cal said. "I'm not in the lending business. Go to a bank."

"A job then," my father said. "Don't tell me you can't use a salesman, I know better." My father's face . . . I had not seen this face before.

"Full up. Let go my damn arm." My father held him. "You should be ashamed," Cal said. "A public place, your own kid sitting there—" My father shoved him, hard. He did not fall, but he staggered. The loose change in his pockets chinked, and a mechanical pencil fell out of Cal Rocker's shirt pocket. "Well you," is all he said. My father was not looking at him. A telephone behind the bar was ringing.

"Mr. Rocker?" the bartender called out, holding his hand over the receiver.

"Now who in the hell," Cal said as he picked up his pencil and went to take the phone. I spoke to my father because he would not look at me.

"Dad? Daddy?"

"Not now," he said. "You best get away from me in case I decide to wipe up the floor with somebody."

"Listen, mister," the bartender said, having heard. My father turned and looked at him, and that was all he said.

"It's for you, Buck," Cal Rocker said, setting the receiver on the bar, "somebody named Rotter. He apparently called the plant for me to ask about you, and I'd left this number—"

"I just left," my father said. He grabbed his money off the bar, his cigarettes, lighter, took me down from my stool. Cal Rocker came after us as we went to the door. My father pulled me along by the hand.

126

"Now what," Cal said, "is the FBI after you or something?" We faced him.

"Answer one question," he said to Calvin Rocker. "Was it you blew the whistle on me, about Irene, to my daughter? Back in Milwaukee. You remember."

"I don't know what you're talking about," Cal said. "You must be nuts. You make me sorry I ever liked you. Don't ever call me again, Hansen." My father let go my hand.

"How would you like it if I was to put you through that wall there," he said, taking a step toward Rocker. Calvin Rocker stepped back. "Keep out of my goddamn way unless you damn well want your clock cleaned for you." The bartender came out from behind the bar. "Let's go, sonny," my father said to me. He took my hand again, and we left, leaving Calvin Rocker with no particular expression on his face.

We sneaked out of the LaSalle Hotel that evening, without paying. "Did you pay when we stayed by Great Lakes?" I asked.

"Yep. They'd put the Gestapo after you, but they're too big for that here. Never you mind. Cut your losses and run if you want to keep kicking, that's the way, boy."

"Why did you take all the towels?"

"Souvenirs," he said. "Don't talk so much. Your old man's head hurts. The old gray mare ain't what etcetera."

"Where are we going, Daddy?"

"Home," he said. He meant his home, in Indiana, where he was born and raised.

VI

So much of it, so very much, is merely talk. I cannot always
remember. Are we racing eastward out of Chicago, across the
viaducts (they remind me of the industrial valley on the way to
Jane's house) leading to the Indiana border, to Goshen, or is this
some flat, green, baked stretch in Ohio, or the grim, dingy
roadcuts along the Pennsylvania Turnpike? Exact times and places
confuse me, but the talk comes, always, as clear as if I were sitting
quietly in the back seat of an eternal 1941 Chrysler, listening to
my father and myself up front.

East then, from Chicago:

Gary—"This stinks worse than by Jane's house, Dad."
"You're telling me. That's your steel mills though. What the hell
would you have if you didn't have any steel mills producing?"

Michigan City—"Are we in Michigan?" "It's just the name of

the town. Anything goes. Probably the most wide-open city in the country. It's worth your life to flash a roll in a bar here."

South Bend—"They have a girl's basketball team here. I read about it." "Is that so. This is where they make Studebakers."

Elkhart—"Do you belong to the Elks Lodge and the Masons too, then?" "No, I'm a Mason, but I'm telling you so you'll understand what Elkhart is. The Elks own a big spread here. They keep it for orphans, if their parents were in the Elks." "I couldn't go then if I was an orphan, could I?" "No. You're not an orphan either, though, are you."

Goshen—"Keep your eyes peeled now, sonny, you'll see my old stomping grounds when I was a kid your age."

Toward Goshen. There is only talk.

"Is this the way to Milwaukee?"

"Nope."

"You said."

"I said most likely. If we made out with Cal Rocker. You saw what happened."

"Should I write to Jane again?"

"All in due time. What's the matter with you? Are you all fired up to get home all of a sudden?"

"No. I was just asking."

"Do you know what a fair-weather friend is?"

"No."

"Don't be one. Cal Rocker's a fair-weather friend. Putting it as nicely as I can."

"I won't."

"Good man. Come on, buck up. You ever seen a farm before in your life? Oh, you'll get a bang out of it. I grew up there until I was damn near eighteen years old."

"Do they have a horse I can ride?"

"I couldn't say. I doubt it. Your uncle raises vegetables. Potatoes. Wait'll you set your choppers in a fresh beefsteak tomato. There ain't nothing like it, let me tell you."

"I don't remember my Uncle Thurston and my Aunt Marie."

"You wouldn't, you were a-way too young. He's a nice enough old coot."

"What's coot?"

"It means he's a hardhead old country Swede son of a bitch, but he's my brother and your uncle. So ask me no questions, I'll tell you no lies about your aunt and uncle."

"Okay."

"Buck up, things got to get better before they can be any worse."

"How's come your name's Buck. If I'm a junior, then your name's supposed to be the same."

"It's not. It's a nickname."

"How'd you get it? They call Andy Pafko the Flash because he comes from Boyceville, Wisconsin. The Boyceville Flash, I mean."

"It figures, doesn't it? I'm a Cards fan myself. The Cubs were lucky. You wait and see come this September. Put your money on the Cardinals."

"I like Brooklyn too. But how'd you get the nickname?"

"I didn't get it, I took it. I just decided one day, I guess."

"Why?"

"You talk too much. Because I didn't like my name I was born with. Satisfied?"

"Then why'd you give it to me if you didn't think it was any good?"

"Jesus, boy. That's not what I said. It's as good as any, I reckon. I just didn't happen to like it. It wasn't me hung it on you, best I can recall. Save that one for your mother."

"Do you know why she did?"

"You don't seem to listen good. When we get to the farm I'll give you old Anton Gustav's earwax treatment, on the house."

"Who's he?"

"Your grandfather on my side. My old man."

"How's come he didn't name you the same as him?"

"I was named after a brother of his. My uncle. And your uncle was named after a cousin back in the old country, some such thing. Hold all this for your uncle, will you? He's got the papers to prove it all."

"Okay. But you never said if you know why Mom gave me your name."

"Balls! Okay. It's a custom. A habit with people. You name a boy after his father. Or after his uncle, or his grandfather, some damn thing. Don't ask me why. It keeps the name going, I guess. Same way, if it's a girl you can name her after her mother or whatever, see?"

"Going where?"

"Going—the name's still here when the person's gone. Dead. *Kaput*."

"Like me and you."

"That's the idea. Let's talk about something else. Let's talk about baseball. You tell me why you like the Cubs, I'll argue for Saint Louis. You start."

"I wish I had a nickname."

"Phooey. Take what you get and be happy with it. It won't make a bit of difference when you're my age, I promise you."

Talk, toward Goshen. Gary, Michigan City, South Bend, Elkhart. Just talk, but, you see, it defined him, and through him, me. I was defining the new universe—the one I have lived in ever since.

It was before South Bend. I had asked, and he took off his Masonic ring and gave it to me. I turned it over in my fingers, sorting the answers he gave to my questions about it: Hiram Abiff, builder of the temple, murdered by a blow on the head. If I wanted, when the day came, his membership was my entry into the fraternity. He said he had forgotten too much of the ritual to ever visit a lodge again. He wanted, still, to be buried by them. I ran the fleshy pad of my fingertip over the raised insignia, the absolutely smooth onyx setting. It became mine, the ring, the scraps of futile, irrelevant information. And then I looked up and saw the car just ahead of us on the highway.

"Pay up!" I cried. "Pay up, pay up, I saw it first! Gimme, gimme!" I held out my hand for the nickel. He did not understand. "Green Studie," I said. "Five cents please."

"We'll just see about that," he said. He did not mean the nickel he had promised in the forgotten game. He put both hands on the wheel and speeded up, closing on the new green Studebaker until he could read the license plate, get a look at the driver.

It was not Sheldon Rotter. It was an old man with glasses; he turned his head, stared at us, eyes unblinking, as my father slowly, very slowly, passed him. I had to ask again to get the nickel.

The commercial district of Saint Paul was empty. Without people, cars, delivery vans, the street where he rented office space looked shabby. Windows were smeary in the bright morning sunlight, entranceways shadowy, the gutters and sidewalks littered, stained. The few parked autos looked abandoned. The building facades were uniformly smoky, dirty, ledges populated with roosting pigeons. This is the way a city looks, Buck thought, when the plague hits. When the air raid siren sounds—how many times, in how many cities, he wondered, had he been driving in the

131

Chrysler when the practice air alerts had sounded? He drove, and suddenly the sirens went off, high, shrill, and street lights disappeared, whole blocks went dark. He pulled over and switched off the Chrysler's headlights to wait it out. The buses and streetcars kept on going. It had always griped him. So who was going to bomb us? The Germans, they said, had shelled the New Jersey coast from a submarine, early in '42, and there was a rumor that a Jap plane had strafed some little town in Washington or Oregon. But that was only rumor. He remembered a block warden coming up to the parked and idling Chrysler, poking his goddamn flashlight in at Buck's face, some creep wearing a silly white helmet and a civil defense armband—*Let's turn our motor off till the all-clear sounds, Mac,* he said to Buck. *Up your bucket!* Buck told him.

This must be how it looks if it's real, he thought, driving the deserted commercial district of Saint Paul on a Sunday morning. When the water supply is poisoned by the fifth column at the reservoirs, and the stricken population uses its last strength to crawl off in the woods like sick dogs, to die, bloated and groaning. When the police and the army are gone, and the gangs of hunkies and niggers come out to look and rape and kill anybody too old or too slow to get out ahead of them. "Not this guy," Buck Hansen said aloud to the quiet, Sunday streets of Saint Paul.

His building was a dump. He remembered how good he'd felt signing the lease with the real estate agent. "It'll do until something better comes along," he'd said, just to keep the agent from drooling over him. Buck Hansen: his very own business address! No wonder he failed (and the goddamn kike-loving, nigger-loving Rosenfeldt-Truman government, the goddamn end of the goddamn war...). The square, dirty gray stone building reminded him of a giant gravestone—dirty gray stone like the stone put up for Georgie Braeder back—when? 1913? The hell with that. The unclean stone facade was mottled with weathering and pigeon droppings. The gold leaf signs on the insides of the unwashed windows were flaked and peeling. *Lawyer. Dentist. Bail Bonds. Chiropractor.* A permanent plaque next to the front door announced prime floor space available, remodeled to suit. Always room for one more fly-by-night sucker. *Hansen Engineering,* painted on the drawn shade, third floor. Now he could sense the disappointment and distrust a potential customer must have known when he came for an appointment. No wonder. His passkey let him into the unlighted central lobby. It smelled, of dirty mops, of the sour solution janitors used to wipe down the cracked marble wall panels; his heels rang on the tile floor.

He was surprised to find his name still up on the directory next to the elevators. *Hansen Engineering, 304A,* white plastic letters on black felt, like a church bulletin board, the glass case dusty enough to draw pictures on. *Wash me,* Buck wrote with his forefinger. The elevators were locked. Just as well. A ride in one of those creaking, thumping cages, the cables twanging, was enough to do in a cardiac case. No wonder. He climbed the worn stairs. On the frosted glass panel in his office door, the symbol of his own design was still intact. A green diamond bordered in black, *Hansen,* also in black, a very expensive, a very flourishing, a very confident script, smack dab in the middle. Buck had labored over the design. The day the painter came in to put it on the glass, working from Buck's original pattern, Buck had stood back in the hall to watch, admire, dream. He saw it famous, one with Lucky Strike Green (gone to war), Arm & Hammer, the little boy with the candle and a Fisk tire. He reached out now with his key and scratched it.

Inside, he tried the light switch, but either they shut off the electric for the whole building on Sundays, or else the power and gas company had given up on him at long last. Just as he reached his desk in the inner office, the phone rang. He was going to let it go, determined not to give his whereabouts away to a soul, when he remembered that a summons could not be legally served on the Lord's Day.

"I have a long distance call from Mineola, New York, for a Mr. Buck Hansen."

"Put her on," he said. "I'm him. Lillie?"

"Buck honey? Honey, I tried to get you at home, sweetie, but you weren't there so I just had to try your office. What are you doing now working on a Sunday, Buck?"

"Where were you last night?"

"What? Buck?"

"I said where were you last night? I called until after midnight, your place, the beauty shop, where the hell were you, Lil?"

"Hon, I was just down with Ben and this one friend of his, downstairs. Buck? Where did you think I'd be so late and all now?"

"How in hell should I know. Who am I to ask you to report to me where you go."

"Buck. That's not nice."

"I called Ben's too, damnit! You weren't there any more than the man in the moon. Now listen, if you want to give me the runaround, that's your business, but I'm damned—"

"Buck," Lillie Broadfoot said, "we were all out sitting on the front porch. Honest, it was just godawful muggy and hot here last night, Buck. We all went out on the porch and had a drink and talked and all. Buck?"

"I'm supposed to believe that?" he said.

"Why should I lie to you, Buck? For heaven's sake. Would I call you here on a Sunday, try to find you at home, try to find you at your office, if I was just going to fib you? Now would I?"

"I don't guess," he said. He did not believe her. He imagined her in a cocktail lounge, accepting a light for her cigarette (she held his wrist with both hands, her palms dry and cool, fingers long, nails done perfectly, long and delicate as needles, as he held the flame to her cigarette . . .). She accepted a light, accepted a drink (Rhine wine and Vichy water, blackberry brandy and soda), held hands, let her thigh rest against the man's leg, went for a ride, went up to her place for a nightcap. Her brother Ben would drop in for coffee in the morning, not blinking an eye at the stranger who sat at the breakfast bar with nothing on under his bathrobe. Buck's stomach sank. He did not believe her for a minute.

"I could ask you the same thing, sweetie," Lillie Broadfoot said.

"What? What did you say?"

"Now I tried to call you near all day yesterday, Buck. I called your office again and again. I called your apartment once, too. I never did get anybody to answer."

"I was out of the office all day. I was out on business, Lillie."

"Well why don't your secretary answer the phone? Is that gal deaf or something, Buck?"

"She's on vacation," he said. "Just for a couple days. There wasn't time to get anybody else, see?" Buck had let his secretary go a month ago. Half the time she did nothing but knit argyle socks for boyfriends (because half the time there was no work in the office to give her). She called in sick, regularly, three days a month with female trouble. Worse, he could not bear to pass her desk, feel her watching him, knowing she knew the business was going under, faster than he could bail.

"Listen, Lillie," he said. "I'm sorry. I didn't mean to be so short with you. Listen. Lillie? Lillie, I have some good news. I may have some business in New York. It depends. I have to see a

134

character in Chicago the next couple of days. But if it works out right, I could be dropping in to see you, the next week or ten days, maybe. Will you like that?"

"Buck!" she said, "that's just wonderful!" If she could have asked for something, it would have been just that, she said. She could not wait to tell her brother. Ben would be so glad to hear it too, said Lillie Broadfoot of Mineola, New York. It was purely a most wonderful surprise! said Lillie Broadfoot, formerly of North Carolina. Buck Hansen believed it.

Lillian Beatrice Broadfoot had thick, very black hair. Buck loved to touch her hair, insert his fingers in it at the back of her head and pull her gently close to him. Her hair was clean and cool, soft to his touch. When he put his face close to her hair and smelled it, it smelled of fragrant shampoo, and even more faintly of the heady Shalimar perfume she wore on her throat and wrists, in the cleavage of her breasts. Her black eyebrows were shaped by plucking, her eyes a pale, so pale green that caught the light, framed by her long, black lashes. When she painted her nails her full lips were tinted to match them. Her ears were pierced, and from them hung elaborate earrings with much filigree. She wore noisy, gaudy, glorious bangle bracelets that rang and clanked as she moved her expressive hands, when she reached up with both hands to softly touch Buck's face as she kissed him. She had fine, long legs, and when she sat on a couch or an easy chair she drew them up under her gracefully, and Buck saw, always, a tantalizing flash of nylon on her inner thigh. She wore black brassieres and panties and garter belts, and her skin—her skin! Oh, Buck Hansen thought, her skin!

He said, softly, "I love you, Lillie."

"Buck, I love you too." Jesus! he thought, that was more than enough right there to make a man want to live! She hoped it would work out, that he would come, and soon. Bank on it, he told her. Hell or high water, he would make it to New York.

"If I've got you, Lillie, I can do anything. You know that, don't you?" he said. They kissed, first Lillie, then Buck, not at all embarrassed after she did it first, into the telephones, and then they said good-bye.

He grabbed what he wanted, impatient to be off and doing, closing gaps, after talking to Lillie Broadfoot. The picture of Oskar Jr., the L.C. Smith typewriter, some unbroken boxes of letterhead stationery and envelopes, his engineer's handbook (sixth edition), a file of the full-color brochures advertising machine tool lines he'd sold, his accountant's statements for the past two years. He answered the phone immediately when it rang, but let the caller speak first.

"Hello? I'm calling the Hansen Engineering Company. May I speak to Mr. Hansen, please? Hello?" They couldn't, Buck thought, slap him with a summons on Sunday, could they.

"This is Mr. Hansen speaking. Who is this?"

"Mr. Hansen? I'm sorry to have to bother you at your office, but after your call last night I've been trying—"

"That's all right," Buck said. He recognized the doctor's voice. He'd gone with Irene on her last few visits, and there was one long discussion in private when he convinced Buck she needed to be committed for intensive observation and bedrest. What Buck recalled of that conference was the doctor rehashing all the symptoms that Buck had told him about in the first place, ticking them off on his fingers to show the overall pattern indicating commitment, while Buck sat waiting, impatient for a chance to speak, to get a chance to turn the discussion to some other matters. He had wanted to ask the doctor if he would advise Buck to check in for a full medical examination, stem to stern; he wanted to point-blank ask the doctor if he thought Buck looked younger, about right, or older than his age. He never got the chance. The doctor was a busy and brisk man.

"How's my wife doing?" Buck said. How high, he wondered, had the tab on Irene out there run by this time?

"Of course that's what I called about, Mr. Hansen. Can you possibly come down here sometime today? Perhaps this afternoon sometime."

"Tell me over the phone. I can't make it, I'm tied up today."

"Well, there's little I can say briefly like this except to say your wife is significantly worse, Mr. Hansen. I really would like to see you and discuss this in some detail."

"How worse?" Buck said. Did they have her in a straitjacket, padded cell? Paraffin baths? Wet sheets?

"Generally, I think she's just degenerated faster than we ever conceived she might. Paranoid to an alarming degree, in fact. I think if you'd come and see her it might do her a world of good. That's another reason I'd like you to come in."

"Oh no," Buck said quickly, automatically. "That I can't. That's out of the question. There's nothing I can do for her."

"I'm sorry you feel that way," the doctor said. "I disagree of course. The fact of the matter is, and I know you'll forgive me for being frank, Mr. Hansen—the probable fact is that you may not

136

have the opportunity, very much longer, to visit with your wife. I know you'll forgive me for speaking this way."

"What? How's that? What's that mean?" What the hell did they do, lock her in solitary after a certain point? Did they toss them out in the street for nonpayment of bills? Throw mad women in some debtors' jail?

"I begin to think the problem here is medical, Mr. Hansen."

"You said it was her change. You said it would pass sooner or later. You said—" He had not thought, not once *really* thought (no matter how often he had wished it) that Irene might be dying.

"I know what I said. We have to revise that, I'm thinking. It's rather unusual in a woman as young as your wife, but—"

"How revise? Aren't you telling me here she's liable not to recover? To die?"

"We call it an embolism," the doctor said.

"Meaning?"

"Think of it as a clot, Mr. Hansen." He tried. "A clot in the brain, in the blood vessel." Buck saw it, a red, waxy lump, tucked snugly into the gray white folds of Irene's brain. "It can be a number of things. Sometimes a minute particle of bone is broken off, dislodged in a fall, some trauma."

"She never fell. Nobody ever hit her on the head if that's what you're saying," Buck said.

"Certainly not. It can be a number of things. It lodges, the clot I'm speaking of lodges in the right place and the individual begins to behave like your wife has. Do you follow me?"

"I follow." Buck watched the embolism tumble as it flowed through a blood vessel, a darker red bead in a translucent red tube. It skipped, failed to turn a corner or leap an obstacle, stopped, wedged tight.

"Loss of coherent memory, neurotic syndrome, general change, pejoration of personality, decline in health—" Was he reading from notes? What was, what happened, Buck understood, was that the individual, the woman, Irene, went mad as a hatter. And maybe she died.

"No cure? Can you do an operation? How about all the new wonder drugs they got out of the war?"

"I'm sorry," the doctor said. "She could go on the way she is now, or she could get worse, deteriorate, or again, she may die at any time. I'm sorry to have to be so blunt with you. We have no way of knowing for certain. I must in all honesty say it does not look encouraging in your wife's case."

"Then how can you know that? If it's all so iffy, how are you predicting?"

"She's become quite paranoid. Do you have that word? Good. Quite paranoid, Mr. Hansen. She very often, *most* often, refuses nourishment. We've had to go to intravenous now and again. She believes we're all conspiring to kill her. That's typical enough of the syndrome. I really regret having to speak like this, you know." Had he, Buck wondered, wished her dead a hundred times? A thousand?

"That's ridiculous," Buck said.

"*We* know that. I'm afraid it's very real to her. And in a way, you know, it's funny, she's right. I mean funny-strange. She is dying. At least I happen to think so. She knows it, she senses it, you see. And so she believes it's the people around her who are responsible. It's an instinct to refuse to believe one can die, I suppose. The mind is a rather complex thing, Mr. Hansen."

"I'd say."

"That's why I ask you to come and see her if you could possibly manage it. It might just reassure her a bit. There's no promise it will, understand, but I thought under the circumstances you'd want to do all you can. Mr. Hansen?" Yeah sure. Reassure her. Hi, Irene! Give us a kiss, I can't stay but a few minutes. They tell me you're giving them hell here. Now cut that out, will you? Straighten up and fly right. Be a good girl and I'll bring you something nice next time I hit town. Hell yes, on the road again. I made it there once, Irene, you remember when I was coining it, and I can do it again. Don't worry about a thing. So I'm moving out on you and a couple dozen heavy creditors, so what? A man's got to go his own way when it comes to survival, right? Ain't it the truth. Where? Oh, hell, I can't even be positive. Chicago for one. Maybe stop and see my kids in Milwaukee—the hell with what Anne thinks of me. I still don't blame you for that, Irene, much as I'd like to. So okay, have it your own way. New York if I can possibly swing it. I'll swing it. I'm not traveling broke, lady, believe you me. I've turned everything wasn't bolted down into ready cash. Moola. Kale. Rasbuckniks. Long Island. There's a woman there may be just what I need to get up on my hind legs and fight again. A looker, Irene! Come off it, you suspected all along. 'Fess up now, you know, right? The hell you say! Well, like I told you, don't give these people any more heat, they have your best interests at heart. Okay, give us a kiss. So long, Irene. Don't believe more than half what you hear about me, huh?

"I'll try to come by later this morning if I can," Buck said.

He doubted he would, but there was something in hearing she was going to die (but it did leave the way clear for Lillie now, didn't it!) made him say it. A little thing, anything, and you had a time bomb bobbing around in your head. It didn't pay to say anything that made it look like you were asking for it. Buck Hansen tried to listen to the inside of his head—anything, tossing around loose in there, and blooey!

"I'm glad," the doctor said. "Oh, and by the way, Mr. Hansen, I had a memo from our business office here. Something about billing your account. It sounds crass, I know, but they seem not to have gotten a response from you for this last quarter."

"That check went in the mail first thing this morning," Buck said. The doctor apologized. "Say no more," Buck said. "Quite all right. Perfectly understandable. If the post office is on its toes you should have it tomorrow afternoon the latest. Right you are. I'll be in if I can. Good-bye to you, sir."

He stood over the telephone for what seemed to him like a long time, wondering just what would be right for him to feel. He knew he should, wanted, to weep for Irene's madness, and now, her probable death, but he could not. He could make himself picture her laid out for viewing in a casket, smell the heavy scent of flowers, hear muted organ music, but still no tears would come to his eyes. A prayer then. But he could not remember any of the prayers he had learned by heart for his confirmation in the Swedish Lutheran Church of Goshen, thirty-seven years before. Would the Apostles' Creed do?

All he got was inappropriate, disjointed fragments. Pastor Nordquist, wearing the old country ruffled lace collar; the way his shouts echoed in the church basement when they were set free after the interminable Saturday morning of instruction; doodles drawn in pencil in the margins of his copy of Luther's catechism (an elaborately illuminated *B, This book belongs to Buck Hansen*); the nodding head, the cold voice of his father as he drilled him on the passages given by Pastor Nordquist for memorization; his brother telling him, as they lay side by side in bed upstairs, to quit kicking and memorize the stuff if it would get their father off Buck's neck . . . He would have liked, since he could not make himself cry for her (he was sniggering softly to himself there in the empty office of Hansen Engineering, in the sudden reliving of the dark bedroom horseplay shared with Thurston after the old man had said good-night and gone downstairs with the kerosene lamp), to say a prayer for Irene's soul—just in case it turned out people had them after all. "Well I'm sorry as hell, anyway," Buck said aloud in the empty office. And, "Don't blame me. I wouldn't wish it on my own worst enemy, I swear."

Then he left the empty office. How much? A hundred thousand? Hundred and twenty, easy. And what he had to show for it, what he left behind for the bone-pickers, was just so many square feet of junk. Correspondence files that traced an unswerving, accelerating chart of failure. Promotional brochures and technical manuals describing products already obsolete. Desk and wall calendars with past days and months showing. A handful of cheap, jammed mechanical pencils, like the few ashtrays, stamped with the names of firms gone already in failures and mergers. A set of third-hand furniture (the inflated doughnut taken from the swivel chair—Buck's hemorrhoids came first!). The scavengers, falling over each other to slap plasters on it, pawing each other in search of convertible assets, would be lucky to find an uncancelled postage stamp. The only light coming from the rain-streaked window, the pigeon-shit-smeared window, it looked like the inside of a burial vault, where a man was buried with the totem tools of his daily life.

Here lies Buck Hansen, laid out flat on the desk top, the disconnected phone propped on his chest—make a pyre out of bills past due. The grim flat-painted walls, the dark, chilly corners; here was a place where failure could live, would wait after Buck was gone for the next fly-by-night to come in, grab him firmly but gently with a cold fist.

And on the way out, on a small deal table in one corner, a dying geranium plant, abandoned by Buck's secretary when he let her go. He left his keys on the secretary's desk, the door open, when he went.

The office salvage was loaded, he was ready to head for the open road, before he noticed the car parked down the block. It was not there when he came, nor after the first trip down to the Chrysler. It was one of the new Studebakers, both ends looking like they could be the front—go to you, come from you. Buck had thought idly of owning one, impressed with the design, when they were first advertised. He'd made inquiries about the new Tucker too, but that turned out to be another swindle dreamed up to fleece investors. But Buck was a confirmed Chrysler man. You got what you paid for. He had settled on the plan of buying a new Chrysler every year, once they got back into postwar production; of course, like everything else, that went up in smoke. He was tapped out by the time the new lines were announced for this year. What the hell.

140

While he studied the new Studebaker, appreciating it, eyeing it, it started forward, approached and stopped just short of him at the curb. A man got out and walked over to Buck.

"Hansen?"

"Do I know you?" The man did not look like the owner of a new 1946 Studebaker Commander. He was small, chubby, a little dirty looking, poorly dressed. Prewar suit, too heavy for the weather, a crooked bow tie Buck wouldn't have worn to a bohunk wedding, scuffed two-tone ventilated summer shoes. The man's face did not look as old as the man did. His hair was going fast, wisps combed over oily scalp in front. His cheeks and jaws were shadowed, dotted by the stubs of his beard, though he was clean shaven. He was a man who needed to shave at least twice a day, and did not. There was something wet and sickly about the look of his mouth. His teeth were stained, stumpy, worn looking, and he was a man whose teeth showed as he spoke. His hands were small and white, too small for his thick, pudgy body, the backs heavily and darkly hairy. He was a man, Buck knew, who would have hair everywhere on his body except on his head. With his too-small hands and his little dancer's feet in the scuffy two-tone summer sport shoes, his wrinkled cold weather suit, he looked like a man who dealt in broken lots and off-sizes, not a man to own or drive a new Studebaker Commander.

"Where you think you're going, Hansen?" the man said. He put one of his small, pale, ugly-hairy hands on the fender of Buck's Chrysler, the other on his fat, high-waisted hip, and he crossed one foot in front of the other like a corner loiterer, an average, out-of-date jitterbug who lacked the money or the touch to have a pimp chain to swing as he watched girls pass in short dresses. The repulsive hand on the Chrysler's fender held the chewed, unlit butt of a cigar. His fingernails were clean, but bitten to the quick, fingers blunt, too short for the palm.

"You better let me have that again," Buck said. "Who the hell are you?" Buck took a step back from him. He felt as if the ugly little man was going to want to touch him.

"You wouldn't know me," the man said. "And you're surprised I know you. Well." The man paused to suck at something in his mouth, turn his head, spit the invisible something out. "I know plenty about you, mister. Like that you're not going anywhere very far, since your wife is in a hospital of a sort at the moment. Surprise you?"

"If I don't get the satisfaction of an identification here in a minute," Buck said, "it's a toss-up if I leave you standing here with your yap open or I knock you on your can. What's it to you? Who the hell are you?" It was funny. If he had imagined it, such a man, coming on him like this, saying these things, he would have been terrified, but the man, here, now, was somehow interesting, and he wanted the man to bring it to a head, give him an excuse to run him off or punch his face in. And the man did not seem shocked or scared at talk of being decked—he shrugged a little, smiled a little, showed again so many of his bad teeth.

"I don't think so," he said. "You don't know me, Hansen, but I think maybe you know my boss. Bosses, I should say. Easy Finance? Union Finance? Builders Empire Savings and Loan? Corn Exchange Bank? Ring any bells for you?"

"You still haven't identified yourself." The man showed all his teeth as he reached, grimacing, for his wallet. Sweat ran down his neck into his collar, and as he swung back the wing of his jacket to get at his hip pocket, Buck saw the huge, soaked crescent of sweat in his armpit. He handed Buck the card with the same hand that held the cigar butt. Buck could smell it as he held the card out to him. *Rotter Collection Service. Sheldon Rotter.* Buck tossed the card away.

"I've got plenty more of those," Rotter said.

"If you've got something to say, say it. Otherwise get the goddamn hell out of my way unless you want to be run over."

"Go," Rotter said. "All I'm paid to do is watch you for now. When I say the word, my bosses take default judgment on you. Then I do what I'm good at."

"I'll just bet you are at that," Buck said. He looked both ways to see if the street was empty. He didn't dare risk getting picked up for assault and battery. He closed the fingers of his right hand into a fist—his right hand felt heavy and solid as a brick to him. "The last time I remember it was still against the law for your kind to do business on a Sunday."

"My kind?" Sheldon Rotter the collector stood up straight, palms out and up. "So what's my kind? Skip chaser? Okay. People like you make my job for me, Hansen—"

"*Mr.* Hansen," Buck said. He took half a step sideways to set his feet firmly for a swing at the kike's head.

"—does that make me some kind of vulture, that I run down deadbeats for people who trusted—" He did not get to finish. Buck grabbed him by the wide lapels of his cheap prewar suit, hoisted Rotter the skip chaser to his toes, jammed his fists up into his throat, slammed him back into the side of the Chrysler and held

142

him there like that. Rotter's eyes bulged. His lips were pulled back over his dirty teeth, showing the wetness of his gums, his tongue. He gargled, trying for air to speak. He kept his hands at his sides, never once touching Buck with his hands, never defending himself.

"Who the goddamn hell are you talking to!" Buck said, his face a bare inch or two from the collector's face. "Who the hell do you think you are, talking to me—I'm Buck Hansen!" he said. "My name is *Mr*. Hansen to you. You're talking to Buck Hansen, understand that? I paid forty thousand dollars in income tax a year ago. I could have bought you and your business and your whole damn clan, every year for five years! Your *kind*, I'll tell you. Kike, kike bastard, your kind! I've got a boy fought a war to keep your kind out of a furnace while you worked your sheeney cheap business! You hear me? Do you hear me, I'm Buck Hansen! You hear that!"

Rotter the skip chaser's face was red. His breath came loudly through his large, hairy nostrils. He tried to speak, but Buck's fists under his jaw, his forearms and elbows pressed into his chest and stomach prevented it. Buck held him there against the Chrysler for a moment. The little man was trying to say something, trying to get his mouth open far enough, his tongue moving, but only a strangling came, broken, from his throat. Buck remembered the Jehovah's Witness in the hotel in Minneapolis, unruffled, unafraid of him; this man was terrified, as though Buck meant to kill him. Then he let him go, afraid himself that he would choke him to death.

He pulled him away from the Chrysler, pushed him toward the Studebaker. He was not shoved hard enough to fall, but he stumbled and fell to one knee before he could catch his balance. Buck waited, ready if the collector wanted to make a donnybrook of it. He waited, and now he wanted him, wanted a fight, wanted this little hebe to wear his fists out on. But Sheldon Rotter was not fighting. He got up slowly, so slowly that Buck thought for a moment he had really hurt him. His trouser leg was torn at the knee. He rubbed his throat with both hands before he could speak, coughing and swallowing, moving his head in slow, complete circles to ease the tightness in his neck. It embarrassed Buck to stand, watching him work to get his voice back. The collector trembled, his whole body jerking in quick spasms. Near Buck's shoe lay the dead cigar butt; he stepped on it to keep from seeing it. The Jew took out a handkerchief and wiped his face, very methodically; Buck felt himself sweating fiercely.

"Come ahead," Buck said, unable to bear waiting any longer for Rotter to recover. "I spot you a good fifteen years at least, and I haven't really fought a man for over twenty."

"I was saying for your own good," Rotter said. There was nothing wrong with his voice when he spoke at last. Buck raised his fists—his fingers felt locked, permanently frozen into fists—and moved toward him. Rotter retreated.

"I didn't think so," Buck said.

"I forget what you call me, Mr. Hansen," Rotter said. "I purposely forget. I can afford to." He turned to run, but Buck went no closer to him. "I'll get satisfaction just doing my job. Go on. Try and skip out! I'll find you. You'll pay up through the nose, mister. I'll just do my job, then see who's so tough. Skip out," he said. "I'll be right behind you!" He got into his Studebaker, still with one hand, massaging his throat.

"Not if you know when you're healthy," Buck said, but he knew he was not heard over the sound of the Studebaker's engine. Rotter started a car like an old woman, gas pedal on the floorboard, then ground his gears. Buck got quickly into his car, suddenly afraid the collector would try to run him down. "Twin Cities Businessman Victim of Hit-Run" he thought, seeing the *Tribune* headline. But Rotter backed his car, cramped the wheels tightly to go wide around Buck's Chrysler. He stopped alongside, leaned over to shout out the window. Buck expected to be cursed.

"You can look at it a good way, Mr. Hansen," Rotter said. His whole face glistened with sweat. "We have confidence in you, my bosses, actually. When they put me watching you it means they think you're still good for the money, see?"

"Blow it up your bucket, hebe," Buck said. He was puzzled by the expression on Rotter's face at that. For the first time, the Jew looked hurt—not scared or angry. He looked truly insulted for the first time.

"I mean it," Rotter said. "Why should I lie? I'll be seeing you, Mr. Hansen." And he left.

So now he was being followed, Buck thought. Rotter's clients would go into civil court Monday, take default judgment against Buck, unopposed, then turn the papers over to Rotter to gut him for anything left worth the trouble. The hell! They'd find damn little meat on his bones. And they had to catch him first if they wanted to serve any plasters, by Christ! He slipped the Chrysler smoothly into gear and pulled away from the curb.

144

VII

Goshen. Surely there are thousands of such towns in America, but we never see them. They were always off the best roads, and now our superhighways skirt them, and we see nothing but the green and white sign at an exit most of us never dream of turning into. We know the exit we pass is not the number we seek. We do not usually even bother to read the name of the town on the green and white signboard. They are there, still, the towns like Goshen, Indiana. But if we did, if we did leave the marvelous modern roads, today, the towns like Goshen will be changed from what they were. Even then, for my father, it had changed enough.

"This is where you grew up, isn't it?" I said.

"I was about to say it was the same old place, but I'll be goddamned if it is. The main drag used to be cobblestones," he said. The main street of Goshen was macadamized, and the center line and the lines for parking were a brilliant, fresh yellow in the sun of early morning—we had stayed the night at a small hotel in Elkhart (yes, he paid the lodging there).

"Where is everybody?" I said.

"At work," he said, "this isn't Chicago. When one of these hicks punches in in the morning, he stays there until they ring his dinner bell. You'll see it in the evening, all the sodbusters come in in their pickups. You know," he said, "they used to park diagonally here in town. I wonder what monkey's behind that." There were some people. There was a policeman standing at the corner where there was a four-way stop. He seemed to look a long time at the Chrysler. "Up yours," my father whispered as we pulled away, and, to me, "They live off out-of-state plates in a burg like this. Wide spot in the road," he said. There were a few people on the street, and when we circled the elm-shaded square to get on the other side of the courthouse, there were half a dozen scarecrow shapes, old men wearing hats, canes across their laps, seated on the benches. There were two Civil War cannons on the courthouse lawn, and on one corner, a statue of a Civil War soldier, wearing a stone cape, seeming to sight on the spear of the bayonet that stuck up in front of his face, the butt of his musket resting on the pedestal between the toes of his high boots.

"There's some people," I said.

"Nobody'd remember me, likely," he said, "or visa versa."

"It's a pretty nice town, I guess. That's a pretty nice park there."

"I can remember when it was the backup from the grist mill. My brother and I used to haul bullheads out of there hand over fist. With a cane pole and a gob of night crawlers for bait," he said.

"I never was fishing, or hunting, or anything," I said, but he did not seem to want to talk.

It was a pretty nice town. The streets were shaded by canopies of elm branches that grew up over the road from both sides. The hot sun, coming through the dark leaf tents overhead, dappled the newly laid macadam. The houses were all painted white, set back from the street to give them generous yards. Most yards were fenced with white stake fences, and nearly all the white houses had porches, often bent around both front corners of the houses. I could not see into the houses because there were heavy curtains on the windows, and the windows usually had blue or green or brown shutters laid back against the white walls. Often there were three or four yards hidden from the street by unbroken hedges that were not squarely trimmed, like the hedges in

146

Milwaukee were. In the yards I could see, there were most often flower beds up close to the porches, and often flower boxes on the porch railings, or potted green plants hanging on delicate strands of chain, like the courting swings that were on so many porches. When we passed a side street, I always turned to look. The side streets were still paved with red granite cobblestones, but the elm trees and the hedges and the white houses were like those on the main street.

"That's all they is, they ain't no more," my father said, and we were at once out of Goshen, with no gradual trailing off of houses between wider and wider vacant lots, as there was in leaving Milwaukee. There was a last house, with a last hedge in front, a last row of trees to shield the house from the year-round wind that blew over the flat farmland, and then there was a post with signs of the Kiwanis, Rotary, Odd Fellows, and Elks, all inviting us to return again soon. And then a sign giving the new speed limit for the open road.

"Your mother and I were back through here once in the early twenties," he said, "and some dodo from the Klan had a sign up when you came in going north. I guess the State Police came and tore it down. The Ku Klux Klan," he said. "Your sister was just a baby." I did not ask what the Klan was, because he did not want to talk to me.

Outside town, it was immediately hotter in the car without the shade of the elms. The sigh of our slipstream came in the open windows as we speeded up. The land was very flat, divided into rectangular fields, the fields fenced against the road, separated from each other by hedgerows to keep the constant wind off the crops that surged thick in the fields under the hot sun, in the humid air. "How's come there's no corn, Dad?"

"Too wet." Most of the fields were in potatoes, the white buds of the young plants like a dusting of new snow, many in clover to feed stock. In the ditches at the side of the highway, buckwheat and dill and asparagus grew wild. The farmhouses and outbuildings were always concealed by stands of oak and elm to break the winds. We reached the four-way stop at the state highway. There was a red blinker above the stop sign. "Real progress," my father said, "hoity-toity. This way even if the squarehead's dead drunk up in the wagon box, at least the horse can know to stop, huh?"

"I guess," I said.

"This must be the place," he said, slowing to turn left off the county road. "I'll be a son of a gun?" The access road to my

147

uncle's farm was now paved also. "Wonder's never cease," my father said.

"Are we here?"

"This must be the place." He stopped at the drive, pulling up close to the mailbox for the slice of shade that lay across the road. The mailbox was set on a post, the post set in a concrete-filled milk can, the can painted white. The box had *Hansen T.* stenciled on its silver side. On the side of the wooden post was screwed a blue metal cylinder, *Elkhart Leader* in dull orange against the blue. "Let's get our stories straight," my father said.

"Mum's the word, I know."

"Okay. But be careful, will you? I mean it, boy. That brother of mine's just screwy enough to call the Gestapo on me if he knew what was what. Get me? Let your old man do the talking and we'll do fine. Right?"

"I hope they have a pony or a horse I can ride," I said. We drove in.

The drive was cool, lined on both sides with huge elms, dark gray blue in the deep shade. There were parallel dirt ruts from the Chrysler's wheels, the grass between them on the lump long and dark green. The car bucked and tipped a little as we drove in.

(Once more, he is renewed! His hands grip the wheel resolutely—he is not smiling, or laughing, but whatever there was in his face to keep me from babbling questions all through Goshen, all along the country road where tin plates wired to fences advertised Red Man chewing tobacco, is gone as we approach the house where he was born. His home. We are home.)

The drive curved left and then quickly disappeared, flattening out into a bare-earth parking area. A Ford Model T, its body chopped away in back to make room for the wooden box set on the rear, sat between two trees, just enough room left for my father to nose the Chrysler in beside it. Then I saw the house, the glider in the yard, the outbuildings beyond the house. There was a large doghouse near us, another bare patch of ground in front of it, but no dog came barking out of the dark hole of its entrance. Turning on the seat, looking back, I could see the green, heat-dancing fields we had come through on the county road. It was cool and absolutely silent in the heavily shaded yard.

"Where is everybody?" I said. My father had turned off the ignition. He turned it back on and pressed the horn ring on the steering wheel. The Chrysler's air horns demolished the silence. A door shut inside the house and then the back screen door on the large summer porch opened, and my Aunt Marie came out.

"Well, we're here," my father said when she met us halfway between the house and the car.

"I thought you'd send word so we could be expecting," Aunt Marie said. She looked at me. "Now who's this? I sure wasn't expecting this," she said.

"My boy. Who else? This is the little one."

"He ain't so awful little anymore, is he?" she said, as if calculating the food I would eat. She looked at me, but she did not stoop or kneel to meet me, did not take my hand, try to touch me. I think I whispered, *Pleased to meet you*, but I may only have thought it. "Thurston!" she yelled. I looked out at the shimmering potato fields, where her hard voice rolled into the heat waves, the fluttering rows of white blossoms, then disappeared.

"I heard!" my uncle called back, coming around the corner of a far building. He took off his hat and waved to us, more a slapping gesture than a wave, a harried, irritated motion he knew would not make us all go away, but still he must make it.

"He's been working out to the shed," Aunt Marie said. My father flipped his Pall Mall away in the shaded grass. She followed its flight with her eyes, stared at the spot where it landed and lay, sending up a spume of last smoke as it burned out. We said nothing, waited for my father's brother to reach us. He walked very slowly.

And do such people still exist, in and outside all the small towns like Goshen, Indiana?

Aunt Marie is a tall woman, about as tall as my sister (your Aunt Jane; your Great-Aunt Marie—no, you never saw her). She is a woman who does not change until she dies. That permanence is her identity, at once her rare, unsought treasure, and the close walls that are the limits of her possibility. I will see childhood, girlhood pictures of her that evening, and save for a little softness in the child, a bit more amplitude of flesh and hair in the girl, they differ almost not at all from the woman in her middle fifties who met us in the farmyard. The child, Marie Gebhardt, only daughter of parents said to have blood relatives among the mysterious Amish, who ward evil away from their crops and stock with hex signs painted on their red barns, is no less certain or sober than the woman. Her softer-only face looks directly out of the oval-cut photographs, pasted on heavy cardboard. This child will not sulk or laugh or stick out her tongue at any camera. It is a soft, plain little face that already knows who it is, without having or caring to know it knows. This child already knows she will become the wife of Thurston Bengt Hansen—she will have no children, will prosper mildly as the value of land increases, will die of a sudden and massive stroke aged sixty-four, preceding her husband by exactly a year and one day. She is not photographed often because it is not a thing to be done often. A girl, a young woman, she appears always in the company of others. This is a girl, a young woman, with no vanity to betray her. Her last portrait is with her husband, her wedding day. He stands, she sits. He looks down at her, as if there were lint on his coat sleeve or the shoulder of her dress on which his hand rests. But she continues to confront us directly, without boldness or subtle intent. There is nothing in her hardened face to suggest even that she allowed herself to feel the least satisfaction that she has in fact become the wife of Thurston Bengt Hansen, as she has known, always, she would be. Doubtless, she is childless because of her age at marriage, thirty-six.

What, without arrogance, I believe (now) she never knew, is that when she dies, quickly, painlessly, of a massive and sudden stroke, the boy she insists on ignoring will think of her, and mourn. Though he will not know why.

"Well you come like you said, didn't you?" my uncle said when he reached us. He took my father's hand.

"Good seeing you again after so long," my father said. They shook hands a long time, and then continued to hold each other's hand for several seconds before parting. "I can't say as how you change much," my father said.

This is not true. They look very much alike in the old pictures. Thurston is seven years my father's senior, so in the early pictures he always dominates, bigger, his arm protectively and possessively around his younger brother. But Thurston at nine or fourteen or sixteen is nearly indistinguishable from my father at those ages. The moods are different, Thurston is serious, relaxed. My father glowers or smiles or, an infant in a long dress and a lace skullcap, chews his lip, while there is only quiet and obedient benevolence in the face of the older brother who holds him securely on his lap.

They have simply taken different paths. The hair visible under the rain-spotted felt hat my uncle claps on like a reflex when he leaves the house is still brown, flecks of gray visible only when the light is right. He is much slimmer. There is a gentle slope to his stomach under his blue work shirt, but he has still the wiry frame of my father at seventeen. He looks younger than my father. His face and forearms are deeply tanned, the back of his neck almost dark brown. He has (I think he has) his own teeth. For all his leanness, there is a solidity lacking, by comparison, in my father. Perhaps it is the carpenter's Levis, a loop for a hammer, a narrow pocket for a pencil, or the black, ankle-high work shoes with thick soles and blocky heels that make his stance, his grip on the ground he walks, seem so firm. Side by side, these brothers are some living before-and-after illustration, but there are no terms to define it.

"Hello there, boy," Uncle Thurston said to me. He put one hand on his knee, bent, took my hand. It was a farmer's hand, a worker's palm abrasive with the whitish pads of callous, fingers rough with the soil worked into every crease, networks of cracks on the tips, nails short, lined with dirt. I meant to drop his hand after the ritual pumps taught by my father, but he held on to me. "I remember this boy when he's just a tiny baby. Now how's he come to be with you, Buck?" His neck was lean, the Adam's apple prominent. The creases went only skin-deep as he turned his head and looked up at my father. I tugged, and he released my hand. "I thought that was kind of out," he said. "You know."

"No problem," my father said. "I was doing a little pleasure with business, so I stopped by and asked Anne if she'd mind if I took the boy on a little trip. That's all. We're divorced, we didn't get a formal declaration of war," he said. At the mention of my mother's name, Aunt Marie turned and went toward the house.

"I didn't know to expect you, either one," she said, "so I ain't got no dinner planned. Come in if you want to snack something when you're done talking." She walked very fast, the screen door banging once, twice, after her.

"That woman knows all about this?" He meant Irene, my father's second wife.

"That *woman* is in the hospital, like I told you over the phone. Certainly she knows."

"Still? This must be something real serious, huh? How can you be taking pleasure with business all over the country when she's bad sick?"

"Let's talk about it some other time, Thurston." He looked at me, and my uncle looked at me, and my uncle nodded and scraped at the grass with his shoes.

"I never was on a farm before in my life," I said quickly. "Do you have any horses here?"

"He wants a ride on a horse," my father said.

"One I keep for a kid in town, but he's mean," my uncle said.

"I'd like a horse ride."

"We'll see," my father said.

"Never once been on a farm? What kind of kid you raising, Buck? Boy," he said to me, "you go in get settled with your pa, get something to eat if you're hungry at all, then I'll show what's a farm, okay by you?"

"Okay. Good deal." My uncle smiled enough to show his teeth. I started for the house.

"Thank you, Thurston," my father said.

"For what? Didn't I say you got your rights around here? Go on get settled. You can have upstairs. Where we slept, you and me. Think you can find it?"

"Blindfolded," my father said.

Perhaps my father was afraid to ask Aunt Marie to fix us a snack (I was hungry!)—but we did not eat. We carried the grips to the upstairs room, unpacked, and my father changed out of his tan suit. We went out again, past Aunt Marie in the kitchen ("I'll be showing the boy around," my father told her as we hurried out.). We did not tour the farm. We found my uncle back at work under a shed, knocking apart old flats, pulling the nails with a claw hammer, pounding them straight on a piece of brick, tossing them, when they satisfied his eye, in a coffee tin to save for use again next spring.

"Mind if we kibitz?"

"Course not," my uncle said. The whole slats from the dismantled flats were neatly piled for reuse, broken pieces tossed on a kindling pile. They had converted the house to oil heat the year before, but the fireplaces, three of them, still worked. "You want a taste?" he said to my father. He took out the can of Copenhagen snuff that bulged his shirt pocket. My father sniffed it, then took a pinch and placed it behind his lower lip. My uncle put his on his tongue, rolled it back in his cheek. He did not smoke. "Smell?" he said to me.

"It's sort of sweet," I said. It smelled rich, like coffee and oil, like spices burning.

"You put you a drop of schnapps on there to keep it good," Uncle Thurston said. He clapped the lid on the can, dropped it in his pocket, buttoned the flap as he reached for another gardener's flat with his free hand.

"Good snoose," my father said, winking, stepping halfway out the shed to spit. "A pro like your uncle just swallers it all," he said. My uncle laughed.

"I never saw anybody chew tobacco before," I said.

"You been living in them cities too long," he said. In a few minutes my father went outside to spit his out, so he could smoke his Pall Malls. We did not talk much. We watched my uncle work, and when he drove out to one of his fields in the converted Model T truck, we did not go along. My father sat on the glider in the yard. When I got tired of moving the glider, standing on the platform, holding on with both hands, using my entire body to get it going, I got off and sat on the grass. The shaded grass felt cold through the seat of my new Chicago slacks. As the afternoon wore on, the air grew stiller and stiller, and it was too warm even in the heavy shade.

"It's a nice farm," I said.

"It's pleasant all right."

"Let's look around some. Okay?" We went to the barn and looked at the mean buckskin my uncle boarded for some horsy teen-age town girl. I could not ride him, but my father pulled back his lips and showed me how to count a horse's age. When we came out he wiped his hand on the grass. We were both very glad when we heard the sputter of the returning Model T. We both knew, sensed, I think, that Aunt Marie kept a close watch on us from the kitchen porch.

"I told you I didn't have nothing special," Aunt Marie said as we washed up, taking turns at the graniteware basin on the porch. They still pumped their water by hand at the sink. In the refrigerator (so old the coils were on top the cabinet), they kept a bottle cold for drinking. Poured in a jelly glass, it stung my tongue and throat, made my teeth hurt.

"We're just folks," my father said.

"We'll fill you up, don't you fret," my uncle told me. We ate in the kitchen, no cloth on the table.

"This is like old home week, man," my father said as we sat on the straight-backed wooden chairs. "You ain't never ate like this before, boy," he said to me, "not so's you'd remember, anyway."

"I just bet how you must eat, Buck," my uncle said.

"What is it, Daddy?"

"Tell him what it is, you're his pa," Uncle Thurston said.

"The elephant never forgets," my father said. "Like back home. That there now, the piece de résistance," he said, "is your *inlagd sill*. Salt herring. Pickled herring. With coffee, that can make you a breakfast you can fight all day on." Aunt Marie stayed away from the table while he spoke, but my uncle seemed to enjoy this: my father's good-natured proof that he remembered the Swedish names of the food, that for all the time and distance between them, here, in this place and way of life they had once shared, their bond, their *brotherhood*, still held. "*Sylta*," my father said, "what the krauts call headcheese. Ask your aunt sometime how long it took her to whip this squarehead stuff." Aunt Marie did not join us. "Lingonberries. It's just like cranberries, only better. *Korv*," he said, "*Potatis korv*. And, if my nose don't deceive me, that would be *limpa*." He reached for the sliced brown bread on the plate, to pick up a piece, I think, and smell it dramatically (it is sweet, nutty!). Aunt Marie sat quickly at the table.

"Thurston," she said; she folded her hands over her plate and bowed her head. I followed—I had listened to grace said at meals in the house of one of my friends (once, just once—I do not recall who, where, when) in Milwaukee. My father drew his hand back from the *limpa* bread. My uncle waited for him to get his hands in his lap before beginning.

"*Jag ar fattig Gud . . .*" he prayed: I am poor and God is rich. If I pray to him he shall help me and if I pray to him right, then he will help me in Jesus' name. "Amen." Aunt Marie joined him in saying. I watched them as he prayed, my hands folded before me, looking up from under my brows. My aunt and uncle closed their eyes. He looked like a man asleep, but his wife pressed her lids shut tight, her forehead pinched, teeth set, her folded hands trembling almost imperceptibly. My father, sitting across from me, stared out over my head. His hands were in his lap, but I doubt he folded them for prayer.

My uncle served each of us, taking our plates one at a time. They did not talk while they ate. "I like the cranberries," I said.

"*Lat maten tysta mun*," my father said. He winked at his brother. "Right, Thurston?"

"That's right."

"It means eat more and talk less," my father said to me, and to his brother. "How many times did the old man jump down my throat with that, huh?"

"You was always talking at dinner's why," Uncle Thurston said.

"To hear him tell it, anyway," my father said.

"Thanks very much for the good supper," I said to my aunt when we were done. She got up to clear the dishes.

"It's all good for you," she said. I think she feared my father had set me somehow against it with the foreign names. I wondered how long it did take her to learn to cook the food her husband knew when they were married.

There was a large living room, but the lights were not turned on. We continued to sit at the kitchen table after the dishes were cleared, the surface wiped vigorously by my aunt. She served egg coffee, and I was allowed a cup, heavily diluted with cream from their own milker cow. My father smoked, my uncle drank his coffee, sighed often, and my aunt washed the dishes with water heated in a whistling kettle on the iron stove. "I hate like the dickens to be a burden, but I'm going to need a jar lid or something to put my ashes in," my father said, and Aunt Marie brought him a saucer. "I do thank you, kind lady," he said.

"Are we going to sit in the living room pretty soon?" I said. My father laughed.

"We're family, boy," he said. "When company comes we'll open up the parlor. Not before, right, brother?"

"We can sit anyplace you like," he said, but we stayed at the kitchen table. My uncle pushed back his chair. "You use a little touch?" he said to my father.

"If you got it I can, damn bet you." Uncle Thurston went to the pantry for the crockery bottle of potato schnapps. The bottle was gray, the surface freckled. He poured the colorless spirits out in two tall shot glasses. He held the bottle up to his wife, but she shook her head and poured more coffee for herself.

"You could sell that thing for an antique," my father said.

"I reckon. This here one a fella give me, but we got one in the fruit cellar was Pa's, I think."

"Skoal," my father said, and they drank. "Hot damn," he said, licking his lips. "Taste," he said to me. The fumes up my nose choked me. It was like a pure, tasteless fire, with an after-odor of potatoes, damp and sprouting in a bin. "Drink not only water," my father said. He finished his, and when offered another said, "Can't walk home on one leg." My uncle drank half his glass, then ignored it a very long time before he finished it in a single, head-jerking gulp.

"They'll nail you yet for moonshining," my father said.

"The government can't be bothering none with me unless the damn Democrats decide to take it all," Uncle Thurston said. They were silent while my aunt finished the dishes, my father smoking, my uncle reaching out occasionally to turn his half-full shot glass with his thumb and forefinger, as if to examine it for some faint tinge of color. Then he got up again and said to me, "I'll show you something," and went to get . . . well, his *things*. His pictures, the few papers, the documents that were the basis of what he understood of his life—the skeleton on which I hung the flesh of my, my father's, our lives.

(Do? I sat all this time, a good boy, not fidgeting. I watched my father and my uncle, I stole glances at my aunt, who rattled the dishes in the pan, rinsed them on the drainboard with boiling water from the teakettle. I traced the perfect grain in the smooth top of the oak table. I tumbled the exotic Swedish words in my mind: *korv . . . limpa . . . Lat maten tysta mun . . .*)

"Tomorrow now I'll have time to fix us some special supper," Aunt Marie said, holding her coffee cup with both hands.

"Oh boy, here we go," my father said as Uncle Thurston returned.

"*Den som vantar pa nagot gott vantar aldrig for lange,*" he said. My father snorted. "You wait for something good, you don't wait so very long," my uncle said to me.

"That's what he used to tell me," my father said. He meant their father, Anton Gustav.

"It always makes it feel like it's longer for me," I said.

"You and me both, buster," my father said.

"You get a kick out of this, I bet," Uncle Thurston said to me. "Don't mind what your pa says none. He even forgot how to speak Swede already."

"In a pig's eye," my father said, but we were not paying attention to him any longer. He poured himself another shot glass of the potato schnapps.

He must, as a life rule, have saved everything. This is not a family that takes many pictures, not a family to entangle itself in the systems, the institutions that create documents. But they, he, my Uncle Thurston Bengt Hansen, he saves all there is. Without elaboration: there are no neatly trimmed, mounted exhibits. It is a jumble, most of the photographs kept in a folder, nearly as large as the kitchen tabletop, covers stiff cardboard, tied with heavy cloth ribbon. We open it, lay back the cover, sort, pick, choose at random. The few papers are folded, wearing badly in the creases; they crackle as he delicately unfolds them in his vegetable farmer's horny fingers. And the prize, the core, a Swedish Bible big as a library's dictionary, leatherbound covers gone yellow brown with age, so dry they have begun to buckle and split. The Bible is held shut with two straps that have withered to half their original width, the brass clasps tarnished black. There is the dry sound of papers rustled, the dry smell of past generations, like the after-odor of a desiccated sachet in an empty drawer.

"Here we are," my uncle says, opening the Bible, the first pages left blank by the printer to record births, marriages, deaths. "We can go all the way back to what's your great-great-grand-father"— he says it grand*fader*— "in here. If I was rich like your pa

156

I'd go back to the Old Country and look up some more. They keep everything in the churches there, you know, they ain't got no governments keeping track of you there."

"Ho ho, rich," my father says, but he is smoking Pall Malls and drinking potato schnapps.

"See here," says my uncle. I follow the tracing of his broad, still dirt-edged fingernail. The ink is brown, or has gone brown in time, like the invisible writing with lemon juice, brought out with the flame of a match, once showed me by my brother Arn. "See there," he says, "Olaf. That's your great-great-grandfather. He's the one started this book." The writing, all of it Swedish—it goes on for six, seven pages, the brown lines of the inks shading darker as we approach ourselves in time—is a spidery, alien rune; it wavers under my eyes, seems to merge in a chaotic tangle, threatens to make me dizzy.

"They wrote funny," I say, to gain some point, some spot in which to stand and begin to see it all.

"That's most probably with a quill pen, that far back. Steel pens, like you dip, later they used. My own pa used a steel dip pen when I seen him write your pa's name in when he was born. I can remember that clear as anything. Right in this kitchen he done it the day your pa was christened at Swedish Lutheran." I look at my father, but he is smoking, not appearing to hear.

"What's that say?"

"In Jesus' name. Like I said in the prayer."

"Where's my dad?"

"Here." He turned, turned to the last page. "This is me. This is your pa. See there, Oskar Torwaldsen, that's him."

"Don't remind me," my father says, but we ignore him.

"Is this the same then, in Jesus' name?"

"No sir. That's a little sister we had. She died a baby just in a few days. Your pa was still too little to remember her. That's why he don't know his mother, too. She died having our sister. From having the baby."

"She'd be my aunt," I say. He nods. I look at my Aunt Marie to see her quickly, imagine another woman, this dead-infant-aunt, place her at the table with us. I look at my father.

"You trying to give him bad dreams, Thurston?" he says.

"It don't hurt nothing," says my uncle.

"And that's all?" I say.

"I didn't have no children," he says. "If it was your pa kept the book, then you'd be written in here the same. But he went off."

"All right. All right," my father says. He is pouring more schnapps from the crockery bottle. Aunt Marie gets up, leaves the kitchen.

"Let's look at some pictures. I can show you most everybody from the book," says Uncle Thurston. "Not that Olaf now. He never left the Old Country. My pa was the one came over. I bet you don't know how he came to come over. You probably think your name is Hansen, huh?" My father relishes the schnapps on his tongue, lower lip out, shaking his head slightly as if to signal none of this is true, or if true, not worth the trouble to know.

"Sure it is," I say.

"That's what you think. That Olaf was a soldier in the Swedish army. Like forty years or something like that. They didn't have no last names, in the Old Country then. There was maybe a thousand Olafs in the Swedish army, so they give him a name for roll call." I look again to my father, but he does not care that our name is not really Hansen, that I am not who I thought I was. He does not seem to care at all! "They gave him the name Skjold," my uncle says.

"Means shield. Who says I can't talk Swede with the best of them," my father says to no one.

"That's right. So he can answer his name at roll call without all them Olafs answering too."

"Skjold," I say. It pronounces *huld*.

"That's close enough," my uncle says. "That's why we call ourselves Hansen. My grandfather, your pa's grandfather, is Hans, see?" The story is simple. My grandfather changed his name after immigrating because no one in America seemed able to pronounce it correctly. Olaf the soldier receives a royal farm, a position as overseer of a royal farm, as pension for service to the crown. His son inherits it. His son, this Hans, sells it to pay the way for Anton Gustav to the New World. And because American tongues, lips, throats, cannot contract to say Skjold, we are Hansen. Because of this, a clumsy, homely anecdote told by my uncle, I am a different Oskar Hansen Jr., in a farmhouse kitchen in Indiana in 1946—my uncle crackles documents in his fingers, sorts through the photographs that are the old world, my new world.

Now the faces. The flesh. Anton Gustav, his brother Oskar, his brother Bengt, who dies in his twenties. His sisters, who raise families in the country, whose families move to southern Indiana, the plains of Illinois and Iowa, to start farms, raise families. Photographs printed on tin, on thick cardboard. Poses formal, high collars, brushed hair, seated on upholstered benches, before

gathered drapes. Infants. Infants in lace caps and gowns twice the
length of their bodies, propped on pillows, cradled in arms, small
Bibles placed next them to indicate christening days. No, no
picture of the dead-aunt-little-sister—she dies too soon for christening. And now my uncle, sitting Indian-fashion on the floor
between his father's feet, father seated, holding my father, their
mother standing. My Grandmother Hansen, her very blonde hair
drawn tightly back from her face, a bun at her neck. Let her hair
fall, and there will be my sister Jane. Now my father a boy, my
age . . . he could be me, I could be him! My eyes swim, my head is
light. There he is aged ten, twelve, fifteen, seventeen, as I will be in
that looming impossibility, the future! He stands, one of six boys,
four girls, in the graduating class of Goshen Township Consolidated High School, 1914.

"Except he never graduated," my uncle says.

"I'll say I never," my father says.

"How's come?"

"You get your pa to tell you that one."

"This is neither the time nor the place," he says.

"Oh your pa was some guy," says my uncle. He drops the
graduation picture on the messy heap in the middle of the table.
"He was going to play baseball for money once, you know."

"Were you? Really?"

"Semipro," my father says, "but I couldn't field a bunt. I got
spiked by some hunky sonofabitch fielding a bunt. I got shy, so
they bunted me to death."

"Did you play too?"

"I never had the time," my uncle says. "I was working a
farm, you know. Your pa was a big music player too. Don't he tell
you nothing?"

"Butt out," my father says.

"What did you play?"

"Anything the way he tells it," Uncle Thurston says. I look
to my father for confirmation, but he has turned his chair away,
drinking with his back to us. "Them spuds could rot in the field
while he plays baseball for all he cares." My father mumbles into
his glass. "What?" Uncle Thurston says.

"I said who in goddamn hell kept all the goddamn machinery
going when there wasn't money in the house," my father says
loudly. His chair scrapes as he turns back to us, sets his empty
glass down hard on the table.

"He had money. He was just saving it."

"Yeah he was. To bury himself for the Christ's sakes."

159

"He was afraid of dying on the poor farm is all," my uncle says.

"Any luck and we'd all been there."

"You never missed no meals, did you?" My father straightens up, inhales, sets his jaw, looks his brother squarely in the face.

"What's the damn use of yammering," is all he says when ready.

"I'd say," my uncle says, rises. "It's about my time."

"It's real interesting," I say, patting the photographs, touching softly the paper that bears my grandfather's signature, swearing the end of his allegiance to the sovereign of Sweden, tapping the dry, hard, splitting cover of the Bible.

"They're most all of them buried right here. We could go out and see the markers tomorrow if you want."

"Why are you so goddamn morbid, brother?" says my father.

"I'd like to."

"We'll go if your pa feels good enough in the morning. That stuff's not so good for you, so much of it, Buck."

"Does anybody ever laugh in this neck of the woods?" asks my father. My uncle turns to go, to join his wife in some dark part of the house, to bed, to sleep. "Where's the banjo?" says my father.

"What?"

"The goddamn banjo. You didn't hock it, did you? I want my banjo."

"I don't hock nothing."

"Then get me my banjo, will you? Everybody doesn't have to go to bed with the damn chickens when you do, do they? I'll quit if I keep you awake. I want to play my banjo, Thurston. I want to see if I can make my kid here smile a little." Uncle Thurston went, returned with the banjo.

"I'll say my good-night," he said, and left the kitchen. My father carefully tuned the banjo, cigarette in his mouth, one eye closed against the smoke, his ear close to the instrument to catch the pitch of the strings.

It was . . . confusion. I did not know the source of their antagonism, but I knew my uncle had been taunting him, had brought out the pictures, the Bible, to provoke. I was lost in the chaos of the alien, quill-steel pen handwriting, the faces and times in the photographs, the ghostly presence-in-absence of the sister-aunt who died a baby, the name Hansen that was Skjold and not Hansen. I was so tired I wanted to cry.

We sat up in the farmhouse kitchen. My father played some

songs that had, he said, made Eddie Peabody famous not so many years ago at that. If my aunt and uncle were kept awake, they did not complain. At last he put down the banjo and we went up to the third-floor bedroom and went to bed.

"Dad."

"What?"

"Are you mad?"

"Never."

"Know what?"

"You tell me."

"You forgot to call Jane like you said we would."

"Remind me tomorrow. When my brother's not around, if you please." He fell asleep almost at once, snoring loudly. Then I slept, and later in the night, woke, cold and frightened to be where I was, doing what I was, and he took me in his bed with him to warm and comfort me. He went back to sleep, and before I slept I had solved the confusion. I understood, as I drifted to sleep in his embrace, what had happened. I had discovered myself—found my past, and if I could not recite it, had no records of it, no pictures, no Bible, not even the words to express it then—nevertheless I *felt* it. It was mine. For the rest, for all that, I had a lifetime.

I preceded my father downstairs in the morning. "Good morning, Aunt Marie," I said. She was, then, always, busy, preoccupied, inward, and yet without the nervous dissatisfaction or impatience of the thinker, the worrier.

"Go get yourself washed up. It's time almost to eat."

"Where's my uncle?"

"Out already. We don't sleep so late here. Is your father up?" We heard him coming down the stairs. Quickly, she said, "Is that the only clothes you have to wear? Don't you have no other clothes for yourself in them bags of his?"

"He's going to buy me some more," I said, and then he came into the kitchen, and my aunt said no more. I went to wash on the porch. The water was warm from the stove. I splashed my face, dried on the single strip of toweling hung on a hook on the wall. Already, as I looked out through the cover of shade made by the elms surrounding the house, the potato fields shimmered in the sun.

"There's the big sleeper," Uncle Thurston said as he came in. The felt hat he wore always left a line cutting across his forehead, in the hair around the back of his head. He hung up his hat and we went in to eat breakfast. This time my father waited for Grace to be said, even lowered his chin a trifle while my uncle spoke.

161

"*Lyckan kommer, lyckan gar—*" he prayed before the morning meal: luck comes and luck goes, but God's love brings luck.

"You decide not to sleep all day?" he said to my father.

"I'm on vacation, remember? And yes, my head feels just fine, if you're figuring on asking that."

"I didn't say nothing," he said, and to me, "Go ahead eat, boy, it's all good for you."

"Eat now," my aunt said.

(Breakfast. It is like . . . it is, after my awareness in my father's arms the night before—it is like waking up to find I am a member of a rare and ancient order of people devoted to rituals running back in time to our founder, Olaf the Soldier. Breakfast is our first small worship of the day, homage through the very food we eat . . . *risgryngrot, gafel biter, knacke brod,* and a cup of egg coffee diluted for me, with real cream from the one milk cow still kept for the very purpose of my gradual initiation into the rites of our order.)

"I never ate fish for breakfast before," I said.

"Good for you," Uncle Thurston said. "Fish is brain food. That's why us Swedes are so smart—" he tapped the side of his head—"all that fish we're eating."

"Tell that one to the Marines too," my father said.

"Supper I'm planning real special," my aunt said as she passed more coffee, cleared. "You'll like it fine." My father smoked, and my uncle sipped his coffee while she did the dishes.

"You need your ears lowered there, sonny," my father said. And my uncle got their father's barber tools out, and my father cut my hair. When it was over, my uncle got up and put his hand on the back of my neck.

"You coming with, Buck?" he said.

"Where's that?"

"Me and the boy here's going to see the graves."

"I thought you were kidding," my father said. "You don't want to go parading around some morbid damn marble orchard, do you, boy?"

"You can stay if you like," my uncle said. "I don't guess it would hurt you none to see your folks' graves once more."

"This is what they do for entertainment around here," my father said to me as we left the kitchen.

"Aren't you coming?" I asked my aunt.

"I got plenty to do right here," she said. "You should have a hat to keep the sunstroke off you."

162

It was still very cool inside the Chrysler, and it was a pleasant ride to Goshen, with air coming in the open windows to take the night's and the shade's chill off the car. I sat in the middle. We had to throw things in the back seat to make room for all three of us up front. "You sure carry a lot of stuff when you go off on this pleasure and business trips, Buck," my uncle said, but my father did not answer.

"You sure grow lots of potatoes," I said as we passed between the fields on the county road.

"There ain't hardly enough money in it to make it pay anymore," he said.

"Crap," my father said. "Land values are going up in leaps and bounds all over the country."

"That's not the same thing," Uncle Thurston said. "That's the damn Democrats again." The fertile fields seemed to steam under the sun. The white blossoms nodded. We passed an Amish family in a buggy.

It was as if I were watching a period movie. We came over a rise, and there was the high, top-heavy bulk of the buggy in the middle of the road. I thought my father would slow, but he cut around them to the left, very close to the drainage ditch. The buggy was closed in back—as we whipped by them I saw the father and teen-age son up front, identically dressed in black coats, wide-brimmed, flat hats, blue work shirts buttoned to the neck, the father's full-brown beard the only distinction between them. The mother and two girls sat in back, faces hidden by their black bonnets, like three black brides loaded for market in the rear of the buggy. The women did not turn their heads, but the boy in front looked, his face startled, eyes wide, as if our Chrysler was as impossible, as unheard of in his world as their horse and buggy was in mine. The father turned his head, but he was not surprised. He gripped the reins to hold in his frighted horse, mouth closed, bearded jaw defiant. My uncle raised his hand to them, and the father nodded, once, up and down, and then we were past them.

"Holy cow," I said.

"That's Gersbach. He's got land near mine," my uncle said.

"He's never seen them close up before," my father said. I got up on the seat to look back out the rear window as they shrank behind us, disappeared below another rise, the horse's head bobbing in rhythm to his trot.

"They're real interesting people," Uncle Thurston said.

"Screwballs," my father said. "They don't even speak a good

163

German. I learned my German from them, you know," he said to
me. He braked the Chrysler as we reached the reduced speed limit
for Goshen.

"Think you can find it?" Uncle Thurston said.

"I'll give you can-I-find-it," he said.

The Swedish Lutheran Church of Goshen was on the side of
town that had not expanded. It was a white building, like all the
houses in Goshen, a little longer and lower than the houses, with a
very short bell tower. It was not shielded from the street by
bushes, and there were no shade trees around it. The hours of
services were posted in a glass-covered case set about midway on
the lawn between the sidewalk and the church. The fenced
cemetery behind it was barely visible as we got out of the car. The
town ended there, and beyond the cemetery were pastures and
clover fields. Out of the car, walking, I was aware how quiet it was
in the heat, and then I could hear the churning of the cicadas.

My father climbed the steps and tried the door. "Locked," he
said. "What's inside worth stealing?"

"Your pa's griped because he got kicked out from confirmation class," Uncle Thurston said, and to my father, "Come Sunday
we can all go and see for yourself."

"Thank you but no thank you." He came down and we went
around to the back, through the gate in the low wrought-iron
cemetery fence. "Grass needs cutting," my father said, kicking at
it. "The old man left something for perpetual care, didn't he? Who
keeps it up?"

"We got a committee does that. We'll cut the grass before
long, I guess." The Swedish cemetery was full. My uncle explained
that there was a city cemetery now, where everyone, except the
Amish, who buried their dead on their own land, in family plots,
went. "There ain't even room for me no more, I guess," he said.

"You won't know it," my father said. I followed them in.
The Swedish settlers of Goshen, Indiana, were not extravagant or
elaborate for their dead. There were no tall columns over graves,
no statues of angels blowing slender trumpets, no mausoleums for
the richest farmers, no granite polished to a rust-colored mirror
finish. Nor were they spare or parsimonious; there were no plain
Shakers' slabs of weatherworn sandstone. They were . . . they
marked their graves with square-cut, solid stones, rectangles with
firm, broad bases. They gave full names, and dates, and occasionally a short prayer or Bible quotation. Most were in Swedish. It was
very hot in the open middle of the cemetery, the long grass dry.

164

Burrs stuck to my socks and the cuffs of my slacks. When my uncle spoke I was not sure if it was to me or my father, who, after all, knew all this.

"This here's Pa, and this is Mama. The small one next here is Karen"— he pronounced it *Koh-ren*—"the baby who died, like I said. I was ten, about ten when Mama left us, so I remember her real good. I saw the baby the day she was born, and then for the funeral here in church, too. They wouldn't let me go see her the rest of the time because she was sick and they didn't want me catching from her." The earth over the graves was very, very slightly raised. There were withered flowers in fruit jars next to the stones of all three graves. When I looked up and down the row, I saw, here and there, iron markers in the centers of graves of war veterans, many inscribed with the gold initials of the Grand Army of the Republic. I looked at my father. His forehead was beaded with sweat, his upper lip wet. He looked at his brother, who also watched him.

He said, "What I remember is this sensation of maybe standing close to her, you know, holding onto her dress, probably. I get this sensation of my face touching cloth." My uncle shook his head, as if to say, yes, yes, that would likely be true, a true memory, one honest and possible at once. Then he looked away at the other graves in the row. My father coughed.

"Is there some more?" I said.

"More?" my uncle said. "Oh yes. You got all kinds of relatives here, boy. My uncles and aunts, some cousins too. But this is your grandfolks here." He looked once more at the three graves, then led us to the graves of other relatives. He named them, and I read the names, and the dates of births and deaths, and he translated the few inscriptions, and we kept walking up and down the rows. I began seeing only names and dates, sweating and panting in the heat, and then only looking at the dates, because I had never seen so many years; it was like seeing the leaves of a calendar flipped by a wind to indicate the swift passage of time in a movie. It was very, very hot, and dry and dusty. I stopped next to my uncle to wait for my father while he lit a cigarette.

I looked at the gravestone. It said *Braeder* at the top of the stone, and below that, *Our Beloved George*. The dates were *1897-1913*. "He was only seventeen," I said as my father came up to us.

"Sixteen," Uncle Thurston said. "That's Georgie Braeder."

"Did you know him?"

"Not so good as your pa did."

"Let's get the hell out of here, shall we?" my father said. "It's hotter than hell's half-acre."

"That's about the one out of all of them isn't no Swede in here," my uncle said.

"How's come?"

"Your pa can tell you better than me."

"How's come, Dad?" I said.

It was supposed to be one of the best days in his life. Yesterday they all wore Sunday best to school to get their graduation picture taken, and the afternoon was a holiday for the graduating class. They were supposed to meet to elect class officers and decide on the gift. That was so much hooey, because every graduating class chipped in for an elm tree from Gust Swenson's nursery, and since Gus Jr. was graduating this year, the tree was free. So they held their meeting in the mill pond grove, elected class officers and that was it, the rest of the afternoon off.

Buck was nominated for vice-president, but they elected Phil Braeder, which griped Buck just a little. Phil Braeder was a jerk who didn't even wear socks when he came dressed up to take the graduation picture. Old Hoffman made sure Phil's work shoes and bare ankles were hidden behind one of the girl's dresses when the picture was taken. Then they go and elect him vice-president of the class. The girls did that, because they were sorry for Phil Braeder. After they elected officers they tried to get the girls to do something with them for the afternoon, but Mary Rasmussen was class secretary. She had to go home, or to the new Carnegie town library, or somewhere, and write up the class will and the senior class prophecy and the humorous class prophecy. And she took the other girls with her.

"Want to see what I put for you?" she asked him. He didn't have any interest in Mary Rasmussen *a-tall*. He didn't know if she liked him or she was just a jerk.

"That means I'm going to," Buck said. She ran off by the other girls, like a jerk, while he read it. *Oskar Hansen leaves his big smile and his big laugh to Mr. Hoffman, because he says nobody needs it more.* Oh boy. That would go over just fine with Old Hoffman, with the old man sitting out there to hear it too. Some jerk. The humorous prophecy was that in twenty-five years Oskar Hansen would be richer than Andrew Carnegie, and would come back to Goshen and tear down the public library and build the town a new one twice as big. Sure I will, Buck thought. The

166

serious prophecy was that Oskar Hansen would become famous as a musician.

"This is all wrong," he told Mary when she came back to get her notes. "I'm gonna play baseball for money. I'm already as good as Joe Jackson, ain't you heard?" Like a jerk she took her notes and ran off without saying anything. It must be, he thought, she liked him more than he'd figured. So he spent the holiday afternoon sitting around in the mill pond grove in his good clothes, sharing his Sweet Caps with Gus Swenson Jr. and Ollie Berntson and Stig Hammer. Which was a waste, but what could he do dressed in Sunday best? The only good thing was that the old man didn't know from anything about a holiday afternoon, so Buck could wait it out long enough to let his brother take care of the milkers, just like a regular school day. It was a little fun later. Buck played his ocarina and they sang a few songs.

But it was a bust, pretty much. Which was why he played hooky the next afternoon. Here he was graduating high school in three days, and there was a party tonight. To sit through another dumb day in school wasn't worth it. If this was supposed to be such a great time in his life, like Thurston and the old man were forever harping at him, then Buck was for damn sure going to enjoy it.

"The hell with it, let's take off," Buck said to Gus Swenson Jr. while they ate their lunch from paper bags in the shade of the new public library.

"Not me. We're too close to horse around."

"Don't be a jerk," Buck said, "there's nothing left to do, is there? So, dopus, what's the sense? We can get your old man's shotgun and go out back of the grist pond. I saw a heron in there a week or so ago."

"It's bad enough I'm sneaking it for tonight. He finds out, he'll strap me." Buck got up, crumpled his lunch bag and tossed it into the farther shadows. "You don't have to face my old man."

"I have to face mine, don't I?" Buck said. "You're bigger than your old man. Take the damn razor strop away from him and wrap it around his neck, why don't you."

"Swell chance," Gus Jr. said.

"Be a jerk," Buck said. "I'm out of coffin nails. I'll be thinking of you having a lot of real fun in school."

So he went over two blocks to Sondergaard's store and bought some cigarettes. For a few minutes it was one of the best days of his life. He was telling Sondergaard about the guy from the Three-I League in Evansville who'd been to see him. He was laying it on thick for old Sondergaard, and they were talking about Joe Jackson, and old Sondergaard was telling how he'd seen Nap Lajoie play in exhibition once. Buck was sitting up on the counter, a Sweet Cap stuck in the corner of his mouth.

Then old Dieter Hoffman walked by, big as life, loping along with one shoulder higher than the other in that black coat like some damn Amishman. They looked right into each other's eyes through the front window of Sondergaard's store. Hoffman came right in without breaking stride. Buck got down off the counter.

"Just tell me what you're doing here, I'd like to know," Hoffman said to him. His face twitched, the way it did if you said something in German to him and then quick ducked, or if you skipped a pebble across the floor while he was trying to find his place in the book in music class. Old Dieter Hoffman was probably the biggest jerk in the state of Indiana, and maybe the whole world. They called him Amish for the long black coat he wore because he was the big deal principal of Goshen Township Consolidated High School. He'd gotten his back twisted up in some farm accident before he went off to the normal school to be a teacher—because he couldn't do farm work with the lopsided shoulder of his. He taught the music classes. He had to give Buck 95 or 96 in music, but he gave him unsatisfactory in deportment, which didn't help with Buck's old man. He was a real jerk. He was principal and music teacher, and he did the girls' sports and games classes too. He got outside with them and led calisthenics with that big black Amishman's coat flopping over his hinder; Buck always got a laugh—he put his head out the second-floor window, cupped his hands at his mouth and yelled, *Hey Amish!* or *Weisst du was, wenn es regnet, dann ist nass.* Like it was a big secret Hoffman spoke German at home with his wife. He was the worst jerk in the world.

"What's it look like?" Buck said. That set the twitch going like crazy on his face. Hoffman took off his steel-rimmed specs and leaned forward like he was having trouble seeing Buck's face.

"Crack wise with me, you get yourself in trouble, youngster."

"Is that so," Buck said. He tried to see out of the corner of his eye if Sondergaard was catching this, but he couldn't. He wasn't so sure why he'd decided to tell old Hoffman where to get off. He wanted to give Sondergaard a show, sure, but there was more to it. He was enjoying himself, playing hooky, and he was fed up to the gills with his old man and his brother yammering about how great it was graduating high school, and he was sick of his friends making such a big deal. He was sick of a jerk like Dieter Hoffman—Buck could have broken him in half with one arm tied behind his back—being able to tell him what to do. Piss on it, Buck thought.

"Okay," Hoffman said. He put his specs back on, shoved them up his nose to set them in the red pinch-marks on each side of his bony nose. "Make out that cigarette and come on back with me. To school." Buck might have done it if he'd let it go at that. "I'll write a letter for you to take your father about this," Hoffman said.

"You can go to hell," Buck said.

"What?"

"*Geh zur Hölle,*" Buck said. "Understand me better in Dutch?"

"Apologize," Hoffman said calmly.

"Maybe if it snows tomorrow. Maybe not." Hoffman lifted his hands, like he was going to grab and try and haul him out of Sondergaard's. Buck made a fist with his right hand; just try, he thought. He would cold-cock old Hoffman into the middle of next week.

"Crack wise. Impudent," the principal said. "Okay. When you decide you apologize to me, then you graduate. Not unless. Tell your father for me—"

"Tell him yourself."

"—we can have graduation without Oskar Hansen unless he apologizes. You tell him." Then Hoffman clomped out, his shoulder going up and down like a tractor piston, back to the high school. What the hell was he doing out of the school in the first place?

"Oh oh," Sondergaard said. "Now you're in for it I bet."

"That's what you think," Buck Hansen said. It was funny; he was expecting to feel rotten about it, but he didn't. It gave him a good reason to get drunker than anyone else at the party that night. He got Thurston to decoy the old man outside while he snuck the shotgun. That made two with Gus Swenson's, three if Stig got his old man's. They'd give Phil Braeder the jerk a scare like he never would forget.

The party wasn't so hot. Buck had kept up talking all the time about asking at least some of the girls to go, but he knew they never would. That way he could blame the others because there were no girls along. They were supposed to get Swenson's old man's truck too, but that was more baloney. They rode, seven

169

of them, for Christ's sake, thirteen goddamn miles in Swenson's wagon on the shitty Elkhart road to the tavern for beer. They could have just as well camped out in a field with the schnapps they drank to and from the tavern in the wagon. Buck got the spot up on the seat next to Gus Jr. When Stig tried to get it Buck asked him if he wanted to make something out of it; Stig backed down. But he could still smell the rotting wet odor of the peat moss clinging to the boards of the wagon bed. Hell!

They had some fun. At the tavern, they were getting a lot of bad looks from the proprietor until Buck took a couple of spoons, sat down and played them just like they were ham bones. And on the way back he played his ocarina until breathing through his nose made him a little sick feeling with the schnapps sloshing around in his stomach. Then he told Gus Jr. about the run-in with Hoffman.

"You think he really means it?"

"I reckon so."

"You tell your old man?"

"Hell no. He's sure to find out soon enough, I guess."

"That's pretty bad, Oskar, if he don't let you graduate and—"

"My name is *Buck* Hansen!" he said. He turned, reached down and grabbed the schnapps bottle out of Bob Lundgren's hand. "Buck Hansen wants a damn drink," he said. "Anybody calls me that dumb squarehead name gets his ass beat by Buck Hansen personally. Right? Right! You keeping my gun out of the manure there? You better."

"I hope he was kidding for your sake is all," Gus Jr. said.

"He can go diddle a pig, too," Buck said. "Some party. Wake up back there! Whop that horse in the fanny one, will you? I'm gonna give Philly Braeder a rousting like you never saw."

"We get caught, boy, we're—"

"They can't run fast enough to catch Buck Hansen. Besides, we'll be way outside town. You can ditch the wagon if you're scared. Cheap sonofabitch can't even scrape up to come on a party with us, I wish I had rock salt, I'd stuff it up his keyhole and shoot it off." Gus Jr. laughed, and the others laughed back in the wagon. "We should of got some girls along," Buck said. "And I'll load my own damn gun, too. I don't want my face half blowed off."

It was not Buck's idea to begin with. They all felt about the same about Philly Braeder. When he was sitting down, thinking it through, later, Buck couldn't pinpoint who it was first suggested it. It was all mixed up with the end of school, graduation, the trip to the tavern on the Elkhart road to celebrate it all with tavern beer and home-brew schnapps. Even before they asked Phil Braeder and he refused, somebody had said, let's hoo-rah Philly Braeder's house, just for the hell of it. It had nothing to do with his being German, because there was nothing wrong with being German in Goshen as long as you weren't Amish. Of the seven of them who went through with it, two, Miller Auerhahn and Axel Gruber, were Germans, went to the same Heilige Baptisten Kirche with the Braeder family. Later, some people in town tried to make something out of that: the Swedes going after some Germans out of pure squarehead meanness, but that was hogwash.

Phil Braeder was the oldest boy in the graduation class, a man, really, just short of his twentieth birthday. The oldest, possibly the dumbest, next to Stig Hammer, who was getting to graduate because it was easier than not for old Dieter Hoffman. Phil Braeder was just a jerk who had a dirty neck nine-tenths of the time, whose teeth were half gone because old man Braeder was afraid of dentist's ether, who wasn't interested in girls, who wouldn't come along on a graduation party because he was against drinking. That kind of jerk. It just seemed like a good way to top off the party—take a couple of shotguns, surround the Braeder house out on the Peggy Track, make, on a signal, one hell of a lot of noise. Maybe they'd see old man Braeder come out, yelling it was Judgment Day at last. It was just for the fun of it.

The Peggy Track was just a two-rut road running out of the southwest corner of town, ending in the cranberry marsh out behind the Braeder house, which was no house, but a shack. There were nine of them living in that rattrap, counting old man Braeder's mother, who never came into town. People said she spoke a German almost impossible to understand. The old lady, Mr. and Mrs. Braeder, the six kids. Georgie was the next oldest after Phil. For some reason Georgie had left school after eighth grade. Philly was the only Braeder maybe smart enough to be educated. Which was maybe why he acted like it was such a big deal graduating, which was part of why Buck got burned up every time he saw or thought of Phil Braeder.

When they got to the Peggy Track and got off the wagon to load the shotguns, Buck felt pretty mean about it. "We ought to light some fires around, make 'em think they're really done," he said.

"Jeez no," somebody said in the dark. "We could get in real trouble." There were three guns, Buck's, Gus Jr.'s, Stig's. They didn't surround the house. They fanned out in front of it in the yard; Buck was close to the washtubs Mrs. Braeder had right out in her front yard. When it all went wrong, Buck found cover behind the washtubs.

It was kind of fun, walking up the Peggy Track, Indian file, spreading out, the bare dirt yard between them and the ramshackle house lit by moonlight. The house was dark. They were crouched or laid low on the ground, and Buck could hear his friends' breathing, his own breathing, see their forms to his left and right. Then he realized they had forgotten to agree on a signal to start. "Jesus Christ!" Buck said. Somebody shushed him. So he hoisted his old man's double-barrel twelve gauge. It felt, as he pulled the triggers, suddenly very heavy. The barrels went off so close together it sounded like one giant blast. "Yagh!" Buck screamed, but it was lost in the sound of the twelve gauge going off.

It happened so fast. Stig and Gus were firing, and Buck was down on one knee, half behind the washtubs, to reload. He'll probably count his shells, he was thinking of his father, fumbling for the shells in his pocket. The others, with no guns to fire, were yelling like banshees, heaving pebbles at the front windows of the house. "Wake up, you Dutchman sonsabitches!" Buck raised his head to shout. That's when he saw light in the house—it was a kerosene lamp, because the light moved with whoever was carrying it. He was having trouble getting reloaded—he wanted to shoot at least once again. The light came to the door, and now Buck was watching to see who it was came out, and Stig and Gus had reloaded, were firing again. They never settled who it was hit the house. The last window on the far right just caved in. Stig and Gus both swore it must have been the other. Get out of here! Buck thought. He got the gun reloaded, but he never did fire again.

He was about to cut and run when the front door opened and at least one person (Phil or George, it was never settled) ran out, either running for fear or going after whoever had attacked their house. Then the gun was fired from the house the first time. Buck heard the whistle of the buckshot in the branches of the trees behind them, saw the muzzle flash in the doorway. It was old man Braeder, thinking they were out to kill his family. He had a single-shot. There was a long pause before he could get reloaded and fire again. That's when Buck got down behind the washtubs for cover. Buck, Stig, Gus, Axel Gruber, they were all yelling "Don't shoot!" It must have sounded like threats to the old man, or else he was too excited to hear anything clearly. In the meantime, somebody else (Phil or George) slipped out the front door. It could have been either of them. Phil told how he was just running around the yard, trying to see who it was out there.

Old man Braeder got the single-shot reloaded, fired out into the blackness beyond the fan of moonlit yard, and hit his son George in the back of the head.

It took only an afternoon in the county courthouse in town. They all testified, and all the Braeders except the old man's mother testified. The barkeep from the Elkhart road testified. The town constable didn't trust himself to question Buck or the others, so they were questioned by the high sheriff and an officer of the state police in the pre-investigation. There was nothing to lie about, and everyone agreed George Braeder was killed by his father.

And it took the afternoon of Georgie's funeral at the Heilige Baptisten Kirche. Thurston waited outside with the wagon. Buck's father called him to hurry up or they would be late. Buck came down the stairs and met him in the kitchen. He could not remember seeing his father wear a collar before. He didn't bother with the shiny, celluloid collar on Sundays when they went to Swedish Lutheran. "We'll be late," his father said.

"You know you make it look like I was the one responsible, don't you?" Buck said. "They got room in their own cemetery for him."

"You ever think they ain't got the money, Oskar?" his father said.

"Why you! How come not Swenson or Hammer's pa? Your giving it sticks it right on me, like I was behind it. Didn't you believe me when I said it wasn't my idea?"

"I don't know for sure what I believe no more," his father said.

"I'm not forgetting," Buck said.

"We can talk after," his father said.

"That's too late." But his father went out to the wagon, and Buck had to follow.

The funeral service did not bother him so much. The coffin was closed. For a while he had been afraid they would leave the coffin open, and they would have had to wrap Georgie Braeder's head to keep from showing what little was left of it. But it was closed. The hymns and the sermon were in German, so Buck could keep himself from hearing that if he tried. The little bit, the snatches that came through anyway, were the usual words about God and the future life hereafter. He was afraid the pastor was going to tack on a little thank-you to his father for giving the plot for the grave in the Swedish cemetery, but he didn't. He listened to the organ, to see how it was different from the music at Swedish Lutheran; it was not much different. They both used "A Mighty Fortress," for one. The organist at Swedish Lutheran was better by a mile.

The hard part of the funeral was seeing the backs of the Braeder family up front, seven of them, because the old woman didn't come out even for death in the family. Worse was looking around to keep from having to look at the Braeders. Nobody else seemed to be looking around, but wherever he looked, Buck saw one of the others, Stig's family, the Swensons, Gruber and all his little sisters, Auerhahn and his widowed mother. When he'd see one of them in the crowded pews he wanted to smile, like he'd been caught in a dumb place only a jerk would be, and he felt stupid, wanting to smile a shit-eating grin at a friend. Near the end there were a lot of prayers led by the pastor, up in the high pulpit. This German Baptist pastor wore a dumb black hat. No hat on Pastor Nordquist at Swedish Lutheran. There were a lot of prayers, and here was Buck's old man, on his left, folding his hands and closing his eyes, like he was praying right along when he couldn't go beyond asking where the privy was in German. Buck was about to jab Thurston, on his right, in the ribs and show him, but when he saw Thurston's face, he didn't. His brother wasn't faking like he was praying along, but he wasn't in the mood for joking.

By the time the procession of wagons and sputtering produce trucks reached the Swedish cemetery, Buck was just disgusted, uncomfortable in the heat. He listened to their shoes swishing through the grass as they followed the pallbearers to the open grave site. They passed his mother's grave, and he read her name, her dates. It meant no more to him than it did whenever the old man laid down the law that he go along to place flowers each year on her birthday.

Until he saw the fresh, wet, black earth heaped in a long, low pile next to the perfectly cut hole that was going to be Georgie's grave. The pallbearers set the coffin in the box waiting for it next to the grave, and the screws were turned down. The Braeder family got up as close as they could, and the Baptist pastor with his black hat got out his Bible to read and pray some more. Then was when it came on him—inside the coffin inside the box was Georgie Braeder, who ran around half the year with no shoes, his tail half hanging out of the torn seat of his overalls, his hair looking like the old man cut it with a cultivating hoe . . .

When they were done with the reading and praying and singing they were going to lower the box with Georgie Braeder in it into the perfect hole, and then they would shovel all that damp soil in on top of him, pound it flat with the blades of their shovels, put up a stone like the stones here, like the stone on his mother's grave, and nobody would ever see Georgie Braeder again. Buck looked around at all the people in Sunday best, heads down praying. He looked up at the glowing disc of the sun. He looked at his father's folded hands, at Thurston's hands hanging at his sides, at all the gravestones and the plots waiting for the sexton to dig them open.

It came to him that everyone there would be buried sooner or later, and then that he would be in a box like Georgie Braeder's box, lowered on ropes, covered. He thought it was the heat, he couldn't breathe so good, then he felt his father's arm around him, hugging, shaking him to get him to stop. He was crying, Thurston was looking at him, people looking up from their prayers to stare at him crying.

What he wanted to do was push his father away, but he was crying too hard for that, thinking, you bastard, leave me alone! It made it worse to have his father trying to make him stop. Goddamn you to hell! he thought. He had to get his father's arm off him to get at the handkerchief kept in his jacket pocket.

They had it out at last the next day. "I'd just as soon," he told his father. His father picked the lamp up off the kitchen table and carried it into the parlor. Buck followed. Oh boy, he thought, in the good room—in *die gute Stube*. He would make, he thought, as big a deal as he possibly could. He made up his mind, sitting down, to tell his old man where to get off at. He figured the old man would call Thurston in too, just to witness, but he heard Thurston go upstairs.

"I don't want to talk no more about Braeder," the old man said.

"I don't care what you say. I told you what I thought about giving them the plot. It still goes for me. You laid all the blame on me with that. I'm not forgetting that, just so you know." The old man rubbed his eyes. His hands were still dirty from working, still wearing his collarless work shirt, his coveralls. Tomorrow was Saturday, so he needed a shave.

"What am I going to do with you, Oskar?"

"Nothing."

"What?"

"Nothing. I'll do it myself."

"Braeder," the old man said, "this graduating from school."

"I said I wouldn't say I'm sorry to Hoffman. Even if there was any chance, not no more with Braeder and all." His father looked at him for a long time, closed his eyes finally, looked again. Buck held himself, did not flinch.

"I can't have this," the old man said. "I can't have you, you curse all the time, you smoke them cigarettes, you say going to a party, then drinking schnapps—"

"You drink schnapps," Buck said.

"I should strap you!" his father said.

"Just you try it once," Buck said. His father stood up, and he stood up, but he knew he could not make himself strike his father. His father did not move to touch him, but Buck could have done nothing to prevent him if he had.

"I can't live with you this way," he said at last.

"I'm going anyway," Buck said. "All you want is bossing me. The hell with it. You want me to work the farm, you want me not to drink, that. I'm getting away."

"Don't do that," his father said.

"I will too! You never . . . you never once said something good about me. I ain't staying here to dig up damn potatoes all my life. Eat, sleep, kick the damn bucket. I'm getting away. I mean it."

"Oskar," his father said as he walked out of the parlor.

"You'll see!" Buck said. If it had not been night, if there had been a way, a place to go, he would have continued on out of the house. All there was was to go up the stairs and go to bed. Thurston was naturally still awake, waiting to talk to him. He had been listening. He heard it all clear as a bell.

"Oskar?"

"You blame it on me too, don't you?"

"For Georgie? I don't. I heard what you said. Go down and say you're sorry before he goes to bed."

"Are you kidding or something? I meant what I said. I'm getting out of here. Tomorrow. The only way I'm ever coming back here is dead." Buck got into bed. He felt really good for the first time since the cemetery, watching George Braeder be buried. He would go down to Evansville, see that guy for a tryout—maybe

176

he could play outfield, where they didn't have to field bunts with the runner coming down on you with his cleats out to cut your hands off. Or Chicago. He could hobo his way to Chicago, find a job easy.

"I think you don't really mean it, Oskar," his brother said.

"Wait till morning. Don't hold your breath waiting on me to come back. I mean it."

"Even if you do—" Thurston started to say.

"Even, hell, I will!"

"Even if you do, though. Go. Say you're sorry to him. Please."

"I'll think some about it." Then they were silent, and he thought his brother had fallen asleep.

"You ain't got no money. What are you gonna do to eat and all?" Thurston said.

"I can do a lot of stuff. I can play baseball at Evansville if that character's still there. I can get a job playing music somewhere. I'm the best musician in this county, and you know it. Everybody knows it. Mechanic's work," Buck said, "I can fix any machine that moves. They're crying for mechanical people in places like Chicago and Hammond, where they build the railroad engines. Berntson's uncle works in the railroad shops in Hammond."

"Maybe you just could," Thurston said.

"The one thing you won't catch me at is digging spuds out of the same ground they plant you in."

"I couldn't," Thurston said. "Farming's what I know, I guess."

What Buck Hansen was thinking of, at the age of eighteen, was how big the world was. All of a sudden, Goshen was nothing. He could go to Evansville, Hammond, Chicago. He could go anywhere in the world he damn pleased! "Thurston," he said; he was going to tell his brother he could get work on the ore boats on the Great Lakes if he wanted, or hobo to California and ship out, hobo all the way around the world, if he wanted. But his brother was asleep, so he turned over on his side and slept himself.

The next morning was the morning of the day he was to have graduated from Goshen Township Consolidated High School. He did not leave that day. He got up, like always, with Thurston when the old man yelled from the foot of the stairs, and he helped with the milkers, and he put in a day's work. The same the next day.

But he was figuring. He decided on Hammond, on seeing Berntson's uncle for a job in the railroad shops. The next day he asked the old man to stake him.

"I guess not," his father said. "I thought you was all over that foolishness."

"Oh no," Buck said, "I'm going. I can go without your helping me if I have to. All I'm asking for is a loan. You'll get it back every penny. It ain't like you don't have it, either. Fifty bucks. Twenty bucks. I can get the train then."

"I guess not," his father said. "I ain't got money for no boy running away from his home. No sir." It was about as close as Buck came to crying about it. He stood in front of the old man in the kitchen. Thurston was out on the mud porch, listening. The old man just looked at him. He knew, short of hitting him, there was nothing going to change the set of his eyes, mouth, jaw. There was nothing Buck could do but go. And he knew his father would not weep if he went. He knew he would not hit him. He could not hit his father.

"Why won't you do nothing for me?" Buck said to his father. "You got the first damn dime you got off the boat with hidden away someplace here."

"I ain't listening to you. You don't know how to talk to your father," his father said. He turned his back on Buck, but did not leave the kitchen.

"Okay, Pa," Buck said. "You keep your money hid away so no gypsies steal you blind some night. I'll make it okay myself. It's a cold day in hell you'll see me back here. When I come back—if I ever come back you'll see. Thanks for nothing."

"I ain't listening," is all the old man would say. When he left, lugging the wicker suitcase that had lain in a closet since Buck could remember, he just walked out past him, sitting at the kitchen table, on outside. He was damned if he would so much as ask if his brother could drive him to town in the wagon. He left the yard, reached the mailbox, before Thurston caught up with him. It struck him, as he watched Thurston coming, that he had not seen his brother run so fast in a long time. If it had been the old man coming after him, he was mad enough, he would have hit him with the suitcase (he knew as he thought it that he would not. He could not strike his father—because he was his father). His brother was huffing, had to swallow and shake his head before he could get it out.

"Come on back, Oskar," he said. "Don't run off from him like this."

"Bunk," Buck said. "Him and Hoffman are the same kind. They should of been born Amish, they'd be happier. I'll send you a letter from Hammond if you want." His brother touched his shoulder.

"You break his heart, Oskar," he said.

"That's his tough luck. You heard, not even money for the train. So I'll hobo. If you were smart you'd get out too." He turned to go. His brother grabbed his shirt. "Leggo me, you jerk!" Buck said.

"I should smack you one."

"You ain't big enough. Try it and see. I'm sorry, I didn't mean that." Thurston let go of him. "You got any money you can let me loan?"

"I ain't helping you any in this."

"Okay," Buck said. He started on the road. "Stay here with him. They'll plow you under with the potato tops one year."

"When you coming back?" His brother did not come after him, did not go beyond the mailbox.

"When hell freezes over!" Buck said. "When I'm rich and famous, maybe, so I can throw it in his dumb face!"

So how was he to know the old man would die in less than four years? Die of some cancer in his stomach. He couldn't eat, Thurston wrote, so they kept him alive in the hospital by feeding him through a tube in his rectum—beer they fed him on until he died. Thurston wrote, a scrawl like a child's. The old man did not talk about Buck, but Thurston knew he would like to see him. Come back and see him, Thurston wrote, before he goes. But Buck was thinking about getting married, in the army, stationed way to hell and gone at Fort Sill, Oklahoma, and could not have gotten away for love nor money, even if he had had the money.

My Aunt Marie had had time to prepare something a little special for us—*rockersaltav skinka, lut fisk, cardamom kaka, pepperkakar,* the ever-present *limpa* bread, lingonberries . . . how long, I wonder, did it take her to make her husband's traditions her own? I watched my father as we sat to table, waiting for, expecting, wanting his small, loud show of appreciation, his naming of dishes, the winks, the rolling of the head as he tasted each in order, but it did not come. He sat without a word, endured my uncle's prayer (I tried to pray with him, make it mine, the way I would sing along with the car radio, only a word or two behind in a song I did not know), ate all he was given, but asked for no second helpings.

He spoke during the meal only when spoken to. He did not look at us. He chewed, swallowed, stopped from time to time to fix his eyes on nothing somewhere out in the darkened parlor, at my back. Once he set down his fork and simply sat with one hand in his lap, the other on the table, mouth closed on the half-chewed morsel, looking beyond me into the parlor, as if trying to catch something threatening to move.

"Have more *skinka*," Aunt Marie said.

"I guess not," he said. "No thank you, Marie."

"You can't get such ham in the town I bet," she said.

"I'll have some more, please," I said. I thought he would be pleased, even proud of me, to see me take to this alien food that was our heritage, but he seemed not to notice. And I spoke, in part, to take her attention. I knew he did not want to talk. "It's real good," I said. My aunt nodded as she served me, as if to give, with the gesture, her authoritarian approval of what could be only a speculation of taste on my part.

We finished (for dessert there were the spicy *pepperkakar*, washed down with my aunt's egg coffee, the coffee poured from a large, enameled pot, the pot decorated with gaudy, crowing roosters, Swedish folk signs of domestic good fortune), and my aunt cleared and began to wash the dishes, and my uncle got the crockery schnapps bottle from the narrow pantry. He put out two glasses, poured his own, then hesitated over my father's.

"You like a touch?"

"As long as you are," my father said. My uncle drank half his at a toss, but my father's sat untouched before him on the table. My uncle stretched, sighed, as a man who has done a good day's work will sigh, though my uncle had worked only the afternoon, after our return from the cemetery. His sigh, his arms out-stretched, broke my father's mood. He looked at his brother.

"Another day," my father said. He got his cigarettes out.

"I'll say," my uncle said. "What'd you two do all afternoon? I didn't see you where I was."

"Poked around," my father said.

"We were in town for a while," I said—we had called my sister again. My father had called her while I waited outside the telephone exchange office. He did not tell me what they said to each other, but it was a long call, much longer than the one from the tourist cabins north of Chicago. "And then we walked all around my dad's old stomping grounds. His name's on the war memorial in town too." My uncle smiled.

"Is that for a fact?" he said.

"Thurston," my father said, "those were pretty good days, weren't they?" It was a question; he was not sure. It was a question.

"What days is that?" my uncle said.

"Here, when we were kids. We walked all over town. I don't recognize half of it, or else I don't remember, I don't know. What I remember of it, all those years, they were some good times for all of us."

"I seen some since is worse. It wasn't no paradise, though, for sure." My father lit his Pall Mall, reached out and took his glass of schnapps, pulled his chair up closer to the table.

"Really though," my father said. "You think back on it, it was a pretty good life." He smiled, as if he were that instant thinking back, knowing the goodness again.

"I think you remember pretty much what you want, I mean, a fella does." I noticed my aunt had stopped her activity; she stayed at the sink, her hands in the hot water with the supper dishes, but she had stopped working to watch and listen. I wonder, now, how she could have known where it was leading.

"I know what you mean," my father said. He was no longer smiling. "And I still say they were good days for us. Us. You, me, the old man too. I know what you mean, all right, but that's the bunk. I remember it all pretty clearly, and we lived a damn good life."

"You go on believe what you want," Uncle Thurston said.

"Don't give me that hooey—"

"It was hard times, lots of it," my uncle interrupted—he looked at my father, but I felt he spoke to me, that what he had to say was like the portfolio of pictures, the box of documents, something he wanted me to have. "We worked our tail off," he said, "even you when I could keep track where you run off to all the time."

"I worked just as hard—"

"I said, we all worked our tail off," my uncle went on, "and we didn't even have the electric or the toilet inside, that stuff. And it wasn't so good what you did to your pa, either." I turned to my father. To give him his turn. Aunt Marie took her hands out of the water, dried them on her apron.

"I think the old man understood why I had to go, once I was gone," my father said.

"That's what you say. Now. You didn't live with him no more, like I did. You weren't by when he was dying, either."

"I was in the goddamn army in Oklahoma," my father said.

181

He had lowered his head, his voice barely audible, as if my uncle had taken away the power to sit straight, speak forcefully.

"I'm damned!" my uncle said. I did not believe a man who walked so slow, who spoke so calmly and surely, would be able to move, speak that way. His fist struck the table, his voice boomed, without windup, warning. My aunt came close to his chair, behind him, as if he were a man subject to rare fits, and she must be close to restrain him if he were suddenly taken. My father sat back from the table.

"The hell with what you say, what you want me to say," Uncle Thurston said. "You think I'll say what ain't true because your boy sits here to listen?" I hunched on my chair, wishing to be tiny, invisible. "You know what you done to your own pa! You broke his *heart*, damn you! I'm sitting here, and I say I heard you curse him over more than once. Then you run away to be some big shot someplace, but you couldn't even come home when he's dying from the cancer! Don't give me none of your baloney you use to be a big businessman, Oskar," he said. And then the anger went out of him, as quickly as it had come, as he watched my father. He half smiled, shook his head. He noticed his wife close to him, smiled at her, as though apologizing, shook his head again. He drank off the rest of his schnapps, poured another.

"There were some good times, too," my father said.

"Sure, sure," Uncle Thurston said. "There was that. I don't forget some good things. It all works out okay for the best anyway, I guess. You got what you wanted. You're a big success now. Hell, you done better than anybody else in this place, that's sure too. Sometimes I talk too damn much." My father did not weep. His eyes shone as he spoke, as if he were about to weep, but he did not lose control of himself.

"What makes you think I'm a big success, brother?" my father said.

"Aw, look at you, big car and all," he said.

"That car's almost six years old. It's got a lien on it big enough to break your back," my father said. "They gutted me, Thurston," he said. "You're looking at a man's had it. The boy and I just came from Chicago, man there turned me down flat. Brother, I'm about the biggest failure ever came out of north Indiana, bar none." He drank his schnapps, coughed, reached for the bottle.

"What are you telling me here now," Uncle Thurston said.

"Like I said man!" He tried to laugh, could not do it. "Oh, it's truth time," he said. "Truth time. Take a good look, brother.

Here I sit. I'm stony broke but for what I've got in my wallet, Thurston." He looked up at Aunt Marie. "I'm telling it straight from the horse's mouth, I swear. Nobody knows it better than me." He drank more schnapps. "This stuff gets better the more you drink. No bull, though. Irene," he said, "you know, that *woman,* you call her, she's kicking the bucket this very second for all I know up in a nuthouse. I swear it."

"You didn't say nothing when you called," my uncle said.

"A man's got a little pride left, brother. Well here I am. Take a good long look. Broke, in debt up to my ears and then some. Hell, Thurston, I'm on the run. I swear it! There's a kike skip chaser probably looking your address up this very minute. If a Jew shows up on your doorstep asking for me, you don't know where I'm gone. I'm forever grateful if you'll remember that and act accordingly."

"How come you came here, Oskar?"

"He asked on the phone if there was trouble," Aunt Marie said. Now, this moment, here is the girl I had seen in the photographs—it was just a matter of getting the truth, to her. She would always know what to do.

"Beats me all to hell," my father said. He was smiling now. "Broke, in debt, Irene about to go, carting the boy here all over hell's half-acre—"

"Why doesn't he have any clothes?" my aunt said. "I looked. I cleaned upstairs today, there isn't clothes, nothing for him."

"Oh, lady," my father said.

"You told me all there is?" Uncle Thurston said.

"Couldn't if I wanted to. Wouldn't if I could. Not to save my damn life, brother."

"Come on, Oskar."

"Buck's the name, remember? Let's say his mother didn't exactly give me the official blessing when we shoved off." They looked at me, my father, Uncle Thurston, Aunt Marie—I might have been a spirit, an essence, materialized without warning or welcome in the kitchen.

"I'm having a good time with my dad," I said quickly. But only my father seemed to care.

"You took your boy from his mother?"

"This is trouble," my aunt said.

"He's all I got left, brother! Hear that? He's enjoying himself. We get along swell together."

"I guess I won't never understand you," my uncle said.

"I guess not for sure," my father said.

"You can't stay here and get us in this," my aunt said.

"How do you do something like that?" Uncle Thurston said.

"I lie," my father said. "An old road salesman can lie his way up one side of you and down the other."

"I'm helping," I said. Nobody was listening to me. They talked on, my uncle trying to get a sense of the whole, the feel of his brother's life, his situation. My aunt said little, but in the gaps, returned always to the fact: we could not stay with them. My father, I suppose, told them no more than what they knew by then. Until it was time to go to bed. My aunt had already left the room.

"Don't count me out yet, brother," he said. "A liar always has one more up his sleeve, just in case. I'm not dead yet."

"How's that? What are you talking about?"

"Hold on to your hat, mister," he said. "Old Buck's got a live one waiting out for him on the East Coast. A woman I'm talking about. I hope to tell you. I've got me a gal out there, young, looks good enough to knock your eye out, money of her own. You wait, Thurston. When she's got me on my feet I'll bring her around for you to see, if Marie doesn't object, of course."

"You got some other woman too?" my uncle said.

"You bet. A man's got to scramble to get a little happiness in this life, brother." My uncle shook his head. "You take my word for it," my father said.

"I don't want to hear any more," Uncle Thurston said. He got up to leave. "Think some time what you're doing to your boy, Oskar."

"He who hesitates is lost," my father said. "I'd give you the Swedish for that, but I can't for the life of me remember."

"Good night," my uncle said.

"And a good night to you too. Let's hit the hay, son," he said to me. Upstairs I waited until we were in our beds.

"Is he mad at you, Dad?"

"Huh? Search me. Get to sleep. We're getting out of here early. I don't want to try and outstare Marie over breakfast."

"What did Jane say?"

"About what?"

"I mean, are we going home tomorrow? Does she want me to come home now?"

"You know, sonny," he said, "right now I really don't have the vaguest what I'm going to do. And to tell you the God's truth, I don't give a damn. Night-night." We slept, and I woke, having to

184

go to the toilet. I crept past my sleeping father, down the stairs. When I came out of the bathroom, my uncle called to me.

"Oskar? That's you," he said, "I thought first it was your pa."

"I had to go bathroom."

"Come in here once." I joined him in the kitchen, where he sat in the dark at the table. I could make out the bathrobe he wore, his felt slippers. He took hold of my arm.

"It's still nighttime," I said.

"Yeah. Listen to me once, now. What I said to your pa, all that, that isn't everything, you know," he said.

"I know." I wanted to be back in the warm bed upstairs.

"It's important you listen to me, boy. I don't want you getting the wrong idea from what I say. Your pa was one of the best kids in this county, see?"

"Yes."

"He was about the smartest kid I ever saw, all my life. I'm lots older, but I was scared, almost, of him, he was so smart when he was a kid, see? He plays all kinds of musical instruments, you know."

"I know."

"He was about good enough at baseball to get paid for playing."

"He told me."

"Your pa's right, for damn sure, too," my uncle said to me. "There was plenty of good times. Back when we was two kids and all. You listening to me good?"

"I'm listening."

"Don't forget none of that. He's made trouble for your mother, that, but he could of been a hell of a good man, see? Okay?"

"I won't forget it," I said. He let go my arm, and I started for the stairs.

"Boy?" I stopped to listen to him. "Is there anything you want to tell me about this trip you're on with your pa? Is there some trouble he didn't tell me about?"

"No," I said, and I went upstairs, back to sleep. You had to scramble, my father had said. You had to lie. If he needed it, I would lie for him. Whatever it took.

VIII

East, toward Lillie. East to Long Island. Maumee, Elyria, Berea, Youngstown, then the gray ribbon of the turnpike, bypassing Pittsburgh, Carlisle, Harrisburg, turning north, Allentown and Bethlehem, then Newark, Manhattan (a brief, choked dash across the heart of the city), and Long Island: Queens, Jamaica, Mineola. And Lillie at last.

"We're not going home," I said.

"Says who."

"Because if the sun rises in the east, then we're going east because the sun's in my eyes, and going home is west."

"You're a real mine of information, aren't you?"

"I know where all the states are on the map and everything. Indiana is north, up on the map. South is down. If you pretend

186

you're standing in the middle, then east is on your right hand, and Wisconsin is left."

"That's real useful if you're lost in the woods, provided you can find a map to stand on, huh?"

"You can follow the sun, because it always goes up in the east and comes down in the west. At night you can follow the North Star."

"How do you find it if it's cloudy?"

"I don't know yet. Maybe there's still something else."

"I wonder," my father said.

"But we aren't going home, are we? I mean to Mom."

"Not just yet. Have you got ants in your pants or something? I heard you say yourself you were having a good time."

"I just wondered why, I guess."

"Trust me," he said. "Can you trust your old man?" He was not ready, not able, to talk about it yet, explain it to me.

We drove. In the heat of the day, we were often silent for long periods. My father sprawled behind the wheel, shifting his left foot about to relieve cramps, smoking steadily, keeping the Chrysler on our side of the line with only two fingers on the steering wheel, hanging them there, really, on the bottom of the wheel, his shirt open at the neck, sleeves rolled back. I counted cows and horses and sheep and pigs, counted cars (always waiting for the green 1946 Studebaker, never seeing one—they seemed all red, or maroon, or brown or black that model year of 1946). I listened to the radio, hummed or sang along with Perry Como, Georgia Gibbs, Jo Stafford. I climbed over the back of the seat to poke among the few books, touch the keys of the typewriter; he did not like this: "Son, will you not screw things up back there? That's my life I've got packed up there. Take some of those business cards if you want something to play with. Come on up here, I'll give you a pencil and you can draw pictures or practice your writing or something, okay?"

Or I dreamed, half dozing. Of course I thought of my mother, my brother and sister, her children. I thought of them often, always, but they existed statically, locked into the previous existence I had left behind when I went with my father. My mother still wore her housecoat, old shoes, cutoff stockings rolled down below her ankles. She still knelt on the bare floors of the new Cramer Street house, wielding a razor blade, laying open the cartons containing the relics of a yet more previous existence. She stopped in her work from time to time, to sigh with exhaustion, to wipe at her brow or blow a stray hair away from her eyes, to glare in frustrated anger at a universe that gave her so much trouble to shape it. My brother Arn still wore his khaki uniform shirt, the shadow of the buck sergeant's chevrons still on the sleeves, the crescents of sweat in his armpits, the pillar of sweat in the middle of his back. He sucked unconsciously at his teeth, struck bitterly defiant poses, hands on hips, feet wide apart, breaking them only to turn aside to spit or swallow a curse. Jane remained in her basement apartment, wrapped, armored in her robe, feeding on cigarettes and sudden, private insights, keeping watch over her oblivious, playing children, her mind's eyes serene in the midst of all those pictures of dead Richard Hackbarth.

Oh, I thought of them always, but for them, the time of this trip, this flight, they held no life for me. They were past. The highways of Ohio, the turnpike, were a tired, deliberate present, a strength gathering, an assessment taking in preparation for the future. The future was Lillie Broadfoot, Mineola, Long Island, New York.

We did not stop the first night, because, he said, we could make better time on the road at night. His money, I think, was going faster than he had thought it would. He dared not let his money run out before he had his chance with Lillie Broadfoot. I curled up on the seat, covered with his jacket, slept fitfully. I woke in the middle of our first tunnel on the Pennsylvania Turnpike, just beyond Donegal.

I do not know what woke me. I woke, and the car was filled with the exhaust fumes that lingered in the long, low tunnel through the mountain. And the car was filled with the pale wash of electric light from the globes in the tunnel ceiling overhead. I woke, the exhaust fumes in my nose, my lungs, and saw my father, strangely illuminated, both hands gripping the wheel, his face set, as if he meant to ram the car into some immovable object in the road ahead of us. I heard the roaring of the Chrysler's engine echo against the tunnel walls. The noise increased, and I sat up to look out, saw a semitrailer coming toward us, its lights flicking as it lumbered through the tunnel. It seemed to fill the tunnel like a barrier. It loomed, it grew, as we came closer. The roaring noise, the stench of automobile exhaust intensified, and as the truck passed us the Chrysler vibrated. I cried out.

And in the instant of my crying out we passed out of the tunnel—the noise ceased, the light left the interior of the car, the air came fresh from the open wings. "Jesus, boy," my father said. "You want to get us crashed?" I looked at him, but it was too dark now to see his face well. I looked at the glowing instrument lights on the dash, saw the sudden sharpness and dying of the glowing end of his cigarette. I touched the fabric of upholstery, picked up his suit jacket. It was safe. It was all right. I was with my father, on the Pennsylvania Turnpike, headed for Long Island. I could lay back down on the front seat and go to sleep again.

We stopped the next afternoon, to complete our preparations. It was near Allentown. We bathed, and the Chrysler was washed and waxed, and he bought me some clothes to wear to Lillie's. We must look our best, he said, if we did not want to send everything up the spout with Lillie Broadfoot. He meant his life.

"Am I getting through to you at all?" he said. "Tell me if I'm confusing you, it's important to me that you understand."

"I won't let the cat out of the bag. I promise," I said.

"That's not what I mean. I know you won't say anything that's going to futz us. I mean *why*. Do you understand *why*?"

"How can you get married if you already are?"

"Irene?"

"The second wife. Mom said she doesn't like her."

"Your mother had no business saying that about her, but that's neither here nor there. No, I can't get married right now. But if I'm not married anymore, later, then I can get married to Lillie Broadfoot, right? Right?"

"Are you having a divorce again?"

"Something like that. Okay. Yes, like that."

"What's a divorce, really?"

"Stick to the subject, will you? I want to marry this woman, boy. I need her, see?"

"Why?"

"This isn't the time or the place to go into it all. Skip the details for a second. Are you paying attention good?"

"I'm listening."

"Like I told your sister. I'm forty-nine years old, see? You know how old that is? It's old enough, believe me. You'll see when you're forty-nine. I'm not saying it's ancient, but it's getting along a little bit. I'm not young anymore, can you see that? Okay. If I don't marry Lillie Broadfoot, then I don't have anything worth getting old for. I've got to have something. You don't just live, you know, son."

"I don't get it exactly," I said.

"No." We crossed the bridge, and we were in New York. "Listen," he said. "She's a wonderful gal. She was married common-law to some screwball made her rue the day."

"Did she have a divorce too?"

"No. He was killed in service, which was a blessing in disguise if you hear her tell it."

"Like Richard Hackbarth."

"Like? Jane's husband, that's right. So she's been over the road a little herself. She's had a damn tough row to hoe of it, I'll tell you. She's got a son about your age too, you know."

"Will I get to see him?"

"No. I've never seen him. He lives with an aunt or some such, down in North Carolina." I was disappointed. There seemed to be nothing for me in it. "She was running around with some Air Force yahoo before I met her. She broke it off after we got together."

"How did you meet her?"

"How? I was out here on business, I guess you'd say. We just happened to get together is all. That sort of thing happens, you know. I met her brother first, as a matter of fact."

"How old is he?"

"Old? Oh. Not your age if that's what you're thinking. Hell no, he's nearly my age. But you'll like him. He's a hell of a swell fella. He thinks the world of his sister too. I think maybe he has a piece of her business, for that matter. You'll see." He waited for me to ask more questions, and when I did not, he said, "So how do you like Manhattan? Did you ever think you'd be in New York City someday?"

"It's neat," I said. "It's like some pictures I saw once of it."

"More Jews than you can shake a stick at," he said, "and boogies. If we get a chance I'll take you on a spin through Harlem. It's worse than Chicago or Detroit." I was hoping we would get to go to the top of the Empire State Building. But we were in a hurry to get to Lillie, on Long Island.

"Here we go," my father said. It was a disappointment to me at first. He had spoken of Lillie Broadfoot, at such length, in such terms and tone, that I was sure even the setting in which she was to be found must surely be lavish, exotic, somehow sparkling and special. I kept waiting for the sudden change that must come over the top of the next hill, around the next bend in the road. The grass, the trees, surely they would be a deeper, darker green. The mottled sky stretching out over Long Island Sound would break instantly blue, set off only by tufts of fleecy white clouds floating here and there in some artistic arrangement. The wind off the

190

sound would cease magically, the air change to a bakery richness, the omnipresent, rotting odor of salt water purged miraculously. And the house—I thought we were going directly to her house—visions of the house were beyond me (it was enough that nature should have made a locale sufficient to the glory of her promise for my father, for us), but, surely, I felt as he stopped the car, it should not have been, could not be this.

On a side street, a residential street, we stopped in front of Lillie Broadfoot's beauty shop. It was early afternoon, just after lunch, and she would be hard at work, my father said. It was only an ordinary street, with some few small trees, and the beauty shop was no proper shop, but an ordinary wooden duplex, converted to a shop. The white boards needed scraping and repainting. The sign swung in the breeze, a sign such as lawyers or dentists may once have called a shingle. The sign was not professionally painted. *Moderne Beauty Salon*. Hours, days of the week. There was a huge picture window, but it was covered by Venetian blinds that looked undusted from outside. In seeing it I felt disappointed; I would have been satisfied by . . . oh, perhaps neon lights, ornamental palm trees, music piped outside, I cannot say. There was a parking lot of sorts, the lawn peeled off, replaced with crushed gravel that crunched under our shoes as we walked. We parked at the curb because the lawn lot was full, her customers parked in a fanlike pattern facing the duplex, the way cars park at a roadhouse or a resort dance hall.

"Be a good boy for me," he said as we got out of the car. He carried a gift-wrapped bottle of Shalimar perfume carefully, so as not to drop it or disturb the bow.

I was disappointed. Lillie Broadfoot's son would not be here, and her beauty shop was an ordinary, weathered house in Mineola, and the sun kept moving in and out of the clouds, changing the cast of the day, at random, from light and clear and cheerful to a sodden-smelling dullness that must have depressed my father as well. But we walked between the customers' parked cars, over the noisy gravel, to the entrance on the side, and a new quality came into him, like some aura or essence emanating from Lillie Broadfoot, making him a new and still different kind of man as I watched.

His walk became a swagger, his shoulders stiffened and squared (he puts the bottle of Shalimar behind his back—it will be a surprise), his jaw lifted—no, I cannot grasp this with details; it is too faint, too subtly complete. Say only that this is not the crisp

191

facade constructed to vanquish Mr. Cal Rocker, not the brief, intense flare of frantic anger that explodes in the faces of other motorists, clumsy gas station attendants, a brother who will not lie with and for him to make even a temporary peace. The suicidal depression of my mother's Cramer Street house, the whining insistence of the Sans Souci Bar, the meek humility of an early morning departure from Goshen, all are past modes, moods, identities of the past. I watch him approach, as he opens the door of the Moderne Beauty Salon, a possible permanence, a future, and the resolution that animates him is the knowledge that he must win it if he is to live.

He swings open the door, and a tiny bell tinkles overhead. I am disappointed, reminded of penny-candy mama-and-papa grocery stores in Milwaukee. There is nothing in it, I believe, for me.

The bell tinkled over our heads, lost in the noise of the shop's activity. It was a busy, functional beauty shop. There was a whirring, a steady sound of blowing, heating, from the row of egg-shaped hair dryers, a row of women's laps, magazines being held, stockinged legs extending into the central aisle of the shop. It was warmer than outside, the air heated and moistened by the dryers. It was like walking into a hospital ward, an impression of nurses, Lillie Broadfoot's assistants, walking, quick and purposeful, dressed in white uniform dresses, white shoes. They were young women, three or four of them, and they did not seem to notice us, did not look our way as my father closed the door behind us, and the tiny bell tinkled again. They were young, trim women, dressed in white like nurses, their hair done in elaborate arrangements, their lashes, brows, lips starkly defined with makeup. The shop smelled strongly of sweet wave set, of the sour neutralizing solutions used in permanent waves, of the simmered smell of drying hair. I reached for my father's hand—I remembered walking alone once in the quiet, empty basement corridors of my school, opening a door, being suddenly in the boiler room with its seared air, the roar of furnaces, the face of a janitor who only looked back at me without speaking.

But my father had turned away, to the high reception counter just to the right of the door, behind which sat Lillie Broadfoot, absorbed in her appointment schedule book. I went quickly to his side. I was not tall enough to see over the counter. He leaned over the counter, still holding the gift-wrapped perfume behind his back, as if it were flowers or a decorated cake, and he made a joke. "Vash my heinie here, lady?" he said.

I heard her say, "Buck!" She laughed, then stood up, and

192

they kissed, lightly, over the reception counter. They kissed like children, leaning forward awkwardly from the waist to meet, their lips in exaggerated puckers. She leaned back, and they grinned at each other, and she said "Good God, why don't you ever call a person," and she took his hand and came out from behind the reception desk. My father moved around me, his extended arm passing over my head, as they walked like two children holding hands over a fence. I thought they might walk away, through the shop into some back room to talk in private, leave me alone in the shop. I saw a woman seated on a stool, her head over a sink, towel draped around her shoulders, one of Lillie's assistants rinsing her hair with a spray from a short rubber hose. The woman sputtered, shook her head.

"How's my gal?" my father was saying. He reached back with his gift-holding hand to touch me, bring me with them.

"I thought sure you'd call me, Buck!" Lillie was saying. She wore a white uniform dress, like her assistants, her eyes, brows, lips so defined, so brightly, sharply marked that at first I could not see her green eyes. Her hair, piled high on her head, was jet black. She was quite tall, her feet in white shoes. My father turned her to introduce me. I do not think she had seen me until then.

"Here's one surprise for you," he said. "This is my youngest boy. Oskar's his name."

"Buck, he's a doll," she said. I waited for her to stoop, to put out her hand, but she did not.

"Pleased to meet you, Lillie," I said. She laughed, and said again to my father that I was a doll, and I followed them to a leather-covered sofa, a low, round coffee table covered with tattered magazines in front of it. I stood by and watched them until she got back up to go on with her work, having unwrapped her perfume. They held hands all the while, my father's tanned, large fingers interlaced with her very pale fingers. Her nails were thickly lacquered, the largest solitary diamond I ever saw on her ring finger. I stood, watching and listening. She never looked at me, that day, that night, all the while we were in Mineola, unless I spoke to her, or my father called her attention to me. Her future, as it turned out, lay as promisingly in my father as his did in her, and neither of them could distract themselves long with me.

"Honestly, when you called me from Indiana I was sure you wouldn't get here for at least a week, Buck," she said. This was the first I knew he had called her from the telephone exchange in Goshen. It was not, is not, surprising he should have, after what my sister had said to him.

"I don't fool around, Lil," he said. "Christ, it's good to see you."

"Ben's going to just die," she said. "I've got to call him this minute. We'll have to have a little celebration," she said.

"How soon can you get the hell out of here where we can talk?" my father said. An hour, no more than an hour and a half, Lillie Broadfoot said. Already an assistant stood a few feet away, smiling, bored, trying to get the boss's attention. I touched my father's shoulder.

"I think she wants to talk to Lillie Broadfoot," I said. Lillie turned to her and the assistant's smile deepened, apologetic.

"Oh my God," Lillie said. "Buck, sit here, honey, I'll make it as fast as I can," and she was up, away with the assistant whose smile had evaporated. I sat down next to my father on the sofa.

"What'd I tell you?" he said.

"What?"

"Her, Lillie. Isn't she the nuts?"

"I guess so. I mean, I don't know what you mean. She's pretty nice, I guess."

"It's a good thing I got you the hell out of there," he said, "you're starting to talk like your uncle. Here, read yourself a magazine or something." I picked up the magazine, opened it, but did not try to read or look at the pictures.

"She's real nice," I said.

"What?"

"Lillie's real nice."

"We'll talk about it some other time." He was still irritated at my failure to give him, immediately, what he needed. And he was too busy watching Lillie Broadfoot move about the shop. It may have been the first, though not the last time he regretted having me with him when so much was at stake here. I hid behind my open magazine and watched.

I was embarrassed for him, because he was not. He unbuttoned his jacket, smoothed its lay, crossed one leg over the other, lit a Pall Mall, striking a posture in readiness for Lillie Broadfoot whenever she might look our way. When she was busy, he held his head up, his eyes on the ceiling, pretending a distracted meditation, a peace and contentment, unflappable. But he kept an eye on her, always. When she looked our way, he smiled, tightened his mouth, lifted his chin to diminish his dewlap, expanded his chest. She would smile, a quick show of her many small teeth. Once she waved, wiggled her fingers (the enormous solitary diamond), and my father winked at her.

194

It was a busy shop. There were women in a sedate row under the egg-shaped dryer heads, their crossed ankles visible to me in a row, like women waiting for a shoe salesman to come and kneel at their feet. There were women in elevated chairs, waiting for the dryers, their heads armored with metal curlers, strange looking without their halos or caps of hair. In one chair a woman sat to have her rolled hair saturated with a neutralizing rinse, Lillie's assistant dribbling it on from a bottle; its smell cut across the room, through the smoke of my father's cigarette to me. In another, an assistant made short, chopping motions with a straight razor, as if she intended to decapitate the customer, but must first cut through her protective hair. In another, Lillie Broadfoot herself combed out a lady's set, stroking delicately with the broad, black comb, lifting the curled edge of the woman's hair, as though she was afraid it would collapse, fall straight if left untended. When Lillie Broadfoot bent or stretched I could see the outline of her brassiere across her tapered back.

She greeted new customers at the door (the tiny bell tinkled), answered the phone, wrote in her appointment book, collected money that went into a drawer behind the reception counter. She came over to us once. "Are you getting all antsy?" she said to my father.

"Take your time," he said.

"Hello doll baby," she said to me.

"Cat got your tongue?" my father said when she had gone, squeezing his extended hand before she let it go.

"I couldn't think of anything to say."

"I hope to Christ you're not having a sulk," he said.

The dryers whooshed, the faucets splashed, hoses sprayed. Women of all ages, their hair combed out, paid Lillie Broadfoot and left, most covering their new hair with scarves before presenting it to the damp salt breeze off Long Island Sound. Women came in, checked in with Lillie Broadfoot at the counter. Often they had to wait. They sat near my father and me, often glancing with interest or surprise at the well-dressed man and the small boy who looked at his shoes or his fingers rather than meet their eyes. But my father did not notice them. He watched Lillie Broadfoot.

(Yes, I can smell it now, the acrid neutralizing solutions, the faintly scorching smell of drying hair. I can hear the egg-shaped dryers, the sharp spray of water from the nozzled end of a rubber hose. I see women, their dresses covered with towels, heads crowned with mounds of shampoo, white-uniformed, nurselike

195

assistants with firm, nyloned legs running down to white crepe-soled shoes, massaging their scalps. I see the outlines of their brassieres through the backs of their dresses, the lines above their hems where their slips end. I peep over the rim of my dummy magazine, to look, full and direct, into the eyes of a waiting customer—I shrink, from her, the smells, sounds, the memory, embarrassed for my father who does not seem to see anything in this alien place but Lillie Broadfoot. Don't, I told myself, have a sulk!)

"I called Ben," she said when she came, ready to go, "he nearly fell off his chair when I told him you were here. He'll meet us up at my place."

"So how the hell is old Ben anyway?" my father said, and to me, "Come on, boy, don't dawdle." We followed her in the Chrysler, to the two-flat that was just an ordinary two-flat in Mineola, New York. She had gotten out of her car, looking back to smile at us, as we pulled up behind her. The white skirt of her uniform dress hiked up her thigh as she slipped out from behind the wheel.

"Can I pick 'em or can I pick 'em," my father said, but I could think of no answer for him.

"I'll give odds he's got a bottle of something up there waiting," she said, looking up at the second-floor windows.

"Wouldn't surprise me in the least," he said. They held hands going up the walk, up the porch stairs, where he had to let her go so she could get her key out. Ben Broadfoot was waiting upstairs for us. My father was his future too.

"I can't wait to get changed," Lillie said.

The afternoon-evening celebration of my father's arrival—what better, more fitting way to mark the end point of our flight, the furthest reach of my father's absurd aspiration, and my share in it? A calculated, impromptu party, laid on in haste by Benjamin Broadfoot, a quick investment as unsound as my father's hope of security, of survival. Some bottles of rye and bourbon, some Vichy water, some crackers and cheese spread . . . little enough to pay for the truth after their weeks, months of greedy anticipation. The fault lies . . . well, the fault lies in their seeing him, in him, no more nor less than he in them. Of the celebrants, who are either dead or scattered in final anonymity, only I saw the whole of it. Only I, of the living, cared, care enough to remember it.

I celebrate, my son, our celebration there in Lillie Broadfoot's upstairs flat in Mineola, New York, in the early

196

summer of 1946. We have laid to last rest a feasible present in Chicago, a rejected, lost past in Goshen, and there remains the futile clutching for a future, in the drunken, angry party that celebrates my father's unexpected arrival.

"You're just exactly the very man I was thinking about this morning!" says Ben Broadfoot as he snatches my father's hand.

"Let me go change," says Lillie. "I'll only be a minute."

"It's good to see you," says my father.

There is no coherence, except in the uneven, stumbling revelation of their mutual truth. There is detail, specification, limitation, but so often without total shape. The bustling beauty shop and the cheap flat sit on almost identical, nondescript side streets. The whoosh of dryers, the smell of lotions and lacquers and chemical solutions impinge on the sound of ice cubes rattling in highball glasses, the snap of a Ritz cracker in my teeth, the tickle of carbonated soda in my nostrils. The occasional questioning, uncertain looks I get from brother and sister Broadfoot superimpose, merge with the annoyed eyes of a lady waiting to have her hair done. The culmination, the end, begins with my father's "Here we go," over the crunching walk on crushed gravel to the side entrance of the Moderne Beauty Salon. It ends in the Mineola Municipal Police Station—no, ends finally with Sheldon Rotter, but the zenith is this celebration in honor of my father's having reached his destination. I am only a minor diversion, a minor irritation.

"This is my littlest boy," my father said to Ben Broadfoot. "He wanted to see what the country looks like, so I brought him along. I may just stick him on the train if it works out for me to stick around out here any length of time."

"How you doing, son?" Ben said to me.

"I'm having a good time with my dad."

"Boy, have I been doing some thinking since we talked, Buck," he said. Ben Broadfoot does not look at all like his sister. He may be younger or older. He is that uncertain age caused by disparate elements—he is bald, quite bald save for a neat low fringe as exact as a monk's tonsure, but clearly too young to be bald. Where Lillie is pale, he is tanned. Even his scalp is tanned, faintly freckled. The skin of his face is taut, tanned, but there is a tooth missing in front, a space where he picks with the tip of his tongue when he listens intently to my father. He wears clean, pressed wash pants, a short-sleeved shirt with the sleeves rolled up almost all the way. He is thin, but very muscled. His veins stand out strongly along his hands, round biceps, his lean forearms. His waist is as narrow as his sister's. He has a way of folding his arms across his chest as he sits, exaggerating the bulge of his biceps. His chin is very sharp, his Adam's apple prominent. When he swallows or chews, the planes of his face move from his recessed temples to the edge of his jaws. He wears soft moccasins on his feet.

"I've been doing some thinking myself," my father said.

"We've got to get our heads together here, now. I'm serious," says Ben Broadfoot. He has very thin lips, a very small mouth. "Let's us build something tall and cold here right off," he says. The rye and bourbon and Vichy are on a teacart that he rolls in front of my father. The ice cubes are heaped in a clear glass bowl. I watch them, as the celebration proceeds, until by the time I follow my father out to grieve with him, there is only a shallow, tepid puddle left in the bottom of the bowl. "Rye, right?" says Ben.

"I'll leave the bourbon to you backwoods people," says my father. And they laugh, joined by laughing Lillie, who has completed her change of clothes.

"You boys better not forget me." In place of the white uniform is a blouse as green as her eyes, a wide, black cinch belt with an ornamental buckle, a tight skirt of paler green. There are no shoes on her stockinged feet. The bangle bracelets on her wrists clink like chimes as she walks past me. There is a whisper of nylon as her thighs touch. She sits beside my father to take her drink, her white, diamond-ring hand in his. I am given a glass of Vichy that I am afraid to taste because Ben Broadfoot has fished the ice cubes out of the bowl with his fingers.

"Skoal," says my father.

"Here's to the future."

"Happy, happy," says Lillie.

"You're supposed to drink up when a man makes a toast, son," my father says, but they do not watch long enough to make me touch it to my lips.

"What have you heard about Levittown, Buck?" says Ben.

"Never heard of him. Christ, this tastes good!"

"Seriously?" says Ben. Lillie tucks one long leg up under her. "Then let me fill you in on what could be a real tremendous thing for the right people."

"I'm all ears," says my father, looking at Lillie Broadfoot.

Here follows the story of the great builder Levitt, as seen by the eyes of Benjamin Broadfoot, of North Carolina. The good things of the war, believes Ben Broadfoot, are far from over. V-J Day was a beginning, not an end. "How many vets would you guess at a rough estimate are gonna get married and buy one of them GI loan houses, Buck?"

"All I read about are the ones shooting their wives under the unwritten law," says my father. He does not want to listen. In time he will want to talk, but for now, with Pall Malls, rye and soda and ice, he wants to hold Lillie's hand, look at her, be looked at, rest, relax in this momentary haven.

"Millions," says Ben Broadfoot. Here follow the details of what will be done by the great builder Levitt. In the newspapers it is a housing shortage, but to Levitt, and men in the know, it is a bonanza. "A goddamn bonanza's waiting out there for them who can see it, Buck." There is the builder Levitt, there is a consortium of builders led by the builder Levitt, there is government financing, there will be a city where now is pasture, or crop land, here, on Long Island. "Right here on Long Island, I'm telling you!"

"More power to them," my father says.

"Wait'll you hear the rest of it, man." There will be a city, like none before it. "The whole gimmick is mass production, Buck." There will come crews, like small armies, bands of architects, to survey, draw the plans for houses, lay out the streets, the business districts, suburbs, the works. There will come convoys of bulldozers and earth-carriers to prepare the land, trenching machines, steam shovels, road graders. There will come platoons of cement layers and finishers to set the slab foundations, one after another. Behind them, keeping pace, will be carpenters, bricklayers, roofers, plasterers, cabinetmakers. There will work, side by side, the men to pave the streets, to lay sewer tile, to lay sidewalks and driveways. The houses will rise the way autos come off the assembly line in Detroit.

"Sounds good," says my father. "Don't wrap it, I'll eat it here."

"I'm serious now, Buck. Think of this just for a minute."

"Honey, my feet ache," he says to Lillie, who pours another drink.

"Get this now," says Ben. Everything will be worked out in advance. The population will be estimated, the number of children. "Think for a minute how many kids there's gonna be the next five, ten years, Buck, will you?" Schools will be placed strategically, complete with athletic fields. Recreation areas will be ordained. Business centers. "Your business won't be stuck all over here and there, Buck. No sir. All in one place. For a city maybe fifty thousand people. Think about that for a minute."

"I bet you won't believe me if I told you I came out here to forget my business for a while," my father says.

"Christ, I'm sorry," says Ben. "Here, let me fix that up for you. Hell, Lillie here can tell you, I'm all fired up on this thing. The public don't hardly know it yet, but man, this is the way it's gonna be. No kidding. Here, tell me if I didn't get it strong enough for you."

"Jes' fine," my father says.

"It's all Ben talks about, I swear, Buck," says Lillie.

"How's things going for you back home, Buck?" When he listens, Ben Broadfoot thinks with his tongue at the gap in his teeth. He leans forward slightly, arms muscularly folded across his chest. Lillie listens; she is a very good listener, her hand anchored in my father's. They listen, wait their turn at a future. My father lies consummately to them. He does not glance at me for a quick reassurance that I will keep quiet, swear to his lies with my silence—by now, by the time of Mineola, New York, he feels he can count on me, come what may.

"There's a lull right now. I'm in the process of settling back and taking a little stock of the situation before I decide which way to jump next," my father says. Ben unfolds his arms, rests his chin, after a score of vigorous, silent nods of affirmation, on his knuckles. Lillie freshens the drinks all around. My father sips, sinks appreciatively. "I can go any number of ways," he says. "I can sit tight there and ride it out, for instance, or I can sell out the whole shooting match and go elsewhere." Ben's eyes ignite. He shares his sister's green eyes. My father looks at Lillie. She squeezes his hand, answers his wink. "Or, for that matter, as one more alternative, I suppose I could get some capital together and expand in the vacuum we've got right now. Get set up for when it's over. That son of a bitch Truman won't be in forever, you know."

"You're in a position to do what you pretty much want to," says Ben Broadfoot. "You take this Levitt deal I was talking about for a minute." And we are told again of the great builder.

Who will blame Ben Broadfoot? He wants only what he has seen, what the business and financial sections of *The New York Times* hint at, what the *Wall Street Journal* treats cavalierly. He is a man for the mailing lists of insiders' tips, for newsletters that snickeringly reveal nascent trends, for coffee conversations with

200

men who turn first to the daily stock averages in the early editions. He is a man who, in a small North Carolina town, would have made something of himself. It will happen: generations of poor Piedmont farmers will inexplicably produce him—one indistinguishable from portraits of the family line, but somehow born with, not dissatisfaction, but simple romantic greed deeply buried in him, like a mustard seed. Frustrate him and he will become dark, brutal. Give him luck and he will own a sawmill or a garage or a farm implement franchise. But cut him loose, tear him away from what he understands and you produce a Ben Broadfoot.

"My brother was in the war," I interrupt—he speaks of what the war has done for us all—"my brother was in the Air Corps. Were you in the war?"

"Merchant Marine," he says.

"My brother was in the Air Corps three years."

"I had a bad back, son. I got out sooner than that."

"Let me get us some fresh drinks," says Lillie.

Take him out of the Piedmont to mingle with sharper, money-wise men, to stand at the curb and watch chauffeured limousines whip past, to hear the accents of regions he has never dreamed of, to listen to men who squint as they discuss rumors of things to come, the builder Levitt. Given this dislocation, this jarring of his universe, given a sister stranded in New York after a bad common-law marriage, given the flesh-and-blood Buck Hansen, who lies glibly of selling, consolidating, expanding, who will blame Ben Broadfoot for dreaming? I will not.

"It depends a good deal on what Lillie here has in mind, I'd say." Ben laughs. "You do your own talking to Lillie, Buck, I can't speak for her there." Lillie laughs.

"I have to go to the bathroom," I say. It is as if they have steadily built a warm dome around themselves, of short, easy laughs, of whiskey and cigarettes, of their lies. My speaking shatters it, and they stop to stare at me, as if I have let in rude light and cold, broken their spell. My father sighs, covers his mouth by drinking deep.

"Straight on back there, hon," says Lillie, pointing a bangled arm; when she moves her arms, her bracelets slide, clinking, from wrist to elbow and back again. When she nods or laughs, her pendulous earrings sway.

The bathroom smelled of pine oil air sweetener and colored soap. It was neat, clean, but filled with Lillie Broadfoot's combs, hairnets, shampoos, bottles of perfume (Shalimar!), and toilet water vials. It was sensuous. I imagined my father's open travel kit on the back of the commode, next to her toothbrush and the methodically squeezed tube of toothpaste. I saw him working up a lather in his hands with one of the little pastel balls of soap in a clear-glass cup on the sink, leaning forward to examine his skin in the oval mirror. Would the clicking slap of his Rolls Razor echo out into the kitchen, the parlor? I slid back the curtains, saw her shower cap on a peg, a long-handled brush for scrubbing her back. I imagined him seated on the commode, trousers bunched around his ankles, smoking. I felt embarrassed for him, threatened for him, as if he had announced his intention to live or work in her beauty shop, to wear a white uniform, wash and cut women's hair.

When I came out of the bathroom I stood and listened to their voices to be sure I was not missed. I surveyed the bedroom, then the kitchen. I decided, I think, nothing. I did not decide: I must prevent this, must save him from Lillie and her brother. It was simply that I felt—even if I did not know—what, how much, he needed. And I felt this would not do, was not enough in quality or quantity. On the sink's drainboard sat a half-full bottle of Waterfill and Frazier whiskey. My eyes teared and I was robbed of breath for a moment, but then it warmly crowded my stomach, lightened my arms and legs.

I was as sure of myself (without *knowing*, without *thinking*) as I walked unsteadily into the parlor again as if I were in the kitchen of my Uncle Thurston's farm, with him beside me for support. They could not prevail against me. Would it have been kinder to have let them discover it all for themselves, to have let him discover it alone?

(No, none of this can be true—I was nine, I could not have felt any of this! I do it now, but it is as if it was then. This present truth will suffice for our past, my son.)

"Just what is the situation with your wife now, Buck," Ben said. "I'm not at all meaning to pry, but Lillie has mentioned it a little to me."

"That's all in process of being untangled," my father said.

"Have you told her about me, Buck?"

"We've talked—" my father started to say.

"Irene's sick in the hospital," I said. And now they could not remake their dome, could not exclude me. My father looked at me. Lillie and Ben waited for him to explain, clarify. My father looked at me—it was nothing he could not fit in, incorporate into whatever hopelessly simple fabric of lies he had spun for them while I was out of the room. "She's pretty sick I think," I said.

202

"I was getting to that," my father said to them. It was different now. As Ben listened, he still tongued the gap in his front teeth, still nodded with certainty in facile agreement, but his eyes would dart to me, as though he were trying to catch my father through me, catch me with my mouth open, be ready for me as I blurted out some new secret. Lillie still kept her hand in my father's, but she leaned away to light her cigarettes, to pick up her drink, to cough or clear her throat. "Let me put it to you this way," my father said. "One way or another I'll have no responsibilities to Irene in the very near future."

"Let's follow this a little further on down the road then, Buck," Ben said. He locked eyes with his sister, up now to make more drinks.

"I think Ben just wants to look out real careful for me, hon," she said.

"Shoot," my father said. "I've got nothing to hide."

Nor will I blame Lillie Broadfoot. Such a woman has very little on which to trade. When she ventures and loses, she will cling to the strength of her brother, reach for straws as frail as my father. A course at a beauty culture school in Charlotte or Raleigh is more vista than many can hope for. Lillie Broadfoot marries common law, for whatever reasons she has. Like her brother, a world war sets her free, first her husband, then, her, leaving behind a son there is not time or temperament to take along. Her husband gone, never coming back, she is left with the skills for cutting and waving hair, and beyond that, only herself to trade. It is no wonder that she agrees to let her brother play her pimp for whatever it will bring.

"We want to have all this all out straight in front of us," Ben said. "I mean, before you two go taking any big steps, I think we should all see where we're at, right, Buck?"

"I'm amenable," my father said, watching me.

"Ben just wants to discuss it all, Buck," Lillie said.

"So you're getting your divorce and all, right?" Ben said. "So far so good. Now when or how do you know if you'll stay out west there or maybe move here?"

"I haven't decided."

"So when do you?"

"When and if I get a firm commitment from the woman I'd like to marry, for one."

"Did you tell them about Cal Rocker?" I said.

"Keep out of this, will you, sonny? Maybe we'd better hold off on this until tomorrow, Ben. I'm a mite woozy from the drinks. The boy's worn out from the trip. I'm getting him on a train home here in a couple of—"

"Hold it now," Ben said. "Let's just hold it." He got up, unfolded his arms.

"Ben just wants to talk, Buck," Lillie said.

"Who's this Cal Rocker?" Ben said. "Is this something we need to know?"

"I better go to the toilet?" I said. The swig of whiskey I had taken suddenly gathered, churning, in my stomach. My mouth began to water, my head gone light, as if pumped full with warm, dry air.

"You look a little green around the gills, boy," my father said, getting up.

"Is he getting sick or something?" Ben said.

"Let me take him, Buck," Lillie said. Nausea struck me, and I closed my eyes to be sick. I felt her long fingernails through my shirt sleeve, heard her stockinged feet as she walked beside me, holding me up. Behind us the strident voices of her brother and my father faded out. I opened my eyes to the light of the scented bathroom. "Go ahead, honey boy," she said. "You'll feel lots better." I very deliberately put my hands on my knees and lowered my head to just above the toilet bowl. Lillie bent with me, next to me, keeping me from losing my feet. "You'll be a new man in a minute," she said. "You must have eaten something bad." I turned to look at her, looked straight down her dress, saw her drooping breasts as she bent over to hold me up. I looked at her breasts, overcome with her perfume, infected by her, I think, as my father was. I retched in long spasms that threatened to rise and end in one supreme convulsion. All the while I vomited, Lillie cooed softly to me to go ahead, get it out, it would make me feel heaps better.

She sat me on the toilet seat when it was done, rinsed a washcloth in cold water and wiped my face. "Better now?" she said.

"I think so. I feel real weaky all over." My hands lay in my lap. My head teetered, wanted to drop on my chest.

"Just sit a bit until you feel better. Will you do me a big favor, honey boy?" With a great effort, I lifted my head and looked into her green eyes. She put her hands on my cheeks.

"What?"

"You're not mad at me, are you?"

"No. I guess not. I don't know."

"I didn't ever do anything bad to you, did I? Please say you'll do Lillie a great big favor just this once?"

"I'm not mad at you. What favor?"

"Don't say anything more when we go back there now? Whatever your Daddy says, or whatever my big brother says to you, don't you say anything, please."

"Why not?"

"Honey," Lillie Broadfoot said to me, "if you say something that gets my brother Ben all mad at me and all I'm afraid he'll kill me. You know what I mean?"

"My dad's telling some lies."

"Oh please, no. I don't know what's all going to happen, but you please promise Lillie not to say anything to get my brother after me. Please?"

"I don't want my dad to marry you," I said.

"Doll baby, I wouldn't marry the last man in the world if I didn't have to," Lillie Broadfoot said.

"I guess I promise," I said.

"You're a good boy," she said, and led me back into the parlor. I could walk, but there was no stiffness left in my arms or legs, no strength in me. I had no will left to speak, to betray my father, bring Ben's wrath on his sister for whatever reason.

They were not talking when we came back into the parlor. Ben sat on a straight chair, near the windows, his arms folded, small mouth shut tight, his temples, the bones of his face lifting and falling as if in rhythm with his breathing. My father was still on the sofa he had shared with Lillie. He was already betrayed.

The resolution, the belief, the hope, were drained away. His age and fatigue seemed to spring out from his limp cheeks and jaw, to roll down from his distended belly, to settle in his spread thighs and swollen ankles. The facts were not out yet, but he knew it was over. Lillie sat me down next to my father, went to my chair. I wanted to touch my father, pat his hand, tell him it would be all right.

"Now maybe we can get this settled for good and all," Ben said.

"That boy needs to be put to bed, Ben," Lillie said.

"Buck?"

"Are you feeling okay now, sonny?" he said to me.

"I'm okay."

"Then let's be real honest with each other," Ben said, "let's just all put our cards out on the table face up."

"Don't, Ben," Lillie said.

"I'm fine," I said, "I feel fine."

"What's the goddamn difference," my father said.

"Then I'll speak my piece first," Ben said. He stood as he talked, his arms folded again, concentrating sometimes on my father, sometimes on his sister, checking me often, to see if I was ready to add anything more. But I had said all I needed to—I had blundered enough to make Ben Broadfoot suspicious, enough to remind my father he had no basis left on which to dream a future.

"The thing is," Ben Broadfoot said, "what's between you and my sister is just between the two of you looking at it one way. That's all fine and dandy, up to just so far."

"Which is?" my father said.

"Please, Ben," she said. Her brother continued as if he had not heard her.

"Which is where I come in. And that's just exactly, purely, this way. When it starts affecting what I got tied up in it. Now I been fairly close to you all the times you been shining around here, Buck, and if you'll recall rightly it was me introduced you to Lillie to start—" my father nodded—"so I got a good idea just how much maybe you know about us all. And how much you don't know yet. Lillie's got responsibilities. She's got that boy down there home needs taking care of—"

"I know all about him," my father said. I hoped Ben would tell about him anyway—I wanted to know.

"And she's got certain debts she owes me," Ben said. "Who you think took care of a lot of that when the boy came along and her with no man worth counting there?"

"Buck knows all that, Ben," she said.

"He don't know it all, not by a lot."

"Get on with it, I'm getting sleepy," my father said.

"She's owing me for a good bit more as well. Who you think went into it near over his head for that beauty salon business, Buck?"

"I figured you had a piece of it," my father said.

"A piece? Hear that, Lillie?"

"I wish you just wouldn't," she said. Don't worry, Lillie, I thought. I won't say anything. It's coming out okay, now, I can tell, and it will be all better. Trust me, Lillie.

"A piece you say," Ben said. "Well, call it all mine and you'll have the truth of it." I tried to see Ben Broadfoot at work in the shop, but he would not go, would not fit.

"So what's your beef?" my father said. "You must be coining it."

"That's what you probably think," Ben said. "Well it isn't near enough for what I got in mind."

"That's the truth, Buck," Lillie said, "it doesn't pay all that much."

"I don't see where I'm concerned," my father said. "If I marry Lillie I don't want her working to begin with. You've still got yourself a going concern, right?" Ben Broadfoot laughed. "Then for God's sake spit it out," my father said.

"I'll tell you all right," Ben said. "This Levittown I was telling you about?" Lillie put her head in her hands. As Ben spoke, spelled out the terms of the future he needed to see, the anger and suspicion left him. His voice went soft, he sat down, pulling his chair closer to my father, he unfolded his arms to use his hands, to shape vaguely the intangible wealth he saw waiting for them both, but a few short years away in time. It must have been amusing, horrifying, for my father to watch him, listen to him. It must have been like watching himself.

"I told you they're going to just build a whole new city, fifty thousand, sixty thousand houses, one fell swoop," he said. "I'm not talking through my hat, Buck, this is what's going to sure enough certain *be!* It's even in *The New York Times* if you want proof. They'll build these here business centers, all your stores and shops and what all in one location for each neighborhood, see?"

"I see," my father said.

"Ben," Lillie said.

"You shut up for two minutes straight, will you!" he told her. "Now think a second, Buck. What business do I know something about?"

"I'd be guessing."

"Beauty parlors, man! Who you think does all the books and managing and all?" He looked at Lillie. "She doesn't know beyond what she does on customers." Lillie looked away, at me, past me. "So I know how to run this kind of business, what's more, I learned it the hard way, when I sold out what my own daddy left me down home to come up here north and take care of my baby sister. You see what I'm driving at, Buck?" My father stubbed out his cigarette in the ashtray, very slow and methodical about it.

"I get the feeling I come into the picture pretty quick," he said.

"I'll say. Put it together and what do you get, man? It's almost too perfect to be true, isn't it? Here's a whole new city going up, needing a whole new set of fresh business for all those veterans going to come in buying houses on government loans! Sixty thousand homes is sixty thousand women coming anywhere from once a month to twice a week getting their hair done, Buck! See? I'm the man knows how to set up and run a shop. I know all the guys can give me discounts, everything! See why I need you?"

"Tell me," my father said, "just for the hell of it."

"Capital," Ben Broadfoot said. "I can't get financing, Buck, but you sure as damn hell can! You said you might be selling out out there, coming east. Well here it is, Buck!" He raised his arms, like an orchestra conductor—he reminded me of Calvin Rocker. "Here it all is!" he said. "Here's this Levittown going to be up on the island, here's a business deal for you to get right into, right up on top of the pile, Buck. Here's Lillie here!" he said. Lillie was crying, very quietly, her hands over her face. Her brother had turned to her, pointed her out like a carnival barker running through a quick peep at what waited inside his tent for the crowd, but he had not seen she was crying. Nor had my father. He was staring at Ben Broadfoot. The lights had not been turned on in the flat when the sun began to go. Ben Broadfoot was almost a silhouette against the windows. My father appeared to fade into the cushions of the sofa, but his face was distinct to me. He was staring at Ben Broadfoot, and he was beginning to smile.

"It's just about natural, Buck," Ben said. "You got the money and all your years in business, you'd know how to organize a big deal like this. You can talk to people won't even give me the right time of day, man. We got a thing here," he said, "we got us a once-in-a-lifetime genuine shot at that bluebird, Buck!"

"And I'm guessing it's Lillie you've got, isn't it?" my father said, and he was smiling more broadly, his face picked out, spotlighted with the last of the sun coming through the front windows.

"It doesn't have to be said like that," Ben said. He frowned, watching my father's smile. "None of this means what Lillie's said, how she feels about you and all, it don't mean any of it isn't true, Buck. Lillie'll swear to that, I know." He looked at his sister, perhaps to check, be sure she was ready and waiting to swear to whatever she had told my father of her feelings for him. Then he saw she was crying, and he looked quickly back at my father, who had begun to laugh. It was a perfect laugh, exquisite stage laughter, beginning in the flicker of a smile at the corners of his mouth, spreading to a broad, open smile of delight, bubbling up in chuckles, snickers, snorts, rolling out in heavy comic laughter, roaring out, a tear-wrenching, belly-hurting laugh like the laughter a man will give on hearing the funniest dirty story he has heard in years. It was infectious. I grinned like an idiot boy, leaning forward to catch hold of my father's mood and follow him into it, through it. Ben Broadfoot kept talking until my father's laughter and Lillie's weeping made his words ludicrous.

"What's to stop us?" he said. "So you got this sick wife to get shut of. That's not forever, is it? You get free of that wife, sell off your business there in Saint Paul, come on out and we're waiting for you with open arms. What's so goddamn funny about it? You think I don't know what I'm talking about? You read it in the papers, I'm telling you. Ask Lillie if you don't trust me! Tell him, Lillie. Stop your damn caterwauling and tell Buck what I say's the damn gospel truth!"

Lillie tried to stop crying, but my father heaved himself up out of the sofa like a cripple, still laughing. I got up to stand next to him. He put one hand on my head to steady himself, choking off his laughter with his fist now, almost sobbing. "You're not even listening to me," Ben Broadfoot said. My father fished out his handkerchief, leaned across me and gave it to Lillie.

"Oh, I listened, Ben, I heard every last word," he said.

"Just tell me what's so funny. How's it funny? Are you insulting me or something?"

"Ben," my father said. He ended his laughter with coughs, wiping the corners of his eyes dry. I still felt the urge to smile, wished there was some excuse for me to continue the laughter; it was over, I had won, and if he could laugh at it, then there was no grudge in him for my stupid betrayal. "Ben. Ben me bucko," my father said. "This is the best one I've heard yet. I thank you. I really do. We'll be going now, if you'll excuse us." He nudged me, and I started toward the door.

"Just hold it," Ben said. "Are you walking out on us? Let me get this right. You're calling everything off? You owe me an answer at least, Buck."

"You won't like it," my father said.

"I'll decide that."

209

"Let him go, Ben," Lillie said.

"You shut to hell up! What's the big idea here, Buck?"

"Don't be too rough on your sister, Ben," my father said. He reached out his hand as if to touch her, pat her hair, but did not. "She doesn't know any better than you do yourself."

"Know what? What in hell are you giving me?"

"Snafu, Ben," my father said. "You poor sap, you're worth probably three times what I am this very minute. Don't you get it, you poor dumb cracker? Good Christ, man, I'm broke! I've got a wife dying in a sanitarium, I've got an ex-wife and three kids—" he touched the top of my head with his fingertips—"I owe support and I've not the slightest idea where I can get it. Wise up, Ben! Get wise to yourself. You own a nice little business, you have a sister here to work it for you. Stay to hell out of business, Ben, or they'll clean you like they did me. Come on, sonny, we're wearing out our welcome here, I'd say."

"Don't lie to me, Buck," Ben said.

"Never," my father said. "It's truth time, Ben me boy! Not a lie in a carload, pure as the driven snow. I'm gutted, picked clean. I was counting on you and Lillie to bail me out." We were at the door. "That's the way she goes, Ben. Better luck next time. Don't take it so hard," he said to Lillie who wept now without restraint. "Things'll get better for you if they don't get worse."

"You dumb bitch!" I heard Ben call his sister as my father closed the door behind us, and we went down the stairs, out to the Chrysler, where it was almost full dark now. Behind us, Lillie's sobbing, her brother's curses, receded into silence.

We got in and drove away, to some other ordinary street in Mineola, New York, where we parked and sat, while my father smoked cigarettes and looked out the window at the houses on the block, thinking, I suppose, of no more than the finality of the fact that it was over, there was nothing more for him to do, no place to go. It must have been an hour at least before he took it into his mind to go back to Lillie's flat and see if she was all right, be sure that Ben had done nothing drastic.

"I'm sorry, Dad."

"No more than I am, boy. It was fun sometimes while it lasted, wasn't it?"

"I mean for saying stuff I wasn't supposed to."

"That," he said. "Forget it. It doesn't make a bit of difference. You can't blame me for trying. Remember that, will you?"

210

"Sure. Dad?"

"I'm listening."

"Were you really going to send me home on a train? Like you said? Or was it fibbing?"

"When's that? Oh, that's just talk. I was dealing, see? It's too complicated to explain."

"Are you going to call Jane again?"

"If you want me to."

"Mom'll worry if you don't. She might get mad."

"She might at that."

"I'm glad though you're not going to get married with Lillie Broadfoot."

"I wonder a little if I don't feel the same way myself." He started to laugh again.

"Is it funny?" I said.

"Depends on where you're standing, boy. Let's talk about something else. Let's not talk at all for a while. Okay by you?"

"If you want to." So we did not talk for a while, and after a while he started the car. "Are we going to a hotel to sleep now?"

"Before too long," he said. "I thought we'd sort of cruise past Lillie's and see if everything's okay. Redneck son of a bitch like that might just take it into his head to rough her up a little."

"How's come?"

"Some people don't take real good to losing till they get used to it, son," he said.

So we cruised past Lillie's, and there was a police car there. A neighbor called them when the noise grew too loud. Ben had given her a beating, and another police car had just that moment left with Ben in handcuffs. Lillie was not a pretty sight, her eyes blacked and swollen, her hair undone. "I'll go down there and let him know he'll deal with me if he ever lays a hand on you again," my father said. "I guess I can do that much for you, Lillie." She insisted on coming along, and we made room for her on the cluttered front seat of the Chrysler. When we reached the Mineola Municipal Police Station, I went in with my father because I was afraid to sit in the car with Lillie looking like that.

"Ben put me up to all this, Buck," she said as we got out. "I hope you don't hate me for all this."

"It's nobody's fault, Lillie," he said. "Sit tight while I go scare the bejesus out of that brother of yours."

"I'm coming too," I said.

"Just keep out of my way then," my father said. We went in,

and they talked, and struggled, and a policeman broke the fourth finger on my father's right hand, swinging his club at Ben Broadfoot. We called a doctor Lillie knew, and we all went to his house, where he splinted and bandaged my father's finger, and looked at Lillie's face, and then we took Lillie home and left her there.

"Now what do we do, Dad?"

"Well, now. Give me a minute to think. I don't know. I guess maybe I'll take you home. Would you like that?"

"If we have to. Is there anyplace we could go?"

"Not that I can think of, boy. I think I'm all played out, to tell you the truth."

"Does your finger hurt a lot?"

"That's not what I meant. It throbs some when I move it. I'm just finished is all. I better get you home to your mother."

"What are you going to do? I mean after you take me home?"

"If I had my druthers I guess I'd crawl off in a corner somewhere and let the rest of the world go to hell in a hand basket. Let's talk about something else."

IX

It requires only that we complete the circle, finish, return to the point of our beginning, that we reach our departure for the journey to be done.

What I make for you is the mystery of a life, mystery if only because all ends in death, all stories end, abruptly, in a death. Son, if we can make a life for my father, then we make the meaning of his death. Believe in this, and we can surely believe in ourselves. He was my father, you are my son, and I stand between you to tell this lie that it might make us one. I trespass fact that you and I might know what we cannot know. Listen.

Buck Hansen. What drives a man at the end of a life? What had he truly fled, racing with me toward Long Island, toward Lillie? What had he hoped I might give him? In the depth of him, what shall we find? Listen.

We imagine what we can never know, and if we can, if we *will* believe, then we can live as he died, in a peace with the mystery of our ends in death. We will have made a meaning, you and I, worth our living.

Listen.

Since the day he committed her, drove there himself in the Chrysler, signed the final papers, Buck had stayed away from the sanitarium. It lay on one of the routes he could take between the apartment and his office in Saint Paul, but he never went that way after he'd committed Irene. A big part of it was just the way it looked; it didn't look like what it was. A real hospital now—one that looked like a hospital, with open grounds, three or six or ten stories, modern wings added on, nurses and medical students walking the streets in capes and white jackets, signs pointing out emergency ambulance entrances and visitors' parking areas—a real hospital didn't bother him. This place was something else.

It was a converted mansion, and it still looked like a mansion, like the beautifully maintained mansion of some nineteenth-century milling or mining baron who made his pile before income and inheritance taxes, before fixed prices and production quotas. Passing by, you could think the milling or mining baron had maybe left a clause in his will requiring his descendants to live on there if they wanted to spend his fortune. The other mansions on the long, shaded block were already broken up into multiple living units, renting out at prices way over the old OPA limits to veterans' families. Instead of nurses and medical students, the sidewalks teemed with pregnant young women pushing baby buggies, accompanied by young men still wearing fatigue caps or khaki trousers, because with new, growing families and outrageous rents to pay, wardrobes were way down the list of priorities in their futures.

That was a big part of it. It didn't look like what it was. You could bring in your wife or your mother or your grandfather, and they wouldn't have the foggiest what was happening to them until you put them inside the front door and an orderly took over if they kicked up a fuss. It looked like a once opulent residential area, gone old and decrepit, taken over by the new hordes of young and struggling families. And smack in the middle of it was this place you took the old and the sick to leave them to die. Like Irene.

Buck remembered the poor farm outside Goshen. You knew what you were about. It had been a piano factory way back, gone broke when Buck's father was a young man. It looked a little like the high school. But there was a sign, big and bold, *County Home*, and you knew what you were dealing with. The fear of it made Buck's old man a miser. *What are you saving it for?* he'd shout at the old man when he turned him down. *So maybe I don't die a burden on my boys, or out by the poor farm,* the old man said. Some people, busted farmers, went there while they were still in their fifties, and they worked the vegetable garden, kept a few cows, looked after a few cows, looked after the grounds, the building, the sheds. The real old workers were lucky to get outside in good weather. They sat on benches in the shade of the main building, the old piano factory, or they walked the grounds a little, in pairs, holding each other steady. If you were out and not nuts, and your family couldn't or wouldn't keep you locked up at home, they shipped you off to the state home, but there were a few of the real old-timers, the senile, who were kept inside, tied in bed, some of them, and you could hear their voices carry on a clear day, screeching, crying, cursing like banshees, some of them. It had scared Buck's old man, scared the hell out of him, but at least you knew what you were getting if they hauled you off to the county poor farm in Goshen.

Buck Hansen imagined himself an old man. Really old. He'd be fifty in September. Sixty in 1956, seventy in '66, in '76, eighty. In 1976 I'll be eighty. An old, old man, eighty, unable to contain bladder or bowels, deaf as a post, shaking like a leaf, without the strength or desire to do anything but sit whole afternoons in the sun with an afghan over his legs, mumbling about . . . what would he mumble about?

He remembered old men in Goshen, some of them who got dressed up in uniform for GAR picnics on the Fourth of July in the city park. They mumbled and nattered and worried over the Civil War, Lincoln, what should have been done with Negroes, about Democratic politicians nobody else could remember. Buck Hansen: sitting with an afghan over his legs, mumbling about the first war, about flying a Spad over Texas and Oklahoma, about the depression, about cost-plus and shipment priorities, Roosevelt and Truman—Jesus! he thought.

He would not let them do it to him! One of his sons, Oskar, a grown man of forty, would take him out for a drive. *Where the hell are we going?* Buck would ask (did old, old men still talk like that, curse, demand?). *Relax, Dad,* Oskar said, a man of forty. *We're just taking a little drive down this nice shady street here. It's just a big house, like the rest of the houses on the block, isn't it?*

215

There, nothing to be afraid of, just come in with me for a minute, will you? That's how they would try to trick him inside, when he was an old man, Buck thought.

They would never get away with it, not if he had to hang himself, cut his own throat, to beat them! Never! He imagined a *Tribune* headline: "Elderly Retired Businessman Resists Confinement In Nursing Home, Escapes, Flees." He saw himself struggling with his forty-year-old son, a white-coated orderly. They tried to drag him across a barbered lawn to a coach entrance, but he knocked them down with haymakers, ran, disappeared through a hedge.

Just you try it and see what you get, Buck thought. He took his right hand off the steering wheel and made a fist with it, reassured by its bulk and solidity. He wished that little kike, Sheldon Rotter, were still in front of him, so he could smash him in the face, break his can opener of a nose with his fist, to show everyone what they would get if they were thinking of ever trying to trick Buck Hansen into one of those places that didn't look like what they were. He wished to hell he had slugged that little kike!

He turned the Chrysler into the circular drive, left it sitting under the massive stone and brick overhang. From the outside it looked empty, deserted. Where were they, he wondered, all the people who could afford the tab for a parent, grandparent, maiden aunt, in this place? He'd seen one group, the day he committed Irene. A black Lincoln Continental, long as your arm, chauffeur-driven, a nigger in a gray uniform to chauffeur them, come to pick up mother or grandmother for a little drive or dinner at home or maybe bringing flowers in person for a birthday or anniversary. Class. Now there was some consolation: Irene's madness and death would occur in the company of some really hoity-toity people. Unless and until they checked out Buck's credit rating. Then they'd ship her off to the charity ward, to die with niggers and bohunks. I've come to see if I can cheer you up, Irene, he thought.

There was one, sitting on a bench just inside the door, next to the knee-high vase that held a supply of canes and sticks and umbrellas for the ones who could still walk.

"A lovely warm day, isn't it?" she said to Buck, and smiled. She could have been anything from seventy to a hundred, dressed to the nines, her neck, wrists, ears, fingers clotted with jewelry. Her face was heavily powdered, rouged, her eyebrows penciled, hair rinsed a hideous polack red blonde. She wore open-toe high heels, her bluish toothpick legs in nylons. Her arms were bare, white as cigarette ash, her stomach bloated under her gay summer dress, the bulge of a goiter showing above and below her choker necklace. Her eyelashes were too long and curled to be real. There was a faint white fuzz of beard on her cheeks, upper lip, chin. Buck caught himself staring at her as if she couldn't see him, the way he stared at blind men led by German shepherds or tapping across intersections with white canes. She looked like a woman with her face made up in advance for the viewing in the casket.

"It is that," he said, trying hard to match the porcelain smile of her even rows of false teeth. He pushed open the heavy glass inner door before she could speak to him. She would be waiting, he figured, for the family to take her out for the day, a warm Sunday afternoon in June. The jewelry she wore looked good enough to liquidate his debts. "Wealthy Woman Robbed At Sanitarium, Police Hunt Thief." There was a woman in a nurse's uniform at a small desk, but before Buck could ask for him, Irene's doctor appeared from behind one of the large potted ferns sitting in each corner of the lobby.

"Mr. Hansen," he said, "I'm glad. Will you come with me, please?" The doctor smiled at the nurse, she relayed it to Buck, as if to authenticate it, and Buck followed after the doctor. The doctor walked briskly, quickly. They passed a small alcove where an old man sat in a wheelchair, peeling a banana. Buck trotted to catch up.

"Hold it, hold on a second, hold it up here a second," Buck said. They stood in a long corridor. It had been extensively redone. From the outside, no one would have imagined such a long, clean, white tiled corridor. "Where are you taking me? I don't want to go in there right off like this," he said. He found himself whispering. The brown doors all along the corridor were rooms for patients, and he did not want to wake, disturb, rouse them. He had a horrible vision of all the brown doors opening, patients pouring out to engulf him in the corridor, walking, crouching, dragging paralyzed legs.

"Now I thought we'd agreed over the telephone." The doctor frowned. He didn't whisper, but his voice was soft, naturally muted, as if at a special, professional pitch used only inside these walls.

"We did. That's right, but at least give me a little information, brief me or something."

"There's nothing to be said beyond what I told you, Mr. Hansen. Just go in and say hello to her as you would in any ordinary circumstance. Ask her how she feels, cheer her up a little—"

"Look, Jesus," Buck said, "I don't know quite what to expect."

"There's nothing to be apprehensive about, surely."

"I'm not apprehensive!" Buck said. He was shocked at how loud he had spoken; he listened for movements on the other sides of all the brown doors before continuing. "What the hell should I be afraid of?" he whispered, his face close to the doctor's. "Do I look afraid to you?"

"Well then," the doctor said, smiling again as he had for the nurse at the desk, "why don't we just go in and see your wife, shall we?"

"You're coming in too, aren't you?"

"If you wish. Of course. I'll leave you alone after a bit, of course. You'll want to speak privately with her, I know." Buck was afraid to ask him not to leave him alone with Irene. As they walked to Irene's brown door, Buck ran his hand over his face, as if he could wipe away any telltale trace of his fear, leave it clean for a face of confidence, of cheerful affection and concern. They came to Irene's brown door, the doctor opened it, and they both smiled for her as they entered.

He hadn't any idea she would look so different, so quickly, look so very different. He had an impulse to turn to the doctor, see if this wasn't a mistake, the wrong room, but the doctor was smiling down at Irene in the bed. "Well see here who's come to see you today, Mrs. Hansen," the doctor said. Buck smiled harder, looked at her.

It was the shrinking, the drying up and withering to a hard, brittle core of what she'd been, like the old woman on the bench by the entrance. He remembered his brother writing him, down at Fort Sill, how the old man lost weight as the cancer in his innards grew and ate away at him. "And how are we doing today?" the doctor said when she didn't respond. She didn't even look up at Buck, didn't seem to know he was there. She was propped, sitting up, several pillows behind her back. A breakfast tray, untouched, the food cold and congealed, was set on a wooden bed-table across her legs. She hadn't been taking nourishment, the doctor told him over the phone.

"Hello Irene," he said, but she did not look up at him, did not answer. She had been a slim woman, a tall thinnish woman with wide hips, but now she was reduced, compressed, wasted. She was badly jaundiced, her color almost light yellow around her eyes, the corners of her mouth. She looked like one of the starving Chinese he was always seeing on relief posters during the war. Her eyes were impossibly large, protruding, in her sunken face, the sockets, her cheekbones gruesomely raised. Knobs of bone stuck out at her wrists and elbows, below the hospital gown she wore. Her neck seemed stretched, elongated. Her hair was uncombed, with far more, deeper, gray than he remembered. Was it a month? Six weeks? The doctor was looking at Buck. "Aren't you going to say hello, Irene?" he said to get the doctor's eyes off him.

"I can't eat this," she said to the doctor. She rolled her globular eyes at the tray, pointed with a long, crone's finger. She still wore the diamond Buck had given her when they were married. He'd tried to talk her out of that the day she checked in, told her it would be safer at the apartment, but she wouldn't give it up—he had not been thinking, not precisely, definitely, then, of pawning it. It shamed him to see it now on her finger, not be able to stop wondering how much it would bring in hock. She still had not looked at him.

"Let's see what's on the menu today," the doctor said. While she glared at his head, he bent, lifted the cover off the main dish, sniffed at it like a child smelling a flower. Buck looked over his shoulder. It was some sort of patty, Salisbury steak maybe—for the money, they could do better than that, he thought. "You've let it get cold," the doctor said. "Now just what seems to be wrong with it? You need to keep up your strength, you know." He spoke in a singsong, like a nursery schoolteacher.

"You know as well as me," Irene said. She rolled her eyes upward, folded her skinny arms over her flat chest, triumphant, as if she had scored in some protracted argument.

"Hello, Irene, I—" Buck started to say.

"Suppose you tell me, just for fun," the doctor said.

"Poison," she said, closing her eyes, as though the word hurt her, gave her a headache.

"Come now."

"Irene—"

"Poison! All of it." She opened her eyes. They shone, fevered, glassy. "Do you think I'm some goddamn idiot? Kill me with poison. You'd like that, wouldn't you?" Buck stiffened, but he could see she was not talking to him. "Eat it and die," she said, "so simple. I'm too damn smart for that, mister." She closed her eyes again. The doctor looked at Buck and shrugged. A hopeless case, clearly.

"All righty," he said, "what would you think if I tasted it for you, would that ease your mind?" Irene opened one eye, a grotesque parody of a long, leering wink. "Better yet," the doctor said, "we'll have your husband taste it, how would that be?" She opened the other eye and turned her head toward Buck, but still there was no sign she knew him. The doctor hesitated over the breakfast tray, like a man asked to pick a card, any card; he picked up a small dish of something, a pudding. It was tapioca—tapioca for breakfast, Buck thought, what the hell am I paying for around here! The doctor found the spoon wrapped in the paper napkin, handed it to Buck. I'm not really hungry at all, Buck wanted to say, but the doctor was smiling hard at him, Irene watching very closely.

It was tapioca, a cold and bland white muck. He thought he would be sick, but spooned it up and ate it, feeling like a cranky child being forced to finish his dinner if he wanted the dessert. The slick beads of the pudding stuck to his bridgework and the roof of his mouth, but he kept on spooning, swallowing, close to gagging, and then the spoon clicked on the bottom of the shallow dish, and he stood holding spoon and dish, looking to the doctor for approval. "All right now," the doctor said. "Is *he* poisoned?" Am I? Buck wondered. "Man Eats Stale Pudding, Sickens, Dies In Agony," the headline read. He set the dish and spoon on Irene's bedside table, wiped with the back of his hand at the sticky feeling on his lips, breathed deep through his mouth to cleanse away the pudding's aftertaste.

"Okay," Irene said, and they stood together at her bed and watched her eat every last morsel of food on the tray. When she was done she scrubbed her lips with the napkin, wadded it up and dropped it in her juice glass. "There!" she said, and closed her eyes tightly again, as if the sunlight hurt them.

"I'll just step out now," the doctor said, "and let you talk." Buck caught his arm before he reached the door.

"Don't," he whispered over his rigid lips. "Not yet."

"It's all right. Just speak to her. See if you can get her to agree to eat her meals. Tell her how good she's looking."

"She doesn't know me, she doesn't even know I'm here—"

"Don't be fooled," the doctor said, "she knows," and then he winked at Buck, as though it were some elaborate game they all played—it was as if Buck suddenly realized they were all mad, Irene, the banana-peeling old cocker in the wheelchair, the old bat dripping jewels at the door, the nurse-receptionist, the doctor himself. It was one big looney bin, and Buck had wandered in unaware, wanting to do something decent, and now they wouldn't let him leave. The doctor ducked out, silent in his crepe-soled shoes. When Buck turned back to the bed, Irene had one eye open, watching him. He stayed far enough away from her bed to avoid her if she tried to touch him.

"Irene," he said. "It's me, Buck." How many times had he had to say that, telephoning, announce to those who should know, brother, daughter, Lillie, that he was himself, Buck Hansen? The walls had come tumbling down, the woods were on fire, and he had to go about calling his own name to be sure he was not lost.

"I know it's you," she said. The doctor knew his business. She did not exactly smile, but it was as if she were trying to make one on her face. "Don't you think I know who you are? Sit by me, Buck." She patted the edge of the bed with her wasted claw of a hand. He sat, making sure he did not touch against her, touch the sheet-covered leg; he remembered his dream of lying next to her in a hospital bed, feared it would all happen. Lillie, his dead father appearing to play out the dream. Before he could jerk it away, she reached out and took his hand, held it tight in both of hers, hugged it to her chest. "I knew it was you all the time. I only did that to keep *him* from hearing." She rolled her eyes at the door. "I don't want *them* to know anything."

"What are you talking—the food—" Buck said.

"I *knew* it wasn't poisoned! They don't poison my food, Buck." She did smile now, and he did his best to return it. "It's got something in it to make me sleep," Irene said. "Sleeping pills." She leaned her head close to whisper this to him. Her breath smelled terrible. What kind of care did they take in this place? She smelled like she needed a bath, her hair needed washing—what the hell was he supposed to get for his money? "They want me to sleep at night so they can come in and kill me, Buck." He pulled his head back, feeling suffocated by the smell of her.

"Who? What are you—"

"*Them!*" she whispered hoarsely. "Didn't you see them in the hall? They hid from you. They're waiting out there to come in and choke me, I know it, Buck, they want me to sleep, and I don't dare sleep, I can't eat their poisoned food." He couldn't think of anything to say—what in God's name was there to say! She stared at him, squeezing his hand, then began to cry like a small child. "Oh Buck," she said, "they want to kill me. I'm afraid they'll kill me if I fall asleep, oh God, Buck, help me, help me, please—" She began to sob, hiccuping, blubbering like a small child. He moved to evade her, but her hands grasped his arms, touched his face, his hair. Then she was holding him by the shoulders, pulling him over her on the bed. She buried her face in the hollow of his neck and shoulder; he felt her tears, a tepidly warm wetness, run onto his skin.

"For God's sake, Irene, stop it. Stop it!" he said. He forced himself to take hold of her and set her firmly back against the propped pillows. There was so little left of her. He seemed to have to grope through folds of bed sheet, the coarse linen of her hospital gown to find her scrawny, brittle-feeling shoulders, arms. "Stop it now, stop it now, stop it now," he soothed. When they had begun to argue frequently after their marriage, over money, over where he spent his time, over anything, she cried, but he never tolerated it. *You can turn off the waterworks*, he would tell her, *this is one man it won't do for. Turn it off, Irene, I've been through it all before.* It only made her cry harder, but saying it kept him from being affected by her tears. He would have liked to tell her that now, give her a good shake, slap her face, but knew he could not. There was nothing he could do.

Finally she stopped of her own accord, ran out of breath, energy, choking to a halt, at last sitting quietly against the pillows, face wet, a runny nose. "I'm sorry, Buck," she said. "I know you hate me when I do that."

"Heaven knows I don't hate you, Irene."

"Yes. Oh yes, yes, yes, you do, I know. I know you hate me. You wish I was dead."

"I never wished anyone—" he tried quickly to interrupt, but she did not wait for him to finish.

"But I don't care if you do, Buck. I can't help it if you hate me anymore. I tried to make you not hate me, but I can't help it anymore, Buck. I'm sorry I made you hate me. I'm sorry you think I wrecked your life for you. I didn't mean to. But I'm afraid to die, Buck, I can't die just to make you happy—" Buck tried to see the door from the corner of his eye; had the doctor left it ajar? Could anyone hear her? "Please help me, Buck. They're killing me, help me just this once and I promise I'll go away from you and never bother you again. They give me drugs all the time, Buck—"

"You're sick, Irene," he said. "You're ill, and you have to stay here and get well. It won't be long. You're better every day, the doctor told me himself." He tried to think of things to say, to keep talking so she wouldn't get started again about his hate for her, wishing her dead. But he was afraid to go on lying to her. He was afraid he would be heard, out in the hall, behind all those other brown doors, where all the others lay waiting to die—he feared they would come out, screeching in some mad chorus, *Liar! Liar! Liar!*

"Him!" Irene said.

"Who?" He turned to see if someone had come in behind him; the brown door was shut.

"That doctor! He's the one, Buck, he wants to kill me, and everyone is helping him."

"Irene."

"Won't you help me, Buck? You're the strong one. You're never afraid of anything. You're never afraid. Help me, please, Buck."

"What can I do?" he asked, more of himself than of his wife. A mad, dying woman: he hated her, pitied her, wished her dead or safe and well, so long as she was away from him, he from her. "I don't know what you expect me to do, Irene. I don't know anything to do." She began to cry again, gently and quietly this time, as if she understood, not that he was powerless, but unwilling to save her. Buck sat on the edge of her bed, unable to find the energy or purpose to get up and leave. He felt he would sit there forever—Irene would weep, he would sit, mute, feeble, because she was dying, everyone in this place was waiting behind a brown door to die, and the doctor and all his staff were insane because they thought they could do something about it, or they tried even if they knew it was useless. And he, Buck Hansen, knew he had to run like hell if he wanted to keep living, but it was all, this place, Irene, what had happened to his life, too much for him to make the effort that would save him.

He was rescued by the doctor's return. He rapped on the door with his knuckles before entering. "How are we doing here?" he said brightly before he saw Irene's face. "Oh my goodness," he said when he saw her. She had shut her eyes, hunched her shoulders the instant he came in, shoved her clenched hands under the sheet. "Oh dear," he said.

"Tell me something I can do for her, for Christ's sake," Buck said.

"I think we'd better let Missus get some rest now." He put his hand on Buck's shoulder, nodded toward the door.

"You won't catch me sleeping!" Irene said through her teeth. She began to tremble violently. Buck got up from the bed.

"What the hell are you a doctor for then?" he said. "Can't you tell me what to do? Is medicine all you know!" Irene opened her eyes.

"You could help me if you wanted to, Buck," she said. "You're always so strong, I wish you would help me." The doctor muttered something under his breath. Buck walked to her side, reached down and took her hand from under the sheet.

"Help me, help me, help me," she said.

"Now, Irene, you take this," he said. He pried her stiff fingers open, one after another, until her open palm lay in his. "This is a magic charm, Irene," he said. He bent, lifted her hand, kissed the center of her palm; it was like kissing a dry surface of a piece of paper, a dry, dead leaf. "Hold it and save it." He closed her fingers for her. "You keep that and save it, keep your hand closed until it's time for you to go to sleep."

"Help me," she said softly.

"You hold it and go to sleep, nothing will happen to you. Understand? Are you listening?" She nodded. "You can sleep any time you want to now. You don't have to be afraid. No one can hurt you while you're asleep now. Irene?"

"I will, I will," she said. He let go her hand. She put her closed fist, the blue veins visible under the taut skin, to her chest, covered it with her other hand, peeked down at it, back at him.

"Good-bye, Irene." He could not tell her he was coming back to see her soon; he would not lie to her anymore.

"Thank you, Buck," she said, "thank you, thank you. I knew you'd help me even if you hated me. You're so strong." He still heard her voice, praising him, as he followed the doctor back down the dim, cool corridor, past all the brown doors, to the lobby. They passed the alcove where the old man in the wheelchair had finished his banana.

"You see what I mean," the doctor said. "I'm not sure it's best to indulge her, but . . . ." In the lobby, Buck faced him.

"You're the one insisted I come down here," he said, "then shove me in there to watch her go to pieces. You sonofabitch, if I ran a business the way you do here I'd go broke."

"Now *wait* a min—." Buck stepped around him to the door.

"Get the goddamn hell out of my way," he said, remembering he had gone broke, was running, had to run to save his own life. "I've got places to go and people to see." The loaded Chrysler waited for him in the blessed shade of the overhang. He scrubbed his lips with the back of his hand, lit a cigarette to clear the taste in his mouth. Thurston, he thought, brother mine, how did you and I turn out so different? Oskar, boy, I'm coming to see you! Lillie! What did I ever do to deserve this?

The engine started, roared, with a touch of the dash button.

He drove down and out the circular drive, away from the sanitarium that didn't look like a sanitarium. Not me! he promised. Not if I have to slit my own gullet! You'll never get Buck Hansen! He headed out of the Twin Cities, where he had failed, toward the Wisconsin border, to see his kids, to see a man who owed him a job or a loan, a break, to see his brother, to see Lillie. He checked the rear-view mirror for Rotter the kike's new Studebaker. He set out to have another crack at it. He'd live, or die trying!

We are sitting in the Chrysler, parked in front of Lillie Broadfoot's flat. There is still a light, veiled by the drawn shades, the front windows; do we wait for her to put out the light, show that she has bathed her blacked eyes, rinsed out the cuts inside her mouth with a warm salt-water solution (as the doctor who splinted my father's finger suggested), gone to bed? I do not know. My father sits behind the wheel, body sagging. His window is halfway open, and the wind off Long Island Sound comes quite cool, still laden with the fish-seaweed stench that seems to permeate Mineola, New York. My father has asked me to change the subject, but there is nothing I know to say, so I wait until somehow he decides what to do, where to go.

He will take me home, he said. He might as well take me home. I think only briefly of my mother, brother, sister . . . they are still caught, stopped in the postures in which we left them, only days, yet ages, worlds ago. I sit as close to my father as I can without touching, disturbing him, and I wait.

We do not hear the man approach the Chrysler. He has been waiting too. There are enough other cars parked on the block to give his Studebaker anonymity. It is too dark to see the colors of automobiles parked on the block. How long did he wait? I am never to know. He has followed, Saint Paul to Milwaukee, to Chicago, to Goshen, here to Lillie Broadfoot's flat in Mineola, New York. He may have been there when we left Lillie's, but he would not come forth, speak, until all was ready for him. He is a cunning man, I suspect, one gifted in knowing, judging the precise time, mood, in which to move. He may have witnessed the arrival of the police in our absence, the arrest and handcuffing of Ben Broadfoot. He may have seen us return. He may have followed us to the police station, followed us to the doctor who set my father's finger. He has followed, waited for my father, and it is the moment now for his approach. Everything, in its way, for him, has led to this, for him. There can be no better time for him.

I look at my father, but I am not watching him, not scrutinizing his expression, not measuring the motions of his arm as he lifts his cigarette to his lips to smoke. I am looking toward him, and there, in an instant, in the half-open car window, is the man's face, as if the window were a screen, his face the projection of a slide flashed on without warning. I do not see the man's face well, but there is a face there, and he peers into the Chrysler with the puzzled curiosity of a man who has come upon a hulk on a deserted beach, some flotsam tossed up by a recent and violent storm. The face peers in, and then his hands come up to place spectacles on his nose (a large, hooked nose, a beak of a nose!), as if they have a special power to clarify images in the darkness. And he speaks, and until then I do not think my father knows he is there.

"Mr. Hansen?" the face in the car window said. My father did not start, did not seem taken unaware, yet I am sure he did not see or sense the man before he spoke. It is that he no longer cared, not who or what. He turned his face to the window (I scramble to my knees to see over my father's shoulder, see the man's face as he speaks). Their faces were only inches apart.

"Mr. Rotter, I'd guess," my father said. The man's head jerked back, as though he were surprised to find someone, something alive, talking in this beach-hulk he has chanced upon. His spectacles caught the light of a streetlamp for an instant, a flare of light like some small, intense explosion in one of his eyes. "What kept you?" my father said.

"I've been looking for you, Mr. Hansen," Sheldon Rotter said. "You led me a real merry chase, you know. That must be the boy there with you," he said.

I wonder how long we might have sat there if he had not come, how long I would have had to wait—or if, without Sheldon Rotter, the Jewish skip chaser, the tracker of deadbeats in the employ of a consortium of money lenders, we might never have moved. Without him, I wonder, Rotter the spur, a goad in my father's flank, would my father have found the energy, a rationale, to start the car and take me home?

"What the hell's it to you?" my father said. He was not angry or defiant. "Hand over the summons or whatever and leave me to hell alone."

"I told you you had me all wrong, Mr. Hansen. I've been doing you a very big turn, actually, even if you don't know it."

My father laughed; it was a laugh without volume, substance, texture, a last laugh, perhaps, hollow, at the confusion of his life. "I mean it, Mr. Hansen."

"Do tell."

"My people wanted to clean you out, you know. There's a lot of unhappy people back in the Twin Cities right today, Mr. Hansen. If it wasn't for me telling them hold off, you'd be in lot worse trouble here. That's the truth, too," Sheldon Rotter said.

"Cut it out, you're breaking my heart. Do what the hell you have to do," my father said.

"That's what I'm saying," he said. He put his fingers over the edge of the window; his face was almost inside the car. "I held them off you so far. We haven't taken any judgments or anything yet, see? Which isn't promising they won't, no matter what I say, but I need you to cooperate if you want to get out of this."

"Save your breath," my father said.

"I've talked to an awful lot of people about you, Mr. Hansen."

"Such as."

"Mr. Rocker there in Chicago." My father laughed again. "He had some good things to say. I talked to some of your family too."

"Did you see my mom?" I said. He looked at me only briefly, surprised again, that I, too, could speak.

"For what it's worth, you could be had on charges for taking the boy, Mr. Hansen," he said.

"I came with my dad," I said, but he was not interested in me.

"Your ex-wife there is pretty upset you know."

"I can well imagine," my father said.

"Did Mom say anything about me?" I said.

"You could be in a lot of trouble, but if you'll cooperate with me, I can help you out of it."

"Not interested," my father said.

"I can get my people to work out something. I checked up on you pretty good, Mr. Hansen. I told you I had confidence in you. It's all in if you want to cooperate or not."

"I'm taking my son back to his mother. After that you can do what the hell you want."

"If I was to call down to the police station now," Sheldon Rotter said, "you'd be in some real trouble, Mr. Hansen."

"I'm with my dad," I said.

"Give me a break," my father said, "let me take the boy home. After, I'm yours to command."

"I can stay with my dad," I said.

"Are you asking me a favor, Mr. Hansen?"

"Call it what you want. Yes. What the hell's it to you? You want to haul me up in front of my creditors to get your commission, okay, I'll go. You got me, on the hoof. Let me take my boy home, Rotter, don't take my boy away from me here."

"This is really something, you asking me," Sheldon Rotter said.

"I want to take my boy home to his mother. Myself. You blow the whistle on me and you won't get a thing out of it, I promise you. Let me go. I'll meet you. You give me the time and place, I'll be there. Come on, Rotter."

"You called me some pretty ugly things, Mr. Hansen."

"My apologies, then. What do I know? Give me a damn break, man. Sheldon, is it?"

"Sheldon's my name. You meant all of it though, what you called me, didn't you?"

"I don't know what I meant. I'm up against it. What do you want, a signed retraction? Type it out, I'll sign. You want my car? I'll give you the car the minute I drop him off in Milwaukee. Come on, Sheldon Rotter, what have you got to lose?"

"You're sorry then, what you called me? All the Jew stuff?"

"Sorry as the day is long. I'm a squarehead Swede myself. Come on, we'll leave tonight. I'll call my daughter and tell her we're coming. Say the word, Mr. Rotter." Their faces were only a few inches apart. Sheldon Rotter looked at him for a long time.

"I can stay with my dad if I want," I said. They did not speak to me, either of them, but I felt my father's hand touch mine. He touched my hand lightly, as if to say: don't speak, don't fret, it will all come out now.

"You guys," Sheldon Rotter said, "you're really funny sometimes."

"What guys is that?"

"You. Always calling people Jew names and everything. You want something, then you sing a real different tune, don't you?"

"What's it going to be, Rotter?"

"You attacked me, don't forget. Why should I do you a big favor? I could get you picked up for the boy there in a minute, too. My people can write off what you owe if they have to. Why should I do it for somebody like you?"

"Put yourself in my shoes," my father said. "You'd ask too, wouldn't you?" Sheldon Rotter thought about that for a moment.

"Okay," he said. "Okay. But I'll just be staying right with you. You call back and tell them you're coming. I'm going to be right with you all the way, Hansen. You try any funny stuff and I'll have to do it the hard way, I'm promising you. If I didn't think I could work this out with my people I wouldn't even try, you know. Consider it a favor."

"Oh I do," my father said. He turned the key in the ignition. "You won't have any trouble, I'm a careful driver."

"Are we going home?" I said.

"You know, I'll tell you something," Sheldon Rotter said. "I sort of enjoyed this, tracing you down. I've never been out here, you know, except when my parents brought me, when they came over from the old country, you know. It's been interesting to see it all."

"Glad to hear it," my father said. He started the car. "I'll be stopping the first place I see open to call my daughter."

"I'll be keeping you in sight," Rotter said. "All these miles are rough on my car though," he said. "It's not the best way to break in a new car."

And so we went home. My father called my sister to tell her. I wanted to speak to her, but he said no, it would only complicate things. We drove, out through Manhattan, New Jersey, Pennsylvania, Ohio, Indiana, Illinois, home. And Sheldon Rotter stayed behind us all the way. He called too, his employers in the Twin Cities, to say when he would have my father there, that my father would submit to whatever could be worked out. We stopped only for needs, to wash and use the bathrooms in gas stations, and I got my sleep on the front seat. We drove that night, and the following day, and into the next night, and the longest we stopped was at Fossland's Restaurant, where I slept on a chair while my father and Sheldon Rotter talked about various schemes that could be worked out to refinance his business and pay his debts. We stayed there several hours, waiting for it to get late enough so we could hit Milwaukee in daylight, at a decent hour. I was dopey a good part of the time, from inadequate and uncertain sleep, and my father must have been exhausted, so we did not talk much. We did not talk much because there was nothing to say.

It was over, except for coming home.

X

My homecoming. My father had to do something for the occasion. The end, the futility of it all would have been too thorough without something to disguise it. The only problem was convincing Sheldon Rotter that he was not reneging on their agreement to return to the Twin Cities as soon as possible.

"You been around this town much, Rotter?" my father said. We have stopped for a light breakfast, coffee, toast, chocolate milk for me—Sheldon Rotter asks for tea, is given a thick, ceramic mug with a chipped handle. The girl behind the counter looks evilly at him as she pours boiling water over the tissuelike tea bag. We are at a White Tower on Wisconsin Avenue. We are home, just west of the downtown area. We are home, because I know where we are, could find my way alone if I had to.

"Just the one time, when I was checking out your family here is all." He held the string, dunked the tea bag rapidly, making little, wet, plopping sounds, crushed the bag against the side of the mug with his spoon.

"Not a bad town," my father said. "A fair town to get a start in. I was years in Chicago, you know."

"I know," Sheldon Rotter said. He blew on his tea.

"That's right, you got all the poop on me from Cal Rocker. Milwaukee though's where I hit it. Big. Fast and fat, Rotter. I could show you copies of my income tax would prove it, too. Good town. Lot of people head for New York. Don't believe it. You from New York? I was born and raised in the Midwest, myself. That's how I settled on the Twin Cities when I went on my own. This is God's country," my father said.

"A lot of people think all Jews come from New York," Rotter said. "I was born in Germany, but my mother and father brought me over when I was about three. They still live in Saint Paul. My father. My mother's deceased."

"You don't say. Sugar?" He reached for the sugar bowl.

"No thank you. My father uses it, but I never did. He uses the lumps. He holds a sugar lump in his teeth and drinks the tea through it."

"Is that a fact? Swedes do that too, you know. With coffee. Stay away from Swede coffee, it spoils you. He drinks it out of a glass, I suppose? Your old man, I mean?"

"Yeah. He drinks tea out of a glass," Sheldon Rotter said. He screwed his face up in anticipation of the hot tea, sucking it through his pursed lips. I had never seen anyone drink tea. I had never seen a Jew drink tea. I wanted to ask him how his father kept the tea from spilling if there was a lump of sugar in the way.

"No offense meant," my father said. "You're too touchy."

"I wasn't taking any," Rotter said, putting down his mug, relaxing his face. "Listen, we should be going, shouldn't we?" he said. Outside, through the large picture window that displayed the row of stools, the counter, to passersby, I could see the cars parked, the maroon, mud-spattered Chrysler, the green, 1946 Studebaker up close behind it. He had not lost sight of us, all the way from Long Island.

"Not at all a bad town," my father said. "You should let me show you around a little. I was very big in this town for a while, Rotter. You wouldn't believe how I hit it here. Wham!" he said. "One minute you're turning parts on a lathe, the next you're sitting pretty, coining it."

"I know all that," Sheldon Rotter said. "I don't want my people waiting any longer than they have to."

"What the hell do you expect?" he said. "What do you want me to do, whiz by the house and drop him out the door? I'm not Al Capone, you know. I'd like to clean up a little before I shine around his mother."

"I get the feeling you're wanting to stall me, Mr. Hansen."

"Not a bit," my father said. He snapped his fingers at the waitress to get the check. She wore a pad on a string, tied to her belt. She wrote, added, tore it off and gave it to him. Sheldon Rotter dug for change. "On me," my father said. "No, I just thought we'd check in someplace, get a bath and whatnot."

"We washed up at the state line, Mr. Hansen. You said we were stopping there to get cleaned up there. Now you're stalling me."

"My God, Rotter, look at him! He looks like the ragpicker's boy. I can't drop him off in that shape." Sheldon Rotter looked at me. I tried to see if the waitress was looking too.

"I can't see how he looks so terrible," he said.

"I didn't have a bath in a long time," I said. Sheldon Rotter looked at me. He never lost the look of surprise, the impression of being startled, that he showed the first time I spoke in his presence. Whenever I said something at the gas stations and restaurants where we stopped along the way, when I asked directions to the bathroom, chose something on a menu, he frowned, jerked his head back, cocked his ear as if to be sure it was not an illusion, that my father was not throwing his voice without moving his lips. For Sheldon Rotter, the skip chaser, I was a lever, a device for controlling my father, like the civil court judgments against him that could be had for the asking. After we left Long Island, my father said no more about him, said no more about the kikes, sheenies, hebes, yids, but I had not forgotten what he said earlier, when he asked me to play the game of spotting a green 1946 Studebaker. I tried to see Sheldon Rotter that way—a man doing something a white man had too much pride to do, I reminded myself. But it generated no feeling against him in me, and I wanted that, to have it to share in with my father.

Sheldon Rotter was just a strange old-young man, short, pudgy though he ate very little, rumpled looking in his clothes, though he was not dirty, an old-young man with a weak nasal voice and small white hands that could have been a girl's except for the dark hair on their backs—he bit his fingernails. Sheldon

232

Rotter was a strange old-young man who had some power over my father I could not begin to understand. He puzzled me, but I could not succeed in hating him.

"I can't take him home looking like something the cat dragged in, Rotter," my father said. "Tell you what. We'll check in at the Schroeder. Now that's a hotel and a half. Get us a couple of rooms, take a long hot bath, get some lunch—"

"Don't try to stall me. Are you trying to get out of it now?" Sheldon Rotter said.

"I'm asking you for the chance to hold my head up like a decent father is all. Don't rob me of a chance to leave him with something decent to remember me by, Rotter. Please." If Sheldon Rotter could smile, a strange old-young man's smile, then he nearly smiled.

"You people," he said.

"At least let me do something for the kid. I gave you my word I'd cooperate with you. You've got Buck Hansen's word, mister. I think that's still worth something, isn't it? If my creditors are still betting on me, then it's not too much to ask of you, is it?"

"All right," Sheldon Rotter said, "but I'm not going for going into any hotel. Buy him a present or something, we can use the washroom somewhere if you want, but just don't try pulling anything on me."

"You'll get stars in your crown, Rotter," my father said. "You should let yourself live a little, though, I'm telling you. You'll be old before your time. How the hell old are you, just for curiosity's sake, Rotter?"

"Twenty-nine years old," Sheldon Rotter said. "I'll be thirty pretty soon."

"Let's get on with it, then," my father said. He put his arm around my shoulder, hugged me to him as we started for the door. Behind us the waitress pocketed her tip and rang up the bill on the register. "Tell you what I'm gonna do, sonny. With your kind permission, sir," to Sheldon Rotter, "I'm gonna real quick like a bunny convert an asset into what's called cash. Legal tender. Dollars American. Then I'm going to take you over to the Boston Store and buy the best damn finest quality blue dress suit can be had for the money. Sound good? You bet you. They won't know you when you get home, boy!"

"What asset's this?" Sheldon Rotter wanted to know. It was his ring. He was going to pawn his diamond ring, the ring we had had cleaned by a jeweler in Ohio, on the drive east to Lillie.

"Here's a stone to knock your eye out, Rotter," my father said. "Take a look the way the light hits it." He twisted it off his finger, held it up to catch the sun. "There's a slight flaw, but only a jeweler can tell. I'll even give you first crack at it. Let's hear your offer." We stood in the middle of the sidewalk, outside the White Tower. People passing had to walk around us. I took my father's free hand.

"I wouldn't know what it's worth. Is that a real diamond? You shouldn't sell a thing like that. You'll never get ahead if you don't use some sense. Put it away. I can't use it. I'm not the type person to wear a ring like that, Mr. Hansen."

"Truer words were never spoken," my father said. "Hear the man, boy? No trouble. No trouble at all. If memory serves, the nearest pawnbroker isn't far. Relax, Rotter, I bought this for a rainy day, and mister, it's coming down in buckets. Leave your car, you can skooch in the back there someplace. Leave it," he said. "Anybody in his right mind'll have brains enough not to steal your car. Come on, boy."

We drove east, turned off Wisconsin Avenue to Wells Street, where all the pawnshops were. "Keep an eye peeled, Rotter, these are your tribe hereabouts. Pick me a winner." He pulled quickly into an open space at the curb. "This'll do." It was not the pawnshop, but the bar next to it he wanted. "Hustle, hustle, you got to hustle if you want to make it, Rotter. We'll just drop in for a quick one here."

"Oh no," Rotter said, "that's what I was afraid of. Let's get going—"

"Come on!" my father said. He took him by the arm, pulled him in the door. Rotter scrambled to keep his feet, moving like a puppet, stuffed with rags or straw, face wincing at the pinch of my father's fingers in the muscle of his upper arm. "Schnapps!" my father called, slapping the bar with the flat of his hand. "One for me, one for my keeper here, and a soda for my boy."

"I don't drink, Mr. Hansen. Will you let go my arm for me?"

"I've heard that someplace," my father said. "Your Jew, like your Mohammedan, won't touch the stuff. Well I do. Amuse yourself. Play the pinball or something. A man needs a drink, Rotter. Even my squarehead brother would tell you that. It ain't easy, mister. It's a rainy day, and I'm starting to feel the cold, I hope to tell you."

It was very different from the Sans Souci in Chicago. The light from the front window was cut in half by the curtains strung

234

on a rod. The floor was bare wood. Besides the bartender, there was only one old man in the room. He wore a railroad engineer's hat, looked up at us only once, then back to his glass. There was no pinball, no jukebox. The bartender said he had no schnapps.

"Top shelf, bottom shelf, I give a damn," my father said. The bartender waited for his money after he poured. He wore suspenders over his undershirt, and went away from us as soon as he had his money. "Hit us again," my father called after him, laying more money on the bar.

"You're not getting intoxicated or anything, are you?" Sheldon Rotter said. He stood close to me, and we watched.

"A bracer only," my father said. "Once again," he said to the bartender. "I tell you it ain't easy, mister. Now this ring—" he took it out of his shirt pocket—"you take this rock. This is not a bad damn stone. I picked it up for just such an occasion. Still it hurts when you come right down to it. I don't mind falling in the shit," he said, "but I do say I don't much like getting my nose rubbed in it, know what I mean?"

"Isn't that enough for you?" Sheldon Rotter said when my father downed his third shot.

"Let's go make some money," he said, and we followed him out, next door to the pawnshop. I liked the pawnshop. The window was filled with gleaming things, knives, watches, binoculars, rings, pins, military badges. One wall was covered with hanging coats, jackets, rain slickers. Under the glass top of the counter were trays of coins, more rings, sterling silverware sets. On tables were shoes, ice skates, army surplus boots, shirts, sweaters, underwear. There was a bell, like Lillie's bell, over the door, and then a fat woman wearing a green eyeshade waddled up from the dark in the rear of the narrow shop, and my father flourished the ring under her nose.

"This is a five-hundred-dollar ring," he said. "The setting I grant you is nil, but examine that stone. Do you have a magnifying glass? You're not buying, you're investing, and I'm letting it go for three-fifty. A steal," he said.

"Where does it come from?" the woman said.

"From out of the earth. You know how diamonds are born? Pressure, heat, blue clay."

"I can't take nothing could be stolen," she said.

"Wait a minute now."

"He didn't steal it, I can vouch for that," Sheldon Rotter said. The woman raised her eyeshade to look at him.

"Don't mix in, you," she said.

"Three hundred bucks," my father said. She was looking at the ring.

"We better go, Mr. Hansen."

"Don't sell it, Dad," I said. I did not know why I said it. I knew nothing of the value of gems . . . I understood nothing.

"There's imperfection," she said.

"You're very astute," my father said. "Intelligence is its own reward. Two-fifty to you, and to you alone. That's my absolute bottom."

"Don't," I said.

"Mr. Hansen, you shouldn't sell it without thinking it over some more," Rotter said.

"Two hundred flat," my father said.

"Take a hundred?" she said.

"Sold!" he said. We did not wait for the ticket.

"That was a foolish thing," Sheldon Rotter said.

"Will you listen to him, sonny?" my father said. "What the hell does he know about the price of eggs, right? Get in, Rotter," he said. "We're going to the Boston Store."

I am home. I *feel* at home! Wisconsin Avenue, broad, crowded with traffic, policemen at the intersections shrilling their whistles, their arms and hands like semaphore flags, wearing pale blue summer shirts, sunglasses, bright black leather puttees. Here are the swarms of shoppers, clusters gathered on the pedestrian islands to wait for clanging, grinding orange streetcars, the department stores, Gimbels, Chapman's, Brill's, the Boston Store, where I will get the best blue suit my father's money will buy. The marquees of movie theaters are lit even in daytime. We park the Chrysler on Plankington Avenue, near the arcade building—in the basement is the Red Room Bar, the Green Room Restaurant, the fountain in the middle of the arcade, a gathering place for drifters, mashers, teen-agers bold enough to smoke cigarettes in public. We walk to the Boston Store, my father holding my hand, Sheldon Rotter hurrying to keep up, his short body forced to an odd, loping jump when he begins to lose us in the streams of people on the sidewalk.

Yes, there is Childs Cafeteria, and there, on the brink of the Milwaukee River, perched above the dark brown pilings, Heinemann's, where my mother takes me for a treat if I have not nagged her shopping—where ice cream sodas are served with two papery wafers, and the long spoon comes sealed in a paper pouch for hygiene . . . I endure an eon of shopping for slips or sheets or

236

salad bowls, eat an ice cream soda and two wafers, wait for the streetcar to take us back to Mrs. Spaulding's attic rooms. How many days, dimensions ago, was it?

"Shake a leg, Rotter," my father said over his shoulder. "You're holding up the show." And we enter the sudden silence of the revolving door; I am jammed against my father's legs, a woman with almost-blue hair on the other side of the glass, back to me. With a rubbery, sucking noise, we emerge in the Boston Store, stand to one side to wait for Sheldon Rotter to catch up. In a moment he appears in the revolving door, his face close to the glass, frantic, certain we are evading; he looks like a man put in a bottle, waiting for the chloroform that precedes the mounting pin, the felt board.

"Mr. Hansen," he said. "Honestly, I don't think—"

"Save it for later," my father said. We swoop through the aisles to an information desk. "Clothes, boys' clothing," my father says. "Suits, jackets with trousers to match, you know the kind of thing." Then up the escalators, a breather, another quiet moment, effortless movement, the faces we pass going down, the random ring of bells calling from one department to the other.

"This is a pretty nice store," Sheldon Rotter said as we got off.

"Would I bring you to a dump?" my father said. "I told you I was big in this town once. Nothing but the best for my boy."

The boys' clothing section was carpeted, quiet again. The customers were women with their sons. I remembered shopping trips with my mother—I was home. My father led us to the register counter, reached over and rang the desk bell a dozen times with the tip of his finger. "Recognize that?" he said to Rotter.

"What?"

"That's Morse code. It means help. Pronto. What the hell kind of an education did they hand out where you went to school?"

"I don't know what you're talking about now, Mr. Hansen." The clerk who came out of the stock room behind the counter was at least my father's age. He wore a glen plaid suit, a black bow tie, and around his neck, dangling down the front of his jacket, a yellow tape measure. Seen with my father and Sheldon Rotter, he looked very ordered, composed, oblivious to the heat and the atmosphere of rushing in the Boston Store. He did not speak, say *Yes sir?* or *Can I help you?*, but pitched forward a fraction of a degree, lifting his eyebrows in open and peaceful expectation, readiness to serve.

237

"A blue suit for the boy here. And make it snappy if you can stand it," my father said. Sheldon Rotter stepped away from us, embarrassed, feigning interest in bins of socks. "What he wants is a suit says class, get me?" We followed the clerk.

"Something on this order?"

"Not near blue enough. More blue," my father said. "He wants a blue says *blue*, and damn all the rest, see? Nothing gives you the feeling you fit right in like a good blue dress suit," he said to me. "That's more like it," he said of the next suit the clerk took off the rack and held up for us. "Now you're talking my language."

"This way," the clerk said.

"Dad?"

"Go ahead. He's going to show you where to try it on. You have to try it on to get the fit right, son. Didn't you ever buy a suit before?"

"I don't think so."

"All the more reason. High time. Hear that, Rotter, this is my son's first suit." Sheldon Rotter looked, nodded, but went quickly back to the socks.

"If you'll come with me," the clerk said.

"Dad?"

"Go on. He won't bite you."

"I don't think I want to, Dad," I said.

"Don't be silly. Come on. Don't make me ashamed of you, sonny." I followed the clerk in the glen plaid suit behind the register counter, a turn to the left, and he opened the door to what looked like a dark, small closet.

"I can't see in there," I said. He reached over my head and pulled the light chain, handed me the suit, closed the door after himself as he left. The dressing cubicle was empty except for a benchlike seat built on the wall, too high for me to sit on and still touch the floor with my feet. The suit was very heavy on the hanger, a dark navy blue, a wool flannel thick and furry to the touch. I stood for several seconds in the dressing cubicle, straining to hold the suit up high enough to keep it off the floor, listening to the muffled sounds of cartons or cases being moved somewhere in the stock room. The air was stifling; I felt sweat break out on my face, my armpits, my crotch. I laid the suit on the bench and undressed. I felt gamey in my dirty underwear, grimy, nauseated by the smell of my body. I pulled the trousers on over my shoes and slipped on the jacket. The stiff flannel itched the skin of my neck, my wrists, thighs and legs. I sweated terribly as I knelt to roll up one leg, then the other, above my shoes. When I threw open the cubicle door at last it was like being able to inhale again after seeing how long you can hold your breath. The clerk was waiting for me.

"Your pop's quite a character, isn't he?" he said. I followed him out, burning with shame, for my father and for myself, dirty and grotesque in this heavy, chafing suit with arms and legs long enough for someone the size of Sheldon Rotter. The clerk marched me to a three-sided mirror, then stood back to make way for my father.

"It's awful hot, Dad," I said.

"Yes indeedy," my father said. "Rotter, give a look, will you? If you're so damn interested in those socks I'll buy you a pair! What do you think? Is that class or isn't it?" I looked at the three images of myself in the mirror—I looked swallowed by the blue flannel suit, engulfed, my wrists and ankles ballooned by the rolled-up material. The clerk went down on one knee beside me to reroll the cuffs and trouser legs, marking possible hems with straight pins he seemed to draw from his mouth as he needed them. His head close to mine, I saw the net, pasted to his scalp at his hairline, of his toupee. "I think I can live with that," my father was saying.

"It looks like a nice piece of material," Sheldon Rotter said, and when my father kept looking at him, waiting for more, he stepped up to me and rubbed the cloth of one sleeve between two of his white, lady's fingers. I tried to retreat within the suit, keep from feeling the pressure of his fingers on my arm. "Very nice," he said for my father.

"You damn bet you." The clerk got up, exhaling loudly, as if he had been holding his breath to keep from smelling me. "We'll wear it out of the store," my father said.

"It makes me itch, Dad, I'm hot," I said.

"I'll have to schedule alterations," the clerk said. "I can have it delivered—"

"Just have it tacked," my father said. "This boy needs a suit. Now tell me the damage and I'll pay up and we can get the hell out of here."

"I'll see what I can do," he said, and I went back to the cubicle to get out of the suit while the hems were tacked up.

Dressed again in the blue suit, I came out carrying my old trousers under my arm. The clerk was waiting for me. "My dad's fine," I said.

"What?"

"I said my dad's fine."

"Whatever you say," he said, and we went out to the counter where my father paid in cash from the money he'd gotten for his diamond ring.

"Hell, I've still got some left. This calls for a drink, Rotter. Throw those pants away, boy," he said to me. "You don't want to carry those home with you." I looked for some place to put them. "Here," my father said. He took them from me and handed them to the clerk, who looked at them as if they would soil his hands. "What say to a quick drink?" my father said.

"Mr. Hansen, if you're trying to stall me off—"

"How about you, boy?"

"I'm pretty thirsty."

"That's good enough for me," my father said. "Come on, Rotter, don't hold us up." He took my hand and we left the Boston Store. I tried to wiggle my shoulders, rub one leg against the other, to relieve the terrible hot itch of the wool against my skin, without letting my father know it.

We went to the Red Room Bar, in the basement of the arcade building.

We sat in a booth in the Red Room Bar. I could look out, past Sheldon Rotter, and see the fountain in the center of the arcade. There were large, fat goldfish in the fountain pool, moving their fins just enough to remain stationary as they scavenged the trash on the bottom—sometimes there were pennies among the gum and cigarette wrappers. A door at one end of the bar opened on the Green Room Restaurant, but all there was to see was the busboys who passed to and from the kitchen with heaped trays on the shoulders of their pea green smocks. Faintly, very faintly, I could hear the fall of pins from the bowling alley at the other end of the arcade. It was cool in the Red Room Bar, not air conditioned, but kept dark, sealed off from the street, and no one rushed or talked loud, so it felt cool. The itching and sweating caused by my abrasive new suit localized in my crotch and armpits, at my throat and wrists. Under the booth's table, I could scratch myself with my nails at will without my father seeing it.

"You ought to take a drink now and again, Rotter," my father said. When you bought a shot of whiskey at the Red Room Bar, they served a glass of ice water with it. Sheldon Rotter and I drank carbonated orange soda. "A little wine for the stomach's sake," my father said.

"I never smoked or drank either one," he said. "It can't be any good for you."

"I guess not."

"I really hope you're not trying to pull a fast one on me, Mr. Hansen. I've put myself out for you with my people, like I said."

"You have my word," my father said. "We'll go in a little bit. You're in no great hurry, are you, son?"

"No." I was home. I had eaten lunch in the Green Room Restaurant once, with my mother and sister, and my sister's two children in high chairs they had for people who brought little children with them. I had not missed my family while we were gone—they were there, always, in the permanent postures we left them in—and now I was home again, and everything on Wisconsin Avenue was the same; there was no reason to hurry for me.

"You really shock me, Mr. Hansen."

"Do I now?"

"You sure do. I wonder if I'd done this, gone along with you on this if I'd known what I know now."

"What do you know, Mr. Rotter?" my father said. The bartender in the Red Room Bar kept a close watch. When my father raised his hand and winked, he sent a waitress over with another shot of whiskey and a glass of water.

"Just the kind of person you are, I guess. It's hard to put rightly. I never thought one of you people would do things like this." He looked at me. "I mean, I was pretty surprised when your family told me about your taking your son with you—"

"I went with my dad," I said. The orange soda made me more thirsty. Under the table, I scrubbed at my crotch with my fingers.

"The longer you live the less surprised you'll be," my father said.

"What I'm saying is, you're the kind of person a lot of people look up to—"

"How's that?" my father said. "Say that again! That's a good one. Come on off it, Rotter."

"I mean that seriously," Sheldon Rotter said. "You were a very successful man at one time, Mr. Hansen. I thought most likely you had some problems with business—"

"Oh I did, I did indeed," my father said.

"—but. Well, doing this kind of thing, your son here, pawning your ring, running all over the country . . ."

"You can't figure that out, can you?"

"Not exactly. Not with the way I had you figured before I left Saint Paul after you." My father signaled for another drink.

"Do tell," he said.

"If I was asked a while back," Sheldon Rotter said, "what my opinion about you was, I'd have said I hated your guts, but still I'd have said you were what you call a respectable person. A businessman, I mean."

"Did you hear that?" my father said, laughing. "Christ on a crutch, that's rich!"

"What's funny, Daddy?"

"Here I am a respectable person, and this is the first time I hear about it," my father said. "Right out of the Jew boy's mouth!" He laughed until his head lay on the table. I looked at Sheldon Rotter, who watched my father, his face with that squinting, curious, awed look it had when he looked in the window of the Chrysler in Mineola, New York.

"It's not all that funny," Sheldon Rotter said, "and I said that was before. Some things you've done, I'd have to revise my opinions. I don't think you're really a respectable person. I wonder how you ever made so much money before in the first place."

"This is more than I can take," my father said, getting out of the booth in the Red Room Bar. "Let's get out of here before I wet my pants!"

"You don't understand," Sheldon Rotter tried to tell my father as he paid the bill at the bar, "I didn't say I ever liked you. You don't understand my meaning. I'm talking about the way I used to think when I was a kid, the way lots of people think. I've seen what kind of a person you really are now. You aren't listening to me, Mr. Hansen."

"Give me change for the phone," my father said to the bartender. "Come on boy, we'll call your sister and tell her we're coming. Don't stand there with your mouth open, Rotter. We've got to deliver this boy and get back on the road, right? We'll take my car," he said.

That, I suppose, was why Sheldon Rotter had held my father's creditors back—he hated my father, and all the men like my father, but there was still a world that seemed to be ready to respect those men if they made money, and were confident in the making of it, confident of themselves. That was why he bothered to chase him across the country, why he did not turn him in, with me, to the police in Mineola, New York. Sheldon Rotter, saved from Hitler by foresighted and prudent parents, reared in alien Minnesota, as detached from the roots of his tradition as my father was, as I am, ran after the same specter of success my father sought so ineptly. Chance and time passed them both, and success and the future fell to the Cal Rockers of this world, and yes, the Arn Hansens, the Uncle Arns, the men with luck or simple tenacity or sheer cunning. Sheldon Rotter would go on, until retirement or death, to chase down the deadbeats there was no longer the faintest reason to respect, just as the Ben Broadfoots of America would suffer bitter frustration upon frustration in the face of a culture they could neither master nor understand.

He sat, Sheldon Rotter, a short, prematurely balding, high-waisted Jew, in the back seat of the Chrysler, silent, pensive, among the salvaged shambles of the Hansen Engineering Company, like an orphan left to play with the broken brick and crumbled mortar of a monument once feared, if only by men who spoke another language. The end of our trip, the end of my father's mystery for me—the stuff of it, not its meaning (this takes years, will take years!)—gave Sheldon Rotter an insight that must have tasted sour. He had thought he understood *those people*. My father drove recklessly north, toward Cramer Street, over all the streets, through all the neighborhoods I knew, because I was home.

"Boy that is rich," he said, steering with his forearms while he lit a Pall Mall, "that is really a hot one. What'd you expect, Rotter, that I was a good Joe even while I was calling you a dirty kike? How to work your can to the bone and end up broke in three easy lessons! We get the boy home and I'm going to tell you the story of my life for starters. You should have bought that ring while you had the chance. It'd give you something to remember me by."

"You aren't interested in understanding what I was trying to tell you, Mr. Hansen," Sheldon Rotter said.

"No, no, not at all!" my father said. "I want to hear it all. This I have got to hear! I mean that sincerely. Hang on, we'll be on our way in a minute. Two shakes of a ram's tail."

"I don't want to talk anymore," Sheldon Rotter said. Then we turned onto Cramer Street.

(This moment, this is the last! This is all there is, the end—hold it, make it ours, cling! We have this much; if we can keep it, hold it, then there is past, continuity, coherence, meaning! We must hold this, my son!)

My father coasts the Chrysler close in to the curb, turns off the ignition, sets the hand brake. "Last stop," he says, "all ashore that's going ashore." I look out the open window at my mother's new Cramer Street house. It is the same house, same street, but I had somehow expected there would still be the signs of our moving in, boxes stacked on the lawn, the porch, the rented trailer at the curb. There are curtains on the windows now—I had expected it to be unchanged to the last minute detail, as if our trip would have occurred in some special warp of time while my mother, brother, sister, lived in suspended animation, without reference to me or my father. But there were curtains on the windows, and the lawn was greener, freshly mowed, and our old Ford must have been parked in the garage in back. "Come on, sonny, let's pay the piper," my father said, and we got out. "Come on," my father says to Sheldon Rotter when he does not move.

"I don't think this is any of my business, Mr. Hansen."

"Come on, this'll be good for your education." And Sheldon Rotter emerges reluctantly from the back seat of the Chrysler. There is an instant, a millisecond, when we stand, the three of us, on the parking strip in front of the car, facing my mother's house. I reach to take my father's hand, but he chooses that moment to raise his arms, stretch, yawn, and he starts first, up the walk to the house.

"Daddy," I say, but it is lost in what happens. I meant to halt him, perhaps give myself time to catch up and take his hand, so that we might face them together, that I might share in the burden of recrimination I expect, be able to give him some small measure of strength to bear it with dignity . . . I cannot say. Perhaps I meant to halt him only to give him time to think of something to say to me, some final, pithy adage on parting that would sustain me in the new universe he has made for me. I cannot say. He did not hear me, or if he did, he had no time to respond.

The screen door opens, bangs back against the side of the house, my brother steps out. No, he has not remained the same, has not been in some sleeping state—his khaki Air Corps clothes are gone, replaced by dress slacks, a white shirt with a tie, cuff links and a clasp that catches the sun. "Hello, Arn," my father says.

"You got a goddamn nerve," my brother says. I am behind my father. He starts up the stairs, and I come after—I am, through all this, running to catch up, to be there among them in what happens, and I never succeed. Jane comes out on the porch behind my brother. She is different, blonde hair swirled high on her head, dressed for church or a party or to greet someone special.

"That's no way—" my father starts to say, holding out his hand to shake. My mother comes out behind my sister, and she too has taken care to dress formally—where is the old housecoat, the worn shoes, the bandana tied on her brow to catch sweat?

"You ruin everything, you can't touch anything without ruining it," Jane says, and Arn slaps my father's hand away.

"Oskar!" my mother cries. "Come here to me!" I am running, I seem to be running up the steps. "I'll get the police after you, so help me God," my mother is saying to my father.

"See the new suit I got him?" my father says. "He looks good, don't you think?"

"Get the hell out of here, Dad, before something happens," Jane says. Where is her warm robe, her cigarette, her babies, her pictures of Richard Hackbarth?

"Mr. Hansen," I hear Sheldon say somewhere behind me.

"Do I get a cup of coffee or do I just put my tail between my legs and run," my father says. He steps toward the door, or moves as if he means to go inside, and my brother hits him.

"Damn you to hell, Buck!" my mother screams. I reach the top of the porch stairs, in time to see my brother hit him full on the mouth. *Bastard,* I think I hear my brother say through his teeth as he swings his fist. "I'll see you in hell!" my mother screams. My father falls next to me, at the edge of the porch, then rolls slowly, almost silently, down the stairs to the walk. And they have me, their hands on me, my mother, my sister.

My father gets up—yes, with dignity! Like a man who has slipped on a banana peel, but will not let the fall humiliate him. He gets up, holding a hand over his mouth, and he looks with surprise and interest at his hand when he lowers it and sees the blood on it. He starts to walk, back toward the Chrysler, but stumbles. He would have fallen but for Sheldon Rotter, who takes him, puts my father's arm around his shoulders and walks him to the Chrysler.

I do not resist their hands. We are there on the porch until they drive away in the Chrysler, my father holding a handkerchief to his mouth, Sheldon Rotter next to him on the front seat, very close to him, face away from us to minister to him. Things are said, shouted, curses, promises, threats, the voice of my sister, my mother, Arn—Arn massages the knuckles of the hand that struck our father. He curses the pain in his hand softly. Did you see the splint on his finger? I want to say. But I say nothing. As long as we stand on the porch, their hands are on me, and I watch, listening for some word, some definition from my father. But there is a handkerchief pressed to his mouth to stop the bleeding, and then they are gone, and I am taken inside.

That is all. There is no more to tell, nothing, my son, for me to say to you. I can tell it again if I must. I will tell it again if you wish. But in its wholeness, all told at last, we have made a truth beyond fact, knowing what we cannot know, and that is ours so long as we believe what we imagine. Between my father and my son, making this lie, I have made a meaning for us all. We live in this, my son, so long as we believe.

Listen.